ACTS OF DECEPTION

ACTS OF DECEPTION

LARRY CARELLO

Braveship
BOOKS

Aura Libertatis Spirat

ACTS OF DECEPTION

Copyright © 2023 by Larry Carello

Braveship Books
www.braveshipbooks.com
Aura Libertatis Spirat

Cover Design by Max von Reinhard

H-60 helicopter image in the cover design used by permission of the photographer, Tomás Del Coro.
Shenyang FC-31 image in the cover design used by permission of the photographer, Danny Yu.

Book layout by Alexandru Diaconescu
www.steadfast-typesetting.eu

ISBN-13: 978-1-64062-161-9
Printed and bound in the United States of America

For my daughters

ACKNOWLEDGEMENTS

Many people contributed to the research that was needed to develop this novel. Among them were the helpful staff at the Navy Office of Information East that assisted me with gaining admittance to a variety of Naval installations and commands. A multitude of active duty and retired naval aviators shared their knowledge of rotary, fixed wing and tiltrotor aircraft, which gave me a better understanding of the challenges faced by today's air warriors. Surface warfare officers briefed me on the ultra-modern Littoral Combat Ship that's featured center stage in the story's plot, and how the vessel's unique capabilities could play a crucial role as part of America's presence in the South China Sea. In summary, without the assistance of the aforementioned professionals, *Acts of Deception* could not have come to life.

It's with deep gratitude that I also recognize Captain Jim Gillcrist, U.S. Navy (Ret), Executive Director of the Naval Helicopter Association, who paved the way for my access to helicopter units on Naval Air Station North Island, California. Having the opportunity to chat face-to-face with talented young pilots was an absolute joy for this retired naval aviator.

I'd be remiss if I didn't acknowledge fellow Braveship authors George Galdorisi and Jeff Edwards who are always there to offer guidance and support as I climb the steep slope of writing a book that readers will want to read. Also, a special shout out to Alex Bear who edited the manuscript with a keen eye toward correcting my spelling, grammar and structure missteps. Thanks, Alex.

And finally, a heartfelt thank you to my wife Connie, and our daughters Katari, Anna and Mary for their love and encouragement. You ladies bring bright sunshine into my cloudy days!

Larry Carello
Jacksonville, Florida

CONTENTS

CHAPTER 1

Sunday
0600 hours
South China Sea

The sight was foreboding—like a highway leading to the edge of a cliff. Lieutenant Lin Yi, call sign "Cardinal," sat in the cockpit of his J-31 Gyrfalcon jet and stared down *Shanghai*'s long flight deck. Absent the "ski jump" takeoff ramps on China's earliest aircraft carriers, *Shanghai* utilized four catapults to launch its airplanes. The "cats" enabled *Shanghai* to launch aircraft faster than by the ramp method, and more importantly, they allowed planes to get airborne with heavier fuel and weapons loads. Lin Yi and his fellow pilots suspected that, like many components on the ship, the catapults had been modeled after proven American technology. Yet despite the advancement of the catapults, Lin missed the unassisted deck run and sensation of being flung into the air by the ramp—the way he'd first experienced the thrill of carrier aviation as a freshly winged *Shao Wei*, or Ensign, in the People's Liberation Army Navy (PLAN). His thoughts drifted back to the obsolete *Liaoning*—China's first aircraft carrier on which he'd made his initial takeoffs and landings. *Shanghai* was his country's latest addition to its growing fleet, and as the ship's political commissar had proclaimed, "another step toward the People's Navy regaining its rightful place in the South China Sea."

The voice in his headset snapped Lin back to the present: "Voodoo One, cleared for launch. Voodoo Two, standby to reposition." Lin acknowledged the radio call from *Shanghai*'s Air Officer—known in common terms as the "Air Boss," or simply, "Boss." Lin watched as his flight leader, Lieutenant Commander Yang Chen, call sign "Thunder," was slung down the catapult and hurled into the air. Yang's afterburners cast an eerie glow against the low cloud layer that cloaked the morning's dark waters. Yang raised the plane's landing gear, extended upwind, and then made a climbing left turn. All hands on the flight deck stood by anticipating what was to follow: Thunder Yang's trademark barrel roll followed by the show-boater's unintelligible scream that sounded like, "Hotta Yee Ha!" over the radio. Whenever asked what he was actually saying, Yang would shrug his shoulders and laugh.

"Voodoo Two, follow signals into position," was the air boss' next transmission. Lin saw that his left hand was trembling as he tried to advance the jet's twin throttle levers; his brain said *push forward*, but the levers wouldn't move. A chilly wave of anxiety swept through his body.

"Voodoo Two, I say again…"

Lin keyed his mike. "Got it, sir. Moving now." Lin realized what had happened: he'd been holding a death grip on the throttles and his left arm had fallen asleep while waiting for Yang to get airborne. He slapped his left wrist with his other hand until feeling returned, then inched the throttles forward and followed the director's hand signals toward the catapult track. As he approached the track, another sailor stood off to one side holding up a large white board. Handwritten on the board with black marker was the aircraft's weight. Lin Yi stopped, set the brakes, and wrote down the number. He compared it to the figure that he'd computed on his own, then gave the board holder a thumbs up. The director resumed guiding the aircraft forward.

When the nose wheel's launch bar dropped into the catapult's shuttle, the "thud" brought Lin's focus where it needed to be. He took a few breaths of pure oxygen through his mask; any anxiety he'd experienced faded.

Lin Yi's next actions were automatic—the result of intense training and the practiced art of detaching his emotions from the task at hand. He completed the final items of the before takeoff checklist then stood by for the director's signal to power up engines. When given the go-ahead, he advanced the throttles to their mechanical limit. He swiped his stick and rudder pedals through a control check, saluted the catapult officer (AKA the "shooter"), and then rested his head against the top of the ejection seat. Satisfied that all systems were ready, the shooter then triggered the steam powered catapult. The force separated a holdback bar from the plane's nose wheel, and the J-31 was sent roaring down the catapult track, its pair of fiery powerplants guzzling fuel and converting it into raw power. G-forces pinned Lin back into his seat as the plane accelerated to over 160 miles per hour in two seconds.

However, once off the deck, Lin sensed something was wrong; he felt it in the seat of his pants as the aircraft began to settle. He raised the landing gear, then scanned his engine instruments, which appeared normal. The sinking feeling eased a little after the gear came up, but the aircraft's vertical speed indicator still showed a descent.

"Pull up, Voodoo, pull up!" the air boss shouted over the radio. Lin pushed on the throttles—but they were already at their stops. He shifted his eyes outside and saw foamy wave tops rising toward him. He could only hope that once the jet settled into ground effect—the condition when an aircraft's wing is close to the surface—the added lift would allow him to trade a few knots of airspeed for more altitude; and that's precisely what happened. Lin eased back on the control stick and coaxed the jet into a shallow climb.

"Voodoo Two, Voodoo Two, say your status!" the air boss shouted. His usual steely demeanor was laced with concern.

"Okay here, Boss," Lin Yi replied. "Might have misset my trim. Everything looks good now."

"Copy that," the air boss said with a relieved tone. "Join up with your playmate."

Lin accelerated, climbed, and banked hard left while keeping Thunder Yang in sight. As he closed the gap, he concentrated on maintaining a steady closure angle, then dipped his jet's nose to pass underneath Thunder's aircraft. After a few delicate flight control and power adjustments, he was tucked into tight formation below and behind Yang's right wing. The rendezvous was complete.

Lin unhooked one side of his oxygen mask and let it dangle from the corner of his helmet. Other than the swooshing sound of rushing air, the cockpit was silent.

Thunder climbed them into an overcast layer while Lin focused on maintaining a snug formation position. When the pair punched through the tops and into clear skies, they lowered their shaded visors as dawn's murky greyness gave way to a dazzling sunrise. Thunder leveled off and keyed his mike. "Two, come up common."

Lin pushed a button that channelized his radio to the preset, private frequency that he and Thunder had agreed on at mission briefing. "Cardinal's up," he said.

Thunder turned his head to the right and looked at his wingman. He raised his visor in hopes of making eye contact with Lin, then said, "Hey, Cardinal, what the hell happened back there?"

Lin Yi took a deep breath. During climb out he had rehearsed in his mind how he'd respond. He knew that Thunder wouldn't let the screw up slide—he never did. Everyone in the air wing shied away from butting heads with the audacious pilot. He had the reputation of a no-nonsense aviator: blunt and degrading toward anyone that he didn't like. Cross Thunder Yang and you were either a "wormy bastard", a "limp-dick fag," or some other lowlife that caused him irritation. Thunder Yang lived atop the peak of aviation's pyramid, and he didn't hesitate to let you know it. Despite being polar opposites, though, he and Lin Yi got along fine, especially when flying together. Lin respected Yang's assertiveness and the pilot's uncanny ability to back up his arrogant boasting; plus he was a great stick. Yang admired Lin's quiet, business-like ways. Their call signs reflected their personalities: Lin Yi had been christened "Cardinal" for his smooth flying style. Likewise for Yang's moniker of "Thunder," which seemed the perfect match for his cocky brashness. But nobody in the air wing knew the real origins of Yang's call sign, not even his classmates at the Chinese Naval Academy. Some figured that he'd likely given himself the tag. Regardless, the call sign fit him to a tee.

"Well, I'm waiting, Professor Einstein," Thunder chided. "We've got a while before descent, so let's hear it."

"Uh... I must have misdialed my trim settings for launch. Not sure. On second thought, my cat shot felt a little weak. Maybe that new—"

"Hold on," Thunder said. "I have to re-sync the destination coordinates in this fucking GPS unit." He focused on the aircraft's navigation system. "Something must have blinked and dumped the damn numbers. There, we're good now. Go ahead."

"Like I said, maybe a bad trim setting or a weak shot. We got a new cat officer last week, didn't we?"

Thunder fired back, "Yeah, matter of fact we did. You know, I don't like that squatty weasel. He had his head up his ass and bumped into me in the chow line this morning; almost dropped my tray." Thunder huffed over the radio. "I'll straighten out that jerk when we get back." He paused a few seconds, then asked, "By the way, I didn't see you at breakfast. Where were you?"

Lin was never known to skip a meal. Despite his slight stature, he had the reputation of a chow hound. "Oh...I overdid it last night with seconds," he said. "My stomach was still full when I woke up, so I just grabbed a cup of tea in the ready room."

"Well, don't go hypoglycemic and pass out on me, ok? I don't want to spend any more time out here than we have to."

Lin clicked his mike button twice, signaling that he understood.

"And heads up, Cardinal, I'm going to throttle back a little to save some gas; we might need it later." Thunder huffed again then said, "But just so you know, we're not slowing down because of that stupid conservation program the Old Man has a hard-on about; I'm throttling back because *I want to*."

Lin saw Thunder shake his head in a disgusted way. He sensed that another one of the pilot's infamous tirades against the establishment was about to hit the airwaves.

"You're a bright guy, Cardinal," Thunder said. "Can you tell me why the hell we're even out here today?"

"Well, like the briefing officer told us, Philippine fishing boats keep clustering around one of our dredging projects. We're supposed to do a flyby and take pictures. With most of our Coast Guard cutters headed toward Taiwan, and —"

Thunder came uncorked. "Yeah, I know all that, wiseass! I was listening. He said some of them aren't fishing for anything and are rigged with electronics for spying. But, hell, why on earth are we building another island anyway? We already have enough of them."

"I agree, Thunder. Good point."

"And what do we care about the Philippines? Hell, those sorry mongrels can't make up their minds if they're Asians or Westerners. Their only leader worth a hoot was that Marcos guy... and rumor has it that his real father was full-blooded Chinese. Maybe that explains it."

A chirping sound in his headset interrupted Thunder's diatribe. He glanced at the jet's heads-up display and saw a flashing alert light. "Alright," he lamented. "Let's start down and get this over with."

Lin Yi said, "Commander, can we hold off for a minute or two? I need to run through a test and transmit the data back to our engineers."

"Really?" Thunder moaned. "Go ahead if you have to, but make it quick. We've got some extra gas, but like I said, we might need it when we get lower."

Thunder Yang wasn't accustomed to being kept in the dark, but in this case, he put his ego aside. All he knew was that Lieutenant Lin Yi was involved with the development of a top secret gadget. The device had been installed on a single J-31 and Lin was the only pilot permitted to fly that aircraft. When not in the air, the plane was parked in *Shanghai's* hangar bay and under armed guard 24/7. The only individuals allowed near it were a band of engineers, a few handpicked mechanics, and Lin. A special security team shadowed the launch crew like overprotective parents when the J-31 was brought up to the flight deck. Lin Yi was sworn to secrecy about the project, and the ship's company was prohibited from asking questions about it.

Lin drifted away from Thunder's aircraft, giving the pair a safe separation before he went "head down" in the cockpit. Thunder glanced over at his wingman—now a good one hundred feet to his right—and watched as a narrow panel retracted from the underbelly of Lin's plane. The J-31's stealthy profile—similar to the Americans' F-35—made the panel nearly invisible until Lin selected it to the open position. A couple seconds later, a sleek lensed device protruded from the cavity, swiveled from side to side, and then came to rest trained down at a forty-five-degree angle.

"Standby for test," Lin announced. Thunder understood the warning and turned his eyes away. "Three, two, one…activate," Lin said as he initiated the firing sequence. He spent the next minute relaying data back to *Shanghai* via a satellite link. Exercise completed, he then retracted the device and closed its access panel. Thunder watched as Lin swung back into formation. "Cardinal is ready," Lin said. He latched up his oxygen mask and prepared for descent.

"Copy," Thunder said as he pushed forward on his control stick. The rising sun disappeared from view as the flight descended into a cloud layer.

Lin stayed tucked in tight. He made a quick scan of his flight instruments: altimeter was unwinding; airspeed was building rapidly. As they sank deeper into the undercast, he felt a light rumble in the J-31's airframe; he glanced again at his airspeed indicator and saw that they were approaching Mach 1. He keyed his mike. "Thunder, check airspeed."

"No worries, kid. Stay with me," Thunder said. At that moment the formation broke out of the clouds 500 feet above the surface. Thunder was following updated guidance that *Shanghai's* intelligence division had uplinked to his nav unit. He verified their data by checking his radar scope. "Looks like those intel pukes were right on for a change: contact is 12 o'clock at one five klicks." He gave a little chuckle then said, "Time to light our hair on fire, Cardinal. Standby for burners…three, two, one, go burners!"

Lin Yi had no choice but to follow Thunder's command. He lit the J-31's afterburners. An instant later, he felt an explosive burst of thrust. Now well beyond the speed of sound, he sighted a white dot on the surface that soon came into focus as a small trawler.

Thunder continued descending and leveled off at 50 feet. Seconds later the flight made a scorching pass over the vessel, almost clipping its masthead.

"What are you doing?" hollered Lin.

Thunder started a shallow left bank and said, "Secure burners." The jets decelerated to subsonic. Thunder then said, "Stay with me, Cardinal, but you might want to go loose trail while we make another pass."

"Another pass? What for? We're only supposed to confirm who they are and take some photos. It looks like your basic fishing boat to me, Thunder. They're not bothering anybody."

"Nah... I think I saw weapons pointing at us when we buzzed them."

"Those weren't weapons, they were booms for their fishing nets. Man alive, Commander, we probably scared the shit out of them; let's call it a day and head home."

But Thunder Yang had other ideas. He tightened his turn and set up for another pass. Thunder's next words left his wingman speechless. "Going guns. I want to give these jokers a warning they won't forget."

Lin Yi eased off power and fell back several dozen yards. Stunned, he watched as Thunder deployed the J-31's cannon and began "walking" a stream of bullets across the surface. The projectiles danced over the water like skipping stones, tracking a path that gave the impression of missing the boat by a safe distance. But then for some reason, the trail of splashes twisted to the left and upward. Lin Yi watched in horror as the bullets inched closer and closer to the vessel's stern. In a sickening instant, the rear part of the trawler exploded. Thunder pulled up and rocketed into the clouds; Lin Yi was blinded by the blast and flew straight into the fireball.

* * *

At first there was dead silence, then Thunder keyed his mike. "Those guys were a threat, damn it; we had to defend ourselves." His breathing became heavier. "You gotta back me up on this one, Cardinal."

Thunder rattled on about being in the right and "taking appropriate action." When he realized that he'd consumed more fuel than planned by lighting the afterburners, he throttled back and punched in *Shanghai*'s coordinates for the return flight. It wasn't until he broke out on top of the clouds that he checked in again with his wingman.

"How you doing, Cardinal?" he said. There was a hint of an apologetic tone in his voice. He glanced to his right but saw nothing but puffy clouds and blue sky; he looked in the other direction; then above and below. Cardinal was nowhere in sight.

Lieutenant Commander Yang Chen fidgeted in his seat, forced a muted laugh and said, "Hey buddy, radio check. Where are you?"

* * *

It was the best job that Salid Alonto had ever had; not just because of the money, but for the chance to escape the abusive life he'd known as a child. As he stood alone on deck and faced the eastern sky, he felt the sun's glowing warmth as it edged upward, steadily burning off a thin layer of morning mist that hugged the surface. Turning west, he saw thick clouds clinging to the shadowy remnants of night.

Salid loved the early morning; other than when he was sleeping, it was the only time of day when he found peace. Soon, the remainder of *Jasmine's* crew would roust out of their bunks, grab breakfast, and lower the nets. Salid and his mates had worked hard for over a week filling the boat's holds. The catch now served as ballast, enabling the pint-sized wooden trawler to ride smoother with added weight below her waterline. With their journey nearing completion, the men looked forward to sailing home to unload, being paid, and then getting drunk.

Salid smelled the greasy aroma of breakfast. He knew that in a few minutes he'd no longer be by himself; he decided to enjoy his last moments of solitude by having a smoke. He reached into his pants pocket and glanced to his right toward the boat's tiny wheelhouse; his eyes were met by the stern glare of *Jasmine's* skipper, a grizzled seadog named Santos.

No words were necessary: Santos waived his finger, and then tilted his head toward the bow. Salid got the message and shuffled forward. With an unlit cigarette pursed between his lips, he shrugged his shoulders sheepishly. Just yesterday Santos had reamed out men who'd congregated near the big cylindrical tank strapped to *Jasmine's* fantail. The crew wondered why the Old Man had agreed to haul the rusty hulk for the length of the trip. When a brave soul had quizzed him, Santos had mumbled something about doing a friend a favor and said that the tank would be dropped off along the way when *Jasmine* returned to her home port, Cebu City. No further questions were asked: everyone knew Santos' reputation as an irritable grouch. Most suspected that the tank was empty; nonetheless, they grudgingly honored the warning, 'NO SMOKING,' painted in red along its side.

Salid dodged a couple of net riggings before finding a quiet place on the bow. As he flicked his lighter, he felt the boat shudder, then heard a low, rumbling sound in the distance. He swiveled his head in all directions. He hadn't noticed signs of foul weather—only the fading mist to the east and the thick cloud layer to the west. He glanced aft and saw that Santos had drifted out from the wheelhouse. The men's eyes connected as they exchanged the same curious expression of *what the hell was that?* Salid looked again to the western horizon; this time he sighted two black dots above the surface. The rumble that he'd first heard morphed into a steady roar. He was mesmerized as the dots grew larger and the noise got louder.

Before he could digest what was happening, two jets burst overhead and banked sharply to the north. A second later there was an ear-splitting boom that shook the boat to its core. Salid spun toward the wheelhouse and saw shards of shattered glass flaking down. He heard *Jasmine's* two diesel engines go quiet as Santos cut them to idle.

By now, the entire crew had scrambled from their bunks and had gathered near the vessel's stern. All eyes transfixed on the jets as they separated from their tight formation and turned back toward the boat. The lead jet headed straight at *Jasmine* while the other fell behind.

Visions of flying fish went through Salid's head as he watched bullets dance across the surface, pulsing closer and closer to *Jasmine's* stern. He had the urge to jump overboard, but his legs felt paralyzed, as if anchored by concrete blocks. His hands dropped to his side and the cigarette fell from his mouth. At that instant a fiery ball erupted on the stern as bullets struck the tank; the ball blossomed into a billowing inferno.

Salid's body went limp as the percussion lifted him over the railing and high into the air. With eyes trained toward the heavens, he prayed that death would be swift.

CHAPTER 2

Lieutenant Commander Dick "Bruiser" Moselli never cared for his call sign. During training as a Navy helicopter pilot in Milton, Florida, an instructor pilot had pinned the nickname "Bruiser" on him; and much to Moselli's displeasure, the moniker stuck like superglue between a handyman's fingers. Moselli was aware that he shared the same hometown of Delphi, Indiana with legendary pro wrestler William "Dick the Bruiser" Afflis, and like Afflis, he'd wrestled and played football; however, the similarities ended there. Despite Moselli's bearish appearance, he was a mild, unassuming soul. His soft-spoken persona had served him well during a Naval career characterized by firm, quiet leadership. Those qualities had elevated him to his present assignment as Officer-in-Charge (OIC) of a U.S. Navy helicopter detachment deployed to the South China Sea. Moselli's Purple Heart and Distinguished Flying Cross (DFC) merely added to his stature.

Moselli and his copilot, Lieutenant Miguel "Don Juan" Aguilar, were wrapping up a late morning sortie delivering mail to a convoy of ships that were steaming at flank speed to the Taiwan Straits. Moselli's own ship, the USS *Grand Rapids*, had been directed to maintain its status operating independently two hundred miles off the west coast of Luzon, Philippines. Moselli and Aguilar had one more task before returning to *Grand Rapids*: deliver the last mail bag and to retrieve the ship's chaplain from a destroyer escort.

Aguilar said, "Let me ask you something, Bruiser: do you get the feeling that we're being cut out of the action?"

Moselli thought for a moment. "Yeah, I sure do. Everyone else is getting into the game while we're stuck selling popcorn in the stands. Guess that's our mission of late: hauling spare parts and mail and being the Holy Helo." He glanced down at the H-60 Seahawk's clock. "Say, I'm getting hungry; I'll be glad to pick up the Padre and head home for chow." Aguilar keyed his mike in agreement. "How's the ear doing, Don Juan? Any issues?"

"Nah, that antibiotic Doc gave me seemed to work right smartly; ear infection is all cleared up," he said with a drawl. "Nice to get back in the saddle.

Shucks, I've been bored stiff sitting around twiddling my thumbs and reading dime store paperbacks; been about as useful as tits on a bull frog."

Moselli laughed. "Well, hayseed, make yourself useful and dial up the destroyer's TACAN[1] so we can make this last stop." Aguilar channelized the aircraft's navigation radio, then shifted his eyes to the cockpit's directional compass; a thin white needle swayed left, then right, before homing in on the signal.

"There she blows, Bruiser, fifty-seven miles off our left side." Aguilar motioned dramatically in that direction, like a police officer directing traffic.

Moselli laughed again. He loved flying with Aguilar and wished that he could do it more often. Don Juan always kept the mood light-hearted, regardless of what intense activities might be swirling around the cockpit. As helicopter aircraft commanders, or HACs, they were seldom teamed together, instead each spending the majority of their flights schooling the detachment's two young second pilots. Unlike Moselli, though, Aguilar's nickname didn't ring as true for the tall, lanky guy from Tennessee. He was the offspring of a Nashville debutante and an Argentinian dental student who'd gotten together during college. Aguilar described the union as "the day Scarlett O'Hara met up with El Gaucho."

Moselli steered a course to the destroyer, and then turned on the helicopter's autopilot. Over his left shoulder he felt the presence of his crew chief, Petty Officer First Class Ed "Crazo" Horton.

Horton leaned in closer and keyed the mike switch attached to a long cord that connected his helmet to the crew chief's communication panel. "Hey, Bruiser, how much longer we got? I've got a hankering for some of that greasy Navy slop myself."

Moselli checked the mileage readout on his instrument panel. "About twenty minutes 'til overhead. How many bags of mail you got, Crazo?"

"Only one. Pretty light load for these guys. Doesn't feel like any chow packages or anything like that, probably just letters. Hey, you want to top off our fuel while we're there?"

"No, I don't think so. Their deck isn't certified for us to land, and I don't want to go through the rigamarole of infight refueling)." Moselli scanned the fuel gauges. "We should have a comfortable reserve by the time we get back to the boat. Just dump the mail and hoist up Padre."

---

[1] Tactical Air Navigation System

"Copy that," Horton acknowledged. He and Moselli had known each other for over a decade and shared a slew of memories, the most poignant being the day that Moselli had earned his Purple Heart and DFC. While flying a rescue mission in the venerable CH-46 off the coast of the Southern Philippines, they'd taken fire from a cult of Muslim rebels known as Abu Sayyaf. One round had pierced the plexiglass window next to Moselli, shattering his right bicep. Had Horton not grabbed a cargo strap and fashioned it into a tourniquet, Moselli would have likely bled to death. The event changed both of their lives: out of respect for Horton, Moselli insisted that his flight crews address each other by first names or call signs, rather than by rank. In Horton's case, the tragedy had convinced him to quit drinking—a vice that had led to him to being "busted" four times during his mercurial Navy career.

"Excuse me, Bruiser," Horton said as he leaned behind Moselli's seat and looked out the pilot's side window. "But is that smoke over there at two o'clock?"

Moselli looked that way. "Can't quite tell. A cloud just blocked my view. Let me dip down a bit." He trimmed the aircraft using its auto flight system, which prompted the H-60's collective lever to lower; the helicopter's two engines unspooled to maintain the 130-knot airspeed that he'd programmed into the unit. They leveled off 200 feet above the water.

"Ain't no denying, that sure is smoke," Aguilar said. "Looks like it's coming from some sorta junk on the surface. What the heck could that be, there's nothing else around us?"

Moselli had to make a decision: either investigate the scene or press on toward the destroyer. He analyzed their fuel state and then sighted the smoke plume again, estimating it to be about ten miles away. "Well, let's take a look," he announced. "But we can't afford to dilly dally more than a couple minutes."

As they got closer it became obvious: what was once a boat had been reduced to a sprawling oil slick littered with smoldering wood and dead fish. A portion of the vessel's small wheelhouse sat bobbing in the center of the debris.

"Most of the smoke has drifted clear," Moselli said. "Let's get a better look." He descended to 100 feet, slowed down and crept closer to the wreck. "My God, what the hell happened here?" As he pulled into a hover, the helicopter's rotor wash spread ripples of white caps across the slimy surface.

Horton slapped Moselli's shoulder. "Jesus Christ, there's somebody floating in the middle of that mess!" Moselli backed away a few yards. As he did, he saw the pathetic image of a man raise his arm, then collapse back onto the flimsy wheelhouse.

"Crazo, rig the hoist! Maybe he can grab on," said Moselli. He regretted accepting the mission with just one crewman. On a dedicated search and rescue flight he'd have two at his disposal: one to put in the water to help the survivor and another to operate the hoist.

"Already on it, sir," Horton answered. The whine of the hoist's hydraulic motor cut through the din of throbbing rotor blades, turbo-shaft engines, and transmission gears. "Easy right and down," Horton said. Moselli hovered the aircraft a few yards down wind of the survivor; he descended to 50 feet. As he did, the helicopter's rotor wash kicked debris into the air and across the water. The man shielded his eyes from the blast while gripping the wheelhouse with his other hand. "Lowering the horse collar," Horton said as the cable unspooled. The padded yellow sling descended toward the surface. "I got it from here, Bruiser," he said. Moselli acknowledged and engaged the Seahawk's auto-hover feature. Horton was then able to control the aircraft's drift with a joystick-like grip, thus fine-tuning the aircraft to where he wanted it.

Moselli twisted his body so that he could watch; Aguilar was blind to what was happening, so Moselli narrated the action.

"He's reaching for the collar... aw damn, he slid off the wreck. I can't see him anymore, he's underwater."

Horton guided the aircraft over the spot where the man had submerged, then paid out more cable as a big swell swept over the wreckage. Suddenly, the fellow's head broke the surface; he began thrashing his arms frantically. When one of his hands grabbed the cable, Horton started reeling in the slack.

"I think he's got it!" Moselli relayed to Aguilar. "Hang on, fella, hang on!"

Horton kept tension on the cable as it slid through man's grip. As the horse collar rose from the water, the guy made a desperate swipe at it. Horton paused the hoist, which allowed the man to get one arm into the collar up to his armpit; he flailed his other arm until it found the collar.

"Bring him up, bring him up!" shouted Moselli.

Horton took a strain on the cable. "Clear of the water, thirty more feet...fifteen, five, almost there..." he said over the intercom. As the survivor approached the door, Horton felt someone at his side. Unbeknownst to him or Moselli, Aguilar had unstrapped and dashed into the cabin. Horton slackened the cable as Aguilar took hold of the survivor's tattered shirt and yanked him inside. The man crumpled onto the deck; he turned his head to one side and upchucked an ugly mixture of sea water, oil, and vomit.

Aguilar returned to his seat as Moselli pulled full power and pushed over the nose; the helicopter rocketed forward. Horton rolled the man onto his back and gave him a reassuring pat on the chest.

Salid Alonto stared at Horton with a bewildered look in his eyes. He managed a weak smile before passing out.

CHAPTER 3

When Thunder Yang realized that Lin Yi hadn't joined up, he reentered the trawler's position into the GPS unit, reversed course and dove for the deck. Yang tried again to raise his wingman on the radio: "Cardinal, Cardinal, say your position." He repeated the transmission a half dozen times.

After he'd descended below the cloud layer, *Jasmine's* smoldering wreck came into view. Yang swallowed hard knowing that he alone, with his reckless stunt-gone-bad, had caused the disaster. He leveled off at 200 feet, slowed down and flew a wide arc around the debris. The few remaining sections of the boat's hull broke apart and sank as he watched. He saw no evidence of survivors.

Yang was prepared to expand the search for Lin when he saw that his aircraft was approaching a low fuel state. *Shanghai's* insistence on launching him with a reduced fuel load, coupled with his decision to go supersonic, had left him with no other alternative: he had to leave the scene and return to the ship. He programmed *Shanghai's* projected coordinates into the GPS and climbed. Once level at cruise altitude he made radio contact with the ship's tower and informed them that his wingman had disappeared. Yang considered asking for a refueling tanker but held off: he didn't want to draw any more attention to himself than he already had.

The return flight was uneventful. He established his aircraft "in the groove" while focusing on the carrier's optical landing system and the LSO's (Landing Signal Officer) commands. He crossed the ship's stern on speed and on profile. As his jet smacked the steel flight deck, he jammed the throttles full forward and prepared to get airborne if the aircraft's hook failed to catch an arresting cable. But the hook engaged and the cable system brought his J-31 to an abrupt stop. Yang pulled the throttles back to idle, then followed directions to parking. While taxiing, he saw a J-15 fighter race down the cat track and into the sky; seconds later its playmate followed.

Yang completed the shutdown checklist, unstrapped and hauled himself out of the cockpit. The usual group of mechanics and support personnel greeted him and began their post flight duties. An off-duty pilot approached and said, "Thunder, Commander Wei wants to see you in the ready room immediately." Yang followed the man to the unit's ready room, where he found Wei seated in the front row of a couple dozen theater-style chairs. Wei's high-backed chair stood out from the rest: it was emblazoned with a special insignia designating him as the squadron's leader. The other pilot departed, leaving Yang and Wei alone.

Wei looked up from a clipboard and said, "You've had quite a morning, Thunder. How are you doing?" The hint of a caring smile crept from the corner of Wei's mouth.

Yang wiped the sweat from his brow and said, "I've had better days, sir." He waited for Wei to tell him to sit down, but the words never came.

"To bring you up to date, we've launched a pair of J-15s in hopes of finding your wingman. A rescue helicopter is standing by when those jets pinpoint Cardinal's location." Wei set the clipboard aside. "And of course, there will be an investigation. Off the record, would you like to tell me what happened?"

"Well, Commander, I'm not really sure. After we completed our mission, I climbed the flight into a cloud layer for return to *Shanghai*, and then…" Yang lowered his eyes to the floor.

Wei detected uncertainty in the pilot, so he said, "Well, no need to get ahead of ourselves. Change out your flight gear and then report to my office after you get cleaned up." Wei checked his watch. "Let's make it twenty minutes from now." Yang nodded and left the ready room.

Commander Wei was new to the squadron, having taken command the previous month. During a pass-down from the outgoing commanding officer, he'd been briefed on the competency of each pilot in his unit. When Yang Chen's name came up, he'd been told, "Keep an eye on Thunder. He is a natural fighter pilot and a great stick, but a real wild card. He's good and he knows it."

Yang Chen was glad that the pilots who shared his stateroom were absent when he walked in. He shed his flight gear, put on a fresh set of blue cammies, then grabbed his shaving kit and a towel; he walked a short distance to the common head facility used by dozens of other officers. After washing up, he went back to the stateroom and sat down. He replayed the flight in his mind, but two items kept crowding his thoughts: the image of the exploding trawler, and the silence that followed his repeated calls to Lin Yi. Commander Wei's knocks startled him back to the present.

"Change in plans," Wei said as he opened the door. "Captain Song and Commissar Han want to interview you; let's go...right now!" Any warmth that Wei had conveyed in the wardroom was gone. Yang noted a pair of *Shanghai's* security guards at Commander Wei's side. Wei led the group up a set of ladders and down a long passageway to an area of the ship that Yang Chen had never been. Wei stopped in front of a door labeled "CONFERENCE." He knocked twice and then entered.

The austere, pale-green space was illuminated by a bank of fluorescent light fixtures recessed in the overhead. Two walls were adorned with blank white boards; colored markers and erasers were arranged evenly spaced on trays at the bottom of the boards. A large 24-hour clock set to Beijing time was mounted above the compartment's entryway. Centered in the room was a long, rectangular conference table, ringed by a dozen dark green upholstered chairs; only two of the chairs were occupied: one by Captain Song, *Shanghai's* commanding officer; the other by Commissar Han, the ship's political officer. A tape recorder sat on the table in front of them.

Captain Song dismissed the guards and motioned Wei to take a seat across the table from Commissar Han and himself. When Yang reached for a chair, Commander Wei grabbed his arm and said, "No. You stand, and stand at attention."

Yang stood rigid and avoided eye contact with the two men across the table. He'd never spoken to either of them but was aware of their reputations, and the scuttlebutt that *Shanghai's* sailors had ginned up about Captain Song and Commissar Han. Like other high-ranking officials, the pair had been given nicknames by the crew; one an affectionate tag, the other not so much. Sailors privately referred to Captain Song as "The Bulldog," not only for his tenaciousness, but also because of his stout, barrel-chested body. Song's fat, jowly face further supported the dubbing. He played the role of a hard-nosed warship captain, yet those close to him knew Song as a kind-hearted man, at least in his personal life. Professionally, though, there were no such sentiments. Song came from a long line of military officers and was a devoted disciple of the Chinese Communist Party.

Seated next to Captain Song was *Shanghai's* political officer, Commissar Han, who like, Song, was a graduate of the Chinese Military Academy. Upon commissioning, both men had opted for service in the PLA's maritime branch, or People's Liberation Army Navy. Commissar Han had commanded China's first aircraft carrier—the venerable *Liaoning*—and with that credential, he possessed the authority to relieve Captain Song if at any time he deemed it necessary. But the men were good friends and worked well together. In private moments they'd even discussed Song resigning his commission and following in Han's footsteps as a commissar. *Shanghai*'s sailors were not as impressed by Han as they were with Captain Song. His gangly, rail-thin body was the opposite of the burly skipper, plus the man had an unusually long neck, a flattened head, and beady eyes—much like a cobra. Han seemed to always have an irritated, sour expression on his face, prompting the crew to tag him as "Lemon-Sucking Snake" or more simply, "Snake." Commissar Han was aware of the label and embraced the slur; he found it humorous, considering that he held the ultimate authority over every person on the ship.

A collection of folders was scattered in front of the two senior officials. Yang stole a glimpse and recognized his personnel file in the commissar's hands. After what seemed like an eternity, Captain Song removed his reading glasses and spoke.

"Lieutenant Commander Yang, we need to know what you observed during your surveillance mission, and why Lieutenant Lin did not return with you. Commissar Han and I have summoned the air operations officer and flight deck crew to obtain their statements as well; however, since it is obvious that you and Lin were the only ones on the mission..." He paused and looked over at Han, who nodded his approval. "Yang, you need to tell us what happened."

Yang glanced down at Wei, then shifted his eyes toward the two most powerful men on the ship. Except for the muted sound of conditioned air pumped through ceiling vents, and the tick, tick, tick of the clock, the room was deathly still. As Yang began to speak, he felt a bead of sweat drip from his check and onto the floor.

"Sir, after we completed our mission, I started to lead the flight back to *Shanghai*. There was a cloud layer that we needed to climb above enroute to cruising altitude. When I broke out, Lieutenant Lin was nowhere in sight. I tried to raise him several times on the radio but got no response, so I decided to fly back to the trawler we'd been assigned to investigate. I did a search of the area for any signs of Lin or his aircraft but came up empty. I saw that I was approaching a low fuel state, so I made the decision to fly back alone." Yang cleared his throat then said, "Sir, we had burned more fuel than planned and I didn't want to put my own aircraft in jeopardy, so—"

Commissar Han shook his head. "No, no, no, Mister Yang." He rocked back in his chair with arms folded. The infamous pained looked spread across his face, like that of someone nursing a bad case of indigestion. "You know what we're asking; what did you observe during your mission?" He held up one of the folders. "Your briefing specified that you were to investigate a surface intruder." He tossed the folder onto the table. "Well, what … did…you … find?"

Yang realized that the commissar wasn't buying what he was selling. As he formulated his words, the vision of the exploding trawler filled his thoughts, followed by the devastation he'd witnessed after making a final pass over the wreckage. *Could anyone have survived that explosion and lived to talk about it?* Possibly, he surmised. *If Lin were still alive, would he fess up about what had really happened?* To that question, he had no idea. Considering all the unknowns, he knew that his next statement would impact his life forever. He looked straight into Han's dark piercing eyes and said, "Commissar, the contact was a fishing vessel, about thirty meters in length, and steaming in a northeasterly direction. Lin and I made two passes to confirm that the boat was not a threat and then departed the area."

Commander Wei raised his hand. "Captain Song, Commissar, may I speak?" Both men nodded their consent. "Yang, why didn't you confirm that Lin had joined up before you entered the cloud layer during climb out?"

"Sir, I was heads down in the cockpit, preparing to fly on my instruments. I assumed that my wingman was still joined up on me; I wanted to provide a steady lead for him while in the clouds." He faced Song and Han again. "The last time I actually sighted Lieutenant Lin's aircraft was when we broke out on descent, and I gave him permission to go loose trail if he desired. Other than the minute or so when he'd done his flight test enroute, he'd been tucked in close for the whole flight; I thought he could use a break."

There was a knock on the door. One of the security guards poked his head inside and said, "Gentlemen, the air officer and members of the flight deck crew are standing by in the passageway. Should I send them in?"

Captain Song held up an open hand. "Not yet, thank you." He leaned in toward Han and the pair exchanged a few words under their breath. Both men rose from their seats; Commander Wei did the same and stood at attention next to Yang.

Captain Song said, "Commander Wei, Yang Chen is grounded until further notice. Other than meals and head calls, he is restricted to his stateroom." Song then turned to Yang, "And you are forbidden to discuss this incident with anyone on the ship. Am I clear, Mister Yang?"

"Yes, Captain," Yang replied.

Captain Song motioned to Han and said, "Anything else, Commissar?" Han shook his head. Song waived his hand toward the door and said, "Gentlemen, you two are dismissed."

Song and Han sat alone in the conference room. Both mulled over their thoughts, each hoping that the other would speak first. As commanding officer of the ship, Captain Song took the initiative. "So, what do you think, Commissar?"

Han stroked his chin. "I suppose we could believe Yang's story about the trawler; he seemed quite sure of himself. On the other hand, it's highly improbable that Lieutenant Lin would just disappear without making a distress call. But if that were the case, it's possible that he lost control and his aircraft bore-holed into the water with such force that it sank before its emergency beacon could deploy. We'd need to launch a subsurface team to investigate that. Any idea how deep the water is in that area?"

"No, not a clue," Song answered. "The navigator can get that data for us."

"Let's hold off on that for now," replied Han. "I'd like to hear from our air officer next. Hopefully, he's heard from the J-15 crews we launched."

Captain Song got up and opened the door, where he was greeted by a half dozen sailors in the passageway, lined up casually against a bulkhead; they snapped to attention when they saw him. *Shanghai*'s air officer, Commander Lu Zhong, was at the head of the pack. Song waved Lu inside.

Commander Lu strode into the room carrying a thick manual, a pair of binders, and a bundle of folders; the binders represented the maintenance records for Yang's and Lin's aircraft. Lu was an imposing figure: he stood tall and erect; his sinewy body filled out the blue camouflage working uniform that he wore. Lu was known for his inexhaustible energy, exemplified by his dedicated jogging routine every morning before reveille; when his afternoon schedule permitted, he was a regular in the ship's weight room. Professionally, he was a pilot's pilot, who'd won numerous awards for his skills during bombing and gunnery exercises; his safety record was flawless. Lu had the respect of *Shanghai*'s airwing, which to a man considered him deserving of the vaulted title of "Air Boss."

Commander Lu didn't wait for questions, but rather charged right into the meat of the matter. "Captain, Commissar, I can report that maintenance records for both birds are clean. In my opinion, it's unlikely that Lin suffered a mechanical failure. There's the remote chance that he experienced a medical issue that incapacitated him, but I consider that unlikely as well."

"Commander Lu, no need to stand," Captain Song said. "Have a seat."

"Thank you, sir. May I continue?"

"Of course."

"Regarding Lin's physical condition, our lead flight surgeon reports that he passed his annual exam with flying colors last month." Lu then pulled out a sheet of paper from his pile of documents. He turned it around so that Song and Han could see it from their side of the table. "On a different subject, though, I've discovered that Lieutenant Lin was launched with significantly more fuel than Yang, which was contrary to the mission plan." He slid his finger down a column of handwritten numbers he'd tabulated. "Gentlemen, you can see here that—"

Captain Song interrupted. "Stop there. Why would they depart with different fuel loads?"

Lu held out both hands in an apologetic way. "Excuse me for not clarifying that. Lin was in fact scheduled to carry an extra one hundred kilos to perform an inflight test, but that's not what I'm referring to." He pointed to his notes again. "It appears that he actually had … an additional four hundred kilos that we were not aware of when he launched."

Han jumped on the error. "How long could he stay airborne with that much extra fuel?"

Lu grabbed the J-31 performance manual and turned to the fuel/range/endurance section. "Sir, I can calculate that." He began jotting down numbers as he studied a chart in the back of the manual.

"No, Commander, we can get to that in due time," Han said. "First, I'd like to know why on earth that amount of extra fuel was pumped into his aircraft."

Lu stood up and motioned toward the door. "Sir, I believe that it can be explained by the sailor who did the fueling, Seaman Feng. May I call him in?"

Captain Song's face turned crimson. "Commander Lu, what you're telling us is starting to sound like a fucking goat rope. Do you realize that?" Lu bit down on his lower lip and braced for another incoming round. Commissar Han tapped gently on the captain's knee. Song paused and took a deep breath. "Yes, bring him in."

Lu ushered in a teenaged-looking sailor. The fellow maintained a rigid posture, but his right hand was shaking like a leaf as he saluted; he appeared on the verge of tears.

Captain Song sensed that he needed to temper his mood if they were to gain any useful information from the kid. "Good day, Seaman Feng. You may stand at ease," he said in a fatherly tone. "Now, please tell us why you added extra fuel to Lieutenant Lin's aircraft."

Feng hesitated and looked up at Commander Lu for guidance. Lu touched his arm. "It's okay, son, like we talked earlier, just tell the truth." Feng nodded and wiped his moist eyes with a sleeve; his shaking had stopped.

"Sir, Lieutenant Lin told me to do it. He was finishing his preflight inspection when I plugged into his aircraft. He said that he'd be testing some inflight gear that would cause him to burn more gas. I told him that I'd been instructed to pump an extra one hundred kilos into his bird compared to Thunder's...er...Lieutenant Commander Yang's aircraft. He said, 'Don't worry about it, I'll straighten it out later. Just give me the gas. Make it an even five hundred kilos.'"

"So, that's what you did?" Han asked.

"Yes, sir, I obeyed Lieutenant Lin's order."

Song followed up. "Did you log the exact kilos you pumped into each aircraft?"

"Yes, sir. I recorded accurate amounts for both planes."

Commissar Han began writing in his notebook. Song glanced over to see what Han had written and then turned to the air officer. "Anything you'd like to add, Commander Lu?"

"No sir. I've counseled Feng that he should have never given Lin the extra fuel without checking with his supervisor on the flight deck."

Song nodded his agreement then said, "Seaman Feng, I trust you understand that you were wrong by not following procedures and checking with your supervisor. Consider this a warning: next time you make such a bad decision, there will be serious consequences." Song stood up, pointed a finger at the youngster and said, "You got that, sailor!"

Feng's body started to tremble. He fought back his emotions and came to attention. "Yes, Captain, I understand."

"Good. I don't want to see you in here again," Song added. "Commander Lu, escort Feng out and bring in the catapult officer."

Lu swept out from the room; a few seconds later he returned with the catapult officer, a man named Dong. Lieutenant Dong had been onboard for only a few weeks, having been transferred from a desk job at the massive naval facility at Zhanjiang, in southern China. Dong had been passed over for promotion and was one of the ship's most senior lieutenants, yet he'd somehow wrangled the billet of catapult officer aboard China's newest aircraft carrier. Neither Lu, nor his staff, understood how that could have transpired. Thus far, his performance had been adequate.

Dong sauntered in and saluted. After being summoned to the meeting, he'd rushed to his stateroom and changed into a fresh uniform, making a valiant effort to look presentable. But the man's dumpy image didn't support his desires: he appeared overweight, tired, and unkempt.

Commissar Han led off the questioning. "Lieutenant, confirm that you were serving as catapult officer when Lieutenant Commander Yang and Lieutenant Lin launched."

"Yes, that's correct, sir."

"Had you received fuel data for both aircraft?"

Dong glanced at the ceiling, took a deep breath, then said, "Yes, but the data I received looked inaccurate, sir."

Han leaned forward in his chair. "What do you mean by that, Lieutenant?"

A sliver of anger flashed over Dong's face. "Well, you see, the other day, I had to fix some of the sloppy numbers the fuel guys had sent to me. When I got the numbers for Yang and Lin, I saw that Lin had a lot more fuel, but since they were going on the same mission as a flight of two, I figured that those clowns…pardon me…I assumed that the fuelers had screwed up again."

"So, you used the same numbers for both aircraft when you set their catapults?" Captain Song asked.

"Yes, sir, that's what I did."

Song pressed on. "You do realize, don't you, that your *assumption* could have caused the loss of an aircraft?"

Commissar Han decided that it was time for him to intervene. Song was his good friend; however, as commissar, he could no longer be silent. He touched Song on the shoulder, then said, "Lieutenant Dong, you are hereby relieved of your duties as catapult officer due to gross negligence. The captain and I are referring your case to the ship's legal officer for appropriate action. You are dismissed."

Dong saluted, nearly tripped while making an awkward pivot, then left. Han and Song held another whispering conference that lasted for over a minute, while Air Officer Lu stood in place; his eyes were focused on the floor. After the long pause, Captain Song said, "Commander Lu, I trust that you have other personnel to launch our planes?"

Lu looked up with an embarrassed but determined expression. "Yes, Captain, we have several good people." He steeled himself for an ass chewing, but one never came.

"Okay," said Song. "Then let's put this behind us and move on. We need to figure out what has happened to our good Lieutenant Lin Yi. I found it unwise with Dong in the room to discuss what Commissar Han and I observed when reviewing the video of Lin's launch." Song peeked over the top of his glasses. "Did you see anything abnormal, Commander?"

"Are you referring to the way Lin settled after getting airborne? Yes, I saw that, but he pulled it out. When I asked on the radio what had happened, he said that he might have misset his elevator trim; he never mentioned a weak cat shot."

"Do you think he misset the trim?" Song asked.

"Maybe, but not likely. Besides being one of the brightest guys on this ship, Lin's an excellent stick…not up there with Yang, but very methodical and very safe. Both his outgoing C.O. and Commander Wei have confided that to me."

Commissar Han continued writing in his notebook as he spoke. "By the way, Mister Lu, you can sit back down. I suspect that we will be in here for a while. Anyway, tell us what you are thinking."

Lu didn't hesitate. "Commissar, in my opinion, there are two possibilities: Lin Yi either flew into the drink before he could join up with Yang, or else he stayed airborne, somehow got disoriented, and had to eject over the water. Those are my best guesses."

Captain Song added, "Or, considering the extra fuel he had…maybe he landed somewhere other than aboard *Shanghai?*"

"Yes, exactly, Skipper," Han said. "That's gives us three scenarios to investigate. Air Officer, would you determine how far Lin could fly with the fuel load he had onboard?"

Lu reached again for the J-31 flight manual he'd brought. As he did, *Shanghai's* executive officer barged in. "Gentlemen, we've just received an advisory over the net. It's from one of our Coast Guard cutters in the area of Yang's mission." He handed the paper to Captain Song. The message was time stamped and included the cutter's latitude/ longitude coordinates:

RADAR DETECTED UNIDENTIFIED AIRCRAFT BEARING 350 DE-
GREES AT 40 KILOMETERS FROM MY LOCATION. AIRCRAFT

HELD LOW LEVEL, STATIC POSITION FOR SEVEN MINUTES, THEN CLIMBED AND DEPARTED NORTHWEST. UPON ANALYSIS, SUSPECT AIRCRAFT TO BE A US HELICOPTER. PROCEEDING TO SAID LOCATION.

Captain Song stood up. "XO, get ahold of those two J-15s we launched earlier."

Air Officer Lu said, "Captain, with all due respect, my I ask—"

"Commander, you provided us with two options, and I provided a third. We will pursue all of them in good time." He looked over at Han for concurrence. "Commissar, the J-15s?"

Han thought for a moment then said, "Yes, I will contact Beijing immediately and recommend that our J-15s intercept that chopper."

CHAPTER 4

Salid wasn't sure if he was awake or in a dream. The helicopter's noisy vibrations reminded him of when he'd sneak below deck and nap inside *Jasmine's* engine room. He had the urge to stand up, but his weakened legs felt numb.

Memories of the explosion pulsed through his mind like an angry mob banging against a locked door. He fought back the thoughts, but the mob persisted, forcing him to relive the nightmare over and over: the deafening blast, flames and heat, followed by the cool relief of water against his singed body. There was smoke, smoke everywhere; then the vision of dark fins circling the chaos and the screams of men being pulled beneath the surface. And finally, the calming peace of floating in silence.

Salid felt a gentle shove against his ribs. He opened his eyes to the sight of a strange man clad in green coveralls and wearing a white helmet; the fellow smiled and offered him a canteen. Salid raised his head and took a few gulps. He pushed away the coarse grey blanket draped over him and tried to stand, but his knees buckled. The man caught him and lifted his soaked body into a seat. Salid felt a warm sensation in his groin; he realized that he'd urinated on himself.

The man in green held out an odd looking cap with earphones attached inside; Salid slipped it on.

"Hey, Crazo, how's he doing?" Moselli said on the interphone, or ICS.

"Well, he came to but looks scared shitless and about to hurl again. By the way, is it okay to burn one?"

"Sure. Smoking lamp is lit, but first, put his boom mike next to his lips. I'll switch the ICS to hot. Oh, and give him something to puke in if he gets sick again."

Horton rummaged through his gear and found a plastic sandwich bag from a box lunch he'd wolfed down days ago. He handed it to Salid, and then mimicked a person throwing up. Salid nodded that he understood. Horton then fished out a crumbled pack of Camels from the left arm pocket of his flight suit.

Moselli announced, "Well, let's give it a try…hello, hello, sir, this is Lieutenant Commander Dick Moselli, your pilot, can you hear me?"

Salid perked up at the sound of Moselli's voice. He looked at Horton with a confused expression. Horton positioned the headset's microphone close to Salid's lips and mimicked a talking gesture by tapping his fingers and thumb together. Salid pressed the mike against his lips and said in a meek voice, "I no Eng-glass, mee Cebuano." He looked up at Horton again for guidance.

"I think he's Filipino. Never heard any of that Cebuano dialect out in Olongapo," Horton said. "Hey, I know some barroom Tagalog. Want me to try—"

Before Horton could finish his sentence, a resounding jolt shook the aircraft, causing Aguilar, who was on the controls, to rise in his seat. "What the hell was that?" he shouted. A second jolt soon followed. Aguilar struggled to keep the helicopter in stable flight.

"Christ sakes, two fighters just buzzed us," Moselli said. "One's at two o'clock now, the other at ten, both in steep turns. That ain't too cool, whatever they're doing."

"I don't think they're friendlies," said Horton. "They sorta looked like F-14s, but with screwy markings and something different up by the nose. We near any carriers?"

"Can't be Tomcats," Moselli said, referring to the U.S. Navy's venerable F-14. "We parked all of them in the boneyard years ago; and they didn't look anything like F-18 Hornets." He reached down to re-tune a radio when from the corner of his eye, he saw one of the jets slide into position along his right side. The aircraft's wing flaps were extended, and its nose was pitched up. Seconds later, the other jet crept in close on the left.

"Damn, those are Chinese J-15 Flying Sharks!" Aguilar said. "I guarantee it. Look at that little airfoil ahead of the wing," he added. "And see the red star on the tail? Holy shit! Did somebody forget to tell us we're at war?"

The jets drifted ahead, unable to match the helicopter's much slower airspeed. They took up a tight formation about a hundred yards in front of the helicopter, and then in unison, the pilots lit off their afterburners. The jets rocketed away and turned in diverging directions. The turbulence generated by their engines and wingtips tossed the American's H-60 into a steep bank; the rotor blades twisted and pounded hard against their stops. Moselli joined Aguilar on the controls as together they battled to stay airborne.

"We got a big problem here," Moselli said after they'd muscled the helicopter back to a stable condition. He re-channeled the radio to *Grand Rapids'* frequency.

Before he could transmit, Aguilar interrupted. "Bruiser, we're still pretty far away from the ship. I doubt if they can hear us from this altitude."

"You're right," said Moselli. "Go ahead and climb two thousand feet. Hopefully we'll regain comms." Aguilar pulled up on the collective and applied back pressure on the cyclic.

After they'd climbed just a few hundred feet, Horton flung his cigarette butt out the cabin door, then hustled forward; he grabbed Moselli by the shoulder. "Bruiser, look to your right. One's coming straight at us!" Wafts of cigarette smoke spewed from his mouth as he spoke.

Aguilar turned to his left. "And here comes his playmate on my side. What are these dickheads doing?"

Moselli and his crew were in a jam; they had no means to engage the fighters: the J-15s were heavily armed, and other than the nine-millimeter pistols that they each carried, the Americans were defenseless. Moselli turned to Aguilar and said, "Just level off and maintain your speed." He dialed in the international emergency frequency of 121.5 megahertz. "Man, I don't believe this," he said under his breath, then keyed the mike: "Chinese aircraft, knock it off! We are unarmed. You are harassing us and in violation of international law. I say again, knock it off!"

A long pause ensued as the fighters inched up alongside a second time. Finally, there was a response. "American heelo-chopper, you... follow... us. Turn now," one of the J-15 pilots said in fractured English. Moselli watched the plane on his right glide by, close enough to note its pilot motioning his hand to the southwest. The pilot then dipped his wing to the left.

Moselli transmitted, "Where are you taking us? We cannot fly far. Minimum fuel."

"You must... follow us," was the response.

Another long pause followed as the jets began flying lazy "S-turns," back and forth, ahead and on either side of Moselli's aircraft; the Americans were trapped.

"Don Juan," Moselli said. "We have no choice; we have to go where they're leading us."

"You fly...one two five kilo meters this way. You...follow...us," the Chinese pilot said.

"A hundred and twenty-five klicks? That's about eighty miles," Aguilar said. "If he's not bullshitting, I think we can make it that far. But where the hell are we going to land?"

Moselli checked the range chart in his pocket checklist and confirmed Aguilar's estimate. "At this airspeed and altitude, I figure we can fly another one hundred twenty miles until we splash." He could only hope that the distance the Chinese had told him was accurate, and that he and his crew would be on deck someplace—anyplace— before flaming out. He compartmentalized his concerns and moved on. "Don Juan, stay between these two jokers. I'll try to raise someone on the radio."

"Copy that, Bruiser," Aguilar said. "Say, how far are we from the ship?"

Moselli entered the last known coordinates for *Grand Rapids* into the aircraft's GPS. "Well, let me put it this way: the number on the distance read out isn't getting any smaller." A chill went through his body. "I don't think we could make it from here."

Aguilar's face blanched as he said, "Thanks. I was just wondering."

Dick Moselli stared out at the horizon; other than the two jets, he saw only endless sky and water. He figured he had nothing to lose by making another radio transmission in the blind: "Mayday, Mayday, Mayday. United States Navy helicopter attached to the USS *Grand Rapids*. Current position is to northwest of Luzon, Philippines. We have been intercepted by two Chinese fighter jets. Proceeding on course two-three-zero. Fuel on board, five zero minutes. Four souls onboard." Moselli repeated the mayday twice. He heard no reply.

Horton came forward and poked his head into the cockpit. A satirical grin spread across his weathered, stubbled face. "Guys, if I'd known my life was going to end like this, I would have never quit drinking."

Despite the tensions, Moselli couldn't keep from laughing. "It could be worse, Crazo, they could have just shot us down. I don't know what the hell is going on, but it's imperative for us to stay composed; we're not at war with these guys. It looks like we've got sufficient fuel onboard to go where they're leading us, and when the ship realizes that we're missing, the gears will kick into action."

Aguilar keyed his mike. "You know, those aircraft don't look half bad. The Chinese engineers probably bought some American model airplanes online and used them as the basis for their design. Never could build anything worth a hoot without stealing somebody's technology."

"Yeah, likely so," Moselli said. "Hey, Crazo, how's our stowaway doing? He puke again?"

Horton turned around to check. "Nah, I think he's alright. Took off the headset a while ago and wrapped himself in the blanket. Looks like he fell back asleep."

"Probably for the better," said Moselli. "God only knows what's in store for us."

CHAPTER 5

Commissar Han had received an immediate response from Beijing: after intercepting the helicopter, the J-15s were to force it down at a Chinese island military installation located at Scarborough Shoals.

Han wasted no time setting up a command post inside the conference room where he and Captain Song had conducted interviews. By the time Air Officer Lu gave a pass down to his assistant in the tower and hustled back to the meeting, Han had assembled a team of officers and senior enlisted sailors. The ship's navigator had spread a large chart on the table, plotting *Shanghai*'s position along with the spot where Lin and Yang had flown their J-31s. He followed up by pinpointing the Coast Guard cutter's location and the coordinates that the cutter's skipper had estimated the suspected U.S. helicopter to have been.

Han motioned Lu to his side at the table. "Captain Song has assumed his station on the bridge," he said. "In case you haven't been informed, we're making flank speed for the Taiwan Straits; tensions are building there."

"No, Commissar, I was not aware of that," Lu said. "Sir, may I ask how this affects the matter of Lieutenant Lin?"

"It does not affect it at all. We will handle both situations simultaneously." Han glanced up at the wall clock. He tugged on Lu's elbow, signaling him over to a corner of the room away from the table. Han got closer and spoke in a whisper. "What do you think of Yang's story? I ordered my clerk to bring you a copy of his statement. Have you read it?"

Lu was taken back by the commissar's frankness. He took it as a compliment that a high-ranking party official would consult him. "Commissar, yes, I read the transcript, but... honestly, sir, I don't know what to make of it." He paused for a moment. "I hate to rat out a fellow officer, but I think there might be more to what happened." Lu stopped there; he hoped that he hadn't overstepped his bounds.

Han looked over at the flurry of activity around the conference table. His team had moved on from plotting Lin's last known position and were now drawing expanding distance rings from that spot. Lieutenant Lin's squadron commander, Commander Wei, had opened the J-31's performance manual and was relaying distances to *Shanghai*'s navigator, who recorded the kilometers, measured them out with a plotting compass, then drew a sweeping arc on the chart. Wei turned to a different section of the manual and called out more numbers; the navigator readjusted his compass and swung another arc. They repeated the process several times.

"Well, let's let these people do their jobs," Han said. He motioned toward the exit, then led Lu out of the conference room and down a passageway. They arrived at a stateroom identified by a simple brass plaque that read, "COMMIS-SAR." Han reached into a pocket, found his key, and unlocked the door. "Excuse the mess; I wasn't expecting visitors today," he said with an embarrassed grin. Commander Lu had been in this part of the ship many times for department head meetings inside Captain Song's office; he'd never been invited to the commissar's private stateroom.

The compartment was spartan: a single bed—unmade, along one wall; a diminutive lavatory comprised of a sink, commode and tiny shower separated from the sleeping area by a narrow folding door. Across from the bed was a metal locker with a few built-in drawers; adjacent to the locker was a fold down table. Like most everything on the ship, the stateroom and its furnishings were painted drab grey.

A single office chair sat in the corner. Han slid the chair forward, motioned Lu to sit while he settled onto the edge of his bed. "Hope that you weren't expecting anything too lavish," the commissar said with a laugh. "As a party official, I'm expected to present a humble existence."

Lu scanned the surroundings. Along the bulkhead above Han's bed were framed photos of all leaders of the Chinese Communist Party since Mao Zedong, with Mao's portrait larger than the others and displayed at the top. On the folding table that served as a desk was a laptop computer plugged in and charging, a few books, plus an empty soft drink can, absent its top. Stuffed inside the can were an assortment of pens, pencils, and colored markers. A small photograph of Han and a woman that Lu assumed to be his wife rested on a shelf next to the bed. The pair were dressed in formal attire; neither of them were smiling.

Commissar Han got right to his point. "Lu, Captain Song and I have had our eyes on you since you reported aboard. We consider you one of the ship's finest officers and a true believer in the Party's objectives. I want to know your gut feelings about Yang's statement." Han leaned back against the wall and propped a pillow under his arm. "So, Air Officer, no holds barred; give it to me straight."

Lu realized that whatever he said would be impactful—not only to his reputation with Commissar Han and Captain Song, but to his military career in general. He took a deep breath, then faced Han, taking special care to look squarely into the man's eyes. "Commissar, I think Yang's story is bullshit." Lu held eye contact. "That's my opinion, sir."

"Any new thoughts about Lin?"

Lu pursed his lips. "I can only hope that he's on that helicopter, or better yet, that he magically appears and makes a safe trap on the boat. But, sir, if you're asking me again what's in my gut... I think we may have lost Lin Yi forever."

"Yes...and his aircraft." Han rubbed his chin while staring at the floor. "The loss of that J-31 would be devastating."

Hearing the commissar's words prompted Lu to recall the potential scenario that Captain Song had presented: that Lin may have had enough extra fuel to land someplace other than aboard *Shanghai*. "Commissar, I'm not privy to details of the equipment on Lin's jet, but would I be correct in assuming that the Party would rather find his aircraft before anyone else does?" Lu regretted asking the question the moment the words left his mouth. His face turned crimson as he braced for the commissar's response.

Han glared at Lu with the same heartless expression that caused the ship's crew to avoid him at all costs. But after a long, tense pause, he smiled and patted Lu on the shoulder. "You are completely correct, Lu Bo," Han said, addressing the officer by his full and proper name. He tossed the pillow aside and stood up from the bed. Lu rose from his chair. "I propose that we return to the conference room to learn the latest developments," the commissar said. "After that, Captain Song and I will summon Lieutenant Commander Yang and offer him the opportunity to, let's say, revise his statement."

But as Han opened the door, his demeanor changed to stone cold sober; any hospitality that he'd extended evaporated faster than water droplets on a hot griddle. The "Snake" narrowed his eyes and got nose-to-nose with Lu. "Commander, the events brewing between our People's Republic and those Taiwanese renegades are of the utmost concern. That being said, the return of Lieutenant Lin and his aircraft may, in its own way, pan out to be equally as important. I ask that you keep our little talk confidential."

* * *

Dick Moselli's mayday calls were finally heard when the crew of a Cathay Pacific airliner flying from Manila to Hong Kong picked up his transmission. By pure coincidence, the Airbus 330 was passing in the vicinity of the American's helicopter at thirty-six thousand feet. The plane's crew relayed the message to their company operations at the Manila airport, which in turn contacted the Philippines' Civil Aviation Authority. Through a string of other governmental agencies, word soon reached the Pentagon, where the Navy's watch team was cut in, prompting them to shoot off an Operational Report (OPREP) message to the U.S. Pacific Fleet Commander. Within minutes of that dispatch being sent, the Commanding Officer of USS *Grand Rapids* was handed a teletyped copy of the message. The entire thread of communications—from Moselli's mayday call, all the way to the White House—took less than thirty minutes.

Oblivious to their instant profile on the world stage, Moselli and crew followed the J-15s to a place unknown. They saw no surface vessels or other aircraft enroute. Forty minutes into their journey, a hazy grouping of images appeared on the horizon. Ed Horton was the first to spot it.

"Bruiser, my eyesight ain't what it used to be…but is that a bunch of boats I see at twelve o'clock?"

Moselli raised his helmet's shaded visor; he squinted hard to focus. Before he could speak, Aguilar butted in. "You're right, Crazo, that *is* something. Wait a minute, yeah…looks like boats clustered inside some sort of lagoon or reef." He adjusted the aircraft's radar antennae and switched the unit to its "ground" mode. "Yup, definitely something out there."

Moments later it became clear. The Chinese fighters had led them to a remote land mass in the middle of the South China Sea. Moselli rubbed his eyes. "Wow. I've read about the Chi-Com's manmade islands, but never thought I'd see one." He checked the fuel gauges. "We've got about fifteen minutes in the tanks before we go swimming. One way or another, we're landing on that sandbox."

One of the J-15s slid back into position on Moselli's side. "American heelochopper, you land there…now," the pilot radioed. He signaled Moselli by pointing his hand toward the island.

Moselli acknowledged by returning a thumbs up, while Aguilar reduced power and put the aircraft into a descent. As the J-15 inched ahead, Moselli couldn't resist keying his mike and saying, "Well thanks so much for the escort,

Charlie Chan. And when you get home, say hello to General Tso; tell him that we love his chicken."

Aguilar and Horton stared at their boss for a second and then burst out laughing. The crew's mood had lightened over the last few minutes. They'd received two confidence boosters: first was a reply from the Cathay Pacific captain with his assurance that he'd relay their distress call; second was the fact that they'd sighted land and wouldn't have to ditch.

Dick Moselli took the controls and began searching for a place to set down. As they got closer, he, Aguilar and Horton were amazed at the site below: what was once a submerged ocean shoal had been transformed into a U-shaped island, appearing several miles long from tip to tip. Nestled inside the "U" were a fleet of barges that had strange looking mechanical rigs attached to them. Moselli leveled off at 200 feet above the surface. He noticed that the J-15s were circling above him.

"Well, we made it to dry land," Moselli said. "And we're not quite down to fumes, so what the hell…let's check this place out." He rolled the aircraft into a shallow bank, slowed to 70 knots, and flew up one side of the U. The crew witnessed partially built structures, bulldozers, cranes, and a pier that extended offshore several hundred feet from one tip of the island.

As they flew over a long string of house trailers, Aguilar saw a handful of people rush out from inside; they waved enthusiastically. "Can't be too hostile," he said. "Looks like they're rolling out the welcome wagon for us."

"Don't count on it," Horton snapped.

Moselli traced a path over the curved part of the U where he noted a square, paved surface, painted bright green, and emblazoned with the international markings of a helicopter landing pad: a white block letter "H" centered inside a triangle. He faced the other end of the island and said, "Good lord, it looks like they're building a runway long enough to handle any type of aircraft." He pointed to an expansive stretch of graded dirt. "That's got to be at least two miles long."

Aguilar got edgy. "We gonna land, Bruiser, or what? Those jets are still orbiting. In case you didn't notice, they had missiles strapped under their wings."

Horton fell forward over the center console and shouted, "Here they come!" The crew watched as the J-15s dove from their holding pattern and bore-sighted the helicopter like a pair of angry starlings protecting their nest. The jets pulled up at the last second, passing just yards away. Moselli yanked his aircraft into a tight bank and headed straight for the helicopter pad; he keyed his mike. "Okay, guys, we get the message. Now leave us alone and go home, damn it!"

He made a soft touchdown on the landing pad as the J-15s joined up in tight formation and rocketed skyward. By the time the H-60's rotor blades came to a stop, the jets had zoomed out of sight.

Aguilar completed shutdown procedures and stowed the checklist. It was dead quiet inside the aircraft. He removed his helmet, tousled his flattened curly hair and turned to Moselli. "Well, fearless leader, what do we do now?"

Before Moselli could answer, the crew saw a dust cloud billowing toward them. A file of military vehicles emerged from the cloud, then encircled the helicopter. Soldiers burst out from the vehicles, assumed prone battle positions, and aimed their rifles at the cockpit.

"Two, four, six...oh, hell, we're outnumbered at least five to one," Moselli said. "Well, Don Juan, there's your welcoming committee."

Moselli glanced over his left shoulder and saw that Horton had unholstered his pistol. "Put it away, Crazo, or you'll get us all killed." He re-assessed the situation outside, then said, "I want you guys to stay in the aircraft and let me do the talking." He then removed his own sidearm, set in on the console, unstrapped, and cracked open his door.

Dick Moselli stepped onto the pavement and raised his hands—not high above his head as if surrendering, but rather at shoulder level. He forced a composed expression and said, "Does anybody here speak English?"

Two men emerged from the crowd that had surrounded the chopper. One was of average height and wearing a short-sleeved, tan jumpsuit drenched in perspiration. Moselli searched for something that identified the man's rank, but the fellow's clothing was so wet, he couldn't discern any markings. The soldier beside him was quite short, and like the others, dressed in green camouflage and toting an automatic rifle. The pair marched in step toward Moselli and assumed a guarded stance a few feet away.

Moselli sized them up: on closer examination, the taller fellow appeared much older, maybe in his late fifties. The man's pocked face dripped with sweat; Moselli winced at the guy's reeking body odor. The soldier looked to be in his twenties; Moselli recognized the man's insignia as that of a Chinese army captain. Despite the sweltering tropical heat, the young officer looked cool and dry.

The sweaty fellow blurted out a streak of words to the captain, who listened attentively and nodded. The captain then turned to Moselli and said in fragmented but clear English, "I speak for my superior. We want Chinese pilot. You give him now!" He waved his weapon toward the helicopter.

Moselli moved closer to the captain and shouted, "I demand that you put me in contact with a United States official!" He jabbed a finger at the man. "And why was I forced to land here?"

The captain ignored Moselli's words and repeated, "We want Chinese pilot. You give him now!"

Dick Moselli motioned to his helicopter. "I don't know what the hell you're talking about; there is no Chinese pilot on my aircraft."

His last statement seemed to aggravate the man in the sweat-soaked jumpsuit; the guy launched into a tirade, directing his wrath at the army captain, not at Moselli. The soldier lowered his head for a moment, then said, "My superior says open hee-lo-copter."

Moselli's patience was wearing thin. He shrugged his shoulders and said with a tired chuckle, "Sure, pal, follow me."

The captain barked an order over his shoulder, which prompted a few of his men to rise from the pavement and join him. The group raised their weapons in unison as Moselli slid open the cabin door.

The captain craned his head inside the helicopter and hollered something in his native tongue. He then stepped up into the aircraft, hollered again, and probed the barrel of his rifle into the rumpled mass wrapped in a blanket. Salid sat up and shielded his eyes from the light. His arms shot into the air at the sight of a gun barrel mere inches from his head.

"Well, mister, is that the guy you're looking for?" Moselli said.

The captain hesitated and then looked to his boss for guidance; the two exchanged heated words. Finally, the captain jumped down from the helicopter while the sweaty fellow stormed off in his vehicle.

Moselli tugged on the captain's arm. "Hey, you need to tell me what's going on; I don't know where we are or why your jets forced us down."

"Wait, please, sir." the captain said. He then backed away, waved his arms and gave an order to the other soldiers circling the helicopter. The men got to their feet, lowered their rifles and stood at ease; they mumbled between themselves with confused looks.

The captain said, "This is big mix up. You stay here...I come back soon." He jogged to an open-air jeep and drove away.

Moselli thought to himself, *Where the hell could we go? We're out of fuel.* He looked back at his aircraft and saw that Aguilar, Horton and Salid were seated on the open doorsill. Horton stood up and walked toward him. His face had a pained look as he leaned in close and said, "Bruiser, I need to burn one like *really, really* bad, but my Zippo is plum out of juice." He tilted his head toward the soldiers. "You mind if I ask one of them for a light?"

Moselli had no idea where he was or how he'd find his way back to the ship. Nonetheless, he and his crew, along with their stowaway, were on deck and intact. The tension that had cloaked his body began to ebb. He put an arm around Horton and said with a weary smile, "Sure, Crazo. If you can talk one those guys out of a match without getting your head blown off, go ahead."

CHAPTER 6

After the news of Dick Moselli's mayday call had reached the highest levels of Washington, the Navy's Seventh Fleet Commander directed USS *Grand Rapids* to a position west of Luzon, Philippines, in the vicinity of where intelligence experts concluded Moselli's helicopter had been forced to land.

CIA imaging satellites had been monitoring China's latest island building project in the area known as Scarborough Shoals. Though the region rested within the Philippines' Exclusive Economic Zone (EEZ)—a concept adopted at the United Nation's Conference on the Law of the Sea in 1982—the Chinese Communist Party had ignored the decree by declaring sovereignty over shallow areas of the South China Sea. The CCP defined the expansive tract of ocean by the nebulous term "Nine-Dashed Line," which started south of Taiwan, paralleled the Philippines' west coast, curved just north of Malaysia, stretched along the east coast of Vietnam, and terminated at China's island province of Hainan Dao. To support its claim, China's military had become more aggressive by interfering with foreign fishing rights, arbitrarily enforcing no-fly zones over the manmade islands, and by obstructing commercial vessels transiting the area. The hijacking of Moselli's aircraft had served as an unprovoked hostile act against the United States.

* * *

Commander Bill Draper, *Grand Rapids'* Commanding Officer, departed Integrated Command and Control One (ICC1) and strode a few steps forward onto the ship's bridge.

"Captain's on the bridge!" a voice called out. Personnel on watch stood a tad more erect; those seated at consoles sat up straighter.

"Carry on, folks," Draper said. A sense of relief spread over the watch team.

The layout of *Grand Rapids'* bridge resembled the control room for a space launch rather than the bridge of a traditional Navy vessel. Most notably was the absence of a helm, or wheel. Instead of a helm, the center of *Grand Rapids'* bridge was dominated by a raised station that wrapped around two officers sitting in what looked like an aircraft cockpit. From this station the Officer of the Deck (OOD) and Junior Officer of the Deck (JOOD) oversaw not only the vessel's internal operations, but navigated the ship and maintained a watch on the seas surrounding them. Computer keyboards, joysticks and complex dials were electronically linked to the vessel's four waterjets; *Grand Rapids* had no propellers. Two gas turbines and a pair of diesel engines powered the water-jets, allowing for remarkable speed and maneuverability. Panoramic windows provided a sweeping view for the watch section.

Captain Draper turned to the OOD, a twenty-six-year-old named Michelle Perks. "How we doing, Lieutenant?" he asked.

"Nothing new to report, Captain. Holding steady at 40 knots. Reminds me of riding my jet ski on Lake Burton, back in Georgia."

Draper smiled. "Yup, this rig can really fly, can't she...or should I say, can't *it?*"

"She, he, it, whatever...the pronoun doesn't matter much to me, sir. I'm just happy that we have calm seas and good weather." The pair gazed at the marvelous sight: an uninterrupted horizon of crystal clear skies and wide open ocean. The ship cut through the ocean's cobalt water, peeling back white waves from its spear-like bow. A roaring blast of foamy spray erupted from the vessel's tri-hulled stern.

Draper checked the electronic navigation plot. "Our navigator says we'll arrive at our new position after dark, about...four and a half hours from now. I wish this speedboat could get us there sooner, but I shouldn't complain; we're about the fastest ship the Navy has in its inventory."

Perks stepped aside to scan the ship's engine performance instruments that were displayed on monitors. Satisfied, she returned and stood next to Draper. "Captain, once on station, when do you expect we'll receive further orders?"

Draper lowered his voice to just above a whisper. "Hard to say at this point. Commodore Torres is on a conference call with her boss in San Diego, and Seventh Fleet in Japan. We should be getting an update very soon—let's hope, anyway."

Draper and Perks continued observing the low-key activity around them. Other than the wisping sound of air piped through the compartment's ventilation system, coupled with the soft, clicking buzz of electronics, the scene was peaceful. But the serene atmosphere came to a halt when the same sailor that had announced Draper's arrival shouted, "Commodore's on deck!"

"Ladies and gents, please carry on," Commodore Katherine Marie Torres said as she marched on to the bridge. The space got quieter by her presence, prompting Torres to quip, "Geez, hope I didn't crash the party." She turned to Draper. "Skipper, should I have called ahead for a reservation?" Light laughter rose from a couple of youngsters. Despite the commodore's authentic effort to put everyone at ease, the crew was guarded. They were keenly aware of the woman's vaulted position in their chain of command, and in addition, a mess deck rumor had spread that Torres—who'd been flown aboard by helicopter yesterday—had been selected for early promotion to rear admiral.

Commodore Torres stood next to Draper, while Perks excused herself and moved to the other side of the bridge. The pair of senior officers could not have presented a more contrasting image: Draper: short, husky, and balding; Torres: trim and tall, with perfectly coiffed, collar length hair. Yet they shared two things in common: their love of the sea, and the gold ring that they each wore as Naval Academy graduates. For Torres, a career in the Navy had been a life-long dream inspired by her father, who'd enlisted in the Navy at age seventeen. Though he'd spent only a single four-year hitch in the military, he'd never lost sight of how the service had elevated him from his humble roots in Queens, New York, to a Second Class Petty Officer, trained to operate complex machinery. Katherine Torres grew up in a modest urban home where her dad had decorated an entire wall with Navy memorabilia: his Honorable Discharge certificate displayed in the middle of photos, framed insignia, and other mementos. When Katherine received an appointment to the Academy, he'd told his daughter that it was the proudest day of his life.

Bill Draper had known Katherine Torres since their days in Annapolis, where she had served as his squad leader during the arduous seven-week training period known as Plebe Summer. Struggling to keep up with his peers, Draper had initiated paperwork to resign from the Academy. But when he'd handed over the forms for her endorsement, Torres stood up from her desk, confronted him squarely, and tore the papers to shreds. "Draper, you'll never forgive your-self if you don't at least stick it out for Plebe year," she'd told him. "Damn it, I will not let you quit... not on my watch!" Years later, Torres had hand-picked Bill Draper to be her executive officer on the first ship she'd commanded. The two remained close friends.

Torres tapped Draper on the shoulder and leaned in close. "Bill, we need to talk." When at sea she preferred to have one-to-one chats in the open air—on one of the bridge wings or on a weather deck; the sights, sounds and smell of the ocean seemed to help her concentrate; but that wasn't the case today. With *Grand Rapids* skimming across the water at high speed, the relative wind was near gale force, and if there was a single bit of femininity that the woman held dearly, it was the neatness of her hair. She glanced outside for an instant, and then nudged Draper again. "How about we go to your office?" she suggested.

Draper followed her and said, "Well, okay, but I forgot to make my bed this morning. You're not going to put me on report, are you ma'am?" The pair burst out laughing as they recalled the numerous times that Midshipman First Class Torres had placed Plebe Draper on report for his messy room.

"Commodore and Captain are off the bridge!" Lieutenant Perks announced as they left.

Draper's stateroom and office were a short walk from the bridge. As he cracked open the door, he said, "See, I warned you." Torres shook her head at the site of the unmade bed and disheveled space.

"Didn't learn a damn thing, did you, Draper?" she lamented.

Draper took a seat at one end of the leather sofa that he'd brought aboard from home; Torres sat at the other end. They were glad to be away from the scrutiny of the bridge crew.

"So, what the fuck, Kathy, where's this mystery leading us to?" Draper said.

"Not quite sure, Bill. The brass in San Diego and Seventh Fleet are non-committal about what action, if any, we should take after we reach our new position. Like we learned earlier, Moselli and his crew were intercepted and forced down." She paused before asking, "Could they have gotten off track and wandered into airspace the Chi-Coms are claiming as theirs?"

"Not a chance," Draper said without hesitation. "They were on a routine utility mission: delivery of mail and spare parts, then hoisting the chaplain from a destroyer; you know the drill. Moselli and Aguilar are the most experienced pilots we have onboard; top of the heap at their home squadron in Coronado." He shook his head. "No, there's got to be something else."

Torres had more on her mind than Moselli's crew. She'd traveled from San Diego to inspect vessels under her charge as Commander, Littoral Combat Ship Squadron Three. The highly automated ships of LCSRON 3 were designed to operate with a minimum crew— less than half the personnel of a comparable size vessel. However, cost overruns, degraded readiness, and uncertainties about the survivability of the ship's aluminum hull had led critics to define "LCS" as "Little Crappy Ship." Katherine Torres aimed to change that perception. A knock on the door interrupted her thoughts.

"It's unlocked, come on in," Draper hollered. A burly petty officer entered, saluted, and stood at attention. The sleeves of the sailor's coveralls were rolled up above the elbow, revealing his massive forearms. He had the build of an NFL linebacker.

"Sir, this message just came into the comm shack," he said, referring to the ship's communications office. He held a red binder marked "Classified." Unsure to whom he should hand it, the sailor looked at the ship's commanding officer, then shot a glance toward the commodore. Torres pointed an index finger to Draper, who accepted the document and acknowledged receipt by scribbling his initials in red ink on its custody record. The sailor left as swiftly as he'd arrived. Draper opened the binder and began reading. There was a long list of recipients, starting with the Chairman of the Joint Chiefs of Staff.

Draper scanned the first couple lines of the message, then dropped the binder to his lap; he sat back with a stunned expression. "Wow, this is a transcript of Moselli's mayday call to the airliner." He wondered how U.S. Intelligence had retrieved the data so quickly; the hanging question didn't occupy his thoughts for long. *Well, I guess that's what our spooks are supposed to do,* he reasoned. After reading further, he and Torres learned that in addition to the mayday call, Moselli revealed he'd made a water rescue before being intercepted by the fighters.

"So, the plot thickens." Torres said. She shook her head. "Bill, none of this makes sense. Why would the Chi-Coms launch on an unarmed U.S. helicopter?"

"God only knows, Commodore," Draper replied. "But I have a hunch we're about to find out."

* * *

The Chinese Coast Guard cutter that had tracked Moselli's aircraft made haste to the location in question. It wasn't difficult; the ship's radar operator had recorded the latitude/longitude on his scope. Plugging those coordinates into the vessel's navigation system was elementary. Extended time had elapsed since the explosion and the debris had drifted; nonetheless, lookouts were successful spotting *Jasmine's* wreckage. The cutter's skipper had considered putting an exploratory boat into the fouled water but decided against it. Instead, he ordered his helmsman to steer an arc around the site, fearful that flotsam and oil might harm his own vessel. After surveying the disaster, he sent another message to the *Shanghai*:

SUBJECT AREA COMPRISES WRECKAGE OF A WOODEN TRAWLER. UNABLE TO DETERMINE COUNTRY OF ORIGIN. SMALL SEC-TIONS OF HULL AND OIL SLICK REMAIN ON SURFACE. WATER SAMPLES TAKEN FOR ANALYSIS. ISOLATED PERSONAL ITEMS RETRIEVED. NO SURVIVORS NOTED.

* * *

After the cutter's message had reached *Shanghai*, Captain Song discussed it with Commissar Han. The pair acknowledged its contents, then concluded that there wasn't anything the ship could do in response; they'd received higher priority instructions from Beijing. Song ordered all of the carrier's oil-fired boilers lit off and for the flattop to make top speed to the Straits of Taiwan, where tensions were building. The J-15s that had intercepted Moselli's helicopter were topped off by a pair of tankers and brought back aboard while *Shanghai*'s air wing remained on high alert.

The majority of Communist China's naval fleet was assembling inside the one-hundred-mile-wide body of water that separated Taiwan from the Chinese mainland. The question persisted: *Would the Communists finally take military action against the democratic nation of Taiwan that for decades it had longed to control?*

With the issue of Taiwan beyond his scope, Commissar Han sat in his state-room and contemplated the whereabouts of Lieutenant Lin Yi. After receiving the news that Lin was not aboard the American helicopter, he summoned Captain Song for his input. Song rapped a pair of perfunctory knocks on the stateroom door and walked in.

Han had poured himself a cup of strong tea and was sitting on the edge of his bed. He motioned for Song to have a seat. "How does that saying go, Bulldog, 'May you live in interesting times?' Guess we're getting our fill of that now, aren't we?"

Captain Song chuckled. "Yes, we are, Snake." He pulled a pack of cigarettes from his breast pocket. "You mind? I know you're trying to quit."

"No, I could use one myself," Han said as he reached for one and lit up. He took a deep drag before speaking. "Where the hell is Lin and that jet?" He drew another hit, held the smoke in his lungs for several seconds before exhaling, then took a sip of tea. He turned to Song. "What are your thoughts, my friend?"

Song shook his head slowly. "I am confused, Snake," he said. "The cutter's message about what it found—there was no mention of aircraft wreckage, just the remnants of a fishing vessel. And in the exact spot where Yang claims that he last saw Lin."

Han shrugged. "Yes, I have my suspicions as well."

Song nodded and said, "We have orders that the Taiwan crisis takes priority." He rubbed his brow and continued. "Our intelligence people report that the Americans have dispatched two carrier strike groups to the region. I suspect that the Australians will also get involved."

"Okay, I understand," Han said. He took another sip of tea. "But back to my question: what are your thoughts about Lin?"

Captain Song lowered his eyes to the deck. "Commissar, this debacle of Lin's disappearance and the decision to intercept the helicopter pale in comparison to what's developing off Taiwan. Regarding Lin, though, I'm not convinced that either he or his jet are lost."

Han got to his feet. "I want to see Yang again, right now."

"Here?" Song asked.

"Yes."

Captain Song reached for the phone mounted on the bulkhead next to the commissar's desk and made the call. Soon, Thunder Yang's footsteps were heard double-timing down the passageway. Han opened the door and waved him in.

"Captain Song and I want to offer you another opportunity to explain what happened," Han said. "Perhaps you've had time to gather your thoughts?"

Yang's heart raced and his breathing quickened. He tried to settle his nerves, but to no end. He'd always prided himself on the ability to cap his emotions and prevent them from interfering with his duties as a fighter pilot. But this situation was different: while inside the cockpit of his jet, he had total control; now, he had none. He knew from the look in Han's eyes that the commissar wasn't buying his story. Yang also realized that he didn't have the ability to dupe the man; Han had the reputation of a hardline Party loyalist who was an expert at routing out the truth. By comparison, Yang felt like a low-level tool; he was putty in the commissar's hands.

"Well, Mister Yang, the captain and I are waiting." Han inched closer; a callous grin edged across his face.

"Commissar, I regret that—"

"Oh, and before you begin," Han said, "Mechanics inspected your aircraft and have confirmed that you expended ammunition during the flight; we've also received word from a Coast Guard cutter that discovered evidence of a sunken vessel in the precise location to which you and Lin were dispatched." Han's grin changed to a warm smile. He held out his arms as if he were welcoming Yang with a hug. "It's all going to come out one way or another, Yang Chen. Save yourself the trouble and just level with us."

Upon hearing the commissar's persuasive words, Yang felt an unexpected sense of relief. He knew that he'd met his match and it was pointless to continue the ruse. He concluded: *if I can't lie any better than this, then I might as well tell the truth.*

So Thunder Yang spilled the entire episode: the supersonic buzzing of the trawler; his ignoring Lin's insistence that the vessel was a defenseless fishing boat and not a spy ship; the reckless way he'd walked a stream of bullets over the water and the fireball that followed; and the fact that he'd left the scene before confirming that Lin had joined up with him.

When he'd finished, Yang glanced at *Shanghai*'s commanding officer. Captain Song sat motionless. At first, he appeared unfazed, but then his complexion reddened. When he spoke, the words came out in a low growl: "Yang, you worthless piece of pig dung!"

In contrast, the commissar seemed to accept Yang's revelation with cavalier nonchalance. "Mister Yang," Han began, "we work in a dangerous business. Accidents sometimes happen." He motioned to Song. "The captain and I appreciate your candor, which will hopefully assist in determining Lieutenant Lin's whereabouts."

Han cracked open the stateroom door; he gripped Yang's shoulder. "What you've confessed will remain confidential. And as I asked before, do not speak to anyone about what you've told us."

"Yes, Commissar," Yang said.

Han concluded by saying, "Yang Chen, you are still restricted to your quarters and will remain grounded. You are dismissed."

It was a long walk for Thunder Yang back to his stateroom. He was devastated by the notion that his military career was probably over; flying fighters was the only thing that gave his life meaning.

However, what weighed heaviest on his heart was not that he'd caused the demise of a harmless fishing boat and its crew, nor the punishment he expected because of his actions. What troubled him most was how he would lose face with his brother aviators. He'd committed a pilot's mortal sin: he had abandoned his wingman. For that, Lieutenant Commander Yang Chen could never forgive himself.

CHAPTER 7

When Thunder Yang had started his second pass at the trawler, Lin Yi slid back several dozen yards from the tight formation he'd maintained during Yang's initial buzzing of the vessel. Lin had decided after the first pass that he wanted no part of Yang's wild stunt. He'd watched as Yang unloaded a stream of bullets in the direction of the trawler's stern, never imagining that the act would go so awry. Yang had the reputation of a swashbuckling, arrogant fighter pilot—a branding that he embraced and considered his calling card. Despite his brash personality, fellow pilots revered the man's courage and superior airmanship, whether during weapons exercises or when performing arrested shipboard landings. Lin figured that Yang's feigned attack would play out like everything else the guy did: he'd fly to within a razor's edge of his limitations and those of his aircraft, and then ease off at the last second to save his hide.

But Lin had guessed wrong. His position behind and to the right of Yang's jet had placed him in the middle of the fireball as it erupted from the propane tank strapped to the vessel's stern; traveling at such a high rate of speed, it was impossible to avoid flying through the inferno. His eyes closed instinctively as the J-31 was engulfed by blackish-red flames. The explosion flung his aircraft up and into a steep bank angle. Once clear of the burst, Lin found himself inverted and descending toward the water. To his good fortune, the J-31's powerful twin turbines never quit. Lin's training took over as he rolled the jet wings level and nudged back on the control stick. He leveled off 300 feet above the surface.

Lin Yi was not a religious person; like many Chinese, he considered himself an agnostic. Yet the experience of being enveloped by fire caused him to flash back to a theology course he'd taken as an elective in graduate school, where his classmates had debated the concept of an afterlife, and the existence of heaven and hell. His passing through the flames had been an epiphany. Any doubts as to what he had to do were erased. He'd carry out the plan that he'd spent weeks conceiving: he would defect and take his airplane with him.

The sequence of events had played out to Lin's advantage. With luck on his side, he'd convinced the young sailor to give him extra fuel; he'd survived the unexpected weak catapult shot, and then, not wanting to bring added attention to himself, he'd lied to the air boss about improperly configuring his aircraft's trim settings for launch. And finally, Yang's failure to recognize that he hadn't joined up had provided Lin additional time to go undetected.

Lin Yi's original plan had been to fake that his jet's oxygen system had become contaminated, thereby incapacitating him while his plane continued flying on autopilot. In that case, he predicted that Yang would follow him for only so long before reaching a critical fuel state and returning to the ship alone.

And yet, there was another scenario, the one that Lin had considered but refused to accept: after being informed that he hadn't rendezvoused with Thunder, *Shanghai*'s commissar would order Yang to shoot him down rather than risk having Lin's jet fall into foreign hands.

The first minutes of Lin's getaway were filled with uncertainties: *Would Shanghai launch another jet to come after him? Could he avoid radar detection by flying low over the water? Would he have enough fuel to make a safe landing, or would he be forced to ditch?*

But Lin's doubts faded as his training and systems knowledge kicked in. He secured electronics that might lead to his stealthy aircraft being tracked: communication and navigation radios were turned off; the J-31's transponder—which identified him on radar— was powered down; and lastly, he switched off the aircraft's satellite navigation unit (SATNAV) that might be used to locate him. However, without those critical electronics, he'd be flying by the seat of his pants, relying solely on his innate sense of direction, and a primitive form of navigation known as "dead reckoning." His fellow cadets at the flight academy had rolled their eyes when required to demonstrate proficiency in the calculating of current position by using a prior known reference point and advancing that point based on estimated speed over elapsed time and course. Most cadets figured that with GPS, ground aids, and radar vectors at their disposal, dead reckoning navigation was an antiquated waste of time. But Lin never cut corners while in flight training. He'd shown the same attention to detail mastering dead reckoning as he'd done with learning more advanced technology.

Any feelings of remorse were compartmentalized and stored in the deep recesses of Lin Yi's brain; he'd made his decision and was dedicated to the completion of his mission. Before switching off the navigation aids, he'd logged the latitude/longitude coordinates of his position. He then turned from the easterly course that he and Yang had flown to the trawler, to a southeasterly heading utilizing the aircraft's magnetic compass—a version of the same unpowered directional device that mariners have used since ancient times. Next, he descended to an altitude just above the water to take advantage of the J-31's sleek profile that was nearly undetectable by radar. As a final step, Lin set the jet's airspeed to "long range cruise." With those parameters in place, he engaged the autopilot, punched the aircraft's clock to start timing, and sat back. He expected to arrive off the west coast of Luzon, Philippines in twenty-seven minutes.

* * *

Commissar Han's team had exhausted their resources while attempting to predict how far Lin could have flown with the extra fuel he had onboard. Squadron Commander Wei, along with Air Officer Lu, were the most knowledgeable pilots on the ship regarding the J-31's capabilities. They'd supervised the plotting of expanding distance rings from Lin's last known position and concluded that he would have had three plausible choices of places to land other than back on the ship. The most favorable option would have been for Lin to track a course to mainland China to a spot northeast of Hong Kong; option two was to head for seldom used Hengchun airport on the southern tip of Taiwan. Though Hengchun's five-thousand-foot runway was marginally suitable for a J-31, Lin would have better odds of avoiding a clash with Taiwanese fighters at remote Hengchun rather than at the heavily populated region of Kaohsiung City airport. Because of the hostilities between China and Taiwan, Wei and Lu disregarded any Taiwan option. And finally, there was option three: the Philippines. Luzon Island was within the last range ring drawn on the chart. Though Philippine-Chinese relations had thawed over the past decades, the country's new president had campaigned on the platform of standing firm against China's dominance in the South China Sea. Wei and Lu considered the Philippines' early warning radar equipment unreliable, which gave Lin a good chance of flying to Luzon undetected.

Han returned and motioned for Lu and Wei to join him in a far corner of the room, out of earshot of the rest. "Air Officer, you go first," Han said. "What are you thinking?"

"Well, Commissar, considering that the Coast Guard cutter didn't find evidence of aircraft wreckage, and we never received a distress call, I think that presents just two possible scenarios: Lin either flew for some distance before crashing, in which case a search effort should be coordinated or, um…"

Han saw that Lu was hedging. "Go ahead, out with it, Lu. Speak your mind."

Lu turned to Wei and then back to the commissar. "My gut feeling is that Lieutenant Lin did not crash and is looking for a place to land."

Han narrowed his beady eyes. "Are you implying defection?"

"Yes, Commissar. We can't get inside the guy's head, but the combination of requesting extra fuel, his failure to join up with Yang after the trawler incident, and the absence of a distress call…I don't think we should rule out defection, especially when considering the value of the weapons system he has onboard." Lu lowered his voice to a just above a whisper. "Delivering a spanking new J-31 with its air-to-air strike capability would give Lin tremendous leverage to negotiate asylum."

Han faced Commander Wei. "And you, Skipper?"

"Commissar, I agree with the Air Officer. There's a strong possibility that he has defected. I've only known Lin for a short time and haven't learned much about his private life; he keeps his cards close to the vest. One thing that hasn't been mentioned, though, is that he spent extended time in the United States as a student and speaks their language."

"Are you thinking he might have a contact in America?" asked Han.

Wei shrugged his shoulders. "We can't know for sure. Our security division monitors communications to and from the ship, but that's not foolproof. Also, the crew has access to foreigners during port visits and these youngsters are adept at using social media." Wei paused then said, "As for Lin's time in the United States… I've found his service record to be vague about that period."

Han stepped aside and approached the men huddled over plotting charts. "Gentlemen, thanks for your efforts," he said. "You are dismissed; please leave the charts, manuals and your work sheets."

Han signaled Wei and Lu to join him as he took a seat. He checked the wall clock, then studied the charts for a moment. "I'll brief Captain Song after leaving you," he said. "But here's the plan: I'm proposing that Beijing deploy more cutters to conduct an extensive search for Lin and his aircraft." He thought for a moment while tapping his fingers on the table. "And I'm also advising my superiors to alert our embassy in Manila that they may have a defector on their hands."

"So, Commissar, you believe Lin has bolted for the Philippines?" Lu asked.

"Short of him being a casualty at sea, that's my best guess. If he'd headed for the mainland, we would have been notified by now. As for Taiwan...possible, but unlikely." Han slapped his hand onto the table. "No, if his aircraft is still intact, Lieutenant Lin Yi is headed for the Philippines."

Wei and Lu faced each other, each silently wondering why such a talented officer would commit an act of treason. Wei spoke first. "Commissar, I honestly never saw this coming. If you wish, I will interview the other pilots to see what they—"

Han interrupted. "Absolutely not, Commander! Rumors will be flying all over the ship about Lin; I do not want to fan the flames. *Shanghai*'s mission is to carry out orders and join our forces in the Straits. Although Lin and his airplane are of major importance, we have bigger fish to fry, so to speak."

Han's eyes narrowed and his neck seemed to stretch longer; he stared at Lu and Wei for several awkward seconds. "I've trusted you gentlemen with some very sensitive information," he said. "Do not breathe a word of our discussion. Am I clear?"

Wei and Lu answered in unison, "Yes, sir!"

"Excellent," Han said as he stood up. "Now return to your jobs."

* * *

There was nothing left for Lin Yi to do: he'd set his plan in motion and was, at least for the time being, a mere passenger aboard a very valuable aircraft. He was confident that the J-31's stealthy profile would provide excellent immunity from radar detection. That fact, coupled his knowledge of the Philippines' outdated equipment, gave him confidence that he had a better than average chance of succeeding.

The low clouds that he and Yang had encountered earlier in the day began to clear, yet land was nowhere in sight. Lin rechecked his compass heading and airspeed, then looked down at the size and direction of the waves. Without use of the aircraft's normal navigation equipment, he was denied access to accurate wind data, so again, as with dead reckoning, he made an educated guess. He drew two vectors on his kneeboard—one representing the aircraft's speed and course, the other what he thought to be the relative wind. He recalculated the numbers: his original prediction of when he'd reach the coast of Luzon still looked reasonable.

Lin let a few more minutes pass, then squinted his eyes and scanned the horizon: still nothing in sight. The sky above had cleared, but a misty haze restricted his straight line visibility. He knew that he had to fly very low to avoid detection; climbing above the haze, even momentarily, might put him in jeopardy. He checked the clock's timer: eleven minutes to go before predicted landfall.

He pulled a water bottle from his helmet bag and took a long draw. He'd packed some nuts, so he nibbled a few of those. The food tasted good, but only served to re-ignite the hunger pangs he suffered by skipping breakfast. He stuffed the bottle and half-eaten snack back into the helmet bag.

Lin looked outside again and saw dark silhouettes begin to form on the horizon. He blinked a few times to confirm it, and then he was sure: he'd reached the coast of Luzon. He noted the time, and then recorded his fuel status. If he was where he'd planned, he'd be a skosh on the plus side of the fuel graph he'd drawn; if he was further north, he'd be on the negative side. He left the autopilot engaged and steered the jet into a gentle right bank, paralleling the coastline about a mile offshore.

As he flew further, the coastline took a dramatic turn to the left. Lin followed in that direction but caught himself; something didn't look right. He noticed that the shoreline continued due south and then wrapped back around to the northwest. He grabbed a map of the Philippines that he'd torn from a National Geographic magazine he'd purchased during a port call in Vietnam. He scrambled to correlate the map to what he saw. After a moment, he realized that he was abeam the Lingayen Gulf; stronger winds than he'd anticipated had pushed him well north of where he wanted to be. He turned off the autopilot, rolled into a tight right bank and rejoined the coastline west of Lingayen.

His miscalculation had cost him precious fuel, but he didn't panic. He'd made it this far and was not about to lose hope. He calculated that he needed to fly another two hundred kilometers to his destination. A quick dead reckoning estimate proved that he could make it—but his fuel margin would be as narrow as a gnat's ass.

He saw more activity the further south that he flew from Lingayen. Tiny coastal villages dotted the landscape that rose from sandy beaches to steep mountains to the east. He rechecked the time; his destination was less than ten minutes away. As he'd expected, the J-31 had penetrated Philippine airspace without evidence of registering a blip on radar and being intercepted. His dream was becoming a reality.

Lin prepared for landing. He switched on a radio and started to dial up the frequency for the Subic airport control tower when he spotted a flock of sea birds swirling off the stern of a fishing boat ahead. He nudged his stick to the right to avoid them, but it was too late; the flock reacted by flying straight up and into his path. He heard a "pop-pop" sound as a cluster of the flock impacted the jet's canopy; their innards splattered into purplish-red smears on the glass. Lin caught his breath, then did what any good pilot would do after a bird strike: he checked his engine instruments. As he did, he felt the aircraft begin to vibrate; it was a low rumble that soon built in intensity. Lin realized that his left engine had ingested some of the birds. The rumble became worse as the turbine's fan blades spun out of balance. Seconds later, the engine's internal section disintegrated, shooting jagged shrapnel through its fuel control unit and severing fuel supply lines. When the vaporized jet fuel encountered the red-hot metal of the damaged engine, it ignited. Lin watched in horror as the aircraft's emergency warning panel lit up like a Chinese New Year celebration.

Lin was faced with another obstacle, and again, he maintained his composure. He carried out memorized procedures that he'd practiced endless times in the J-31's flight simulator: he retarded the left throttle to idle, flipped a switch that shut off fuel to the engine's fuel control unit, then pulled a handle which closed a valve inside the left wing's fuel tank and simultaneously shot a stream of fire suppressing agent into the torched engine cavity. The rumbling stopped, but the fire continued to burn for several seconds before extinguishing.

Lin Yi then focused on the right engine. He attempted to transfer fuel from the dead engine's tank into the right's supply, but the left side was already near empty. The combination of Yang's supersonic stunt over the trawler, coupled with Lin's navigation error and the fire, had placed him in a critically low fuel state. Further complicating his dilemma was the fifty percent loss of power; the jet's airspeed began to decay toward a stall condition. Lin eased the right throttle forward. The plane accelerated, but at the cost of increased fuel consumption.

He had to make a crucial decision: should he continue nursing the aircraft just above the water's surface, or should he climb? He looked to his left, where he saw the rugged terrain of the Zambales Mountains. He considered taking a shortcut to his destination by climbing above the Zambales, but that would further risk being spotted on Philippine radar and intercepted by military jets at nearby Clark Air Base. Lin ruled out traversing the Zambales: he'd evaded detection by staying low. At this juncture, he saw no reason to do otherwise.

The coastline transformed into a ragged series of inlets as he approached the final segment of the flight. He studied his map again, then looked for corresponding landmarks. He identified two prominent features—Nagasasa Bay and Silanquin Cove. The inlets looked exactly as they appeared on the National Geographic map.

With the entry to Subic Bay now in sight, all that remained for him to accomplish was to turn up the bay, then line up for a touchdown on Subic Airport's eastbound runway. He cleared his throat and prepared to broadcast intentions to land, but as he keyed his mike, cockpit warning lights changed from amber to flashing red as the J-31 approached fuel starvation.

* * *

The two air traffic controllers in Subic's tower had welcomed the uneventful morning. Commencing their shift at 0700 hours, they'd taken a relaxing breakfast of coffee and donuts, and then settled in for a quiet Sunday. A lone cargo plane had departed the former U.S. Naval Air Station at 1015 hours, followed by a small Cessna on its way to conduct basic instrument training maneuvers over the water, west of the Bay. A few minutes after the Cessna had taken off, its instructor pilot had questioned the tower about a "strange looking jet flying low along the coast." The controllers had reached for their binoculars and searched the sky. "Contact not in sight," one of them had replied. Satisfied they'd fulfilled their duties, the men grabbed another donut and plopped down on their rolling leather chairs. They never saw the J-31 as it skimmed over Grande Island and lined up for runway 07.

* * *

Lin aimed to get his aircraft on deck in one piece, but to do so he needed a better sight picture of the runway. He inched the right throttle lever forward and pulled back gingerly on the stick, placing the aircraft in a shallow climb. Because of the jet's fuel-depleted weight, he was able to trade a few knots of airspeed for some altitude; he leveled off at 400 feet, dropped the gear and flaps, then started a lazy right hand turn for the runway. But the aircraft began drifting left, overshooting the runway centerline. Lin looked down and saw whitecaps racing across the surface, signaling a strong crosswind. He corrected the overshoot and was back on track when the right engine quit, causing the unpowered airplane to descend at a sickening rate, still well short of the runway threshold. The aircraft barely cleared an elevated string of lead-in lights and was hurtling straight toward the earthen berm at runway 07's approach end.

Lieutenant Lin Yi faced a dire choice: either eject or stay with his aircraft until the bitter end. He did not hesitate, but rather, leveled the J-31's wings and trimmed its nose up to the landing attitude. He then reached between his thighs, gripped a yellow handle and pulled hard with both hands. A split second later the ejection seat's rocket motors fired, the plane's canopy was blasted clear, and he was shot into the air.

* * *

Air traffic controller Rolando "Rollie" de Guzman was three weeks from retirement. He'd requested the job at Subic as his twilight assignment after twenty-seven stressful years at Manila's bustling Ninoy Aquino International Airport. Subic's slow pace suited Rollie just fine and provided him with ample time to rehab his beach bungalow located a short drive away on the Bataan Peninsula. When he'd felt the muffled thud, he assumed that one of the airport's freight trucks had dumped its load on the tarmac near the tower.

"What the hell…" he mumbled through his pastry-filled mouth. He lowered the newspaper he'd been reading, slid himself backwards across the floor and inched up from his seat. His partner, a twenty-two-year-old rookie named Eduardo "Eddie" Domingo, had looked up from his paperback just as Lin Yi had ejected. The sound-proofed, glass tower cabin had isolated them from the clamor of Lin's jet pranging off the runway's paved underrun and then skidding another quarter mile before coming to rest in the grass.

Eddie was tongue tied at first, but soon regained his wits. He shouted, "Rollie, Rollie, outside! Approach end, Seven!"

Rollie sprung from his chair in time to see Lin's parachute mushroom out before it crumpled into the water. He'd witnessed a handful of aviation accidents, and like the others, this one came as a complete surprise. Rollie reached for the large red button on the countertop in front of him, undid the button's protective cover and pounded it, triggering an alarm signal to Subic's Crash, Fire and Rescue (CFR) unit. He then grabbed the tower radio's handheld microphone, took a deep breath and transmitted, "Attention all aircraft! Attention all aircraft!

Subic Bay Airport is now closed. Emergency in progress." He repeated the transmission, then joined Eddie Domingo to watch the scene unfold.

* * *

Lin Yi had never punched out of an aircraft and had to rely on what he'd been told in training. One of his buddies had ejected during flight school after his plane's electrical system had shorted out, resulting in thick smoke and noxious fumes in the cockpit. The pilot had told Lin that after he'd felt the jolting force of the seat's rockets, his surroundings went into slow motion. At the same time, though, his major life events replayed in a blur. Lin Yi experienced the same sensation. Visions of loved ones flashed through his brain: his mother, father, and brother; his squadron mates and close friends. But Lin's most poignant memory was the image of a woman he'd fallen in love with while studying in America. The thought of reconnecting with her gave him hope.

After ejecting he felt a moment of weightlessness, followed by a bone-jarring jerk as his parachute opened. His body swung wildly, one way, then the other, before he slammed face down in the water. The strong crosswind he'd experience during the approach had blown him clear of the runway and into the bay.

Briny water flooded his nostrils; he choked, spit it out and took a single gasp of air before he started to sink. He stroked his arms and flutter kicked his legs, but the parachute's canopy had collapsed on him along with its spidery web of suspension lines, which acted like an anchor pulling him down. He fumbled for the release latches that connected the chute's risers to his body harness; he found one but not the other. He continued sinking until the soles of his boots hit the bay's sandy bottom. Looking up, Lin realized that he was well below the surface. He gave up on locating the other riser and turned his energy toward the pair of toggles on his survival vest, that when pulled, would activate CO_2 cylinders and fill his vest's chambers with compressed air. But his strength began slipping away and his thoughts became foggy. Lin's lungs felt as if they were about to burst. He was on the verge of losing consciousness as images of loved ones filled his mind again. Lin folded his arms and prepared to die.

During an elective theology class at Berkeley, students had debated what it might feel like at the moment of death. Lin had sat without contributing to the discussion. He'd smirked when someone had proposed that a person might experience an ascending feeling as their soul rose toward heaven. Those portentous words were now lodged in his psyche. He assumed that he'd already died, and as the student had suggested, he began to feel the sensation of rising. The ascension began slowly, and then became more rapid. Lin assumed that his earthly body had left the material world and he'd entered a new dimension—until he felt pounding on his chest and slaps against his face. A warm, blinding light filled his eyes, coupled with an overwhelming surge of nausea. He turned his head and heaved.

The two fishermen who'd saved him erupted into excited laughter; they high fived each other, and then finished hauling Lin's limp body into their boat. One man began cutting away the parachute's entanglements with a bolo knife, while the other focused on starting the boat's motor. He yanked and yanked on the outboard's start rope, cursing after each pull until the motor wheezed to life.

The men made a beeline to a spot along the airport's perimeter, not far from where Lin's plane had come to rest. While one man steered, the other hovered over Lin and talked to him. Though Lin couldn't understand the Filipino, he didn't need to: the fellow's calming tone and reassuring taps on the shoulder conveyed the message: *You are safe now; you will be okay.*

The boat ran aground along a stretch of shoreline known as "All Hand's Beach," located between Subic's runway and a shipping container terminal that until the mid-1990s, had served as a pier for U.S. Navy aircraft carriers. A throng of morning sunbathers rushed to the scene but were pushed back when a trio of airport police officers arrived. The lead officer, named Ramos, helped drag the boat's bow onto the sand. Lin tried to stand up, but his legs gave out and he fell backwards; one of the fishermen caught him and guided him to a wooden bench in the middle of the boat. Lin pulled off his helmet and slouched over, resting his head in his hands with elbows on his thighs.

Ramos noted the markings on Lin's helmet and assumed them to be Chinese, so he tried communicating in the few Mandarin words he knew. Lin interrupted the man's mangled phrases and said in clear English, "I defect. Tell the U.S. Ambassador in Manila. I defect." He braced himself and got to his feet. The fishermen held his sides as Ramos took hold of an arm; together, they helped him out of the boat.

The looky-loos swarmed in closer, prompting Ramos to tell his partners, "We need to get him away from here before things get out of hand." He drew his pistol, held it up in plain view, and then shouted a warning in Tagalog. The crowd grumbled, then drifted back to their spots on the beach.

The fishermen handed the rest of Lin's flight gear to the police. They began pushing their boat back into the water until Lin stopped them. "You saved me," he said while shaking their hands. "Thank you." The pair smiled, got into their boat, and slipped quietly out onto the bay.

Ramos ushered Lin into a pickup truck and started driving toward Subic airport's operations building. The route took them close to the jet, where rescue vehicles and emergency personnel were gathering. The aircraft had skidded to a stop with its left landing gear collapsed and its crumpled left wingtip dug into the dirt; somehow, the nose gear and right gear had stayed extended in place. The plane's canopy had been recovered and placed next to the left wingtip. Members of Subic's CFR crew were huddled around the aircraft; one man had climbed into the cockpit and was standing in the void where the ejection seat had been.

Lin Yi perked up as they drove by. "Take me to my plane," he said. His words were more of a demand than a request.

Ramos gave him a dubious look but complied; he pulled off the road and parked next to the aircraft. "We cannot stay long," he said. "I have orders."

Lin bounded out of the truck. He walked around the aircraft, paying extra attention to the condition of its underside. He said something to the man standing in the cockpit. The fellow flashed a thumbs up, then tossed down Lin's helmet bag. After making a full circle, he paused in front of the jet's nose cone, reached up and gave it an affectionate pat. Tears welled in his eyes when the cold, hard truth hit him: he might never get the chance to fly again.

Ramos tugged him by the shoulder and said, "We have to go."

As they drove across the tarmac, an open-air jeep raced by on its way to the crash site; a pair of airport policemen hopped out and began cordoning off the jet. Ramos parked in front of the operations building; he gripped Lin's arm and led him inside.

CHAPTER 8

Sunday morning
Rizal Park Hotel
Manila, Philippines

The coffee was strong and black, the way Admiral Johnny Jack McGirt liked it. He'd found a quiet spot inside the Rizal Park's flowery courtyard and settled in for a leisurely breakfast; he looked forward to reading a copy of the Wall Street Journal that he'd requested at check-in the day before. His meeting at the United States Embassy wasn't scheduled to start for another couple hours, so after shaving and showering, he put on casual clothes: a golf shirt, khaki shorts, and a pair of sandals. Uniform for the afternoon session at the embassy would be "tropical whites."

A wide, ruby-colored umbrella above his table provided shade from the bright morning sun. This wasn't McGirt's first time in the Philippines; he knew that by early afternoon Manila's heat and humidity would turn the surroundings into a virtual sauna. He felt lucky being able to enjoy cooler temperatures while he had the chance.

Admiral McGirt had spent a few nights in this same hotel building during the 70s and 80s, when it was known as the Army-Navy Club. But since then, the venerable landmark had fallen on rough times, deteriorating into a shell of what it had been during its glory days in the early 1900s. After clearing many hurdles, a team of investors took over a restoration project in 2014, spending millions of dollars refurbishing the structure to its current grandeur. The building's majestic alabaster pillars, sweeping staircases and crystal chandeliers were preserved. Gone were its wobbly ceiling fans, flickering television sets, and staticky phones; in their place were central air conditioning, wide-screen plasma entertainment units, and Wi-Fi.

McGirt had taken a couple of bites from his plate of scrambled eggs with bacon when a clerk from the front desk appeared and handed him a note that

59

read: "CALL EMBASSY ASAP". A local phone number was written at the note's bottom. McGirt pulled a cell phone from his pocket and dialed; he was greeted by a pleasant female voice that carried a mild Tagalog accent. "Hello, this is the United States Embassy switchboard. How may I direct your call?"

"This is Rear Admiral McGirt. Please connect me with the Duty Officer."

Seconds later McGirt was speaking with a Marine captain who said, "Admiral, your presence is requested at the embassy as soon as possible. My superiors have instructed me to relay this message; I quote: 'tell the admiral to pack for an overnight stay.'" McGirt read the officer's tone as urgent. The man closed by saying that a driver was on their way to the Rizal.

McGirt signaled his waiter and asked that the meal charge be placed on his bill. He wolfed down a forkful of eggs, drained his coffee cup and headed for his room. Once inside, he surveyed the clothing he'd packed. He glanced at the fresh set of trop whites he'd set out but decided against wearing them. He was unsure of what might lie ahead or where he'd be spending the night, so he hung the whites inside a garment bag, and then reached for a pair of summer khakis. As the military representative on the President's National Security Council, he'd been dispatched to Manila to advise the U.S. Ambassador and the Under Secretary of State for Political Affairs. The trio was slated to meet with their Philippine counterparts the next day to initiate talks concerning the role of Philippine and U.S. forces in the region, specifically how the two nations should respond to China's growing presence in the South China Sea. The Americans had agreed to meet Sunday afternoon to discuss their strategy.

McGirt had a hunch that the instructions to "pack for an overnight stay" would prove to be more important than tomorrow's casual pow-wow between diplomats. He gathered his belongings and repacked the large rollaboard suitcase he'd traveled with, holding out the basics for an overnight; the cloth gym bag he'd tucked inside the rollaboard was well suited for that. He didn't feel right about incurring an extra day room charge, so he left his suitcase and garment bag with the hotel's bell captain, then told the desk clerk that he'd be checking back in the next day.

A military driver whisked him to the embassy; the drive took less than five minutes. McGirt breezed through the embassy's security check point and was met by the Marine captain with whom he'd spoken. The officer wore a crisp, short-sleeved khaki shirt, pressed blue trousers with symbolic blood-red stripe, and an immaculate white frame cap. Stacked above his left breast pocket were several rows of award ribbons; on the right side was a black name plate embossed with white letters that read "MULVANEY." The fellow matched McGirt's six-foot height and had the lean physique of a triathlete. The officer saluted and introduced himself. McGirt returned the salute, then extended his hand. Mulvaney's vise-like grip was no surprise.

"Admiral, right this way please," Mulvaney said as he led McGirt into the building. The Marine's walking pace was just short of a jog. "You're the first one here; Ambassador Remington is traveling from an hour away."

McGirt asked, "And Secretary Demitrio? Has she been notified about this change of plans?"

"We were not instructed to contact her, Admiral; only you and Ambassador Remington."

"I understand," McGirt said. He glanced into empty offices as they made their way down a long corridor. He tugged on Mulvaney's elbow. "Captain, this place looks deserted. Is that normal?"

"Yes, Admiral. We go down to a skeleton crew on Sundays; most clerical and support staff are off 'til tomorrow. My boss, the embassy's military attaché, is on leave."

"So, you're *El Jefe* today?"

Mulvaney laughed and came to a stop. "Afraid so, sir. It's just me and three other grunts on watch."

As the two stood facing each other, McGirt got a closer look at Mulvaney. His eyes focused on the top row of the officer's ribbons where he saw the Navy Cross and a Purple Heart. He also noted a nasty scar that ran from behind Mulvaney's left ear, across the cheek, and terminated in a jagged clump in the center of his chin.

McGirt pointed to the scar and asked, "Son, is that related to how you earned the Navy Cross and Purple Heart?"

Mulvaney's mood changed from cordial to solemn. "Yes, sir. Two tours in Afghanistan. I was the lucky one; everyone else in my MRAP was killed."

McGirt was lost for words. He guessed that Mulvaney was no older than thirty, and now saddled for life with a disfiguring scar, plus the inevitable guilt of being the sole survivor. He reached out, squeezed the Marine's shoulder and said, "Thanks for your sacrifice, Captain." McGirt saw a wide staircase ahead. "So, where are we going?" he asked.

"Second floor video conference room. I've preprogramed the equipment for the president's call." He paused to check his watch. "...in exactly four minutes from now."

McGirt stopped in his tracks. "President? Are you on the level?" He'd met with President Maxwell Black on several occasions, but always in the White House during scheduled meetings with the Secretary of Defense, Joint Chiefs, and other high-ranking players. He glanced at his wristwatch: it read 11:15 a.m. local time. Washington was twelve hours behind at 11:15 p.m. McGirt knew that an unplanned meeting at that late hour was serious business for the president.

Mulvaney ushered him into a room that resembled a small theater. There were two rows of plush chairs: a long, polished mahogany table sat in front of the first row; the back row was equipped with fold down writing tablets.

McGirt scanned the layout and asked, "Where should I sit?"

Captain Mulvaney motioned to the middle of the front row. "Admiral, the camera will be focused there, where the ambassador normally sits. But since he's running late this morning..." The captain stopped in midsentence. McGirt sensed that Mulvaney wanted to say more but had held his tongue about Ambassador Harold J. Remington. He wasn't surprised by the Marine's reluctance to elaborate.

After he and Demitrio had arrived on Saturday, they'd attended a reception hosted by the Executive Secretary of the Philippines, the nation's highest ranking official after its president. McGirt had watched Remington cozy up to a gorgeous Filipina actress. The pair had left together midway through the evening. Although it would be McGirt's first encounter with Remington, he'd heard stories about the wealthy bachelor. Remington had donated a ton of money to Maxwell Black's election campaign, and the choice job of ambassador was his payback. The handsome, middle-aged billionaire was tall, tanned, and talented, prompting D.C. gossip columnists to tag him the "Triple Threat." As for Under Secretary Demitrio, McGirt had spent much of the night listening to the former Ivy League professor brag about her grandchildren. Demitrio had excused herself early, apologizing that she was exhausted after the long flight. McGirt had forced himself to stay until the affair wound down at midnight.

Mulvaney called out from the back of the room. "Here we go, sir. I'll be standing by in the hallway if needed." A couple of seconds later, the big screen blinked a few times, and then an encrypted-looking message scrawled across its bottom. An instant later, President Black appeared on the monitor; to his immediate left sat Secretary of State Roscoe Depew; to Black's right, Secretary of Defense Nathan Croft. Standing behind the trio were the Chairman of the Joint Chiefs of Staff and the Chief of Naval Personnel. McGirt saw his own thumbnail headshot displayed in the upper corner of the screen.

President Black stared into the camera and said, "McGirt, you tough old son-of-a-bitch, how nice to see your ugly face!" The men surrounding Black lowered their heads and turned away in an effort to hide their chuckles.

McGirt was familiar enough with Black to not be startled by the man's frankness. "Hello, Mr. President, nice to see you as well. Unfortunately, I'm on this call at the embassy by myself. I expect Ambassador Remington will join us soon." McGirt had no intention of throwing Remington under the bus. Black read straight through his attempt to stall.

"Well, no big surprise with Harold. It *is* Sunday morning where you're at; we both know Ambassador Remington's...shall we just say, predilections."

McGirt and the president shared more than their graying, brush-cut hair styles. Black had watched McGirt play at middle linebacker for the University of Michigan football team when the Wolverines had traveled to Wisconsin to take on Black's Badgers. With the home team driving for the game's winning touchdown, McGirt had blitzed the quarterback and tackled the guy so viciously that he fumbled. McGirt recovered the ball and Michigan went on to win the game. When Admiral McGirt had first met the president decades later in Washington, Black recounted the event as if the game had been played that day.

While McGirt had pursued a Navy career, Maxwell Black had made a fortune in the construction business, been elected Mayor of Green Bay, then governor of the state, and ultimately elevated to the highest office in the land. The hardnosed Black had campaigned on a platform of cleaning up the country's urban decay, returning America to its manufacturing roots, and restoring pride in being a U.S. citizen. Maxwell Black said what he meant and meant what he said. His blunt, pugnacious ways drove his opponents crazy, but warmed the hearts of his followers. When McGirt's name had come up for a position on the president's national security council, Black had taken the folders of a dozen other contenders and tossed them on the floor. He'd held up McGirt's file and waved it in the air, telling his staff, "This is who I want...get McGirt over here ASAP!"

With pleasantries out of the way, President Black got back on track. "Anyway, let's proceed without Harold. McGirt, we sent you over there to begin discussions about establishing our forces in the Philippines on a more permanent basis. When we pulled our military out after that volcano blew up—"

McGirt heard Secretary of State Depew interrupt in a whisper, "Mount Pinatubo, Mr. President, it erupted in 1991. We had to—"

Black shot a dirty look at the bureaucrat. "Yeah, I *know* that, Roscoe! The freaking thing exploded and buried our military bases in ash. Now, let me finish…"

McGirt sensed that the president and Depew might have shared heated words earlier. Black lacked experience on the international stage and had relied on recommendations of Washington insiders when he'd nominated Depew. But the pair had not meshed well since the president's inauguration eighteen months ago. The two men came from opposite backgrounds: Black, raised by Midwest working class parents and schooled in the public education system; Depew, an only child of wealthy socialites and a product of Harvard. Rumors were circulating that Depew was on the verge of being canned.

President Black undid his necktie and yanked it off. He then rose from his chair, took off his suitcoat and handed it to the Chairman of the Joint Chiefs. An assistant darted forward to retrieve the garments. "There, that's better," Black said. He took a swig of water, shot a glare at Depew, then said, "Hell, McGirt, you know the story; we don't need a history lesson on the Philippines. Let's get down to the facts so we grumpy old men can go to bed." Black nodded toward the Secretary of Defense. "Nate, why don't you take it from here."

Secretary of Defense Nathan Croft opened a folder stuffed with his notes. Like the president, Croft had the reputation of a cut-to-the-chase, no nonsense guy. He'd retired from the Army as a four-star general and had sailed through confirmation hearings. The son of an Army sergeant and a Japanese-American woman, Croft was one of the most respected members of Black's cabinet. "Good evening… or should I say *good morning*, Admiral McGirt," he began. "In addition to what's going on in the Taiwan Straits, we have two unexpected situations brewing in your region." He turned toward Black. "With your permission, Mr. President, I'd like to summarize both events and then open up for questions." Black nodded his approval while Secretary Depew sat mum with the dejected look of a scolded teenager.

Croft continued. "Earlier this morning, your time, we received word that an H-60 helicopter attached to the Littoral Combat Ship *Grand Rapids* was intercepted by two Chinese fighters and forced to land on an island that the Chinese are building, west of Luzon. At present, we have no concrete idea why the intercept took place; we're confident that the chopper was dozens of miles from the island and not in violation of what the Communists have claimed—wrongly, I might add—as sovereign territory. Fortunately, sources report that Lieutenant Commander Moselli and his crew are safely on the ground. Shortly after we learned of the intercept, our intelligence apparatus picked up Chinese message traffic stating that one of their J-31 fighters might be headed toward the Philippine Islands. That suspicion was confirmed after the plane snuck into Philippine airspace and crash landed at the Subic Bay Airport." Croft peeked over his glasses. "Admiral, I understand that you're familiar with the area, is that correct?"

"Yes, Mr. Secretary. My experience in the P.I. goes back to the 1970s when the field was called Naval Air Station Cubi Point."

A grin spread over Croft's face. "Yes, I remember Cubi and Subic very well." McGirt and Croft shared a muffled laugh. President Black shrugged his shoulders and looked up at the brass behind him with a befuddled look, as if a joke had been told and he didn't get the punch line.

"Sorry for the digression, Mr. President," Croft said. "We're not sure if the two incidents are related; nonetheless, Beijing is demanding that the J-31 and its pilot be returned at once. Our intelligence folks suspect that the fighter is constructed with stealth technology superior to ours and may be carrying a laser weapon system unlike anything we have in our inventory."

"I understand, Mr. Secretary," McGirt said. "But with all due respect, where do I fit in with all of this?"

Black took over the conversation. "McGirt, I want you to get your rear end over to Subic as quick as you can." He pounded a fist on the table. "We need some American horsepower on the scene. Nate's staff is arranging your transportation as we speak. Good news is that the Philippines' new president, Diaz, has already reached out to me and he agrees that this may be an opportunity to draw a line in the sand with Beijing over the bullshit they're pulling in the South China Sea. Diaz' predecessor was way too chummy with the Chi-Coms and we aim to change that." Black pointed a finger at the camera. "China can have back their airplane after we strip the damn thing naked. We're sending over a team of Philippine and American defense gurus—Boeing, Raytheon, General Dynamics, and the rest—to break it down and learn as much as they can."

McGirt raised his hand. "What about the pilot?"

"I want you to check him out," Black said. "We don't know what shape he's in; I understand that he landed pretty hard and had to eject. But I'm guessing he's in no hurry to go back to China after running away with one of their fighters."

"Got it, Mr. President. I'll do what I can."

"Good! I'm meeting with the Chinese ambassador and his minions tomorrow morning; we'll see how that goes, but so far, I've found that group about as trustworthy as gas station sushi." Black rotated in his seat and made eye contact with everyone but Depew. "Anything else, guys?" No one responded, so he said, "That's it from here. We'll contact you as things develop. Goodbye."

The video faded off before McGirt could respond. He got up and headed for the door, where he was met by Captain Mulvaney.

"Admiral, I just received word that a Philippine Air Force helicopter is on its way; E.T.A. ten minutes. They'll be landing on our helipad along the seawall."

McGirt followed Mulvaney downstairs, through the building and outside. This wasn't his first time at the embassy's helicopter pad: he'd landed there many times while deployed to the Western Pacific and flying the now-shelved CH-46, typically transporting senior staff members and dignitaries from Subic's military complex to the capital city. Filipino stewards assigned to McGirt's ships would sometimes bum a ride to visit family in Manila, thereby avoiding the three-hour bus ride from Subic.

The two officers found a place in the shade next to the landing pad. McGirt figured that as a flag officer he'd rate one of the country's executive choppers, or at the very least, one of their Air Force's Bell 412s—an updated version of the venerable UH-1 "Huey." He would never have guessed what had been dispatched for his flight to Subic.

Captain Mulvaney heard the sound a few seconds before McGirt: the *pop, pop, pop* of rotor blades cutting through Manila's thick air. The noise grew louder, and the ground began to tremble when all at once, a dark silhouette burst overhead from behind. The pair shielded their eyes from the sun as the helicopter swooped low over the bay, made a steep banked turn, and slowed for its approach.

McGirt roared with laughter. "You gotta be kidding! They sent a Cobra?"

"Oorah!" Mulvaney shouted above the din. "Looks like you're going first class, Admiral." The two officers held their hats in hand and braced for hurricane-force rotor wash as the Philippine AH-1 attack helicopter crossed the seawall and touched down. Seconds later the aircraft's engine was secured and its rotor blades coasted to a stop.

McGirt approached the tandem configured, dual control helicopter as its pilot raised the canopy. He removed his helmet and set it atop the helicopter's cyclic, or control stick. He scrambled down and rendered a crisp salute. "First Lieutenant Anthony Gomez, reporting for duty!" he said in flawless English. "You ready to go flying, sir?" Gomez was short, stocky, and had bushy black hair. A wispy mustache crowned his upper lip.

McGirt greeted Gomez with a handshake. He noticed a blue and silver pin on the collar of the pilot's green flight suit; it had the image of a lightning bolt and the letters *USAFA*. "Air Force Zoomie?" he asked.

"Yes, sir. I was one of three Filipinos in my class at the Academy. Great experience, but those Colorado winters were awfully rough on this homeboy."

McGirt took an instant liking to the kid. "That's a nice-looking machine you got there, Mister. How you like flying it?"

"It's the best, Admiral. Second only to having sex... if you don't mind me saying."

McGirt had heard the phrase comparing flying to sex many times before, yet he couldn't resist soaking up the young pilot's enthusiasm. He glanced at the guy's name tag: it read "Guts Gomez."

"How'd you get that call sign, Guts?"

"Wish I had an exciting story to tell, but I don't. When I got my wings, my buddies prodded me into doing shots after drinking a bunch of beers."

"Let me guess: and you puked your guts out?"

Guts hung his head in mock shame. "Yes, sir. I've learned to be more careful."

"Well, that's good to hear. How'd you draw the lucky job of running me over to Subic?"

"Weekend duty and I'm the junior guy. They wanted to send a Bell 412 but couldn't find one in up status. Sorry."

"Hey, no problem. I just have this one bag," McGirt said as he held up a faded yellow gym bag embossed with the blue letter "M", symbolic of his alma mater. Guts opened a compartment below the cockpit; McGirt tossed the bag inside.

McGirt shimmied into the Cobra's front seat and strapped in. Guts leaned over him. "Any questions, Admiral?"

"No, I think I'll be okay." McGirt had never been in the cockpit of an AH-1, but the layout was intuitive, and similar to other helicopters he'd flown. Guts had brought a set of headphones, so McGirt slipped them on. The pair established communications and canopies were closed; McGirt followed along as Guts mumbled through the start checklist over the intercom. Soon, the engine was lit off and the bird's rotor blades began spinning.

"Ready to go, sir?"

"You betcha, Guts. Let's do it!" McGirt waved to Mulvaney, who snapped to attention and saluted. McGirt returned the salute and gave a double thumbs up.

Guts pulled into a hover and did a slow pedal turn to face the bay. "Your choice, Admiral," he said. "We can take the shortcut across the mountains or fly over Manila Bay by Corregidor and then up the coast."

"Let's take the scenic route up the coast."

"Sure." Guts made a call to Manila traffic control, stated his intentions, and was approved for the visual flight. He dipped the nose, yanked in an armful of power, and they were off.

McGirt looked at his altimeter and noted that they were flying just 100 feet above the water. He felt the aircraft accelerate; soon they were traveling at the Cobra's red line airspeed, over 150 miles per hour. Infamous Corregidor Island—the final allied bastion to fall after the Japanese had captured the Philippines during World War Two—came into view.

"Sir, I noticed those shiny gold wings on your khaki shirt. Think you remember how to fly?"

"You smartass! Wanna see?" McGirt shot back. He hadn't piloted an aircraft on a regular basis since his tour as commanding officer of a CH-46 unit on the West Coast five years ago. Since then, he'd bummed a few hours of stick time here and there, but nothing significant.

"Okay, sir. You can have it when you're ready."

McGirt gripped the cyclic with his right hand, then slid his left over to the collective. The controls felt odd from what he'd known, and yet not that much different. He scanned the flight instruments and waggled his stick. "Okay, I've got it."

Gomez waggled in return and said, "You got it, Admiral."

McGirt made a couple of gentle turns to get a feel for the Cobra, then descended to 50 feet. He dodged a few fishing boats before whizzing past Corregidor at high speed.

He thought to himself: *Damn, how I miss this!*

CHAPTER 9

Dick Moselli and his crew realized that they weren't going anywhere for a while. After they'd landed and been greeted by the Chinese welcoming committee, the Americans and their unexpected passenger sprawled out on the helicopter's cabin flooring; the confines provided shade, but little relief from the scorching mid-day heat.

A half dozen soldiers stood guard over the Americans as an hour passed before the English-speaking Army officer returned. He invited Moselli to join him inside the cargo bed of the troop carrier that had transported his men to the scene. The vehicle's bed had benches on both sides and was covered by a canvas top with flaps that had been pinned open, allowing a breeze to filter through. The two men sat facing each other. Moselli hoped to establish a rapport with the Chinese officer, so he said, "What is your rank? Your insignia suggests that you are an army captain."

"Yes, that is correct. My rank *Shang Wei*; like your army captain or navy lieutenant."

"Ah, then I am one above you," Moselli said. "Lieutenant Commander."

"Okay, we say, *Shao Xiao* for that." The officer leaned closer to read Moselli's name tag. "You *Shao Xiao* Mo...se...lee. Correct?"

The man's accent was strong, but his pronunciation was decent. Moselli focused on the Chinese symbols above the left breast pocket of the officer's fatigues. "I cannot read Chinese," he said while pointing to the symbols. "What is your name?"

The officer sat up proudly. "Family name is Gao. Other name, Ying."

"Okay, then, may I call you Gao?"

"Yes, that is most proper between us."

"Your English is very good."

"We study English in early school years. I speak, but do not write on paper."

Both men smiled in a friendly way. Moselli felt comfortable moving past the small talk. "Captain Gao, can you tell me why I was forced to land my helicopter?"

Gao fidgeted in his seat; the informal mood that Moselli had felt disappeared. Gao stared outside as if he were gathering his thoughts. "Not allowed to say. I only can tell that it was a mistake."

Moselli pressed him. "A mistake? Can you explain?"

Gao hesitated again. He shook his head and then faced Moselli, looking him squarely in the eye. "The other man, not American. My superior thought he is someone else."

Moselli turned toward the helicopter and saw Salid's bare feet hanging outside the cabin door. He was about to ask another question when Gao's radio came alive with a staticky transmission. Gao replied with a single phrase, then got to his feet and jumped down from the truck. "We must go," he said. "Tell your people we must go."

Moselli hollered for Aguilar and Horton to grab their flight gear. Salid put on his soggy shoes and followed. The trio joined Moselli in the back of the troop carrier. Gao rode in front with the driver. The soldiers sat on one bench, Moselli and his group on the other. The two sides studied each other while the truck bounced over a dirt road.

Horton broke the silence. "Well, Commander, this is a fine mess you've gotten us into! Would I be safe to assume that we'll be spending the night on this island paradise?"

Moselli smirked at the sarcasm. "Starting to look like that way, isn't it? I pressed their officer about why we were forced down. He said they thought the guy we pulled out of the drink was somebody else, but he got tight lipped after that."

Aguilar pointed at Salid. "Him? Man, did they get their wires crossed. And what the hell...how'd they know we were in the area?"

"Beats me," Moselli said. "But we need to keep our wits and go with the flow. I'm confident that our mayday call has rattled a few cages by now. Other than that sweaty jackass that met us when we landed, we've been treated okay so far." He tilted his head toward Salid. "He say anything you could understand?"

"Not really," Aguilar said. "He slept for most of the time we were laying in the aircraft. I got that his name is Salad, or Saleed, something like that...and he's Filipino."

The truck came upon a long string of white house trailers; it jerked to a stop at the far end of the row. The buzzing hum of air conditioners filled the air.

Captain Gao appeared at the truck's tailgate. "You should stay in this for now," he said, pointing to the trailer. "I come back with food."

Horton shot his hand in the air. "Hey buddy, we need water too. You know, H2o?"

Gao turned to Moselli. "Yes, I bring food *and* water. You go into there and stay."

Moselli and his group jumped to the ground. The soldiers—minus Gao and his driver—formed a perimeter around the trailer.

"Please do not leave," Gao said to Moselli. He then hopped back in the truck and sped away.

"Preeze do not reeve?" Horton mocked. "Jesus Christ, Bruiser, where the hell would we go?"

Moselli picked up his gear, cracked open the trailer's door and said, "Well, let's see what the Hotel Ritz looks like inside."

* * *

Guts Gomez dialed in Subic's ATIS (Automatic Terminal Information Service) on the radio. The recording said: "This is Subic Bay International information Romeo, time, zero-five-zero-zero Zulu. Subic now closed to all traffic. Contact Subic operations for further information."

McGirt keyed the interphone. "Hey, Guts, ATIS says they're closed. What's the plan?"

"No worries, Admiral. I got prior permission to land before I left Clark."

McGirt was on the controls and feeling comfortable; he'd taken to flying the Cobra like a duck takes to water. As they rounded the northwest edge of Bataan and entered Subic Bay, Grande Island came into view.

"Look familiar?" Guts asked.

"Hell, yes. Hard to get the memories of this place out of my mind. Don't know what you've heard, but in its day, Subic was a hopping place."

Guts laughed. "Yup, heard all the stories; most of them not suited for general audiences."

"Well, yeah, that's true. Sailors couldn't get into town fast enough after the ship tied up. The young ones usually fell in love with some cutie who'd just said goodbye to another guy that was shipping out. Olongapo and Subic City were a young sailor's Disneyland."

"Not like that nowadays. More of a working man's vacation spot."

Guts set Subic's frequency in the radio and keyed his mike. "Subic tower, Cobra One-Zero, approaching Grande Island low level. Over..."

"Cobra One-Zero, Subic, got you in sight. Caution fifty-foot crane abeam runway on northwest corner of the airport. Caution men and equipment on and around the runway. Wind two-one-zero at two-five, cleared to land on the VIP pad."

Guts acknowledged, "Roger tower. Cleared to land on the VIP pad."

McGirt gave the aircraft back to Guts. He felt confident on the controls despite not having flown anything for months; nonetheless, he didn't want to press his luck. As they flew past Lin's jet, he saw that it was being hoisted onto a long flatbed truck. Guts slowed to taxi speed, made a lazy ninety-degree turn, then spun the Cobra's nose into the wind. He followed a marshaller's hand signals and touched down in front of the control tower. The Cobra's turbine engine was secured, and its rotor blades brought to a stop; Guts and McGirt pushed open their canopies and unstrapped.

"Thanks for the lift, Lieutenant," McGirt said as he climbed out of the cockpit and lowered himself to the tarmac. "You need to top off?"

"No, sir. Got plenty of fuel for the flight back to Clark." He unlatched a compartment door to retrieve McGirt's luggage. Guts raised an eyebrow as he held the small satchel. "None of my business, sir, but not much in your bag. Short stay?"

"Yes, that's what they're telling me; just one night. Orders were to get over here ASAP. Rest of my gear is at the hotel in Manila."

"Got anything to do with that wreck we flew over?" Guts motioned toward the operations building. "By the looks of the commotion at Ops, must be something big going down."

McGirt faced the building; he saw a cluster of military vehicles and black sedans parked in front. Two Filipino soldiers guarded the building's entrance. He grabbed Guts' hand and shook it. "Son, I could tell you but…"

Guts flashed a wide smile. "Yeah, I know…but then you'd have to kill me. Right?"

McGirt squeezed a little harder. "You take care, Gomez…and stay safe."

Guts squeezed back. "Thanks, Admiral, you too. Good luck."

McGirt started a slow jog towards operations. The two soldiers came to attention as he approached. He acknowledged them with a nod and reached for the door handle, but the door flew open before he could pull; a medium-build gentleman met him at the threshold. The man wore dark slacks and an open-collar, white Barong Tagalog dress shirt. The shirt had long, sheer sleeves; its front was embroidered with a fine, intricate pattern. His impeccably coiffed silver hair made a striking contrast with his light-caramel skin tone; he could have passed for an Asian movie star. When the fellow grinned, McGirt recognized him immediately.

"Jimmie! Jimmie Posadas!"

"At your service, McGirt...or should I say *Admiral* McGirt. It's been a while, hasn't it?" The pair shook hands and then bearhugged. They'd met during the Marcos regime when McGirt was a junior officer and Posadas worked at the U.S. Embassy in Manila. Jimmie was a Filipino-American who held dual citizenships. He'd been raised in Hawaii, schooled in California, and then employed by various U.S. agencies, specializing in foreign intelligence. His connection to McGirt stemmed from when he'd helped investigate the shootdown of a Navy helicopter by a band of Philippine extremists known as the New People's Army. The shootdown was spun as an accident; McGirt and Posadas knew otherwise.

Jimmie signaled McGirt to follow him inside and down a long hallway. "How much do you know?" he said.

"Just what President Black told me during our video call: a Chinese pilot snuck in under radar and wants asylum in the United States. Immigration isn't my specialty, Jimmie, but he defected to the Philippines, not the U.S. Isn't that a problem?"

"Spot on. That's the tricky thing we're dealing with. But here's the bigger issue: our intelligence folks suspect that his aircraft, a J-31 fighter, may be way ahead of us in both stealth technology and laser weaponry."

"Jesus...are you for real?"

"Yeah, I know. We're lucky, though, the pilot speaks good English. Young guy...says his name is Lin Yi."

"Did he give a reason why he defected?"

"No. Wouldn't reveal much to me other than he wants asylum in the U.S. I think he's hesitant to talk to anyone but a U.S. official."

McGirt frowned. "Whoa, Jimmie, you're an American. Why not you?"

"Can't say for sure. It could be my Asian looks: maybe he doesn't believe I represent the United States. Let's face it, this guy's life is on the line. I don't blame him for being paranoid."

"Yeah, he wouldn't survive long if we ship him back to China. Say, how'd you get here faster than me?"

"I happened to be in Subic with my wife for a weekend at the beach. Got a call to hustle over and meet you."

"Okay, so where is he?"

Posadas led McGirt into a tiny room filled with cleaning supplies and janitorial equipment; a pair of vents blasted cold air into the space; it felt like a meat locker. Lin Yi sat in a metal folding chair, dripping wet and shivering. Two soldiers stood guard over him.

"Christ sakes, Jimmie, can we get this guy something to cover up with!"

"Already on it, Admiral," Posadas said. On cue, another soldier arrived carrying a blanket. Posadas draped it over Lin's shoulders.

"I saw a gaggle of vehicles outside," McGirt said. "Where is everybody?"

"Upstairs. Subic City Chief of Police, the mayor and his posse, and some P.I. military honchos are all huddled in a conference room. They wanted to wait until you got here before doing anything."

McGirt shook his head. "So, in the meantime, just leave this poor bastard down here freezing? That's brilliant."

Posadas felt the urge to say something about P.I. officials being notoriously inefficient. Considering the presence of the two soldiers in the room, though, he held his tongue.

McGirt took charge. He found two other folding chairs leaned against the wall, sat down across from Lin and waved Posadas to join him. He looked up at the guards' steely faces and said, "Jimmie, would you ask these gentlemen to please stand outside in the hallway?" He guessed that the men understood English but figured it better that they got the request from a Filipino. Posadas spoke to the men in Tagalog. They saluted and left.

McGirt faced Lin and said, "My name is Johnny Jack McGirt. I am an admiral in the United States Navy. I understand that you speak English…is that correct?"

Lin shrugged off the blanket and got to his feet; he stood at rigid attention. "I am Lin Yi, a *Shang Wei* in the Chinese Navy. I choose to defect with my jet and request asylum in the United States." He remained at attention with eyes fixed straight ahead.

McGirt stood up and extended his hand. "Pleased to meet you, Mister Lin."

Lin hesitated for a moment, then looked down at McGirt's hand; he took hold and shook it enthusiastically. McGirt turned toward Posadas. "This is my good friend, Mister Jimmie Posadas. He works for both the American and Philippine governments. We are going to do everything in our power to get you to the United States."

Lin's lower lip began to quiver; he swallowed hard, and then took a deep breath. A wide smile spread across his face. "I thank you very much. I can share important information about my airplane. I will provide it when you grant me asylum."

"Mister Lin," McGirt said, "Receiving asylum isn't as easy as you may think—"

Lin interrupted. "I ask that you please address me by rank, Admiral. I hold rank like your Navy lieutenants."

McGirt grinned. "Okay, *Lieutenant*...we will get to your request for asylum... and we can discuss your airplane. But first we need to follow certain protocols. You did not defect to United States territory, you landed at Subic Bay in the Philippines. Do you understand that presents a diplomatic problem?"

"Yes, I understand. May you resolve the matter? I wish to return to the United States."

McGirt and Posadas faced each other with stunned expressions. "Return?" Posadas asked. "So, you have been to the United States?"

"Yes, my country sent me to be a student. I studied in California for two years."

"What school did you attend?" Posadas said.

"University of California Berkeley. I obtained a master's degree in electrical engineering."

"Anything to do with laser technology?" McGirt asked.

"Yes, I wrote a thesis on laser devices. My principles were used to build the weapon on my airplane."

Pieces of the puzzle came together: It was obvious that Lin wanted to trade his technical expertise for asylum in the U.S. McGirt could only guess what had motivated the young pilot to put his life in jeopardy by flying a military jet into a foreign country. He surmised that considering the knowledge he possessed, Lin would have achieved favored status within the Chinese Communist Party.

Posadas stole McGirt's next thought. "Lieutenant, even recognizing the value of what you've told us, we cannot guarantee your freedom. As the admiral said, we will do our best; however, neither of us have the authority to grant you asylum in America. And it's a very big obstacle that you landed in the Philippines."

McGirt added, "We will need to consult with our superiors. For now, let's see if we can get you out of that wet flight suit and into dry clothes." He stood up and began rummaging through the room. He opened a closet and found a set of stained coveralls hanging from a nail; they looked about the right fit for Lin's small frame. On the floor beneath the coveralls were a pair of black sneakers. Likewise, they seemed close to the size of Lin's flight boots, so he grabbed them too. Other than a wide-brimmed straw hat, there was nothing else in the closet but brooms and mops.

"Jimmie, you start the ball rolling to establish comms with President Diaz' office, and then with our Secretary of Defense." McGirt handed his global smart phone to Posadas. He recalled President Black's distain for Secretary of State Roscoe Depew. "My contact list has direct, secure numbers for Nathan Croft and Depew—try Croft first and give him the quick and dirty of what we're doing. Call Depew only if Croft doesn't pick up."

"Got it. What about everybody upstairs?"

McGirt threw his hands in the air. "Hell, make something up…tell them that we're still in the process of verifying Lin's identity, or whatever. The last thing we need is to get more people involved, it will only complicate things."

"You're right. I'll stall them topside, and then start making calls." Posadas checked his watch. "Geez, McGirt, it's the middle of the night in D.C. You really want to wake people up over this?"

"You bet your ass I do. Now, let's get moving!" McGirt considered Jimmie Posadas a good friend and a sharp thinker; nonetheless, he was a career bureaucrat who'd never served in the military, and he functioned with a different sense of urgency.

McGirt handed Lin the coveralls and shoes. "Lieutenant, slip out of that wet zoom bag and put these on for now."

Lin looked at the coveralls suspiciously, then unzipped his flight suit. McGirt turned around to give him privacy. As he did, he noticed the gym bag he'd brought from Manila. He inventoried what he'd packed: toiletries and some undergarments—enough for an overnight stay. He pulled out the undergarments, and offered them to Lin. "Here, take these, I can get others."

Lin inspected the items: a plain white tee shirt, grey boxer shorts, and a pair of khaki uniform socks. McGirt stood an even six feet tall and weighed a solid two hundred pounds; Lin was at least six inches shorter, and at most, weighed one-hundred thirty pounds. His eyes widened as he held up the big boxers.

Sensing Lin's dismay, McGirt shrugged and said, "Hey, they're clean and dry. We'll find something better for you later." Lin stripped down and put everything on.

McGirt wondered if Posadas was having any luck connecting with Philippine President Diaz' staff or anyone in Washington. He figured it would be easier with the Diaz people, but considering the time of day, didn't have the same confidence with the U.S. officials. He felt comfortable dealing with President Black's staff, but he'd never met Diaz and knew little about the man. What McGirt did know about the newly elected Philippine President was, unlike his predecessor, he'd taken a hardline stance against China's trade policies and its increasing presence in the South China Sea. Diaz had welcomed Maxwell Black's offer to expand America's presence in the region to counter China's influence.

Posadas returned and held out McGirt's phone. "Secretary Croft picked up on the first ring. I gave him a quick summary; he wants to speak with you."

McGirt took the phone. "Hello, Mister Secretary, this is Rear Admiral McGirt. My apologies for the oh-dark-thirty call, but I believe it's warranted."

"You're absolutely right that it's warranted, no apologies necessary. FYI, the president has given me the green light to run with this. It's imperative that you get that Chinese pilot out of the Philippines and into U.S. territory ASAP." Croft muffled a laugh, then said, "The Chinese Ambassador is going apeshit on Diaz and Remington, demanding that the pilot be turned over to him immediately." Croft paused; this time he didn't bother to hide his amusement. "And in case you were wondering, the S.O.B. wants the plane back too."

McGirt had held the phone away from his ear so that Posadas could hear the conversation. He said in a whisper, "Jimmie, did you get through to Diaz yet?"

"Yes, spoke to him directly. He's onboard with whatever we can arrange."

McGirt didn't hesitate. "Mister Secretary, it would take extensive coordination to get Lieutenant Lin to Guam or an American military base in Japan on such short notice. If you can get me an aircraft, I propose that we fly him to a U.S Navy ship. That's sovereign territory that the Chi-Coms can't mess with."

"CNO also brought that up after our video call," Croft said. "There's a Littoral Combat Ship, the *Grand Rapids*, in the region with a helicopter available. We thought about dispatching the LCS' chopper, but CNO persists on using *Reagan*'s V-22 Osprey. Said it can fly twice as fast and won't need to refuel." Croft paused then said, "What are your thoughts on that proposal?"

"Yes, Mister Secretary, CNO is correct. The H-60 doesn't have the range nor speed of the Osprey. If time is of the essence, we should go with the Osprey."

"Good, then let's proceed with that plan," Croft said. "CNO suggests that we stash the pilot on *Grand Rapids* for the time being. *Reagan* is on her way to the Straits and I don't want to muddy that situation by dumping the guy on the carrier's skipper: he's got enough on his plate. By the way, McGirt, *Grand Rapids* is the same ship that had their other chopper forced down by those Chinese fighters."

"Huh, interesting," McGirt replied. "Okay, I copy all of that. Sir, any advice on how we should deal with the Chinese ambassador if he gets here before the Osprey?"

There was an extended silence on the line. "Admiral, you and Posadas will have to work that out on your end."

A torrent of thoughts flooded McGirt's mind after hearing Croft's response. He swallowed hard and said, "Mister Secretary, I'm confident we can handle it."

"Good, you've got the ball, now run with it. Oh, one more thing—and this came straight from the president: he wants you to accompany the Chinese pilot and remain with him until further directed. Any questions?"

"No, Mister Secretary. I've got it."

"Excellent. We'll be in touch as things develop, Admiral. Goodbye."

McGirt tucked his phone away, and then glanced over at Lin, who stood with arms folded across his chest, dressed in his new garb. He had a satisfied grin on his face.

"Guess you heard, didn't you?" McGirt asked. Lin nodded.

Posadas said, "I can't stall those guys topside any longer. We need to cut them in on what we're doing, otherwise, they'll find a way to dick things up." McGirt agreed.

The two guards were called back into the room. As Posadas and McGirt climbed the stairs to the building's second floor, McGirt said, "Jimmie, this is turning into a real cluster-rama. I know it's a minor thing, but can you get my gear out of storage at the Rizal and hold on to it?"

"Sure. No problem."

"I told Gina that I'd only be away from D.C. for a week or so. Now, I've got orders to babysit a Chinese defector and haul his ass out to sea."

"Comes with the job, Admiral. That's why they pay you the big bucks."

"Yeah, right," McGirt lamented. "But you know the worst of it?"

"What's that?

"I gave Lin the only freaking pair of underwear I brought with me."

CHAPTER 10

Two V-22 Osprey pilots and a pair of enlisted crew chiefs stand "ready alert" aboard the nuclear-powered aircraft carrier USS *Ronald Reagan*; they file into their squadron's ready room for briefing. The unit's operations officer takes his place in front of a large interactive monitor which depicts *Reagan*'s position in relation to the Philippines. He zooms in on the island of Luzon, changes scale again, and then focuses on the Subic Bay airport. He goes over basics with the crew: weather conditions, fuel load, any significant maintenance issues, and potential security threats. The mission is straightforward: fly to Subic Bay to pick up a Navy two-star admiral and one civilian; transport them to USS *Grand Rapids*, then return to *Reagan*. The flight is well within the Osprey's range capability; refueling at Subic will not be necessary.

The tiltrotor is parked on *Reagan*'s number three elevator aft of "Tilly," the ship's salvage crane. Proprotors and wings have been folded over the aircraft's fuselage to minimize its footprint. Mechanics complete a handful of servicing tasks, while another team of sailors prepare to tow the aircraft into position on the ship's angle deck, where wings and proprotors will be unfolded. The flight's two crew chiefs arrive and begin running through checklists. The cockpit crew soon follows.

The two pilots come from different backgrounds: the aircraft commander is a twelve-year veteran who's transitioned to the Osprey after flying the bulk of his career in the Navy's fixed-wing C-2 Greyhound. The mission's copilot, a Lieutenant Junior Grade, has been assigned to the squadron straight out of flight school. They strap in, go through a series of pre-start checks, and then light the first of the aircraft's two 6150 shaft horsepower turbine engines. Proprotors begin spinning immediately.

Engines are tilted forward to the takeoff setting of 71 degrees, final checks are completed, and the flight receives launch clearance from the tower. Instruments are checked, brakes are released, and the thrust control lever is advanced; the Osprey starts rolling and uses just a fraction of the deck before becoming light on its wheels and getting airborne. Once clear of the bow, the aircraft makes a shallow right turn and climbs. Through a complex set of flight controls and computer signals, it transitions from vertical takeoff and landing mode (VTOL) to airplane mode. Engines are rotated to their 0-degree position; helicopter-like rotors now serve as propellers.

Designated in Navy parlance as the CMV-22B, the Osprey has endured a checkered past. The revolutionary airframe suffered numerous setbacks including several fatal accidents while flying in its initial role as a U.S. Marine transport. *Fortune* magazine once summarized the Osprey's plight in these words: "...the tilt-rotor aircraft has been persistently criticized as wildly expensive, ineffective, and unsafe." Yet tiltrotor supporters persevered. Safety issues were ironed out and joint manufacturers Boeing and Bell received funding to build a Navy derivative of the aircraft. One by one, C-2 Greyhounds were retired, clearing a path for the Osprey to become the Navy's new workhorse for onboard delivery missions.

The Osprey reaches cruising altitude and accelerates to 225 knots. Aided by a tailwind, it's traveling in excess of 300 miles per hour over the water. Subic Bay's coordinates are confirmed in the navigation system, auto flight controls are engaged, and the crew settles in for the flight.

* * *

McGirt and Jimmie Posadas did their best trying to convince the nervous Subic officials that the defecting pilot dilemma was under control. Posadas had placed Philippine President Diaz on his phone's speaker so that the group could hear him in real time: Diaz confirmed that he and President Black had reached a collective decision to evacuate the Chinese pilot by a U.S. military aircraft. Diaz had concluded by saying that Admiral McGirt and Jimmie Posadas had full authority to carry out the action as they saw fit. Reassured by their president's words, the Philippine officials left the building.

McGirt and Posadas hustled down to the janitor's space where Lieutenant Lin was being held. The guards sprang to attention when they walked in.

"Gentlemen, please stand at ease," McGirt said.

Posadas repeated the words in Tagalog, then motioned for the soldiers to huddle in close with him. He whispered a few more sentences, which prompted the men to laugh. Posadas shook their hands, and then held open the door as they resumed their post in the hallway.

Jimmie's phone rang. After a minute of his repeated acknowledgments of "yes," and "okay," he hung up and turned to McGirt. "That was Ambassador Remington. He said that Chinese Ambassador Wu stormed out of his office and is headed to the Manila airport. Wu told him that he's flying his private jet here and will take custody of Lin. President Diaz has granted him diplomatic clearance to land at Subic."

"What the hell?" McGirt hollered. "If they get their hands on Lin, the kid's dead— period. Geez, I thought Diaz was onboard with this."

Posadas bit his lower lip. "Right…I'm not sure what's going on in his head, but I've been around Diaz long enough to know he's a crafty politician. My guess is that he wants to show some deference to China's concerns. But he was firm about Lin: he reassured me that he fully supports our plan."

McGirt stared at the ceiling then said, "Well, if that's the case, tell the tower crew to deny the Chinese landing clearance. Better still, just shut down the damn runway. Has Lin's plane been moved yet?"

"Last time I looked, it was being hoisted onto a flatbed truck. The police told me it's being relocated to a hangar on the other side of the airport."

"Okay, then there's our solution. Get word to that flatbed driver to park his ass in the middle of the runway, like he's having mechanical problems—overheated engine or something. Have the crash crew put a couple of firetrucks out there to make it look authentic. If the runway's clobbered, Wu's plane can't land. Jimmie, do we have an ETA for the Osprey?"

Posadas checked his watch. "I'll call the tower and see if they have an inbound."

"Good. Where the hell is Remington, anyway?" McGirt asked. "We could sure use him here."

"Diaz told me that he's sprung loose his helicopter and is sending it over to the embassy to pick up Remington."

McGirt flashed back to the image of the pretty Filipina glued to Harold Remington's side at last night's soiree. He could only hope that the ambassador's head was screwed on tight when he landed at Subic.

Posadas left the room and flagged down an airport cop that was in the building. The pair hopped into a patrol car and raced out to the runway where the flatbed carrying Lin's jet was inching its way along. The officer brought his car to a screeching halt, blocking the truck's path. Posadas jumped out and explained to the driver what he wanted him to do. The guy shrugged his shoulders as if he didn't care one way or the other. He then got out of his truck, leaned up against a fender and lit a cigarette.

Posadas hitched a ride back to Subic operations, found the airport man-ager—a fifty-ish looking woman named Vera Navarro—and asked her for a direct line to the control tower. Vera pulled out her cell phone and dialed.

Rollie de Guzman answered. "Subic Tower, de Guzman here. Vera, if you're going to ask me how soon before we can reopen, I don't have an answer. The flatbed's stalled on the runway and now I see a couple CFR vehicles driving toward it."

Vera made a quick introduction of Posadas, and then handed the phone over. "Hello, this is Jimmie Posadas. Two questions: do you have an ETA for a Navy CVM-22 and also, one for a civilian jet from Manila?" He heard muffled conversation between de Guzman and his partner.

"Yeah, Navy Titan One-Zero just checked in with Subic approach control. Should be on deck in ten minutes. Approach told them the airport is closed until we can clear the runway."

Posadas put the phone on speaker mode so Vera could hear. "That Navy aircraft needs immediate landing clearance. He's a tiltrotor and can land like a helicopter."

"Huh…didn't know that. I'll need my boss' approval."

Vera grabbed the phone. "Rollie, let the Navy aircraft land on the taxi-way…and tell him to expedite parking close to operations. I'll have a marshalling crew standing by."

"Got it, boss," Rollie said. "Oh, Eddie just told me that the jet from Manila is in range; they're estimating here in five minutes." Rollie paused. "Hey, if that wreck is clear by then, you want me to let him land too?"

Posadas interrupted. "No! No! No! *Do not*, I say again, *do not* allow that aircraft to land until the Navy bird has departed. Do you understand?"

"Sure. If it's okay with Vera, it's okay with me."

Vera jumped in. "That's what I want, Rollie. I'll explain later."

* * *

McGirt paced inside the janitor's room. He had confidence in Jimmie's abilities, yet he knew that timing would be critical; he wanted to get Lin off Philippine soil before the Chinese delegation had a chance to see him. He wasn't sure what yarn Posadas would spin to the group, and hoped that when Remington showed up, he might deflect some of the load falling on Jimmie. He was about to sit down when Posadas burst through the door. He took a second to catch his breath. "The Osprey is almost here; tower is going to clear them to land on a taxiway."

"What about the Chinese?" McGirt asked.

"They're airborne and only five minutes away. I told the flatbed driver to stay put on the runway until we tell him otherwise. Two rescue vehicles are on the runway parked next to him."

McGirt faced Lin, who was sitting with arms across his chest; a sly grin lingered on his face. "Okay, here's the plan, Lieutenant: You and I are going to fly to a U.S. Navy ship. I can't guarantee what will happen from there. All I can say is that you'll be a hell of a lot safer on that ship than you'd ever be in the hands of your own government."

Lin Yi's grin spread into a broad smile. He stood up and started walking toward the door but turned and reached for the tattered straw hat hanging on the wall. He gave it a quick inspection, then put it on, pulling it low over his ears. He stood tall and faced McGirt; the smile had left his face, replaced by a stone-sober expression. "Admiral, I request that you take me to America," he said in his most deliberate English. He concluded with, "Please, sir."

McGirt cracked open the door to the hallway, where the two Philippine Army guards were stationed; they started coming to attention until he signaled them to relax. Other than the guards, the passageway and surrounding spaces appeared empty. McGirt didn't want to move Lin without confirmation that they'd have a clear path to the Osprey. As he stepped into the passageway, he felt a rumble under his feet, followed by the unmistakable sound of the V-22's throbbing proprotors.

"They're here!" Posadas said. "Sweet Jesus, McGirt, this is going to work!"

McGirt shoved Jimmie toward the building's entrance. "Make sure there' s no one out there except the marshallers. After the Osprey parks and the boarding ramp is lowered, let me know."

Posadas stood by the exit as the pounding, mechanical din grew louder and louder. He held the door ajar and waited while the aircraft taxied to a spot in front of the building. It parked with engines still turning and burning; Jimmie coughed as engine exhaust filtered into the hallway. He pushed the door full open and yelled to McGirt, "Go, go now! They're ready!"

McGirt grabbed Lin Yi by the arm, bolted down the hallway and onto the tarmac; he broke into a jog and squeezed Lin's arm harder. Lin's ill-fitting sneakers caused him to stumble; McGirt helped raise him to his feet while one of the crew chiefs jumped off the boarding ramp to guide them aboard. Lin's straw hat went flying off his head from the propwash. It tumbled end over end before coming to rest fifty yards downwind.

The Osprey's pilots wasted no time getting airborne: the aircraft started its takeoff roll on the taxiway; seconds later it was off the deck. The pilot made a tight left turn and reversed course to the west, then initiated the transition to airplane mode. By the time it reached Grande Island at the mouth of Subic Bay, the aircraft had accelerated to over 200 knots.

Jimmie Posadas stood in amazement; he checked his watch. Total time from when the Osprey had landed, boarded its passengers, and had whisked out to sea: less than four minutes. The chaotic scene became eerily quiet.

Vera approached from inside the building. "That was impressive," she said.

Jimmie replied with a simple, "Yes, it was."

Vera pointed to the flatbed carrying Lin's jet and the crash vehicles grouped around it on the runway. "Is it okay for them to start moving?"

"Yes, we're good now," Jimmie said.

Vera called Rollie de Guzman, who relayed the message via radio to the vehicles. Moments later, the caravan turned off the runway and onto a taxiway; the CFR vehicles headed back to the firehouse while the flatbed trudged to a vacant hangar on the airport's east end.

Vera's phone rang; it was Rollie again. "Boss, what about the inbound from Manila? He's been holding to the east for quite a while. Said if he can't land within ten minutes, he'll have to divert."

Jimmie squinted to see the corporate jet orbiting over the Zambales Mountains. Vera turned to him with questioning raised eyebrows. "Sure, let them land," he said. Vera gave the go ahead to Rollie.

Jimmie Posadas stayed on the tarmac while Vera returned to her office. He watched the Chinese ambassador's jet as it lined up for a straight in approach to Subic's west runway. The blustery conditions that Lin Yi had experienced earlier in the day had mellowed into a gentle, late afternoon sea breeze. Jimmie realized that he hadn't spoken to his wife since he'd left their beach cottage in a flurry, hours ago. The couple had planned a romantic sunset happy hour, followed by a peaceful dinner. He wondered how he'd apologize to the woman; he was afraid it would be late evening before he'd see her.

The jet landed and taxied to the same spot where the Osprey had parked. Jimmie looked to the east and hoped that Harold Remington's helicopter would soon appear over the mountains. He had no idea what he'd tell the Chinese.

CHAPTER 11

Dick Moselli was surprised when he stepped into the trailer: the place looked move-in-ready, right down to curtains over the windows and framed still life art on the walls.

"Well, lookie here!" Horton said. "This beats any enlisted barracks I've stayed in and definitely that fart-filled bunk room on the ship." He tossed his flight gear on the floor and then plopped down on a plush teal colored sofa in the living area; the sofa was still wrapped in protective plastic.

Aguilar walked over to the kitchen sink and tested the faucet. "Don't get too excited, Crazo. We don't have water." He looked closer at the stainless steel sink and its fixtures; like the sofa, they appeared fresh from the factory. "I think we're the first ones to stay here… it has that new car smell. Know what I mean?"

Horton shot back, "Yeah, but like you said: don't get too excited. The jackoffs probably bugged the joint."

Moselli returned from the other side of the trailer where he'd discovered three fully made-up bedrooms. "Son of a bitch, they've got this place decked out: sheets on the beds and towels in the head." He opened a kitchen cabinet. "Same here: plates, glasses, the whole nine yards." He glanced at Salid, who was still standing by the doorway; he had the woeful look of a lost child. "Wish we could communicate with this poor guy. He might give us a clue as to what the hell is going on."

Aguilar joined Horton on the sofa. "That sweaty skunk that met us thought we had someone else onboard. Remember when his flunky, the Army officer said, 'We want the Chinese pilot…'"

Moselli couldn't take his eyes off of Salid. He had a hunch that their rescuing of him was the key to why they'd been intercepted by the Chinese fighters. Until now, Moselli had all but ignored the young man; he'd been too busy flying and attempting to put the puzzle together. He motioned Salid to take a seat next to him at the round kitchen table. Like every other piece of furniture, the wooden table and its chairs looked brand spanking new. Salid sat down and hugged his blanket around him; the trailer's conditioned air was frigid.

The men heard three loud knocks on the door. Captain Gao entered; behind him was a string of soldiers carrying boxes teeming with supplies. One soldier lugged two cases of bottled water into the kitchen area and plunked them on the floor. The others set their boxes on the countertop.

Moselli approached the captain. "Thanks for the supplies, but we have no water for the toilet or shower."

"Yes, my apology. People are making correct… will hook up water and, how you say…thee crapper."

Moselli chuckled at Gao's effort to be congenial. He pointed to Salid. "Can you also get him some dry clothing?"

Gao studied the shivering fellow. "Okay. We can do." He barked an order to his men; they saluted and left the trailer.

Moselli invited Gao to join him at the table. He grabbed some water bottles and distributed them to everyone, including Gao. Aguilar and Horton had already torn into the supplies; they dug out cups of dehydrated ramen noodles, added water, and set the cups inside a microwave oven mounted above the kitchen's electric stove top. Moselli gestured toward Salid. "Hey, fellas, nuke one for our guest here, will ya?"

As he sat down, Dick Moselli gathered his thoughts and searched for the right questions to ask Captain Gao. He considered the intercept a hostile act; however, other than the reception by Gao's obnoxious supervisor, he and his men were being treated well.

"Captain Gao," he began. "I want to thank you for the supplies and for your concern about our comfort. However, we are being detained against our will. You need to explain why that is so."

"This man here," Gao said while pointing to Salid. "We thought him to be somebody different. Somebody my country very much wants to find."

Moselli looked at Salid, who was wolfing down his noodles. "We haven't been able to communicate with him. He only tells us that he is Filipino, but we do not speak his language, and he does not speak ours. Do you have any workers here from the Philippines?"

Gao didn't answer the question. Instead, he reached for his radio and made a brief transmission. "We shall see about that," he said. A moment later, the radio erupted with a long string of phrases. Gao gave a short reply and checked his watch. "My superior will be here soon."

Moselli smiled and said, "Thank you." He'd decided that the most effective way to handle the situation was to remain calm and cooperate with his captors.

He and his men were outnumbered, stranded on an unfamiliar island, and hundreds of miles from their ship. His helicopter was nearly out of fuel, plus there was nowhere to flee by foot. He heard commotion in the kitchen: Aguilar and Horton had finished their noodles and were pawing through the rest of the food.

Horton opened a thin, tube-shaped item wrapped in plastic. "Looks kind of like a Slim Jim sausage," he said. But after getting a whiff, he held it at arm's length. "Can't read the damn label, but by the smell, I'd guess it's some sort of dried fish…maybe eel. No thanks!" He heaved it into the sink, and then reached for something else, settling on a canister of potato chips. "Ah, finally some real food!" he mumbled through his stuffed mouth. He poured the chips into a bowl and returned to the sofa.

The crew heard commotion outside, followed by the clumping of boots on the ground. An older gentleman burst in without knocking; he was dressed in long-sleeved camouflage fatigues adorned with odd-looking collar devices. His pant legs were tucked into the tops of polished black boots. Unlike the ball cap style headgear that Gao and his men had on, the fellow wore an oversized, olive drab helmet. Once the man's rank body odor wafted into the trailer, McGirt figured it was the same person that Gao had introduced as his supervisor.

Captain Gao rose and stood at attention. His supervisor surveyed the room, grunted a few words, and then nodded approvingly. He spoke to Gao, who interpreted for Moselli.

"The colonel has brought someone that can speak to your other man," Gao said.

"Colonel?" Moselli asked. "You didn't tell me that this man was an officer; he was dressed as a civilian when we met."

Gao hesitated, then said, "Yes, that is correct." He lowered his voice. "When it is very hot, the colonel choses to wear…other clothing." Gao glanced at the colonel as if expecting a reaction. The colonel seemed unfazed by Gao's words. He stood flat footed with arms crossed over his chest; his sweaty face had a smug expression.

"Okay, now I understand," Moselli said. "What is the colonel's name."

Gao said something that sounded like "Gu Yin Fu Quan Shing."

Moselli asked him to say the name again; Gao did, but Moselli found it too difficult to repeat. "Captain Gao, I do not want to insult the colonel by mispronouncing his name. Would it be proper for me to refer to him simply as, 'Colonel'?"

Gao translated the request to his boss, who nodded approval.

"Okay, fine," Moselli said. He noticed that the colonel had not fully closed the door; through the crack he saw a tiny, dark-skinned man dressed in work clothes; two soldiers stood next to him. The colonel waived the fellow inside. Salid's eyes widened when the man approached him and said something in the Philippine dialect of Cebuano, his native language. The pair chatted for over a minute before the newcomer turned to Moselli and said in broken but decent English, "My name Hashim. We come from same place. His name Salid Alonto. His fishing boat was sunk by airplane. What you want me to ask him?"

Moselli tapped Hashim on the shoulder. "Thank you! We're finally getting somewhere! Ask him to tell you what happened." Aguilar and Horton stopped eating and came closer to listen.

Hashim and Salid continued their conversation. After a rush of sentences, Hashim raised his hand, signaling Salid to stop talking while he translated: first to English, which in turn, Captain Gao relayed to the colonel in Mandarin. The process went on for several minutes while Salid described everything in detail: how he'd moved to the bow of the fishing boat to have a smoke; the thunderous roar of the two jets as they'd first buzzed the vessel; and how they'd circled and come back. Salid's voice quivered as he recalled how the one jet began firing bullets across the surface. At that point, he stopped; tears welled in his eyes.

Moselli was enthralled. "Ask him what happened next; how did he end up in the water?"

Hashim pressed on with questions. Salid regained his composure and told how his mind had gone blank after the explosion and how he'd thought he was going to die when the blast blew him overboard. When he had regained his senses, he realized he'd landed on a piece of the boat's pilothouse. He'd called out to other crewmembers, but no one else had survived.

The colonel appeared caught up in the story. He said something to Gao, who relayed the words to Hashim. "My colonel wants to know what direction the jets went after they fired their weapons."

Salid lowered his eyes; his head swayed from side to side. His words were barely audible. Hashim turned to Gao. "Salid does not remember except for explosion and when helicopter lifted him from water."

Moselli glanced at the colonel. He noticed that the man's demeanor had changed from arrogance to one of sober compassion. The colonel spoke to Gao in a low voice, and then faced Moselli while Gao translated.

"My colonel says that this was a big mistake. We thought this man was someone else. Colonel offers you apologies."

"Please tell the colonel that I accept his apology," Moselli replied. "Now ask him to get fuel for my helicopter so we can fly back to our ship."

Partway through Gao's translation, the colonel cut him off. In fractured English he addressed Moselli directly. "No...I no...not do." He finished his thoughts in Mandarin.

"That is not to be so easy," Gao relayed. He turned to the colonel for guidance but received none. Gao repeated, "...not to be so easy. You must stay here now." With that, the colonel exited the trailer. Hashim extended his hand to Salid and then followed the colonel.

"I will check you in the morning," Gao said. He moved toward the door but paused before opening it. He faced Moselli and said, "I am sorry this has happened." Moselli sensed that Gao wanted to say more but he didn't. Instead, he got into his vehicle and drove away.

Aguilar said, "Guess we're spending the night, huh?" He drew open a window curtain. "It's looking to be a right pretty sunset. Anybody want to join me outside for a special moment?" Horton laughed, grabbed another water bottle, and followed him outside.

Moselli spotted a trash bag next to the door as Aguilar and Horton left; he guessed that one of the soldiers had left it behind. "Well, it's your lucky day, young fella," he said while opening the bag. He handed Salid a clean set of work coveralls—the same as Hashim's—and a pair of thick-soled boots. Salid smiled and went to the trailer's bathroom to change.

Lieutenant Commander "Bruiser" Moselli sat alone at the kitchen table. It dawned on him that the last thing he'd eaten was a soggy omelet and a dry piece of toast in *Grand Rapids'* wardroom twelve hours ago. He eyed the cornucopia of dry goods piled high on the counter. He didn't have much of an appetite but figured that he had better eat something. He knew he'd never get to sleep on an empty stomach.

* * *

Jimmie Posadas stood alone on the tarmac as the Chinese ambassador's airplane came to a stop on Subic's VIP apron. Other than McGirt's Cobra and the Navy Osprey, no other aircraft had arrived since Lin Yi's jet had crash landed.

Posadas didn't know the model of the delegation's plane, but he thought it to be an overkill for the short flight from Manila: the sparkling, three engine bizjet was comparable in size to a small airliner. He wondered if the ambassador had purposefully chosen the big aircraft as way of projecting strength.

As the plane's turbines wound down, the marshalling crew installed chocks around the aircraft's wheels, and then placed a pair of orange safety cones beneath its wingtips. The jet's boarding door was eased opened by a crewmember, followed by the lowering of a short set of stairs that came to rest a few inches above the pavement. Out stepped two very tall Asian men that Posadas assumed were bodyguards. They descended and took positions on either side of the stairs. The men had the no-nonsense air of law enforcement and the lean appearance of athletes. Their black hair was closely cropped in flat-top style; dark aviator glasses shielded their eyes. Underneath the thin, embroidered fabric of their long-sleeved Barong Tagalog shirts, Jimmie detected the unmistakable bulge of holstered sidearms. The men stood motionless, with feet shoulder width apart and relaxed hands folded over their midsections. A few seconds later, China's Ambassador to the Philippine Islands emerged.

Ambassador Wu Zhou paused at the top of the stairs; he scanned the setting from side to side. Wu was of average height and had the stockiness of a middle-aged government official who'd spent most of his time behind a desk. Unlike the guards, he was attired in a Western style blue business suit. His white dress shirt and red tie projected importance. Wu also wore dark sunglasses.

Posadas met Wu with an extended hand. "Welcome to Subic Bay, Mister Ambassador," he said in deliberate English. "My name is James Posadas. I am employed by the Philippine government; I also represent the U. S. State Department."

Wu snubbed Jimmie's handshake. Instead, he removed his glasses, and again, looked from side to side. "I was expecting to be met by an official from the Philippine Defense or Executive branch. Might I ask where they are?" Wu's diction was near perfect: he'd studied at Oxford and had taken on the refined accent of an educated Brit.

Posadas lowered his hand. "Mister Ambassador, I cannot speak for those individuals. It is Sunday... and, as you know, this is a Christian country." He offered an apologetic smile. "Things move at a slower pace on Sundays." Wu laughed and mumbled some words to his guards, who neither flinched nor replied to what he'd said. Posadas continued. "However, Ambassador Remington has offered his services as an intermediary; I expect him any moment. May I escort you to a conference room inside?"

Wu grunted something unintelligible and started for the door; the guards followed at his side, and a half step behind. Posadas double-timed to stay ahead of the trio. He lunged forward to open the door. "Please take the stairway to your left, gentleman," he said. The group brushed by him without saying a word.

When they arrived at the conference room, Jimmie noticed that the place had been spruced up since the Subic officials had met there earlier in the day. The long mahogany table had been polished to a glossy shine; on an adjacent credenza, bottles of cold water had been set out, along with services for coffee and hot tea. He said a silent thank you to Vera Navarro, who'd provided the hospitality. Wu took a seat at the head of the table while the two guards stood on either side of the doorway.

Jimmie motioned toward the credenza. "Mister Ambassador, may I offer you—"

Wu cut him off. "I do not know what position you hold, but it is protocol for an ambassador to be greeted by a person of comparable status." Wu spoke without making eye contact. He checked his watch. "If a Philippine official or Ambassador Remington does not show within ten minutes, I will leave and return to Manila. I will be forced to report this rude affront to my superiors in Beijing." Wu was keenly aware that the Philippines' new president, Emilio Diaz, held a cooler tone toward China than had his predecessor, while at the same time, Diaz had rekindled warm relations with his country's long-standing ally, the United States.

Jimmie stood speechless in the middle of the room. He glanced outside and saw that the sun was about to dip below the horizon. He pictured his wife waiting patiently for him at their beach cottage, cocktails at the ready. He then turned his sights to the pompous foreigner who sat before him. At times like this, he questioned why on earth he'd volunteered to leave his work in the States to accept a job in the country of his ancestors. As his regretful thoughts deepened, he heard the *clap, clap, clap* sound of a distant helicopter. "That must be Ambassador Remington," he said. He bolted from the room and rushed down the stairs.

President Diaz' helicopter, a black corporate Bell 525— trimmed in the Philippine flag's colors of red, white, blue, and gold—landed and taxied to a spot near the operations building. A side door slid open, and Harold Remington jumped out. He was alone and carried nothing with him—not even a briefcase. Posadas met him halfway on the tarmac as the chopper taxied clear.

Remington gave a weak smile and latched on to Jimmie's hand. His coiffed, silver hair settled back into place as the helicopter's rotor wash died down. He wore an open-collar pinstriped shirt, its sleeves rolled up to mid forearm, and a pair of khaki pants. Both shirt and trousers looked unpressed, as if he'd worn them for a couple of days. As they approached the building, Jimmie noticed that Remington needed a shave. The man's strong cologne filled the air as they stepped inside. Posadas wondered if the cologne had been splashed on in hopes of masking the smell of alcohol.

Jimmie Posadas had worked with Harold Remington on a handful of projects involving trade, health care and general relations between the United States and the Philippines. He didn't know Remington very well but was mindful of the billionaire's reputation as a hard-driven international player. Posadas had followed the issue of China's encroachments in the South China Sea; however, as an intermediary between the U.S. and P.I., he hadn't been exposed to the tensions created by the matter. He had a hunch that that was about to change.

"Where is he?" Remington said as he searched the empty hallway. Jimmie led the way as the ambassador bound up the stairs two treads at a time. When Wu's guards blocked his path at the doorway, Remington peeked around them and made eye contact with Wu, who said something in Mandarin; the guards parted and stood aside.

Remington walked into the conference room and examined the layout: long table with a dozen chairs surrounding it and Ambassador Wu sitting at one end. He started for the chair at the other end, but checked himself and chose a seat along the side and next to Wu. Posadas sat beside him. As Remington turned toward him, Jimmie noticed that the man's eyes were bloodshot.

The room was dead quiet for a solid minute until Remington said, "Well, Wu, I'm here. What can I do for you?"

Ambassador Wu chuckled haughtily. "You know the answer to that. I am here to take custody of our Navy pilot, Lieutenant Lin Yi, who has stolen one of the People's aircraft and dishonored his country by fleeing like a coward to the open arms of another nation." Remington set both elbows on the table and slumped forward; his eyes avoided Wu. "And don't try to distract me with your nonsense," Wu added. He pulled out his phone, slid it across the table and said, "Look at this!"

Remington picked up the device. "Ah, thank goodness for the internet," he said under his breath, then pushed the 'play' arrow on the screen of Wu's smart phone. He watched a collage of video snippets that sunbathers on All Hands Beach had posted on social media: Lin descending into the water after ejecting; the two fishermen dragging him into their boat; Lin being whisked away by the airport police; and finally, a two-minute segment depicting Subic's CFR crew craning Lin's jet on to a flatbed, covering it with a tarp, and towing it away.

When the videos were finished, Remington slid the phone back to Wu. "Okay... so like I said, what do you want me to do?"

Wu's face reddened. "This is unacceptable! You are wasting my time." He pointed to Posadas. "You, you there...get me someone from your country, some-one who can carry out my demands."

Posadas cleared his throat and was about to speak when Harold Remington squeezed his forearm, signaling for him to be quiet. "Ambassador Wu, Mister Posadas represents both the United States and the Philippines; however, I believe I can summarize things in a way that you can better understand. When—"

"Do not patronize me!" Wu shouted. "You may stall, but I know you have Lin and the airplane. Where are they?"

Posadas watched as Remington hung his head lower and stared blankly at the table. Jimmie could only wonder why he'd been saddled with this mess; he wished that McGirt would magically reappear and take charge. He knew that the admiral had a knack for prying open diplomatic channels at the highest levels in D.C. By comparison, Harold Remington appeared to be way over his head dealing with the Chinese ambassador. Posadas recognized that it was common practice for an American president to dole out ambassadorships as a form of payback to his biggest donors, but so far, Harold Remington's actions were embarrassing. *And why hadn't President Diaz sent one of his own cabinet members to the meeting?* Jimmie pondered. *Was it a calculated snub of the Chinese?*

After an uncomfortable pause, Remington sat up straight and faced Wu. "I can't help you with Lin, but unless someone has figured a way to get his wrecked plane back in the air, I'd guess that it's someplace on the airport." Reming-ton shrugged his shoulders with a *how would I know?* facial expression: like a teenager claiming that they'd done their homework but hadn't a clue how the papers had disappeared.

Wu's reddened face faded back to normal as he calmed down. He shook his head and smirked at Remington's bullheadedness. "Okay, then, will you and your helper assist me with locating the aircraft? I would like to confirm its condition."

Remington took a deep yawn, then stood up. "Sure, I guess we can do that." He turned to Posadas. "Talk to the airport manager and see if you can get us some wheels, will you, Jimmie?"

Posadas made a beeline for Vera Navarro's office; she was still at her desk. Minutes later, two police cruisers showed up in front of the building. Their blue and red lights pulsed across the dusky tarmac. The pilots of Wu's bizjet had secured the aircraft and settled into the airport's lounge to wait.

Remington and Wu sat in the rear seat of one cruiser while Posadas sat in front with the driver; the ambassador's bodyguards rode inside the other vehicle. The cars exited the airport's main tarmac and proceeded onto a narrow taxiway defined by blue lights along its edges. The taxiway sloped down slightly for a few hundred yards, before making a ninety-degree turn to the right and terminating onto an expansive area where a handful of small aircraft were parked. A pair of hangars sat along one side of the tarmac: one hangar was dark, while lighting filtered through the other's upper windows. The crane and flatbed that had moved Lin's jet were silhouetted at the far end of the tarmac. President Diaz' helicopter was parked in front of the illuminated hangar. Posadas swiveled in his seat with an inquisitive look on his face: he could have sworn that he'd seen Diaz' helicopter fly away after Remington had gotten out.

Someone inside slid open the hangar door a couple of feet to make an entryway. Wu got out of the cruiser and hustled through the opening. Remington and Posadas followed.

Lieutenant Lin Yi's J-31 fighter jet sat in the center of the hangar. Its crumpled landing gear had been removed and an iron jack installed in its place. Bright yellow tape—the kind used to cordon off crime scenes—encircled the jet, except for a small gap that allowed passage into the work area. Next to the opening was a white sign with bold red lettering, "RESTRICTED. AUTHORIZED PERSONNEL ONLY!" A team of mechanics were busy removing airframe panels as a Philippine Air Force general and his aide stood on ladders examining the jet's cockpit. The whine of power tools and ratcheting wrenches filled the air.

Wu tried to bully his way inside the work area but was rebuffed by a pair of Philippine soldiers. He backed off and turned to Remington. "What is the meaning of this!" he hollered. He then faced a befuddled Posadas. "And whoever you are, I demand that you contact Diaz immediately and inform him of this indignation. That airplane is the property of the People's Republic of China!" He then pointed to a man wearing coveralls stenciled with the words "Boeing Aircraft" on the back. "You! Put down your tools and get away from that airplane. All of you, leave the building…now!" The Boeing rep looked at Wu for a second, then went back to work.

Jimmie Posadas started to better understand as pieces of the puzzle came together; why Harold Remington had shown up late for the meeting, and why he'd presented the image of a disheveled, bored incompetent: It had all been a ruse to buy time. Unbeknownst to Posadas, Remington had assembled a team of American and Filipino mechanics assigned to Ninoy Aquino International Airport in Manila; they'd flown to Subic with him on the helicopter. Remington had pulled it off in a matter of a couple hours—and with the full endorsement of presidents Maxwell Black and Emilio Diaz.

Harold Remington stood just inside the hangar doors, clear of the activity; he made eye contact with Jimmie, flashed a wry smile, and then approached the Chinese ambassador. "Don't worry, Wu, President Diaz asked me to assure you that you'll get your airplane back, but it wouldn't be right if the Philippines hands it over in such bad condition." Wu glowered at him; he seemed incapable of a response. Remington pointed to the people hovering around the jet. "I know what you might be thinking: are these men qualified to repair a sophisticated fighter like the J-31? Well, granted, they normally work on big airliners, and not top secret marvels like this. But military technicians will be arriving tomorrow to lend a hand. Like I said, President Diaz wishes to return it in tiptop shape."

Wu said a few words to his bodyguards, who acknowledged and returned to the police cruiser. He then turned to Remington and spoke in a polished, unemotional manner. "Ambassador Remington, I will depart now and return to my residence in Manila. But to be clear, this matter is far from over. My country will not be satisfied until both our airplane and its pilot are returned. And we will seek formal apologies from the United States and the Philippines. This act will not stand." With that, Wu pivoted and left.

Posadas watched as Harold Remington turned away and started chatting up a couple of the mechanics. One of the men stepped outside the yellow ring and lit a cigarette. Remington tapped him on the shoulder and bummed one. The pair joked about something as they enjoyed their smokes.

Until tonight, Jimmie Posadas didn't know much about the American ambassador's persona. He'd figured that Remington, like others in his position, was a privileged billionaire donor who'd been given a primo government position in return for his support. That may have been the case, yet Posadas had learned two unequivocal facts that helped explain how the tycoon had been so successful in business: Harold Remington was sly as a fox and had brass balls the size of cantaloupes.

CHAPTER 12

Admiral Johnny Jack McGirt had never flown on an Osprey, but his first impression upon boarding was that the aircraft cabin felt similar to his beloved H-46—the helicopter on which he'd logged most of his 5000 flight hours. Similar to the '46, the Osprey had accommodations for two dozen passengers. Instead of troop benches, the V-22 had been upgraded with individual, improved crashworthy seats, each with a four-point restraint harness. And like the venerable '46, the Osprey's cabin interior was bare-bones: there were no sound dampening bulkhead or ceiling liners. Thick labyrinths of electrical wires and stainless steel hydraulic piping filled almost every square inch of the cabin's sidewalls and overhead. The H-46 Sea Knight and V-22 Osprey shared another distinctive characteristic: they were both loud—very loud.

A crew chief guided McGirt and Lin to seats across from each other in the forward cabin. The pair barely had time to strap in before the pilot had gotten airborne. The crew chief handed each of them floatation vests to put on over their heads, followed by a flight deck helmet, better known as a "cranial." The headgear was a one-piece combination of canvas, heavy-gauge plastic, and cushioned noise suppressing cups that hugged the ears. McGirt's cranial was equipped with earphones and a boom mike.

The Osprey's helicopter-like vibrations subsided as the aircraft accelerated. McGirt caught the eye of a crew chief and signaled that he'd like to speak with the cockpit crew. The man nodded and plugged one end of a long cord into a nearby jack; he then inserted the cord's other end into a fitting on McGirt's cranial. McGirt found the unit's transmit button, stood up and walked toward the cockpit. As he did, he looked at Lin, who sat with arms folded across his chest and head leaned back; he had a blank stare in his eyes, as if hypnotized or in a daydream. But when he made eye contact with McGirt, his expression changed to a satisfied grin.

McGirt peeked out a cabin window and saw Grande Island whiz by. He stood outside the cockpit, pressed his mike's transmit button and said, "Request permission to come aboard, sir."

The aircraft commander looked up from the clipboard on his lap; his eyes fixated on the two stars pinned to McGirt's shirt collar. "Absolutely, Admiral. Permission granted. Come on in."

McGirt knelt on one knee between the pilots and scanned the cockpit; the layout was nothing like he'd ever seen. He'd bagged flight time in most of the Navy's helicopters, and a couple of prop and jet trainers, but the Osprey's instrument configuration appeared more like that of a spacecraft: two large monitors in front of each pilot, plus another pair of screens nestled atop the center console. He recognized a few of the switches on the console and overhead panel, but most of the items were unfamiliar.

"Rear Admiral Johnny Jack McGirt," he said while extending his hand. He saw the name "STRETCH" stenciled in bold letters across the back of the pilot's helmet. "Nice to meet you, son." It was obvious by Stretch's long, lanky frame how the guy had acquired his call sign. McGirt wondered if he might have ducked his head a little to sneak under the Navy's maximum height limit for aviators: Stretch's seat was in the full aft position while his legs nearly touched the instrument panel.

McGirt then turned to the copilot who was flying the aircraft from the left seat. The fellow had both hands on the controls, so he dipped his head in respect and said, "My pleasure, Admiral." McGirt saw the name "STREAKER" scripted on the youngster's helmet. He thought for a second about asking the moniker's origin but chose not to; he could only imagine. He asked Stretch, "What info did your ops officer give you about this flight?"

"Admiral, we were ordered to fly to Subic, pick up two passengers—you and one civilian—and then rendezvous with *Grand Rapids*, somewhere off the coast of Luzon for drop off. After that, return to *Reagan*."

McGirt was dumbfounded. "You never got the ship's location before launching?"

Stretch shook his head. "No, sir. Ops told us it was TBD[1]. Excuse my French, but that pissed me off to beat the band. I accepted the mission with the caveat that we carry a full bag of gas so I could bingo back to *Reagan* if this got messed up." McGirt heard a chime followed by an alert light on the instrument panel. Stretch pressed a button to display the message and said, "Okay, here we go... 'proceed to LCS 40. Deplane pax. Buster to home plate'...Oh, that's nice... they

---

[1] To be determined

even remembered to give us the ship's lat/long coordinates." He faced McGirt with a frustrated expression. "Admiral, ever since things got hot in the Straits, life on the boat has been, let's just say...pretty hectic."

McGirt had been in more than a few situations like this when the tempo of operations got ahead of thorough planning. He knew that most of the U.S. Pacific fleet was steaming toward the Taiwan Straits in response to China's gearing up its forces in the region. In his judgement, dispatching an aircraft to haul him and Lin only complicated *Reagan's* workload.

Stretch acknowledged the message, then typed *Grand Rapids'* projected latitude and longitude coordinates into the navigation system. Streaker confirmed the numbers, and then engaged the Osprey's auto pilot; the aircraft banked and tracked a new course. Stretch turned toward McGirt while tapping on the aircraft's digital map display. "One hundred seventy-eight nautical miles; we should be overhead in about thirty-nine minutes." McGirt located the flight gauges on Stretch's instrument panel: the Osprey was cruising at an altitude of 10,000 feet; the speed readout said they were traveling over the water at 270 knots—twice as fast as most rotorcraft could fly. He marveled at the aircraft's capability.

"Sir, you might be more comfortable in the jump seat," Stretch said. He waved the Admiral forward. "Step a little further inside and close the door. Now you can fold down the seat; then flip the top part of the door to the side; that way, you can see back into the cabin too." Once seated, McGirt had a pilot's level view of the Osprey's controls and instruments. He breathed a sigh of relief: his legs had been throbbing while he knelt.

"Ah, much better," he said. "This old-timer's bones were getting stiff kneeling like that." He didn't elaborate that he'd had several knee surgeries—the first one occurring while playing football at the University of Michigan. He glanced back at Lin, who appeared to be sleeping. Considering how well the Osprey's crew had responded to the short-fused mission, he decided they deserved to hear the story—at least part of it. "Are your crewmen on the line?" he asked. Stretch did a quick communications check over the aircraft's ICS; both sailors responded. "Good, I want them to hear this also." He wasn't sure if the two crewmen, like the pilots, held adequate security clearances for what he was about to reveal; he decided to give a sanitized account of why they'd been tasked with the mission.

"Men, you've likely figured out that my traveling partner isn't on active duty with the U.S. Navy...or any of our other services for that matter. For security reasons, I can't go into the details; what I can share with you, though, is that he's traveled at great risk to provide invaluable information to the United States and our allies."

McGirt paused to gather his thoughts; Streaker jumped in before he could speak. "Pardon me, Admiral, but is this related to what we've heard about an H-60 being forced to land on one of those unchartered Chinese islands?"

Stretch jabbed Streaker in the arm. "Hey buddy, hold your tongue. If the admiral wants to open this up for questions, he'll let us know."

McGirt smiled. Apparently, the rumor mill had been working overtime on *Reagan*. He put a hand on Streaker's shoulder. "Tell me more, Lieutenant; what's the skinny on the boat?"

Streaker looked guardedly at Stretch, who shrugged and nodded his approval; they both turned to face McGirt. "Sir, at noon chow, my intel buddy told me that one of the ship's radiomen overheard a garbled transmission on the emergency channel. Something about a helicopter being intercepted by jets. The guys in the comm shack tried to raise the helo but got no response."

By now, the two enlisted crew chiefs had come forward and were hanging over McGirt's shoulder. McGirt rotated in his seat and said, "Gentlemen...as I said, this is a very sensitive matter. I can't confirm anything about one of our helicopters being intercepted and forced down."

McGirt stopped short of going any further. He peeked outside and saw that the sun had declined to just above the horizon. "Looks like you'll be logging some night time, fellas." He was glad to change the subject. "This is my first hop in an Osprey; mind if I pick your brains?"

"Sure, Admiral," Stretch said. "We've got another thirty minutes until overhead. Shoot."

"By those gold oak leaves on your flight suit, I'm guessing that at your rank, you've come from another aircraft. What'd you fly?"

"C-2s, sir."

"Ah, the old Greyhound; a wonderful COD[1] aircraft and a real workhorse. I had the pleasure of making a few carrier traps on that bird—as a passenger, of course. Most of my flight time is rotary; CH-46 Sea Knights mainly."

"So, coming from the '46, you're familiar with interconnected drive systems like the Osprey's," Stretch said. "I compared notes with a retired Sea Knight

---

[1] Carrier Onboard Delivery

driver; substitute cables and rods for the Osprey's fly-by-wire setup, and the two systems are quite similar."

"Yeah, losing an engine was not that big of a deal on the '46; both rotor heads kept turning. That feature saved my tail more than once." Early in his career, McGirt had wondered if designers had studied the H-46's tandem, interconnected rotor heads when they'd first conceived the V-22; the tiltrotor concept had been explored for years, but with marginal results. Decades later, the V-22 Osprey served as the crowning result of those efforts.

McGirt added, "But, after watching this thing get airborne in a jiffy and then accelerate to a fast cruising speed, I'd say comparing the Sea Knight to the Osprey is like comparing a wheel barrel to a Formula One racecar. This is an impressive machine; how do you like flying it?" He leaned forward in hopes of getting an accurate take on Stretch's reaction to his question. What he saw was a glint of disappointment.

Stretch shifted his eyes outside, and then back to McGirt. "This is a unique aircraft, Admiral, for sure. Amazing capabilities in both VTOL and airplane modes." He placed his left hand on a complex-looking handle by his left knee. "Thrust control lever, or TCL—instead of the collective that you had on the '46 to affect rotor blade pitch." He mimicked pushing the TCL forward a few inches. "It controls thrust while the rotors spin at 100 percent for takeoff and climb. We trim it back to 84 percent when in full airplane mode; that gives us a smoother ride at cruise." He then pointed out a small grey thumbwheel built into the side of the TCL. "This little gizmo angles the engine nacelles between 0 and 97 degrees of horizontal. That's the magic that allows us to go from helicopter to airplane, and back again."

"Huh, you said 97 degrees?" McGirt asked. "Isn't that beyond vertical?"

"Sure is. That's what allows us to taxi backwards."

McGirt shook his head in amazement. The Osprey was flying on auto pilot, so Stretch gripped the control stick loosely. "Cyclic is similar to what you had on the Sea Knight. Same with the rudder pedals." He then said, "Sir, my short answer to your question is that I'm fortunate to be in this seat. I'm a senior lieutenant commander, and my year group will be up for command screening soon. With that being said, the Osprey is my best career path to a commanding officer billet."

McGirt read Stretch's lukewarm endorsement of the V-22. "Do you miss flying the Greyhound?"

"Yes, I do. The Osprey's a whole different animal, and it has its own set of issues, but with it having been developed for the Marines' inventory— I fear that we Navy types will be the fleet's stepchildren. I was one of the initial C-2 pilots to make the switch over; the first of us Navy guys went through the Marine training program on a Jarhead base. At least Streaker here got trained by our own RAG[1] instructors in San Diego."

After over thirty years in the Navy, McGirt understood what Stretch was saying: Washington's eagerness to get a new program up and running sometimes created unanticipated problems. Guys like Stretch were expected to fill in the gaps and make the program work. "There's never been the launch of a new aircraft that didn't have its speedbumps," he said. "Those wrinkles will get smoothed out."

McGirt glanced at the aircraft's clock. He knew that the crew needed to prepare for landing, but he didn't want to ignore Stretch's copilot. "How about you, Streaker, what do you think of the Osprey?"

Streaker's reaction could not have been more positive: the young officer was exuberant. "Love it admiral. I was born to be an Osprey pilot. Got my orders straight out of primary flight training. Then some basic helicopter flying in the Jet Ranger and advance multi-engine prop down in Corpus Christi. I received my wings and beelined it to San Diego for Osprey training." Streaker was smiling from ear to ear. "Flying the Osprey is a blast. But I have to agree with Stretch: until the Navy gets more airframes, most folks will consider it a Marine machine."

"Fellows, just one more question: you mentioned that the Osprey's drive system resembles the H-46's. How about auto rotations? Do you have that capability?" McGirt's question related to a conventional helicopter's ability to experience a total engine failure, and then descend at a high rate while building up inertia in its windmilling rotors that could be used to cushion a landing.

Both pilots laughed. "Well, you see...autos are not really an option in the Osprey," Stretch explained. "Our proprotors aren't big enough to always generate sufficient energy that can be traded off for a safe touchdown. Experienced flight instructors can complete the maneuver about twenty-five percent of the time—and that's under ideal conditions in the simulator, not in the actual aircraft."

---

[1] Replacement Air Group

"In that case, why can't you do an unpowered glide to a runway, like an airplane?"

"A glide is survivable, sir," Stretch said, "But because of her short wings, the Osprey drops like the space shuttle when unpowered; you'd need several thousand feet of altitude to pull it off. Plus, even if you made a perfect approach, the proprotors will disintegrate when they hit the ground; their arc sweeps lower than the landing gear when in full airplane mode."

"Emergency procedures for a dual engine failure are in our manual," Streaker added. "That said, it's not something we like to dwell on."

"I understand," said McGirt. "We had a few issues like that in H-46. For instance, there was a big nut that secured the rotor heads to their respective transmissions. We called it the 'Jesus Nut:' if it ever broke loose, you better prepare to meet Jesus." He chuckled. "We didn't like to dwell on that either."

"I guess that's why we get flight pay," Stretch joked.

McGirt looked out at the horizon: the vibrant sunset had faded to a dullish, darkening grey sky. In the distance, he spotted the twinkling lights of the USS *Grand Rapids*. He started to unstrap. "Thanks, guys. This was a real treat for me. I'll let you get back to work."

Stretched raised his hand. "Admiral, you're welcome to stay up front a little longer. I'm planning to make a slow pass overhead to check out the ship's deck markings, and then come back around for the approach. You'll need to return to the cabin before we touch down; the jump seat's not certified for landings."

McGirt perked up. "That would be great. I'd love to see how you make the change from plane to helicopter."

Stretch flicked off the auto pilot and took over on the controls while Streaker made radio contact with the ship. The dusk-hour setting was perfect: technically night, but adequate light to make the approach and landing easier for the pilots. Naval aviators referred to this as "pink time."

Stretch said, "Admiral, after we land, please be ready to deplane; I'd like to make this a fast stopover. *Grand Rapids* hasn't been certified for normal Osprey operations; they're still in the 'Emergency Only' category."

McGirt's eyebrows raised. "Are you kidding me?"

"No, sir. I asked about it at our briefing and was assured that they've made the necessary improvements to their flight deck, but our manuals haven't been updated yet; LCSs are still 'Emergency Only.'"

"So, what's the hang up? From the pictures I've seen, the LCS flight deck is huge—it looks large enough to handle a couple of big helicopters at once." McGirt turned to check on Lin Yi, who was awake and sitting upright; his facial expression remained blank.

"I think they had to beef up the flight deck and fortify the standard non-skid coating they use to cover it," Stretch explained. "The Independence-variant LCS is constructed of aluminum. From what I've heard, engineers were concerned that the Osprey's high exhaust temps could damage the flight deck when our engines are at the full vertical position in a hover."

Another unchecked block during the ship's design phase, assumed McGirt. His mind drifted to the numerous times he'd witnessed "the cart coming before the horse" with defense procurements. Streaker's voice interrupted his thought.

"Bronco, Titan One Zero..." Streaker said on the radio.

"Go ahead, Titan," replied the ship's tower operator.

"Yes, requesting a low flyover, then back around for our approach. Two pax to offload. No services required."

"Copy that, Titan. Wind zero three zero relative at twelve knots. Sea state two. You have a green deck."

"Ah, good," Stretch said. "Nice to hear she won't be rocking and rolling much."

McGirt watched as *Grand Rapids* grew larger in the windscreen. He'd only seen photos of the futuristic looking vessel. With its long, spear-like bow and broad tri-hulled design, the ship had a distinctive profile. He'd once overheard someone at the Pentagon joke that the Independence variant looked like the result of a spaceship and a seagull having a child.

"Admiral, we're about to start the conversion," Stretch said. McGirt watched as Stretch gripped the cyclic with his right hand; his left held the TCL. Through a series of coordinated motions, the magic began: He inched back the TCL and tweaked the grey thumb wheel. McGirt glanced over his shoulder and watched the right engine begin moving from its o-degree, full airplane setting. Stretch must have read McGirt's mind when he said, "Engine nacelles are at 60 degrees now, and we're slowing to 120." The ride got rougher as the aircraft's proprotors generated more downward thrust. Stretch paralleled the ship's track to port, flying five hundred feet above the surface. "Looks like they're ready for us," he said as they passed close abeam the flight deck. He started a course reversal. "Okay, turning downwind now."

McGirt took this as his signal to leave. He unstrapped and hustled back to his seat in the cabin. He made eye contact with Lin, whose expression crept from stoic into a full smile. McGirt craned his head to get a better view through a window: he saw the aquamarine, luminescent glow of the ship's churning wake below; the engine nacelles were now positioned in a near vertical position. Cabin noise grew louder and airframe vibrations increased as Stretch established the aircraft in a hover over the deck. He held the hover for a couple of seconds while gauging the ship's roll and pitching movements. When ready, he eased back thrust; the Osprey landed with a solid thump.

The crewmen sprung from their seats: one lowered the boarding ramp, while the other helped McGirt and Lin unstrap. As the pair rose from their seats, three sailors ran onto the aircraft. The lead man was dressed in camouflage utilities and wearing a cranial labelled "Chief MAA" (Master-at-Arms); he held something in one hand. His two partners grabbed Lin by the elbows while the Chief shouted something inaudible to McGirt, and then placed a black hood over Lin's head. He adjusted it so that its eye, nose, and mouth openings were positioned properly. The Chief nodded to his cohorts, shouted again to McGirt, and then led everyone off the aircraft.

McGirt fought to keep up with the group as they jogged across the flight deck. The ship's two hangar doors were closed, so the entourage entered through a hatchway on one side. As he stepped into the dim hangar, he felt a shudder under his feet; the Osprey created a deafening roar as it departed.

Lin Yi stood motionless with his chin lowered against his chest; the two guards stayed glued to his sides. McGirt noted an H-60 Seahawk helicopter secured to the hangar deck. Next to it sat a smaller rotorcraft that he'd never seen before. He faced the Master-at-Arms and said, "Chief, I think we can dismiss the guards and remove the hood. This fellow isn't a threat and he's not going anywhere."

The Chief took off his cranial. "I understand, Admiral, but unless you're willing to pull rank, I'll have to follow the orders of my commodore. She's on her way down here."

McGirt heard a hatch creak open at the far end of the hangar. Two officers emerged from the shadows: one, a stocky male, the other, a tall, slender female. The man didn't look familiar, but McGirt recognized the woman: she was Captain Katherine Torres, whom he'd worked with on a covert mission at the Central Intelligence Agency and had known for many years. Under different circumstances, the unexpected reunion would have been joyous: McGirt and his wife, Gina—a Navy physician—were dear friends with Torres and her partner and had stood as godparents to the couple's child. But this was not the occasion for pleasantries.

McGirt charged at Torres. "Captain, what the hell is going on here?" He pointed to Lin Yi. "This man is not a prisoner."

Torres stood at rigid attention, her face reddened. "Admiral, my sincere apologies for not being on deck when you touched down." She motioned to the navy commander standing next to her. "The skipper and I were on a conference call with my boss in San Diego; there are new developments." She took a measured breath. "Sir...we need to talk."

CHAPTER 13

Sunday evening
USS Grand Rapids

McGirt's blood was boiling. He managed to cap his anger while he, Commodore Torres, and Commanding Officer Bill Draper made their way to Draper's office. Not a word was spoken between them on the way.

Torres had ordered the Master-at-Arms to get Lin off the aircraft with minimal exposure to the ship's crew. Yet despite the precautions, several people had witnessed his arrival: a CPO in *Grand Rapids'* control tower, plus a half dozen flight deck personnel. Lin was shuttled into a small compartment adjacent to the hangar where two sailors stood guard outside the door. Nonetheless, word spread quickly that *Grand Rapids* had taken on a pair of mismatched visitors: a navy flag officer and an Asian man dressed in shabby work clothes.

McGirt paced the floor. He was still fuming as he confronted Torres. "Commodore, bring me up to speed. What the hell has changed since I left Subic?"

"Admiral, the call that Bill and I took directed us to prepare for an at-sea transfer of you and the Chinese pilot to another ship. *Grand Rapids* will likely re-deploy to the Taiwan Straits and your new ship will take you both back to Subic Bay where the pilot can be turned over to China's ambassador in Manila."

McGirt's eyes widened. "Back to Subic...and Washington is on board with this?"

"I can only assume that they are, I don't know for sure," Torres said.

McGirt gave a tired chuckle. "Okay, Commodore, let me ask, is what you *assume* going to make an *ass*, out of *u* and *me*?" The worn out cliché had shot from his mouth before he could catch himself. He realized he was getting punchy: his day had begun with an interrupted poolside breakfast and terminated hundreds of miles out to sea on a warship. He stopped pacing and sat down. "Sorry guys. Between the jet lag and bouncing around from Manila, to Subic, and now the ship, this old seadog's low fuel light is starting to flicker."

Torres began to speak but was soon drowned out by a blaring voice over the ship's main communication system, or 1MC: "Captain to the Bridge, Captain to the Bridge."

Draper excused himself and departed, leaving Torres and McGirt alone.

Commodore Torres was eager to discuss the Lin situation, but, instead, held off. "If it's okay with you, Johnny, I'd like to wait for Bill to return before continuing." McGirt nodded, leaned back in his chair, and yawned. The rigid structure of rank and chain of command dissipated as the pair resumed their relationship as close friends. Torres asked, "So, how's Gina doing in her new billet at Walter Reed?"

McGirt smiled. "Gina's doing great, thanks. She's a shoe in at the next O-7 selection board...at least in my humble opinion."

"Well, you'll both be wearing stars then," Torres said. "Could that be a problem around the house? A clash of egos?"

"Are you kidding, Kathy? You know who runs the show at our place, and it sure ain't me. Things okay for you and Donna in San Diego?"

"Other than the fact that I'm never home, things are fine. My wife runs a tighter ship than I ever could. Maybe that's why we get along so well." She searched for an appropriate segue back to the matter at hand. "I've been planning this inspection of my West-Pac ships for months. How'd this hot mess fall into your lap?"

McGirt gave her a synopsis of his connection to President Black and why he thought the commander-in-chief had hand-picked him for a critical billet on the National Security Council. He was about to describe how his trip to Manila had taken such a dramatic turn, when they heard a faint tap on the door followed by Bill Draper entering the compartment.

"What's up, Skipper?" Torres asked.

"More news from D.C."

McGirt checked his watch—still set to East Coast time. "Makes sense. Everyone's had their coffee and is ready to lead us into battle," he said with a smirk.

Draper handed a clipboard to McGirt. On it was a classified message originating from the Secretary of Defense, addressed to the Commanding Officer USS *Grand Rapids*, and routed via the Chief of Naval Operations. McGirt fumbled with the button on the pocket of his shirt and pulled out a pair of glasses. He read aloud: "'USS *Grand Rapids*, proceed to designated location. Remain on station until otherwise advised.'" He mumbled to himself the latitude and longitude coordinates that were listed, and then peered over his glasses at Torres. "Ah...and here we go, Commodore… I quote: 'Admiral McGirt to remain onboard as intermediary for exchange of Chinese National and Navy helicopter crew being held at Scarborough Shoals facility. Further details to follow.'" He gave the clipboard back to Draper.

Torres sprang from her seat. "Damn it, can't these desk jockeys make up their minds!" She then said to Draper, "Bill, looks like you're staying in this region for a while. Has your navigator been cut in with the coordinates?"

"Yes, ma'am, I carried a copy of the message to him. Those coordinates pinpoint a spot fifty miles from Scarborough Shoals. Intelligence has it that our flight crew is being held on a landmass that the Chi-Coms are building there."

This news confirmed the rumor that Streaker had shared with McGirt on the Osprey flight. As much as he valued his reputation with the president, McGirt wished that the man would have chosen somebody else for this mission. He figured that once he'd delivered Lin to the sovereignty of a U.S. Navy ship, his job would be done; he'd either restart his original assignment with Ambassador Remington or fly back to the States. He tucked away his glasses and said, "Skipper, do we have on ETA at those coordinates?"

"Yes, sir. Should be on station at sunrise…roughly 0545."

"Then may I suggest that we call it a night; there's not much else for us to do." McGirt stood up and extended his hand to Draper. "I appreciate all that you're doing under these circumstances, Skipper; I know it's not easy. I'd like a few minutes with the commodore if you don't mind."

"Of course. I'll be on the bridge," Draper said.

McGirt ran a hand through his salt-and-pepper brush cut, then rubbed his stiff neck muscles. "Kathy, I've got a couple requests that I'd like you to handle through Bill. First, I've been sweating in this uniform all day and could use some new threads. I must smell a little funky by now."

Torres grinned and said as only a friend could say, "Yes, since you brought it up, Johnny, you do."

McGirt blushed. "Ask Bill if his storekeepers can round me up a set of cammies …and some toiletries too. And one more thing: I want to share a stateroom with Lin."

"Really?"

"Yes. He'll be a goner when the Chi-Coms get their mitts on him. I'd like to establish a rapport before we make the exchange. I think there's more to this whole thing than meets the eye."

* * *

Bill Draper had vacated his stateroom so that Commodore Torres could use it; she in turn offered it to Admiral McGirt so he could shower. McGirt had ignored the ship's water conservation policy, figuring that after enduring the last eighteen hours, he rated the indulgence. Instead of alternately 'wetting down, turning off water, soaping up, and then rinsing down,' he'd spent a full five minutes inside the steamy shower stall. While toweling off, he saw that Torres had hung up a fresh set of greenish- brown cammies, adorned with his two-star collar devices, aviator wings, and name tag that she'd transferred from his dirty khakis. McGirt rarely had the occasion to wear the camouflage working uniform, which had been modeled after those used by expeditionary forces like the Navy SEALS. The garb had replaced an older version of blue-grey camouflage attire that sailors had hated since its inception, derisively branding the outfit "Blueberries." On a shelf next to the cammies were two new undershorts and tee shirts, along with a couple pairs of black socks. Torres had also provided a complete set of toiletries. He appreciated how gracious she'd been by coming to his rescue with the clean clothing and supplies, concluding that few male counterparts would have been so thoughtful.

After dressing he propped open the bathroom door to let out steam while giving his hair a second toweling. When he raised his eyes, he saw Kathy Torres seated at Draper's desk. She looked up from a manual she was reading and asked, "Feel better?"

McGirt let out a sigh. "Whew...much better. Can't thank you enough for the threads and the other gear. And you got my sizes spot on."

"You're welcome. You'd do the same for me if the situation were reversed."

McGirt held up the extra pair of boxers, still bound in plastic wrapping. "Yeah, but I wouldn't know where to begin buying this stuff for you." He shook his head. "Geez, you're a girl!"

Torres peeked over the top of her glasses. "Are you referring to me as a... *girl?*"

McGirt blushed beet red and stopped smiling. "Guess I should have up-graded you a notch or two; how about I change that to *lady?*"

"Yes, that's more appropriate... Admiral." She seemed offended.

Despite their close friendship, Johnny Jack McGirt sometimes neglected Kathrine Torres' sensitivities: she'd had to fight and claw her way to the upper echelon of a male dominated profession. He shrugged his shoulders with a forlorn look. "Uh, I'm truly sorry for that, Commodore. Please—"

Torres interrupted him with a cackling laugh reserved solely for dear friends. "Hey, you big lug…I'm busting your balls. Relax!" She pointed to a chair. "Now that you're freshly groomed and more pleasant to be near, have a seat and let's talk."

The guilty expression drained from McGirt's face. He and Torres had worked together on numerous projects, both as line officers and while on staff duty at the Pentagon. They'd always welcomed humor in their dealings—if not for sheer entertainment, then as a method of stress relief. Yet they each knew when to flip the switch from joking to serious.

Torres led off. "Nothing new from Washington. Do you think President Black has been brought up to speed with our situation?"

"Yeah, probably. But I can't gauge how high on his agenda a defecting Chinese pilot ranks, especially with most of our West Pacific fleet steaming to the Straits. During my video call at the embassy, I got the impression that Black didn't want to give up Lin too early. That's why I want to spend some time with the guy." McGirt rubbed his eyes and yawned again. "Where are they keeping him?"

Torres sat back and placed her hands atop her head. "Initially, the MAA hauled him to the decontamination station. Not sure from that point." She reached for the phone on Draper's desk. "Want me to call Bill for an update? He's on the bridge."

McGirt glanced at the clock above the Draper's desk: it read 2300 hours local time. "No, I suspect Bill's plate is overflowing right now; it can wait until morning. Hey, this is his stateroom; did you pull rank and bump him out?"

"Didn't have much of a choice," Torres said. "These new LCSs are designed to operate with a minimum crew; quarters aren't exactly… plentiful. Bill graciously moved to his at-sea cabin, next to the bridge."

"I see. That was big of him."

"Yes, it was. But *Grand Rapids* does have a couple *girl* officers. Guess I could have bunked with one of them. Shoot, we could talk about the latest fashions and giggle while doing each other's hair."

McGirt frowned. "Boy, did I step in it this time or what? You're gonna ride me like a rented mule over this, aren't you?"

Torres flashed a wide smile that conveyed: *You bet your sweet ass I will.* She stood up from the desk and stretched. "That's it for me; time to hit the rack," she said. "By the way, the XO doubled up a couple of junior officers, so your stateroom is ready."

McGirt got up and started for the door. As he did, his stomach let out a God-awful growl.

Torres laughed. "Jesus, when's the last time you ate?"

"This morning, at the hotel in Manila."

"Then march yourself down to the wardroom," she barked in a motherly tone. "The cooks should be whipping up midnight rations."

McGirt had wondered why he was feeling lightheaded during their chat. It wasn't until Torres queried him about eating that he realized he was probably suffering from low blood sugar. Unsure of which direction to go, he left Draper's stateroom and walked along a dim passageway, then down a ladder until his nose took over: the pungent aroma of Navy chow—that always seemed to smell the same regardless of its ingredients—guided him the rest of the way.

Grand Rapids' wardroom was a modest-sized compartment decorated in dark, faux-wood paneling. Captain Draper had ordered its lime-colored tile floor covered with a blue, low pile carpet. The paneling and carpet offered a modicum of warmth to the otherwise institutional setting. There were three brown laminate rectangular dining tables—two in the room's center, the other tucked in a corner. A tiny lounge area was positioned against one bulkhead, separated from the dining space by a half wall. Inside the lounge area were a black Naugahyde sofa and matching coffee table. Atop the table was a tattered acey-deucey board. McGirt gave the compartment a quick scan and thought, *Yup, this feels like every other wardroom I've ever been in.* He stepped back into the passageway, walked to the chow line, and grabbed a tray.

A smiling, heavyset sailor wearing a white tee shirt, matching trousers, and an apron jumped up; his chef's cap was tilted to one side. "Hello, Admiral. I've got a tasty pot of beef stew simmering for mid-rats, but I can fix anything you'd like: eggs, sandwiches, you name it. Got some nice peach cobbler too; baked it myself a few hours ago for dinner."

"Stew smells great. Scoop me up a bowl if you would please."

The cook ladled a bowl and handed it over. McGirt set it on his tray, thanked the fellow, and stepped back into the wardroom. As he did, he noticed a civilian at the corner table, seated with his back to the door. The man had shoulder-length, stringy black hair, and was dressed in a set of grey coveralls. In front of him was a bowl of the stew, a plate piled with slices of wheat bread, and an overflowing bowl of cobbler. The man took a long draw from a tall bottle of Mountain Dew, then let out a hearty belch.

McGirt walked toward him and extended his hand. "Good evening. I'm Admiral Johnny Jack McGirt. And, sir, you are?"

The fellow sat up and reached for a napkin to wipe his mouth. "Sorry, sir, didn't see you come in." McGirt noticed a dog-eared issue of *Popular Mechanics* magazine on the table. A blob of stew stained a page titled, *Artificial Intelligence: Savior of Mankind or Master of its Destruction.*

The man shook McGirt's hand. "Name's Dickle, Leonard Dickle. I'm the tech rep for the MQ-8, you know, the Fire Scout."

"Oh, is that the small chopper I saw parked next to the H-60 in the hangar? It's a drone, right?"

Dickle took a big spoonful of cobbler and said while chewing, "I prefer to call it by its more accurate name of UAV; that stands for Unmanned Aerial Vehicle."

McGirt laughed as he withdrew his hand. "Yes, Mister Dickle, I understand the acronym UAV. But nonetheless, thanks for your explanation."

Dickle got up and removed his thick, black-framed eyeglasses. He stood a solid four inches taller than McGirt's six-foot height. "No worries. So, what *really* brings you aboard this wonderful vessel...Admiral...sir? Rumor has it that you flew in undercover with some Asian dude dressed like a hobo."

McGirt bristled at Dickle's crass familiarity. He'd worked with many civilian contractors, the vast majority of whom were mannerly and respectful of the military. Dickle seemed to exude neither of those qualities. He noticed that without his glasses, Leonard Dickle appeared buggy eyed. Coupled with his thin, lanky frame, he reminded McGirt of a grasshopper.

McGirt ignored Dickle's probing. "Son, I don't know much about the MQ-8 Fire Scout; however, seems like Uncle Sam is pumping plenty of dough into unmanned flight research."

"There's no other choice," Dickle replied. "Pilots as we know them will soon go the way of the dodo bird. Sorry to break the news to you...Admiral."

McGirt couldn't resist the challenge. "You seem pretty confident about that last statement, Lenny. But even without a human in the cockpit, somebody will be needed to control the vehicle."

"You got me on that one, but it doesn't have to be an overpaid, overtrained person wearing a flight suit. Most average gamers can master the skill of piloting these machines—fixed wing or rotary—after only a handful of practice sessions.

If you're onboard for a while I'll prove it to you." Dickle reached for his soda bottle and drained the last few ounces. "And sir, I prefer to be addressed as 'Leonard', not Lenny."

McGirt choked back another laugh. He was too tired to get into a sparring match. Instead, he stared Dickle in the eye and said, "I'll keep that in mind."

The cook cracked open the wardroom door. "Admiral, let me know if I can get you anything else, sir."

"Thanks, I'm good for now," McGirt said. Dickle wolfed down the last of his food, then started to leave. A young officer met him in the doorway and made the clucking sound of a chicken as they passed.

"Face it, Bobby," Dickle mumbled. "You're a dying breed."

The officer clucked again as Dickle slammed the door behind him. "Beg your pardon, Admiral. I did not see you sitting there. My apologies."

McGirt's stew was too hot to eat, so he pushed it aside to cool. He noted the fellow's name embroidered over the breast pocket of his cammies. "On your way to the midwatch, Lieutenant Bale?"

"Yes, sir. Thought I'd grab a coffee and some peach cobbler first. Between the caffeine and sugar, I figure I'll be good and wired 'til my relief shows up at 0400."

"Been there and done that," McGirt said. He motioned to his table. "Have a seat."

Bale sat down, took a sip of coffee, and then dug into his cobbler. McGirt blew across a spoonful of stew and took a cautious bite; the meaty concoction tasted delicious. "So, what was that about with Tech Rep Dickle...the clucking and all?"

Bale fidgeted in his chair. "Well, sir, it's about the drone that Lenny worships; the crew has coined it the 'robot chicken.' Darn thing gets squirrelly in the air sometimes...that is, if we can even get it started and off the deck safely."

"I see," said McGirt.

"Dickle tells us it's because we pilots enter its computer commands in the wrong sequence, but I think it's because the machine is an outdated piece of dog crap. He's onboard to test new systems that will be incorporated on the MQ-8B's replacement. The new MQ-8C model should be a big improvement."

"Huh, that's interesting. Time permitting, I'd enjoy a look-see at how you pilots fly the thing."

Bale polished off the cobbler then said, "That would be my pleasure, Admiral. But you need to know something: when I sit down at the control station, I'm no longer a pilot."

"What do you mean?"

Bale straightened up and puffed out his chest: "I transform from a mere naval aviator to an AVO; that's navy lingo for 'aerial vehicle operator.'"

McGirt chuckled. "Well, whatever, son. I'd still like to see how you fly it."

Bale checked the time. "Excuse me, sir, but I need to head topside and relieve the Junior Officer of the Deck."

"Lieutenant, you're a pilot; why are you taking on double duty by standing bridge watches?"

"Sir, we're grounded until this affair with Lieutenant Commander Moselli and his crew gets sorted out. Thought I'd give the ship's officers a break from their watch rotations."

"Nice gesture, son. That knowledge might come in handy later in your career."

"Hope so," Bale replied. He stood up to leave and said, "It was a pleasure meeting you, Admiral; and it's great to have another *real* pilot onboard."

"The pleasure is all mine, Lieutenant. With regards to Moselli and his crew, I can't tell you much, but our intelligence channels confirm that your buddies are alive and being treated well."

"That's great to hear. Thanks, Admiral."

"Sure," McGirt said as Bale left the wardroom. He finished eating and then wandered over to the lounge area. For grins, he picked up a pair of dice and tossed them down the little wooden chute next to the acey-deucey board; a 'one' and a 'two' tumbled out—the best roll a player could hope for.

McGirt squeezed the dice in his hand. He prayed that the roll would bring good luck.

* * *

All the traveling—coupled with a hardy bowl of stew—finally got the best of him. After tossing the lucky roll, McGirt considered making his way to the stateroom he'd been assigned, but instead slumped down on the wardroom sofa and promptly fell asleep. He woke up to the sounds of clanking pots and pans as the morning cooks prepared breakfast. The pungent aroma of greasy meat, eggs, and potatoes wafted out from the galley. He stood up, rubbed the kink in his neck and checked the wall clock: it read 0555.

A different cook poked his head into the wardroom. "Good morning, Admiral. What can I get you to eat?"

"Nothing, thanks. But I could sure use a black coffee." The cook set down his spatula and started for the coffee urn in a corner of the wardroom. McGirt raised a hand. "I don't mind getting it myself, sailor. Thanks anyway." He poured a cup and sat at one of the tables. "What time do folks show up for chow?"

"Everyone straggles in around 0615 or so, depending on their watch section. The drone guy is normally the first one in line—0600 sharp, every morning."

McGirt's mind flashed back to the mound of food that he'd watched Dickle consume just hours ago. As if on cue, he heard Leonard's loud voice in the passageway. "Hey, Rodriquez, I'll take a three-egg omelet with the works, toast, home fries and a glass of milk...on second thought, make that *chocolate* milk."

"You got it, sir," Rodriquez shouted back. A few moments later, Dickle burst into the wardroom carrying a heaping tray of hot food. He sat at a vacant table.

"You're welcome to join me here," said McGirt as he motioned to a chair.

Dickle seemed surprised by the invite. "Okay, sure. Hope I'm not intruding."

McGirt smiled. "Not in the least. I welcome the company."

Dickle looked disheveled: he hadn't shaved, and his stringy hair needed combing; he appeared as if he'd slept in the same coveralls that he'd worn at mid-rats. Watching the man shovel down the huge breakfast, McGirt couldn't resist saying, "Wish I could eat like you, son. But if I did, I'd probably put on fifty pounds."

Dickle grabbed a slice of toast, piled some omelet and potatoes on it, then took a hefty bite. "Never had a problem with weight," he said with a full mouth. "Doctor tells me I got an issue with my thyroid. I've been the same size since tenth grade: six-four, a hundred and sixty pounds."

McGirt watched as Dickle loaded up another slice of toast. "Well, I guess a young fellow has got to eat."

Dickle looked up from his plate. "Admiral, if I don't, I can't think real straight. And it's hard enough keeping that Fire Scout from flying itself into the drink."

"Tell me more. I'm not very familiar with the machine. My background is helicopters; UAVs weren't very active during my time in the fleet."

"Yeah, I sort of figured that when I saw your rank. Guessing things were pretty steam-driven back then. It's a new digital world, and with artificial intelligence, it's just a matter of time until most everything in the sky, and on the surface, goes unmanned. Pilots don't like to admit it, but with automation, someday they might be replaced by a gamer with good hand-eye coordination."

"Maybe so," McGirt said. "I'm sure there are some youngsters that can push the right buttons and jiggle a joystick effectively…that is, until something goes wrong with the aircraft they're flying. Then what?"

Dickle finished cleaning his plate. He drank half of the chocolate milk then said, "A.I. will solve that too. Once an aircraft's emergency procedures have been programmed into the system, computers will react to the abnormal faster and with less chance of error than a pilot fumbling with a checklist." He chugged the rest of the milk, belched, and leaned back in his chair. "By the way, Admiral, I know that the commodore is with us doing an inspection, but if you don't mind me asking again, why are you onboard…really?" He leaned forward and whispered, "It's got something to do with that Chinaman locked up in the de-con station, right?"

McGirt had had enough of Leonard Dickle's insolence. He considered putting the guy in his place but responded by saying, "That's not a matter of your concern, Leonard."

"Yeah, I understand. Just wondering."

McGirt was glad to change the subject. "Say, I'd like to get a closer look at your Fire Scout when you have some free time."

"Sure, whenever you want. I'll be in the hangar all day."

"Thanks. I'll find you."

* * *

Grand Rapids arrived on station at daybreak. The ship loitered fifty miles from the Chinese installation at a fuel-conserving speed of 10 knots; sea state was low, and the morning sky was clear. The crew resumed their normal at-sea routine: rise at reveille, get dressed, grab some chow, and then muster with division leaders for work. Questions about the ship's current mission, however, persisted in everyone's mind.

Captain Draper had addressed all hands over the 1MC but hadn't revealed much; he reconfirmed that the nimble littoral combat ship had been ordered to remain at its current location until directed otherwise.

McGirt found Commodore Torres seated at the desk inside the skipper's stateroom. "Nothing new from Washington yet, Johnny," she said. "I guess we're playing the old 'hurry up and wait game.'"

McGirt shook his head in frustration. "Kathy, this ordeal is turning into a real goat rope. I left D.C. for what was scheduled to be an easy trip. Now I'm not sure when I'll get home."

"You and me both. On the upside, though, we should be getting an update from Secretary Croft soon. The skipper didn't want to give the crew any false hope, so he left that off of his announcement."

"That's encouraging," McGirt said as he sat down.

Torres slid back her chair; she crossed her long legs. "Hate to tell you this, my friend, but you look like crap. Did you get any sleep last night?"

"A little. I crashed on the wardroom sofa." He stroked his face. "Darn, I better shave and clean up."

"Yeah, I came looking for you in the wardroom; found you zonked out. Didn't have the heart to wake you up." She reached into a pocket and handed him a key. "You're all set; you and Lin have a stateroom. Oh, and I put your gear inside and sent your uniform to the laundry."

"Thanks, Kathy, you're a doll." He cringed after realizing what he'd said.

Torres just shook her head and sighed. "You're hopeless, McGirt."

He smiled at her sheepishly, then studied the metal tag attached to his stateroom key. The tag was stamped with a string of numbers and letters that identified the compartment's location.

"You need help finding it?" Torres asked.

"Nah, I think I can figure it out." He laughed, then said, "But if you see me wandering around like a lost child, please take my hand and show me the way." The ship took some moderate rolls as it came about and reversed course. McGirt grabbed the side of Draper's desk to steady himself. "How long did it take you to get your sea legs back?"

"Never lost them. Why, have you?"

"Let's just say they've been in storage. After all the days sitting on my duff in D.C., it's taking a while. Here's hoping the weather stays good."

Torres feigned a serious expression. "I have some motion sickness pills in my bag if you need them."

McGirt shot her an irritated look. "Nope, not necessary, I'll be fine."

"Well, that's nice to hear. I wouldn't want the crew to see an admiral upchucking over the rail. Not good for your image." A silly grin spread across her face.

"Okay, that's enough...*Commodore.*" McGirt started for the door. "I'll talk to the MAA and ask him to move Lin. I have a hunch that the guy's aching to talk; I think the best way to get reliable information out of him is in a comfortable setting, not the decontamination closet."

Torres stood up and checked her hair in the mirror that hung above Draper's desk. McGirt watched her straighten a couple wayward strands and then pat the sides of her immaculately coiffed hairdo. He'd always found the woman attractive in an odd way: not pretty nor particularly feminine, but still appealing. At nearly six feet tall, her profile was statuesque.

"How about we regroup in about an hour?" he said. "That will give me time to shave and relocate Lin."

"Sounds good. Skipper is on the bridge; that's where I'll be."

* * *

McGirt held both handrails while descending the steep metal ladders; his brittle knees throbbed with every step. After five surgeries, he couldn't remember which leg, the left or right one, had been sliced open more times. He'd electively trashed his body while playing football in college. *If I hadn't loved the game so much, perhaps things would have been different,* he thought to himself. But after a few seconds of regret, he realized that given the opportunity, he'd do it all over again in a New York minute. The rush of adrenaline he'd felt after making a bone-jarring tackle in front of 100,000 screaming fans was a thrill he'd never been able to duplicate, even as a pilot.

He ducked into his stateroom before meeting with Lin. The place was similar to most other compartments he'd holed up in as a junior officer: a set of bunk beds, a handful of drawers and lockers along one bulkhead, and two puny fold-down tables for desks. There were no windows. Dreary beige and grey paint gave the place a dingy feeling. But there was one luxury item: a private head with a toilet, sink and shower—a perk he'd never enjoyed during his early seagoing days. Back then, only the CO and XO of the ship rated their own facilities, while the rest of the officer contingent shared a community head. As he turned to leave, he was met by *Grand Rapids'* Chief Master-at-Arms, a stocky, bullnecked fellow whose nametag read "DURFEE."

"Good morning, Admiral. The captain asked me to escort you to the De-Con station. I've also been instructed to release the prisoner and haul him up to this stateroom." Chief Durfee paused and then asked, "With all due respect, sir, is that what *you* want?"

"Yes, that's exactly what I want, Chief. Not sure what you've been told, but the man is not a prisoner. I accept full responsibility for him."

Durfee acknowledged with a quick nod of his shaved head. "Got it, Admiral. Follow me." The two men navigated another ladder and a series of narrow passageways; McGirt's knee joints pounded, but pride kept him from asking Durfee to slow down. They stopped in front of a slab-like hatch labeled DECONTAM-INATION STATION; the hatch had a single, eye-height window the size of a dinner plate.

"He's in here?" McGirt said.

"Sir, we don't have an old school brig with prison bars like when you and I were newbies." Durfee shrugged his broad shoulders. "Guess the engineers didn't think we needed it—or else the Navy was too cheap to pay for one."

"Okay, thanks, Chief. I'd like a couple minutes inside before we head back to officers' country. And Chief, it won't be necessary to hood him like your guys did when we landed yesterday."

"Copy that, sir. The commodore gave me those same instructions. We'll take a route that's been sanitized: all passageways have been swept; no one will see either of you." Chief Durfee sorted through a wad of keys dangling from his belt until he found the correct ones. He inserted each of them into two separate padlocks and yanked open the heavy hatch. *Grand Rapids'* 'brig' was nothing more than an eight-by-eight-foot compartment. Lin lay upon a thin mattress that had been placed on the mesh metal flooring. He hugged a coarse gray blanket around himself. An industrial shower head was suspended from the ceiling. On the floor was a tray carrying a half empty water bottle and a stack of plain white bread.

McGirt stepped inside. "Good morning, Lieutenant Lin. How are you doing?"

Lin sat up and scowled at him. "This is not what I was promised. I am not a criminal!"

McGirt crouched next to him. "For the record, Lin Yi, no promises were made. This is a very complicated situation."

Lin's face reddened. "Complicated? No, this is *not* complicated! I delivered a *complicated* weapon system to you and your allies; I should be rewarded. Why are my demands not being met?"

McGirt saw that Durfee was standing in the open hatchway. "Chief, shut the hatch; I'll let you know when I'm ready to go."

"Aye, aye, Admiral." He complied and stood at ease on the other side.

McGirt's lack of sleep and painful knees had sapped his patience. "Okay, Lieutenant, listen up and listen up good," he said. "You seem to understand English exceptionally well, so I'll lay it on straight: It's my guess that by now a team of the world's top engineers and mechanics have started to dismantle your aircraft; they'll uncover whatever secrets are hidden inside it...trust me. And you also need to know that your country is holding three Americans as hostages in response to your defection. Negotiations are underway to exchange you for those men." McGirt tried to curb his temper as he said, "So, Lin Yi, you aren't as valuable as you think, and certainly not worth sacrificing three of my countrymen."

Lin shifted his eyes to the floor. "I...I was not aware that your people were being detained."

"How the hell would you know?" McGirt said as he stood up. "Look, for now, I want to get you out of this place. You'll be staying in a guarded stateroom with me." He glanced at Durfee through the window. "This isn't the best place to talk."

CHAPTER 14

After chowing down on the snacks the Chinese had provided, Dick Moselli and his men had ventured a few yards to the water's edge to watch the sunset, then returned and collapsed onto their bunks. The temperature inside their trailer was set at a comfortable 72 degrees when they'd turned in for the night—the whirling drone of the air conditioner's fan had served as a calming backdrop for their sleep. Moselli, Aguilar, and Horton had occupied the trailer's three bedrooms, while Salid had sprawled out on the living room sofa. When the trailer's cooling unit conked out just before sunrise, it took just minutes before the temperature soared inside.

Moselli woke up sweat-soaked and disoriented. "What's going on?" he shouted. "Did we die and go to hell?" He stumbled in the dark to join Horton and Aguilar in the living area; the trio stood bleary-eyed in their skivvies. Salid remained asleep, snoring.

Moselli cracked open the door and looked down the long row of house trailers for clues; the scene was dead silent. "Sounds like everyone's lost power." In the distance he heard the rumbling clatter of heavy equipment as construction crews began work. When he stepped down from the trailer and looked out to sea, he noticed a freighter approaching the island's pier.

Horton called out from the doorway, "Inbound, ten o'clock." Moselli swiveled his head and saw a vehicle racing toward them on the dirt road; it left a billowing dust cloud as it came to a stop. The driver was Captain Gao; he was alone. Moselli met him as he got out of his jeep.

"My apology, Lieutenant Commander, sir," Gao said. "Generator fuel runs low, so electric air comfort shut off."

Dick Moselli's patience was worn thin. A restless night of sleep—coupled with lousy food and the island's sweltering temperature—had stretched him to his limit; he ignored Gao's apology. "I demand to know why we are being held captive like this! God damn it, I want to see your superior, where is he?"

"That would not be possible. Colonel is very occupied."

Moselli took a deep breath and told himself to stay calm. The last twenty-four hours had presented him and his crew with plenty of challenges: the rescue of a shipwrecked fisherman; being hijacked by Chinese fighter jets; and finally, being forced to spend the night in a house trailer on a strange, land-filled ocean reef. Overall, though, he and his men had been treated humanely; they'd been given food, water, and shelter. Rather than taking out his frustrations on the young officer, Moselli chose a milder tactic. "Captain Gao, do you know when the power will return? It's too hot for us to stay in here."

A happy expression spread across Gao's face. "Yes, I might answer that question. The ship by the pier…it brings more supplies and fuel for generators. Colonel shut down power to save fuel for building machines and pumps." He pointed to the activity where cranes, bulldozers and earthmovers were in full motion. The muffled glugging sounds of dredging equipment could be heard in the background.

"So, when will the fucking power come back on?" Horton begged. "I'm sweatin' my balls off!"

Moselli glared at the crew chief, signaling him to stow his attitude. He then turned to Gao. "We will need more drinking water, much more. We are not accustomed to these conditions. And we will need better food."

Gao seemed excited by Moselli's request. He jogged back to his vehicle and lifted a big box from its rear seat. He lugged it to the trailer's steps. "We give you water and food. More will come when ship is unloaded."

Horton stooped down and started pawing through the box. He found two thermos bottles of hot tea, a bulging, grease-stained paper bag, and a large glass jar. When he twisted free the jar's lid, steam wafted into the humid morning air. "What's in here, anyway? It looks like watered down oatmeal or something." He took a cautious sniff. "Doesn't smell too bad," he said while offering it up to Aguilar.

Gao became animated as he reached inside the greasy bag and pulled out a thin, pastry-looking item that resembled fried dough; he dipped it in the jar as if dunking a donut into coffee. He took a bite and rolled his eyes with exaggerated pleasure. "Very good. We call *congee*. You should like too," he said. One by one, the Americans sampled the concoction.

Moselli gobbled down his first pastry and reached for a second. "Hey, you're right, this is pretty good." The anger that he'd felt earlier dissipated; he and his crew seemed to bond with the foreign soldier as they shared food. Horton went back to the trailer and returned with mugs for the tea. He noticed that Salid hadn't budged.

Moselli led them to a shady spot where they sat on the bare ground in their skivvies while leaning against the trailer. The four men finished breakfast in silence. When they'd had their fill, Aguilar said, "Hey, Gao, any chance that you can drive us around the island?"

Horton echoed, "Yeah, not much else for us to do, and I'm not wild about spending the day inside this aluminum oven." He turned to Moselli. "What do you say, Bruiser?"

"That would be up to Captain Gao," said Moselli. "If he's allowed to do it, I'm game."

Gao made a call on his radio. After a minute of what sounded like heated chatter, he stood up, dusted off his uniform pants and said, "My colonel said 'no' to your request."

Moselli said, "Well, we can't stay cooped up like this in the trailer. Gao, would you ask your colonel if we can at least take a walk before it gets too hot." He gestured toward Aguilar and Horton. "Our legs could use some exercise."

Gao made another radio call. His boss' response was terse. "Colonel said okay to walk, but you must be guarded."

"Guarded?" Horton shouted. "Christ sake, where the hell we gonna go?"

Dick Moselli slapped Horton's knee, signaling him to clam up. "Thank you, Captain Gao." He turned to his men and said, "Okay, fellas, let's get dressed."

The crew went back inside to put on their flight suits and boots. When they emerged from the trailer, Gao had already assembled a half-dozen soldiers. "My men will lead you and follow from behind," he said.

"Is there a way to follow from the *front?*" Horton snapped.

Aguilar jabbed Horton in the side and whispered, "Cool it, Crazo, or else you'll screw us over." The Americans walked along a dirt road that led toward the island's pier. Gao's men took positions several yards ahead and behind them.

"This is a different perspective than what we saw from the air," Moselli commented. He pointed to the pier. "The way that freighter is sitting low in the water she must be jammed to the gunwales; and look, there's at least a dozen flatbeds lined up to offload her."

"Yeah, quite the operation," Aguilar said. He reached into an ankle pocket of his flight suit and pulled out a tiny telescope. "Normally I use this for hunting back home." He smiled, then added, "But I like to have it handy for unexpected times like this." He scanned from side to side as they walked. "Yup, like we thought when we flew in, definitely a runway going in over there," he said while pointing to his left. "And I think that's a control tower being built next to it." He then focused on the lagoon where the dredging rigs were. "Man, they're not wasting any time, are they? I see muck being sprayed into big piles onto the shore; and a parade of earthmovers scooping it up and dumping it into trucks." Aguilar offered the telescope to Moselli.

"Hm...looks like those trucks are hauling it to some sort of plant," Moselli said. "I'd guess they're mixing it with cement for the runway and other structures." He adjusted the focus and said, "And I can see a pair of cranes lifting steel panels into place; maybe building fuel storage tanks?" He handed the scope to Horton.

Horton zoomed in on the cranes, then shifted his sights to the pier. "Hey, Don Juan, where the heck are the Chi-Coms getting the dough to do this?"

"Great question, Crazo." Aguilar said with a laugh. "You ever check the labels on the stuff you buy to see where it's made?"

"Lemme guess...probably China, right?"

"You got it; and a large chunk of those profits go straight to their military and projects like this."

Horton rotated his view back toward their trailer. "Uh oh...damn, I think we've been busted." The group turned to see a jeep speeding toward them. The driver slammed on the brakes and jumped out. It was Gao; he appeared more annoyed than angry.

"Hey, Captain Gao, nice to see you again," Horton said with a shit-eating grin.

Gao yanked the telescope from Horton's hands. "No, no, no! This is not allowed. You must return, you must return now!" He waved the crew to get into his jeep.

When they arrived back at the trailer, they saw a pair of vehicles parked in front. The colonel sat in one with arms folded across his chest. Gao parked next to him as the colonel hopped out and went inside. Moselli and his men followed. Once inside they witnessed a group of soldiers ransacking their flight gear. The time for restrained leadership had passed. Moselli got face-to-face with the colonel and hollered, "You can't do this, pal! We're not your fucking prisoners!"

The colonel gripped the handle of his holstered sidearm; he smirked, then turned his back. Gao moved in and pressed his hands against Moselli's chest in a non-threatening way. "Routine inspection, Lieutenant Commander; nothing to be taken unless against the rules."

Dick Moselli collected himself. He knew that the Chinese held all the cards and there was no way to retaliate. In simple terms, the Americans were outmanned and outgunned.

The colonel spoke in a soft tone to his men, then mumbled something to Gao, who came to attention and saluted. The colonel and his entourage got into their vehicles and left.

Gao approached Moselli with an exaggerated, saddened look. "Colonel says you cannot go to your helicopter; not today or ever."

"What?" Moselli said.

Gao replied, "Maybe not the correct word, but I think he says there was disrespect. You disrespect him."

Moselli threw up his hands. "Of course! Yes, I *did* disrespect his stinky ass. You are right, Captain; disrespect is the correct word."

"I am sorry this has happened," Gao said. "I must go back to work. Lunch will be served very soon."

Aguilar and Horton had been at the other end of the trailer checking their belongings during Moselli's confrontation with the colonel. They came forward as Gao left.

Horton picked up on Moselli's frustration. He stood in the open doorway and yelled, "And tell your asshole cook to make some decent chow…no more of that Chinaman shit!"

Moselli grabbed Horton by the collar and pulled him back inside. "Jesus Christ, Crazo, knock it off! They might piss in our food… or do something worse." Horton stomped across the floor and plopped onto the sofa.

Aguilar remained next to Moselli as they watched Gao disappear down the road. "On the bright side, Bruiser, at least our power and air are back on."

Horton lay on his back staring at the ceiling. "Hey, I wonder what happened to that little guy we pulled out of the drink. He ain't here no more." The food they'd left for Salid looked untouched.

Moselli made a perfunctory scan of the space, thinking Salid might reappear. He shrugged his shoulders and sat down. "Well, one thing's for certain: unless he's a great swimmer, he can't go too far."

CHAPTER 15

Monday morning
Subic Bay Airport

Jimmie Posadas never made it back to his wife at their beach cottage. After watching Ambassador Wu storm off from the hangar, Posadas sent her an apologetic text saying that he'd try to join her later in the evening but made no promises. She'd responded with a terse reply stating she planned to pack in the morning and return to their high-rise condo in Manila's posh Makati district. She'd ended with the sentence, "I'll see you when I see you." Jimmie's heart sank; their romantic beach weekend had panned out as a bust.

The J-31 incident at Subic had occurred on a Sunday when Philippine government agencies were closed. Because he happened to be in the area, Posadas had felt obligated to respond to President Diaz' request to serve as the interim on-scene commander. But he was eager to relinquish the job; he'd never enjoyed that role, though he'd been tossed into similar situations a handful of times. With dual U.S. and Philippine citizenships he'd held a variety of positions in Washington and Manila, jetting between the two cities on a regular basis. After three decades, the harried routine had lost its glamour; he was burned out and ready to retire. But Jimmie considered himself lucky compared to his old friend Johnny Jack McGirt. He was a short distance from his home in Manila; McGirt had traveled from the other side of the globe.

Posadas had left the hangar after midnight and caught a ride back to the airport operations building, where he was met by the nighttime security guard. The man recognized him, unlocked the door and waived him inside.

"Looks like I'll be spending the night," Jimmie said with a dejected look. "Mind if I go topside and find a place to crash?"

"Whatever you like, Mr. Posadas," the guard said. "I'm here if you need something." Jimmie thanked him and headed to the building's second floor conference room, hoping to find a spot to lie down. On the way, he passed Vera

Navarro's office. Taking a chance, he turned the door handle; to his surprise, it was unlocked. He stepped inside and flipped on the lights. Across from Vera's desk was a weathered leather sofa, so he stretched out on it and dozed off. After a few restless hours, the sound of a taxiing airplane woke him. He sat up and fumbled for his cell phone: the time was 6:15 a.m.

Jimmie felt miserable: his back ached and his head buzzed as if he'd been on an all- night bender. After splashing cold water on his face in the men's room, he wandered downstairs and found the same guard sitting at his desk drinking coffee. He scanned the fellow's I.D. badge: it read "Rocky Mendoza."

"You got any more of that stuff?" Jimmie asked.

Rocky pointed to a crusty pot on a small table behind the desk. Jimmie filled a Styrofoam cup, blew across the top, and took a sip of the steamy brew; it tasted as he'd expected: bitter and very, very strong. As he sat down next to Rocky, he glanced outside and saw the sun cresting over the mountains; Subic Bay shimmered with a golden tint. "What time do things get busy here?" he asked.

"Well, it's Monday morning; probably a little later today: around eight, eight-thirty, I guess. Tower's been open all night, though. Two small planes flew in from Manila earlier this morning."

Jimmie nodded. "Yeah, I heard them a few minutes ago."

Rocky motioned with his hand. "They parked over there by the flight school hangar. I saw a bunch of people get out carrying what looked like tool bags. They hopped into a couple cars and drove off. I think they went down to that wrecked plane holed up on the east end of the airfield."

Jimmie recalled from last night that someone in the hangar had told him more mechanics would be arriving soon. He wondered how they'd responded so quickly. He said, "Were you working when the plane crashed yesterday?"

"No, but the guy who's going to relieve me was." Rocky yawned and checked his watch. "Should be here in thirty minutes if you've got any questions."

The coffee had cooled enough for Jimmie to swallow a couple more gulps before tossing the cup into a trash can. "Rocky, you mind doing me a favor?"

"Sure, what you need?"

"Dial the airport police. Tell them I'd like a ride to that hangar."

Rocky made the call. A few minutes later a police car pulled up. Jimmie shook Rocky's hand, thanked him for the coffee, and got into the cruiser.

When he arrived at the hangar, the Chinese J-31 was a shell of what he remembered seeing just hours ago. Large sections of its fuselage had been deskinned, exposing the jet's complex inner workings. Extracted components had been laid out in organized rows, each item tagged and labeled. The jet was suspended on jacks placed beneath its wings, nose, and tail, allowing for its right gear and nose tires to dangle above the hangar's concrete flooring. The left gear assembly, which had collapsed during the plane's crash landing, had been removed. Three Filipino soldiers guarded the barrier that had been expanded to make space for the added manpower and collection of aircraft parts.

Jimmie approached one of the soldiers and was about to identify himself when he felt a gentle tug on his shoulder. "Can I help you?" a female voice said from behind. He turned and faced a very tall woman dressed in khaki pants and a short-sleeved emerald golf shirt; she looked to be in her thirties.

"Hello, ma'am, my name is Jimmie Posadas, President Diaz' liaison for this project."

"Glad you finally made it, Jimmie," she said while offering a handshake. "I'm Agent Gwen King with the CIA." Jimmie was surprised by the size of the woman's hand and the firmness of her grip. "I'm the project co-leader, along with Alfonse Castro." She motioned toward a Filipino gentleman who was conversing with two mechanics. The trio was standing on a work platform positioned next to the jet's cockpit.

Jimmie couldn't hold back his yawn. "Sorry about that," he said. He raised his voice above the noise of power tools. "Yesterday was a nightmare. I slept on a lumpy sofa in the airport manager's office."

Gwen laughed. "I feel your pain. They put us on a redeye from Guam to Manila, then we connected to a couple puddle jumpers to get here. Nothing like short-fused government travel. Say, Jimmie, did Remington brief you about what's going on?"

Jimmie felt in the dark; he regretted sneaking off last night to grab a few winks. Gwen read his bewildered look. "Not to worry, I'll bring you up to speed. Follow me."

King fanned herself with both hands and said, "Do you believe this heat? Hell, it's barely sunrise and I'm already sweating like a hooker in church."

Jimmie got a kick out of Gwen's down to earth attitude. He was anxious to get the inside skinny on what Remington had told her, yet he felt compelled to learn more about the lady. "So, you mentioned Guam. Is that your home base?"

"Yes, it is. I've been there for a year. Not too bad for the first few months, until island fever sets in. Spent most of my time in D.C. after the CIA recruited me straight out of college. I had a basketball scholarship to Notre Dame and majored in Mechanical Engineering. How about you?"

Jimmie sighed. "Gee... I've been all over the place; grew up in Hawaii, then off to Stanford where I studied political science. Found my way to D.C. and interviewed for a job with the State Department. Over the last thirty-odd years I've bounced around between different offices at State. Latest gig is working jointly for the U.S. and Philippines. My parents are full-blooded Filipinos, so I hold dual citizenship. Like you, a long way from where I started."

The noise grew louder as a group of mechanics holding air-powered tools clustered around the J-31's nose cone. Gwen shouted, "How about we find a quiet spot to talk?"

Jimmie followed her to a small room off one side of the hangar. The space looked like it hadn't been used in years; there was a shabby wooden desk, an empty bookcase, and two tattered chairs. Gwen dusked off the chairs with a bare hand and sat down. Jimmie closed the door.

Gwen got straight to the point. "Your top secret clearance allows me to tell you this, so here goes: We've been monitoring China's development of laser weapons and suspect that they've ginned up a device unlike anything in our inventory. Until now, airborne lasers have been very limited in their capabilities because of the enormous amount of electrical energy they require. Our intelligence has uncovered info that leads us to believe the Chinese are able to generate a huge amount of energy aboard a ship—hundreds of kilowatts— and then harness it into a super capacitor." She paused. "You with me so far?"

"Yes. I've read a little about lasers capable of jamming radio signals that control drones and aircraft electronics. Is that what you're talking about?"

"Way beyond that, Jimmie. The Israelis mastered the ability to send a 'go home' signal to small drones years ago, and there've been advancements in methods to fry a missile's guidance system with a ground-based laser. But nothing that compares to what we suspect here. Admiral McGirt was yanked from his assignment in Manila to get the plane's pilot under American sovereignty before the Chi-Coms got their hands on him."

"Yes, I helped McGirt coordinate the extraction yesterday."

"And we sincerely thank you for that," Gwen said. "For your information, our operatives have been tracking Lin Yi since he studied at Berkeley. The guy has genius-level smarts, and for a variety of reasons, he appeared eager to leave China. That being said, we were surprised at how and when he defected."

Jimmie began putting it all together: he understood why Lin's aircraft was of such interest to the United States, and Gwen's revelation further explained why McGirt had been ordered to take charge of Lin and hustle him off Philippine soil. He was stunned, however, to learn that the CIA already had data on Lin; McGirt had never mentioned that. But this wasn't Jimmie's first rodeo: he knew the CIA had the reputation of operating outside the realm of other government agencies.

Gwen conducted a "Cliff Notes-style" summation of how U.S. weapons contractors had spent decades attempting to develop lasers for use in air combat. She described how the Air Force, Boeing, and Lockheed Martin had partnered in the early 2000s to create an airborne laser system, or ABL. The project proved its capability to destroy a dummy missile, but there were severe limitations: the bulky Chemical Oxygen Iodine Laser needed to be housed in an aircraft the size of a jumbo jet, plus the ABL's accuracy was unpredictable in varying weather conditions. The Airborne Laser endeavor was ultimately scrapped; its test plane, dubbed the YAL-1, was decommissioned and flown to an aircraft boneyard in Arizona.

"So, what makes the Chinese technology different?" Jimmie said. "Sounds like the idea of airborne lasers came to a dead end."

"That's what those people tearing apart Lin's plane want to find out. The big defense players are sending their top guys to analyze it. Lockheed Martin has explored a laser pod that can be slung under the belly of an F-16 or F-35, but so far, the system is restricted to targeting and surveillance, and not capable of destructive force. Plus, being housed in a sizeable external pod, the aircraft's stealthy-ness is degraded." She waived a finger toward the hangar. "We know there's a laser on that jet, and we know it's carried internally. What we need to find out is how powerful it is."

Jimmie leaned forward in his chair. "What's your take, Gwen, off the record?"

Gwen stared straight ahead as she thought. "Off the record, I suspect there may be sufficient juice in that system to fire a beam capable of penetrating an aircraft's fuselage."

"And then what?"

"Lasers are very hot, tightly focused light. If the beam is strong enough to pierce a plane's skin, it could ignite its fuel tanks and weapons stores."

"So, you're saying Star Wars stuff?"

"Yes, sir, that's exactly what I'm saying. Air-to-air missiles could become as obsolete as the musket." A wry smile crept from the corner of Gwen's mouth. "Of course, that's all off the record."

There was a knock on the door, followed by a man in coveralls poking his head inside the room. "Beg your pardon, Agent King," he said. "But you have to see this."

CHAPTER 16

Aboard Shanghai

Captain Song was edgy. He feared that the nuclear-powered aircraft carrier, USS *Ronald Reagan*, would beat him to the Taiwan Straits. Song lamented over the extra time it had taken to recover the two J-15s he'd dispatched to search for Lieutenant Lin. Though the J-15 pilots had failed to confirm Lin's whereabouts, they had successfully intercepted the U.S. Navy helicopter and forced it to land at Chinese-occupied Scarborough Shoals. Song and Commissar Han had fallen to wishful thinking when they'd wagered that Lin was aboard the chopper. They agreed, however, that the decision to launch the J-15s might prove to be a blessing in disguise: the commandeered Americans were now pawns for bargaining.

What weighed on Song's mind the heaviest, though, was that his ship needed to take on fuel from a lumbering Chinese tanker. *Shanghai*'s outdated boilers guzzled fuel oil like an alcoholic chugs booze at an open bar; if the ship continued sailing at its top speed, it would arrive at the Straits lacking reserves to conduct flight operations. Yet, despite the handicap, *Shanghai* was the most advanced aircraft carrier that China had in its arsenal. Instead of the ski jump ramps employed on the country's first two carriers, *Shanghai* used steam-driven catapults to sling its planes into the air. That advancement enabled it to launch planes with more fuel and heavier armament loads; but until China developed a nuclear-powered carrier with unrestricted range like the American flattops, Song feared that the People's Navy would remain a second-rate maritime power. Commissar Han had once equated China's disadvantage with the analogy of a clumsy old boxer battling an agile young champion.

Song stood on *Shanghai*'s bridge wing and watched as his ship crept into position alongside the tanker at a snail's pace of 12 knots. The time was just after sunrise and the seas were calm. *Shanghai*'s looming shadow dwarfed the smaller vessel as the pair sailed as if tethered together; barely one hundred feet separated their hulls. He'd relinquished control of the ship to a trusted senior officer who gave precise steering and speed commands to the bridge crew to keep *Shanghai* in position with the tanker. The din of grinding winch motors and swaying booms filled the air as the two ships' refueling machinery came to life. A muffled "pop" was heard above the noise when a seaman on the tanker fired a rifle-powered shot line across *Shanghai*'s wide bow, where a gaggle of sailors scrambled to grab it. The thin shot line was then attached to consecutively thicker wires suspended between the vessels; the hookup process concluded with hefty fuel hoses strung above the wave tops. Hose nozzles made a metallic "thud" when mated with *Shanghai*'s receiving ports.

The decks were abuzz with activity as crews made final adjustments to the replenishment riggings. When both vessels were satisfied with the hook ups, refueling began. It was a tedious process: the tanker's pumps could push the petrol only so fast. An impatient Captain Song drummed his fingers as reports streamed in confirming that *Shanghai*'s cavernous tanks were being filled.

Song relaxed and lit a cigarette; his mind drifted to the time when he'd no longer be saddled with the pressures of command. Though he'd still spend time at sea as a commissar, he hoped that the day-to-day demands of that job would be less intense. Song's wife had proposed that he accept an administrative position with the Communist Party, but in her heart, she knew he'd be miserable sitting at a desk. As he'd confessed to her when they'd met: "I am a sailor, and sailors belong at sea."

A messenger tapped Song on the shoulder and delivered a hand-written note from the ship's engineering officer. The note said that a stuck valve had restricted the flow of oil into *Shanghai*'s tanks. The problem would cause a delay of at least an hour.

Captain Song chain-lit another cigarette and checked his watch. He wondered if Commissar Han was awake.

* * *

Eight hours earlier...

Captain Song had looked forward to an uninterrupted night of rest. He realized, though, that the luxury would probably not happen. Phone calls from *Shanghai*'s officer-of-the-deck about weather developments, the proximity of surface contacts, or an anomaly with one of the ship's complex systems—combined with Song's chronic insomnia—would likely lead to a fitful evening. Nonetheless, he stretched out on his bunk. A few moments into dozing, the annoying metallic ring of his phone cut through the stillness. He rolled to one side and saw that a red light was blinking; it was the commissar calling on the direct line that the men shared.

Song fumbled in the dark to grab the receiver. Before he could speak, Han barked, "Get your rear end down here, Captain…we need to talk!" Had the harsh words come from any other commissar, Song might have been intimidated. But the men's friendship traced back to their days as junior officers; they frequently talked trash to one another when in private.

Song got out of bed while still holding the phone. He mumbled, "What is it now, Snake, you royal pain in the ass?" He hadn't a clue why Han would be calling at this hour: *Shanghai* was cruising on smooth seas and her flight deck was quiet.

Han chuckled. "Just get down here, Bulldog," he said before hanging up. Song dressed and walked the short distance to the commissar's stateroom. He didn't bother to knock.

"Thought you might enjoy a little refreshment, old man," Han said as the skipper entered the cluttered stateroom. Han sat at his desk holding a delicate crystal tumbler half-full of whiskey. At his side was a freshly opened bottle of Jack Daniels. He reached for a matching tumbler. "You've been wound too tight these last few days, Comrade. Sit down and have a drink with me."

Captain Song let out a grateful sigh; after Lin Yi's defection and Yang's sinking of the fishing boat, he questioned his future with the Party. He'd hoped that Han might serve as a buffer after the news reached Beijing, yet he was unsure of his tenure as *Shanghai's* commanding officer: he feared that he might be relieved for cause. Song glanced at the pictures of CCP leaders above Han's bunk; he wondered how the officials would view drinking alcohol while underway.

Han must have been thinking the same thought as he said, "And don't worry about having a little snort on the job." He pointed to the pictures. "I'll bet those old bastards did the same when times got tough, maybe even smoked some opium, who knows. And for the record, when I was a C.O., my commissar sometimes invited me to his stateroom for a sip or two; he called it 'attitude adjustment.'" Han poured a tumbler half full and handed it to Song. "Besides, I've been waiting for a good reason to crack open this bottle since we left port." He held up his glass of amber-colored spirit with admiration in his eyes. "We've caught up with the Americans in many areas, but I think they still top us in the liquor department." They clinked glasses and sipped.

The Tennessee sour mash whiskey burned a little as it slid down Song's throat, but he thought to himself, *Snake is right: this tastes damn good.* A few seconds later, the alcohol took effect: a warming comfort draped his body and the tension in his shoulders began to ebb.

Han slouched back in his chair. "Well, where do you want to start: The sunken Philippine trawler, Lin Yi's defection…or maybe what's in store for us when we reach the Straits?"

Song swirled his glass. "You've read me like a book, Snake. May I reply, 'all of the above?'" He took another slug.

"I suggest that we begin with the most serious issue, our role when we reach the Straits of Taiwan. Beijing has been characteristically vague about the Party's intentions. Of course, we will be on full alert: battle stations, aircraft fueled and armed. Whether or not the Americans will engage us, I do not know. But their new president, Maxwell, is nothing like that mealy-mouth coward he replaced. He's not bluffing about supporting Taiwan's right for independence and full membership in the U.N." Commissar Han sneered. "The audacity of those rebels: referring to their puny island as the Republic of China. What arrogance!" Han drained his glass and leaned forward, mere inches from Song's face; he pounded a fist on his desk. "We are *one* sovereign nation: the People's Republic of China!"

Captain Song nodded in agreement. He sensed that Han may have started drinking well before he'd arrived, and wondered if he'd been invited to talk strategy, or to be the commissar's sounding board. Song hoped to lighten the mood as he said, "I believe there's a line from a Western poem that may provide guidance in this situation: 'Ours is not to reason why, ours is but to do and die.'"

Han burst out laughing. "I gather that you're not receptive to the gravity of my words, dear friend. Yes, our ultimate calling is to follow the orders of our superiors… as we should." Han offered more whiskey, but Captain Song waived him off. The commissar understood and smiled. "Then may I suggest that we discuss the issues that relate more directly to us? First would be Lieutenant Lin and his aircraft. News of his defection has spread like wildfire in the media, but it has taken a back seat to the conflict brewing in the Straits. I've received notice that the Lin matter has been delegated to Ambassador Wu in Manila."

"What about his aircraft?" Song asked. "That weapon system is critical to our achieving air superiority; it will be compromised."

Han shook his head slowly. "Maybe." He paused for a second, then said, "The Americans were on a path to advance similar laser technology before Lin's act of treason. But the system has numerous safeguards to prevent tampering. What they gather from the J-31 could expedite the process, but in my view, Lin's expertise is what's most valuable. Before the defection, he'd begun drawing plans for a follow-on system to what's aboard his J-31. Our scientists believe it will take the West another decade to master that newest technology. And for that reason, it's imperative for Wu to negotiate Lin's extradition." Han grinned. "We hold a trump card with the hostages on Scarborough. I doubt if any U.S. president, even Maxwell, would gamble with their lives."

Song stared into his empty glass. "I agree. What could bite us in the tail, though, is the specter of Yang's reckless stunt. I suspect that at a point very soon, questions will be asked about that fishing boat."

"Of course. But I believe we have some time before we're forced to address that." Han turned his laptop so that Song could see the screen. "My latest update tells us that our agents in Manila haven't seen a single news report about the missing vessel. Unless we've been misinformed, the boat was completely obliterated, and its lone survivor is being held with the Americans on Scarborough."

"And he must be kept there...permanently," added Song.

"Yes, that's what I have proposed to Beijing. If there are no surviving witnesses, it will be difficult to trace the sinking back to *Shanghai*."

"Okay, so assume Lin is returned, what about Yang?"

Han took Song's glass and set it in the small sink next to his desk. "Yang is being transferred off the ship." Han rose from his chair and stood erect; the man's long, skinny neck seemed to flatten and extend, like that of a cobra. "I think it best if Thunder Yang cools his heels on the mainland until all of these matters take their course."

CHAPTER 17

Monday afternoon
Subic Bay

Lin Yi's J-31 was unrecognizable. After removing the three layers of airframe skin and insulation that shrouded the laser's power unit, a Raytheon technician assigned to the task had set down his tools and backed away; something didn't look right to him. Whether it was his experience overhauling complex electronics for over thirty years, or pure luck, the decision might have saved his life. He'd pulled a current sensor from the breast pocket of his coveralls and held it at arm's length from the power unit; the sensor lit up like a Christmas tree. "Jesus…" he said under his breath. His face turned ashen as he eased himself off a stepladder and said to his coworkers, "I don't know what's inside that compartment, but I'm sure as hell not touching it."

When Agent King and Jimmie Posadas arrived, the entire crew of engineers and technicians had walked away from the plane and were standing outside the taped-off security perimeter. King approached the lead Boeing engineer and said, "What gives?"

The engineer turned to the fellow who'd made the discovery and said, "Go ahead, tell the lady."

A mechanic emerged from the group and approached King. She read the man's embroidered name tag. "So, Mister Lombardi, what'd you find?"

Lombardi clutched the current sensor in his hand. He stared at it with a bewildered expression. "Ma'am, I've never had this sensor react like it did, and I was a good three feet away from the unit." He held up the sensor. "With typical power units, this doesn't register anything until I'm just a few inches away." He tucked the device back into his coveralls. "And I saw a bunch of digital numbers flashing on top of what we think is the capacitor. They'd blink in unison for a few seconds, then the display would change to a different set of numbers, flash for the same length of time, and then the repeat the process over and over." His expression changed to a nervous smile. "Hope it isn't counting down to detonation." Muted laughs rose from the group as Lombardi stepped farther away from the plane.

Gwen King had taken graduate courses that focused on the creation and transmission of different energy sources, including mechanical, steam, electrical, solar, and nuclear. But like Lombardi, the CIA specialist was baffled. She raised her voice to address the group. "Gentlemen, let's stand down until we can sort this out. It's almost noon; your lunch should be here soon." The work crew drifted away from the jet and huddled together on one side of the hangar.

"Pardon me, Gwen, but this is getting way above my paygrade," Jimmie said. "I agreed to fill in for Ambassador Remington until he could get here yesterday, but I—"

King interrupted. "No worries, Jimmie. You've held down the fort until the cavalry arrived. We've got it covered from here."

Jimmie let out a relieved sigh. "Thanks. Then I'll find a rental car and drive back to Manila."

"How'd you get to Subic in the first place?"

"President Diaz' staff hired a car for me." Posadas explained how his weekend had fallen apart and that his wife had driven home without him. Gwen saw how dejected he was. She pulled out her phone and said, "I noticed an air charter service on the other side of the airport. Let's see if they can fly you over to Manila."

Jimmie raised a hand to object, but before he could speak, Gwen had already found the number and called. As the phone rang, she looked at him and grinned. "Hey, I've got a fat travel budget. This one's on me."

* * *

The movement of Lin Yi from the De-Con station to McGirt's stateroom went off without a hitch. As planned, the ladders and passageways had been sanitized: McGirt, Chief Durfee, and Lieutenant Lin traveled unnoticed by the ship's crew.

Once inside the junior officer stateroom, Lin marveled at the accommodations. "Not so nice on my ship. Many pilots sleep in a small area."

"Well, don't get carried away," McGirt said. "The bunkrooms on our carriers are similar to yours; you'd be sharing a space this size with four or five other pilots. Staterooms on our smaller ships are similar to this one."

Lin sat down on one of the chairs. He pointed to a green vinyl bag in a corner on the floor. "Thank you for saving the sack for my helmet."

McGirt didn't recall Lin bringing his helmet bag on the Osprey flight from Subic. With all that had happened during the last two days, he wasn't surprised by the oversight. He unzipped the bag and peeked inside: he saw Lin's helmet, a pilot's kneeboard for writing, and a booklet of checklists—the same gear that McGirt figured any military pilot would carry. He was surprised that the bag hadn't been lost. "Anything in here I should know about?" he asked.

Lin shrugged. "There is nothing private. But I would like to save it if that is permitted."

McGirt noticed that Lin Yi's eyes were drooping and suspected that he hadn't gotten much sleep either. Plus, he remembered seeing only bread and water in the De-Con station.

"When was the last time you ate?" McGirt asked.

"Two days ago at the evening meal on *Shanghai*."

"What about when you were held in the compartment last night?"

Lin smirked. "I refused to eat that bread. It smelled like chemicals and had mold."

McGirt took a seat. "We can discuss your future later. In the meantime, I will order some decent food." He noted the ratty coveralls and old sneakers Lin was wearing. "And I'll try to find better clothing for you." McGirt got up and cracked open the door. Chief Durfee was leaning against the bulkhead. Seated in a chair next to Durfee was a young petty officer: the sailor wore a sidearm strapped to his waist and carried a two-way radio.

"Hey, Chief, can you do us a favor and fetch some hot food for our guest?"

"Sure, Admiral. Chow line should be opening soon. I'll get him a tray."

McGirt closed the door. "Food is on the way. For your information, there's a guard posted on the other side this door, so do not attempt to leave." He motioned to the stateroom's head. "If you need to do your business, that's the place. I'll be back in a couple hours." Stabbing pains shot through his knees as he stood up. He eyed the steel ladder used to reach the upper bunk. "And if you want to rest, take the top bed."

* * *

The black coffee he'd had in the wardroom helped stymie McGirt's own drowsiness. He'd had success powering through periods of sleep deprivation as a young officer, but after turning fifty, things had changed: he'd found that copious amounts of coffee would keep his eyes open, yet the stimulant didn't always help him stay alert. With Lin secure and the ship in a holding pattern, he decided to kill some time by visiting the hangar.

Upon arriving in the hangar bay he found a handful of wrench turners clustered around the tail section of the Air Detachment's other H-60 Seahawk helicopter. The three male and two female sailors snapped to attention when they saw him.

McGirt said, "Please carry on with your work." He spotted two opened access panels on the aircraft's tail section—one at the base of the tail drive where it angled up, the other located higher by the tail rotor blades. One of the females positioned a ladder under the upper panel, then climbed up while carrying a can of oil. When chest level with the panel, she poured in a measured amount of the lubricant.

A male voice hollered, "Hey, Sheila, make sure you tighten the cap on that tail gearbox reservoir good and snug." Sheila gave a thumbs up and then secured the access panel. She stepped down, moved the ladder to the other side and repeated the task on the lower unit—termed the intermediate gear box—where the tail rotor drive was coupled to a long shaft that led to the helicopter's main transmission.

The scene rekindled a poignant memory for McGirt: he'd lost several friends when their aircraft crashed after experiencing a tail rotor failure. The accident investigation team attributed the mishap to the sudden loss of oil in the tail gear box. Without lubrication, the mechanism had overheated and seized, thereby eliminating the helicopter's ability to counteract torque created by the main rotor blades. The crew had fought a losing battle trying to maintain balanced flight. McGirt was ready to leave the hangar when he heard Leonard Dickle call out, "Hey, Admiral, over here; I'm working on the Fire Scout."

He sidestepped a tall metal locker and saw Dickle sitting on a stool next to the Fire Scout UAV; at Dickle's side was his ever-present bottle of Mountain Dew. "Retorquing the bolts on these landing skids," Dickle said. He stood up, swiped his nose on the sleeve of his coveralls and cleaned his hands with a rag.

McGirt noticed that Dickle was smiling—a stark contrast to the snarky mood he'd displayed during their earlier encounters.

"Nice to see you, Admiral." Dickle said. He nodded toward the H-60. "That whirlybird look familiar?"

McGirt scanned the helicopter from nose to tail. "Sure does. I have some hours in the Seahawk; it's a great machine."

"So, sir, anything special bring you down to aviation central?"

"Thought I'd take a break from my other duties and see what was happening with the Air Detachment...and you."

"Well, thanks Admiral." Dickle noticed that McGirt's eyes were still focused on the H-60. "You miss flying, sir? From what I gather, senior dudes in the Navy don't fly much."

"That's true," McGirt replied. "Honestly, Leonard, the best years of my career were the ones in a squadron, especially as the commanding officer. But now I spend most of my time flying the BMD."

"BMD? Haven't heard of that aircraft. Fixed wing or rotary?"

McGirt forgot that he was talking with a civilian unfamiliar with the acronym. He explained, "Big mahogany desk—*BMD*."

"Oh...I get it." Dickle removed his thick-lensed glasses and rubbed his eyes with the clean corner of a rag. "Yeah, been there and done that. My last job was at the CIA photo lab. I held a top secret clearance and the gig paid good money; it wasn't my cup of tea, though. I was going nutty holed up in the Agency's basement developing film. But I got to see some amazing shots taken from spy planes and satellites. Wouldn't trade those experiences."

McGirt didn't have anything better to do at the moment other than chatting up the tech rep. *Grand Rapids* was awaiting further orders, plus he wanted to leave Lin Yi alone to get some shut eye. He surmised that like many people, Leonard Dickle enjoyed talking about himself and discussing the esoteric details of his job. He decided to extend their conversation. "Leaving a secure government job must have been a big decision, Leonard."

Dickle reached for his Mountain Dew and took a gulp. "Yeah, it was a leap of faith, but I'm single with no strings attached. When this opportunity presented itself, I jumped at it: lots of travel and more in line with my two college majors, computer science and general engineering." He noticed that McGirt's eyes had shifted from the H-60 to the Fire Scout. "No flight ops on the schedule until late afternoon, Admiral. Would you like a tour of the MQ-8?"

"Sure, if you have the time."

Dickle launched into a spiel, that based on its rapid pace, McGirt guessed he'd delivered many times. He described how the small autonomous aircraft was modeled after a manned helicopter designed by Hughes Aircraft, with its manufacturing rights later purchased by a trio of brothers, the Schweizers. In the early 2000s, Northrup Grumman was awarded a contract to adapt the Schweizer 330 to a "tactical unmanned aerial vehicle" for the military. After he'd given the bullet points, Dickle opened a few access panels to expose the Fire Scout's innards.

Admiral McGirt had experience in a wide variety of aircraft, but he'd never seen anything like the guts of the MQ-8. Its cubbyhole-like compartments were packed with radios, sensors, and control servos. "I was about to ask where a human being might fit in there," he said, "but I don't see an empty square inch."

"No, there isn't much spare room," replied Dickle. He pointed to a tiny void inside the nose section. "You might be able to cram a midget inside there, but that's about it. Or maybe, put somebody on a stretcher attached to one of the side fairings, like the Army did with the Bell 47 during the Korean war."

McGirt laughed. "Hey, you're not old enough to remember Korea."

"No, but I watched the TV show M.A.S.H. Every episode began with a chopper flying in with wounded soldiers strapped to its side."

McGirt rubbed his chin. "So, theoretically, the Fire Scout *could* carry a passenger, correct?"

Dickle's expression turned sour, as if he'd swallowed something distasteful. "Well…maybe…but it's highly improbable." He pointed out the aircraft's compact turbine engine. "This little baby puts out a bunch of power, and the airframe might be able to handle the added weight…" He paused for a few seconds, then shook his head. "Nah, passengers are out of the question; too many stability issues."

McGirt recalled the spat between Dickle and Bobby Bale in the wardroom. He thought about bringing up Bale's comment about the MQ-8's nickname, "the robot chicken." Instead, he chose to continue the chat in a positive vein. "Leonard, would you explain how this thing is controlled?"

"Sure can." Dickle's eyes lit up. He chugged more Mountain Dew and then led McGirt to the front of the aircraft, where he pointed out a big camera-looking device mounted below the Fire Scout's tapered nose. "Let me start here; this component is the bird's eye in the sky. Sends back a high resolution signal to the operator."

"So the pilot can fly it by visual reference, right?" McGirt asked.

Dickle frowned. "Yeah, I guess the operator could do that. But you see, the vehicle can takeoff, maneuver, and land automatically. And with GPS navigation, visual references aren't necessary."

McGirt couldn't hold back: he persisted on making his point. "That's all well and good, Leonard…at least until something goes wrong— that's why you need a trained pilot. In the event of a malfunction, we're the last line of defense."

Dickle's expression soured again. "Sorry to relay the news, sir, but a pilot isn't needed to operate an autonomous aerial vehicle." Dickle's attitude had shifted back to the irritable smugness he'd projected when McGirt had first met him in the wardroom.

McGirt ignored the brush off. "I could ask one of the aviators, but I suppose you can explain it also: what are the missions of the Fire Scout and how does it integrate with a manned aircraft like that one?" He pointed over his shoulder to the H-60.

"Most anything a manned helicopter can do, the MQ-8 can do equally as well, and in many cases, more accurately. Intelligence, surveillance, and reconnaissance missions are the first to be explored. Deployment of sub-finding sonobuoys are in the works, as is the carrying of ordnance like rockets and guns. As for the integration between manned and autonomous, a few bugs need to be smoothed out before that's feasible."

"What kind of bugs?" asked McGirt.

Dickle started closing the access panels. "Have you heard of Link 16?"

"Just bits and pieces. Tell me more."

After he'd buttoned up the last panel Dickle said, "Link 16 is a way for airborne assets to communicate between themselves in real time, independently and in a more secure, jam resistant manner than they do now."

"Has *Grand Rapids* been upgraded with that capability?"

"Nope, not yet. To follow up with your question about interplay between aircraft, Link 16 enables simultaneous data exchange between participants. As it stands now, that information has to be relayed through the ship before it's passed to the players."

"So, as I understand it, aircraft can communicate verbally by radio, but since there's not a breathing human in the Fire Scout, that's of no use. Sounds cumbersome and outdated."

"Yes, plus the current limitations hinder situational awareness between the helicopter pilots and the AVO."

"AVO? Oh, you mean another pilot?"

For the first time since they'd met, Leonard Dickle laughed. "Sir, I'm hungry and don't want to argue. I think you'll find today's flight operation interesting. Would you like to join Bale and me at the control station at 1600?"

McGirt patted Dickle on the shoulder. "Sounds like a plan, Leonard...and thanks for the tour, I enjoyed it." Dickle finished putting away his tools, and the H-60 working party knocked off for noon meal. McGirt headed back to his stateroom.

CHAPTER 18

On the way back to his quarters, McGirt swung by the wardroom. A half dozen officers eating noon meal sprang to attention when he walked in. He motioned them to stay seated; they responded with relieved smiles as they sat down and resumed eating. "What's for chow today?" he said.

"Sub sandwiches," answered one of the females.

"Any good?" asked McGirt.

She turned to her table mate for input; he responded with a blasé shoulder shrug and continued chomping on his sub. "I guess it's okay, sir," she said. The woman picked up her half-eaten sandwich and stared at it. "Not sure what kind of meat is inside: either chicken or turkey...and maybe some type of salami." She set the sandwich on her plate. "Potato chips and carrot cake aren't too bad, though."

McGirt laughed. "Well, thanks for the review, Miss." He flashed back to his days at sea. Sub sandwiches were always a favorite for lunch, though its sliced meats were jokingly referred to as "horse cock." The admiral doubted if that terminology had survived the Navy's politically correct watchdogs. He was anxious to check up on Lin Yi, so he poked his head into the kitchen and ordered a sandwich to go.

When he arrived at his stateroom, he found Lin Yi sitting at one of the desks hovering over the tray that Chief Durfee had delivered; it had held the same submarine sandwich, chips and cake served in the wardroom. An empty glass rested on the corner of Lin's tray.

"So what do you think?" McGirt asked. "Is the food alright?"

Lin Yi rested his back against the chair. "I did not eat the bread; it reminded me of what they gave me in the ship's jail. The meat tasted good but smelled of preservatives. I found the chips and cake acceptable."

McGirt pointed to Lin's empty glass. "What did the chief bring you to drink?"

Lin smiled as he said, "Something sweet and... how do you say...tangy?"

"Ah, yes, that must have been what we call bug juice," McGirt offered. Lin's face paled as he held up the glass.

"It's slang for a sweetened beverage served on the ship," McGirt said. He sat down next to Lin. "Don't ask me where the name came from because I haven't a clue. It's always been called bug juice."

"Well, if it was not made from insects, then I guess it tasted okay." Lin seemed more relaxed than when McGirt had left him earlier.

"Good. I'm glad we got that straightened out." McGirt unwrapped his sandwich and took a couple bites. Sensing that Lin Yi was more concerned with his future rather than critiquing the ship's food, he moved to matters at hand. "There are no new instructions from my superiors in Washington." He pointed to his wristwatch. "It's the middle of the night there, people won't be at work for several hours."

Lin tapped his fingers on the desk; he had a far-off gaze in his eyes. "I suppose it is time for you to interrogate me, isn't it, Admiral?" He stared at McGirt and said, "I...I would..." He stopped short of finishing the sentence.

McGirt sensed that Lin had more than lasers and airplanes on his mind, so he didn't interrupt. Almost a minute of silence passed. After the pause turned awkward, he said, "That will happen in good time, Lieutenant, but before discussing your plane and the laser, it would be helpful for me to learn more about you as a person. Tell me about your background: your family, where you grew up...those type of things."

Lin Yi's eyes shifted from McGirt to the floor. It was obvious that McGirt's request had bothered him.

The admiral read Lin Yi's mood and changed lanes. "Well, then, I'd like to tell you about me," he began. "I was born in the Southern United States, in a place called Kentucky, but my parents moved us to another state, Michigan, when I was very young." He smiled and added, "I was just a little guy, only three years old. My sister and I grew up in an industrial town called Ypsilanti, near Detroit."

The mention of Detroit seemed to perk Lin's interest. "Ah, yes, I know of the Motor City." He grinned while gesturing as if steering a car. "I too lived near an automobile center in China."

McGirt seized the opening. "Oh, really? What region of China?"

"My family is from the Guangdong Province, by the city of Guangzhou."

"That's interesting. From what I've heard, Guangzhou is one of China's largest producers of vehicles, is that correct?" Lin nodded, so McGirt pressed on. "My father and uncles worked in automobile plants around Detroit." He hesitated for a moment, then asked, "Did any of your relatives work in the automobile industry?"

A proud expression spread over Lin Yi's face. "Yes, many did, most notably my father; he was a design engineer."

"And your mother?"

Lin Yi looked even more proud at the mention of his mother. "She was a mathematics teacher and very intelligent. My father always told my brother and me that she had the best brain in our family."

"It was the same at our house. My mother did not work at a job, but everyone knew how smart she was." The two men shared a knowing laugh. "So, do your parents still work or are they retired?"

The cheerfulness drained from Lin. "My mother and father are not living." His eyes drifted back to the floor.

McGirt saw anguish in Lin Yi's face. He decided to take the conversation further, so he said, "It's painful to lose our parents. My father died when I was a teenager. He committed suicide with a shotgun."

Lin sat up straight and looked McGirt in the eye. "That must have been a terrible thing for your family to endure."

"Yes, it was."

"Why did he do it?"

McGirt felt a tinge of regret at bringing up the subject. Nonetheless, he hoped that sharing the tragic memory might serve as a way to gain Lin Yi's trust. "My father was an alcoholic. He was driving while drunk and caused an accident which killed a mother and her two small children. I think he was so ashamed, that he chose to take his own life."

"In my culture, people would understand why your father inflicted punishment upon himself," Lin said. "He did the honorable thing."

McGirt shook his head. "My culture does not always share that view. Our family considered it a selfish act."

The two men sat in silence, each emersed in their own bitter memories. After a moment, McGirt stood up and said, "Let me return your meal tray. Also, we need to find you some clean clothes to wear."

As McGirt started for the door, Lin tugged at his arm. "Admiral, I ask that you stay seated. There are things I need to say to you…in private."

"Sure." McGirt set the tray aside and sat down.

"There are several reasons that I chose to flee my country. I was treated very well because of my military rank and position as a fighter pilot, but that was not enough for me. After I spent time in the United States as a student, I saw that your way of life, your freedoms and opportunities, were far greater than what China could ever offer me under its communist ways."

"Yes, despite our flaws, America is still the land of great opportunity," McGirt said.

Lin took a deep breath as he fought back his emotions. "During the big pandemic, my parents were forced to stay inside their apartment. They were treated like caged animals. As with many, many others, they starved to death inside their own home. The government informed me that they had both perished from the virus, but I am positive that was not how they died."

"How do you know for sure?"

"I have a friend that told me the truth. He was tasked with recovering the bodies; he recognized my mother and father. Party members lied because they wanted me to continue working on the laser weapon that I designed. They deposited large sums of money in my bank to keep me happy."

McGirt was stunned by Lin's revelation. "So, the CCP tried to buy your loyalty?"

"That is correct."

"But wait," McGirt said. "I'm confused at why your parents were not in a more protected status. You were in the military, and in a highly respected position. Didn't that benefit them in the eyes of your government?"

"It should have, but it didn't. My parents were swept up in the pandemic. They were victims, like millions of others."

McGirt reflected on how his own country had reacted to the same virus pandemic: questionably effective vaccines; quarantines and mask policies that changed on a daily basis. He could only imagine what life had been like for Lin's parents under a repressive government. "I am truly sorry about what happened to your mother and father," McGirt said. He then asked the obvious question: "Would you have defected if your parents were still alive?"

"Of course not. They would have been punished for my actions."

"You said that you have a brother...what about him? Aren't you worried about putting him in jeopardy?"

Lin Yi leaned back with hands clasped behind his head. "They will never find my brother," he said with conviction. "He moved to the mountains in the western part of China. He lives...how do you say...as a hermit."

"I didn't think it was possible to hide in your country," said McGirt.

"It is difficult to do so, but my brother is most resourceful. I have never worried about him; he is a special person who lives by his own set of rules. I think you would like him, Admiral. When we were young, he would lead me outside the city to the wooded areas where we would spend nights in a tent. I was never very comfortable doing that; sleeping on the hard ground and eating burnt food cooked over a fire was not fun for me."

"So, you and your brother are quite different. Did he ever go to college like you did?"

"Ah, my brother and education," Lin said with a laugh. "My parents were so frustrated by him. He would score very high on aptitude tests that every Chinese student must take, but his school grades were very terrible, which was an embarrassment for my parents, especially my mother who was a teacher." Lin shook his head. "And he would get angry with me because I was the opposite: I studied hard every night and followed the rules."

"When was the last time that you saw your brother?"

"I have not seen him for several years. He sent a letter home to my mother and said he found a job guiding tourists along hiking trails, but I am not certain he was telling the truth. Maybe he did that job for a little while, until he got bored." Lin smiled as he reflected. "When I told my friends at Berkeley about my brother, they said that he paraded to his own drum, or something like that."

"Your brother sounds like a good man," McGirt said. "I think I would like him. Are there any other relatives or friends that will be put in harm's way by your defection?"

The deep affection that Lin Yi had shown while speaking of his brother faded. A cold look of determination took its place. "No. There is no one else that I care about." Lin's motivation seemed crystal clear: he had nothing to lose by defecting, and his technical knowledge of the J-31's laser weapon was his ticket to America.

McGirt got to his feet. "We can talk later after I speak with my superiors in Washington about our next step. Is there anything that I can get you in the meantime?"

Before Lin could answer, there were three loud knocks. McGirt cracked open the door and was greeted by Chief Durfee, who handed him a plastic bag. "Here's the gear you requested, Admiral. Let me know if there's anything else you need."

McGirt thanked Durfee and closed the door. He peeked into the bag and said, "Well, you can finally get out of those rags." He shook the bag over the lower bunk: a set of blue fire-retardant variant coveralls (FRVs), black boots, socks, and white undergarments tumbled out.

Lin Yi got to his feet and stripped off the janitor's garb he'd been wearing for two days. "After I take a shower, it would be pleasant to leave this room and breathe fresh air." He held up his new clothing. "Do you think I will appear as part of the ship's personnel?"

McGirt was flabbergasted by the question. "Lin Yi, I'll see if I can arrange a few minutes of supervised time outside for you. But don't think for a moment that you're a member of the crew."

* * *

Before leaving the stateroom, McGirt fished out a vial of pain killers from his shaving kit. His crippled knees throbbed after climbing up and down *Grand Rapids'* steep ladders. He hobbled to the ship's communications office where he found Captain Draper and Commodore Torres huddled over a printer; the machine hummed through the last words of a message.

"We were just about to call you, Admiral," Torres said as she turned to greet him. She tore the message from the printer and handed it over. "Looks like another all-nighter for the folks at the Navy Command Center," she said.

McGirt pulled the readers from his pocket and scanned the news. "Okay, this is good…things are moving along." He mumbled a few sentences as he read to himself. "So…I'll be video conferencing with the Big Guy and his staff at fourteen hundred GMT." He checked the digital clock on the bulkhead. "Twenty-one hundred local time…let's see…about five and a half hours from now." He tapped Torres on the shoulder. "Want to join us, Commodore? When's the last time you had face time with the Prez?"

Torres laughed. "I'd love to, Admiral, but a movement order came across the wire detaching me to another one of my ships I'm scheduled to inspect. They're sending a chopper to pick me up."

McGirt regretted having to say goodbye to Torres. He considered her more than a close friend; she was one of the sharpest naval officers he knew. "Sure you can't stay aboard a little longer and back me up as this Lin drama plays out?"

"No, sir. My boss was emphatic that I'm to finish my duties and return to San Diego. They've already booked me on a flight out of Manila. I'll be heading stateside in a couple days."

"Well, I guess the Navy's work grinds on no matter what," McGirt said. "No problem, I've got another great wingman," he said while patting Draper on the back. "Skipper, where will this video thing go down?"

"Admiral, we'll be doing it from ICC2. The space will be sanitized: all personnel cleared out, and a security detail posted at both entrances."

McGirt started to speak but was drowned out by the ship's 1MC: *"Now flight quarters, flight quarters. All hands, man your stations."* He remembered Dickle's invitation to observe the Fire Scout operation.

The commodore excused herself while McGirt and Draper stayed behind. "Any news on your hijacked helicopter, Skipper?"

"Afraid not, sir. I'm hoping that your video conference will shed some light on that."

"Me too. Bill, it goes without saying that I want you by my side when we get dialed in with the president. Those are your guys being held prisoner."

"Thanks, Admiral. I'd appreciate that."

McGirt empathized with Draper. The comradery he'd experienced as a commanding officer was the highlight of his own naval career; but the job had been stressful. He'd completed the tour with a clean record: free of aircraft accidents, but more importantly, without a loss of life. McGirt's greatest fear had been the specter of having to write a letter to the surviving kin of a sailor who'd died under his command. He prayed that Bill Draper would be spared that dreadful task.

CHAPTER 19

McGirt found a secluded corner of the hangar to watch the arrival of Torres' helicopter. He saw a cabinet where the extra cranials were stored, so he grabbed one and put it on; he knew that the setting was about to get very loud.

Word had filtered through the ship that he'd been saddled with guaranteeing the safety of the Chinese national onboard. At first, the crew knew nothing of Lin Yi's defection or why he'd been flown out to sea in a clandestine fashion. But rumors began to swirl as some hypothesized that Lin's presence might be tied to Moselli's missing aircraft. Captain Draper had made a general announcement about the ship's location and confirmed that Moselli's helicopter had landed safely; he made no mention of the Chinese military base at Scarborough Shoals or the presence of Lin Yi aboard.

McGirt heard the *whomp, whomp, whomp* sound of the chopper's rotor blades before he spotted it approaching from the stern. A green deck status light was given, the helicopter came to hover and made a soft touch down.

Katherine Torres entered the hangar and started an easy jog toward the aircraft; a junior sailor toted her brief case and rollaboard luggage. Torres saw McGirt leaning against the bulkhead next to the open hangar door and approached him. McGirt smiled and pulled away one of his cranial's earcups to hear her.

"Wish I could stay longer, Admiral," she shouted above the noise. "Good luck, I hope this all works out." McGirt returned her salute, then reached to shake her hand when Torres suddenly pressed closer and wrapped him in a tight hug. "Please be careful, Johnny...*please*." When they parted, he saw tears in her eyes. He considered Katherine Torres one of the strongest-willed officers he knew—but he'd never witnessed the woman display her softer side in public.

Minutes later, the helicopter lifted off and roared into the bright blue sky. What had been the scene of noisy controlled chaos transitioned to a quiet day in the South China Sea. The launch team scurried back into the hangar and gathered around the MQ-8 Fire Scout, where they jacked the UAV onto a custom designed hand cart and prepared to push it onto the flight deck.

Once the vehicle was secured in place, pre-flight procedures began: the refueling gang dragged a hose across the deck to fill the MQ-8's tanks; another group plugged a cable into the left side of the UAV, then attached the other lead to a laptop-looking computer. The drone's four rotor blades were unfolded and a series of pre-launch checks were completed. McGirt watched the activity for a while, then went one deck below to meet up with Leonard Dickle.

He was glad to see Lieutenant Bobby Bale seated next to Dickle at the Fire Scout's control station. Had McGirt not known better, he would have thought they were preparing to play a sophisticated arcade game. They sat side-by-side at a workstation comprised of video monitors, joysticks, and computer keyboards. One monitor displayed a bird's-eye view of the Fire Scout from a camera located above the flight deck. Another monitor displayed an image projected from the UAV's nose mounted camera. Rows of switches and circuit breakers surrounded the monitors.

Dickle's fingers danced across a keyboard; his face had an excited, engaged expression. He smiled and said, "Hello, Admiral. Pull up a chair."

Bobby Bale glanced at Dickle, shook his head and smirked, then motioned for McGirt to sit next to him. "Sir, I will be the AVO for this flight. The mission should take about an hour."

McGirt peeked at his wristwatch; the White House staff would be shuttling in to work about the same time flight quarters were secured; he figured he'd have enough time to get something to eat, check on Lin Yi, and prepare for the conference with President Black. He sat next to Bale and marveled at the technology before him. "I'll try not to get in the way or ask too many questions," he said. "Can you give me a quick rundown before you start?"

Dickle jumped in before Bale could speak. "Admiral, we're going to test a new system." He never looked up from his typing. "And that's why Uncle Sam flew me halfway around the world: to make sure that everything does what it's designed to do." He removed his glasses and used them as a pointer. "If you look closely at the vehicle, you'll see a series of sensors attached to the underbelly." He zoomed in on the monitor that displayed the MQ-8 from the tower, and then entered a few commands on his keyboard. "Ah, shoot…you can't see them from this angle, but take my word for it, they're there."

"I believe you, Leonard," McGirt said.

"Anyway… those are listening devices that we'll drop from low altitude, then attempt to retrieve underwater data which will then—"

Bale rolled his eyes; he raised a hand to interrupt. "Lenny, I'll take it from here."

Dickle sat back with a pouting expression; he mumbled, "It's *Leonard*, not *Lenny!*"

Bale continued. "Sir, we'll be deploying an updated model of sonobuoys that we're testing for the ASW[1] guys." Bale nodded toward Dickle. "Mr. Wizard here helped develop them."

"You bet I did," Dickle chimed. "Along with the enhanced navigation system that I'll gladly demonstrate if the admiral would like." Leonard shot Bale a smug look.

It didn't take long for McGirt to confirm that relations between Dickle and Bale hadn't improved since Bobby's comment about the robot chicken the previous night. He couldn't clear his mind from the image of a mechanical hen hopping across the flight deck.

The trio watched as the launch crew removed tiedown chains from the UAV. Bale started the Fire Scout's engine and completed a handful of checks, then switched to another display on one of the monitors. He pointed out a cluster of gauges that displayed the status of the Fire Scout's systems. Satisfied, he requested and was granted takeoff clearance from the control tower.

"Here we go," Bale said as he typed in a couple commands and then pushed a button labeled "launch." McGirt focused on the video monitors as the MQ-8 got light on its skids and lifted into a hover. "Admiral, we call this the perch position," Bale said. He typed in another command. "Now entering 'perch proceed,' which will turn us to the direction I've programmed—in this case, left—and begin a climb out to…" He punched a couple more keystrokes. "Climbing to eight hundred feet."

McGirt pointed to the joystick, which hadn't been touched. "Aren't you going to hand fly this thing?"

Bale shifted his focus away from the computer screens. "No can do, sir; it's totally automatic: I program what I want it to do by using a keyboard and this tracking ball thingy, that's sort of like a mouse on your standard laptop."

"Then what's the stick for?"

"On an actual mission, we'd have a mission payload operator, who's also an air crewman, seated here with the joystick. They'd use that to slew the BRITE

---

[1] Anti Submarine Warfare

Star camera, which is a derivative of the FLIR, or forward looking infra-red camera."

McGirt said, "Hey, smart ass, this isn't my first rodeo; I know what a FLIR is."

Bale's face reddened. "Sorry, Admiral. No disrespect intended. Anyway, Lenny will fill you in on the BRITE Star."

Dickle's head lowered. He said through clenched teeth, "It's *Leonard*. Don't call me that *other name!*" The two officers fought back laughter.

"Okay, I'll try to remember next time," Bobby said.

McGirt switched his focus to the monitor displaying a live signal from the Fire Scout's camera. "Hey, it almost looks as if we're in the cockpit! No instrument panel in front of us, but darn, we're definitely airborne." He tapped Bale on the arm. "Pretty cool, mister!"

Bobby Bale grinned. "Yes, sir, we *are* flying. Not in the way that I'd prefer, but I'll admit, it's still a kick in the butt." He pointed to another monitor. "As for the instrument panel, here are all of our basic flight instruments, engine gauges and warning systems. My biggest complaint is that it takes a while to get used to controlling an aircraft without a seat-of-the-pants sensation."

Dickle and Bale then began working as a team; McGirt noted that the rivalry between them appeared to have vanished. Dickle typed on his keyboard, while Bale relayed flight data and engine readings to him.

"We've programmed a position twenty-five miles ahead of the ship," Bale said. "At our present speed of one hundred knots, we'll be overhead in approximately fifteen minutes."

"What are you using for navigation?" McGirt asked. "Is the ship's TACAN up and running?"

"Not sure about the TACAN's status, Admiral. GPS signals are strong today, so we don't need any shipboard navaids." Bale tilted his head toward Dickle and said, "*Leonard* is our GPS guru; he can tell you more about that and our data link system."

Dickle emerged from his moodiness. He slugged down a few gulps of Mountain Dew, sat up straight and began explaining how the MQ-8's sensor data would be relayed back to the ship—not by line-of-sight radio signals, but via a satellite link. McGirt feigned interest while not understanding all of Dickle's techno-gab. When Leonard had finished talking, McGirt patted both men on their shoulder and said, "Glad we've got people like you operating this machine. I'm a little embarrassed: I feel like a low tech guy in a high tech world."

Bale and Dickle discussed their plan to deploy a string of sonobuoys and then monitor the devices as their signals were transmitted from the ocean's surface, back to the Fire Scout, and then beamed to the ship via a relay satellite orbiting above earth.

Images of the robot chicken kept sneaking into McGirt's mind, despite the fact that the MQ-8 appeared to be flying smoothly and free of quirks. Once at the designated latitude and longitude coordinates, Bale slowed the aircraft and descended to a lower altitude. He then programmed it into a shallow bank angle, which flew it in a wide circular pattern over the surface. Leonard dropped the sonobuoys at timed intervals to obtain the desired signal pattern. Water-activated switches triggered each sonobuoy to begin transmitting its own unique signature. Moments later, the data was fed back to the UAV, uplinked to a satellite, and relayed to the ship.

McGirt was intrigued by the chain of events. "Are the sonobuoys' signals distance limited?" he asked.

"Yes, they're limited by line-of-sight for now," Dickle said. He beamed like a proud new father as he added, "But they won't be for much longer, not after I put the finishing touches on my latest project. Soon, that is, provided my grant money comes through, these sensors, or any similar type of device, will be capable of talking straight to the satellite." He looked over to Bobby Bale. "Plus, an on-station pilot won't be needed. Several UAVs will be controlled by one operator from a single location, dependent only on having adequate satellite coverage." His smile grew wider. "Operators can be trained for pennies on the dollar compared to what we're spending on pilots. I've already developed a training syllabus that can make that happen." Dickle nodded confidently and said, "Yes, automation will change the world."

McGirt was skeptical. "Wait a minute, Leonard, hasn't a form of this capability been around for years? Heck, we've been remotely piloting vehicles like the Predator and the MQ-9 Reaper for years. And don't forget the QH50 DASH: hell, that was a drone helicopter that flew back in the 1960s." He waved a dismissive hand at the display monitors. "What makes this thing so special?"

Dickle fidgeted in his seat as he formulated a response. "You have a point, Admiral. What you see here is merely a test bed. Future MQ-8s, like the updated 'C' model, will be much more sophisticated in terms of automation and performance." He continued to drive home his point. "There's really no need to spend taxpayer dollars on expensive pilot training like we do now." He leaned back with arms folded across his chest and stared at Bale. "I predict that within fifty years, everything in the air will be pilot-free, even airliners."

McGirt laughed. "Heck, I'll probably be pushing up daisies by then. No way would I hop on a plane without a real pilot in the cockpit."

Bobby Bale had been quiet during the discussion. "Excuse me...*Leonard*... we should start preparing for return and landing."

Dickle shuffled some forms, raced his fingers over a keyboard and acknowledged, "Roger that, Captain Bobby!' McGirt saw a satisfied, cocky expression on the tech rep's face. But it was a challenge arguing with Dickle; the fellow had countered everything McGirt could offer in defense of pilots.

Bale reversed course, climbed to a higher altitude, and radioed the ship that he'd be overhead in a few minutes. He had the calm, relaxed aura of someone that loved his job; he wasn't in the cockpit of an actual aircraft, yet he still considered this an exercise in doing what he was trained to do. He turned to McGirt and said, "Sir, any questions before we land the vehicle?"

McGirt scanned the control station; he understood the basic setup, but the MQ-8's automation was much more advanced than any aircraft—rotary or fixed-wing—that he'd ever flown. "No questions. I'm looking forward to watching the Fire Scout make an automated approach and landing." From the corner of his eye he saw Dickle nodding enthusiastically.

"Sure, how about we do a couple of them?" Bale proposed.

"Sounds good to me, provided it's okay with the ship," said McGirt.

Bale cleared the request with *Grand Rapids'* tower operator. As the vessel's wake came into view on the Fire Scout's camera, Bale programmed the MQ-8 to capture the ship's approach signal, which would guide the UAV to a hover over the flight deck. McGirt and Dickle watched the monitor as the image of the ship's fantail came into view; seconds later, they heard the muffled *whomp, whomp, whomp* of the Fire Scout's rotor blades outside. The UAV came to rock solid hover over the center of the deck as Bale reached for the "land" button on his console.

Dickle said, "Oh, yeah...look at this. She's locked on!" It appeared that the automated, pilotless aircraft was proving Dickle right: it was performing as good as Bale, or any other pilot could. The MQ-8 started a slow, graceful descent to the deck—until things went haywire. It yawed wildly to the right and drifted toward the flight deck's edge in a steep, nose down attitude. McGirt alternated his sights between two monitors: the BRITE Star's screen displayed an image filled with blue water and wave tops, while the flight deck camera showed the Fire Scout on the verge of plummeting overboard.

Dickle jumped from his seat. "What the…I don't believe this!" he screamed.

Bobby Bale typed furiously. "I got it, I got it!" he yelled. The UAV flew clear of the ship's stern and started to climb. "Programming another approach and landing sequence," he said. His voice was calm and deliberate. "Okay…let's try this again."

Dickle pounded his fist. "Damn it, I thought my software patch fixed that anomaly!"

McGirt kept his eyes on the monitors as the UAV leveled off and made a 360-degree turn. Bale typed a command to capture the ship's signal again, which guided the bird down and into another hover; the "land" button was pushed, and the Fire Scout settled onto the deck. Sailors hustled out with chains to secure it. After he'd cut off fuel to the vehicle's engine and its rotor blades had coasted to a stop, Bale ran through the shutdown checklist.

Dickle stormed off. "I'm going to the flight deck," he yelled over his shoulder. "I've got to check this out."

"Jesus…" said McGirt. "What a real cluster-you-know-what."

Bale let out a sigh. "Whew…that was interesting. I wish the other guys were here; they would have loved to see Dickle eating crow…or should I say, some robot chicken."

McGirt chuckled in agreement. "Lieutenant, when I was your age, auto flight systems were not as advanced, so we never put our full trust in them." He paused while remembering the advice of a crusty instructor pilot who'd taught him during primary training in Pensacola. He decided to share the nugget. "Bobby, an old salt from the Vietnam War once told me how he felt about automation. I quote: 'All that magic shit works great…until it doesn't.'"

"Well, sir, that guy was spot on today." Bale got up from the console and wiped sweaty palms across his pant legs.

Watching the young pilot manipulate the UAV had made McGirt nostalgic. Sure, they weren't sitting inside an actual aircraft or flying by "stick and rudder," yet after witnessing how Bale had used his skills to save the MQ-8, the admiral realized how much he missed the challenge of flying and being back at sea in the heart of the action.

McGirt had some extra time before his videoconference with President Black; he'd planned to check on Lin Yi, and then eat dinner. But those things could wait; right now he felt the urge to sit down and share some camaraderie with a fellow aviator. As they left the control station, he squeezed Bale's shoulder and said, "You did a hell of a job saving that aircraft, son. How about we get us a cup of coffee and talk about it?"

CHAPTER 20

After he and Bobby Bale had kibitzed over coffee and had dinner, McGirt went to his stateroom to check on Lin Yi. He was greeted by the sailor who'd been assigned guard duty in the passageway. The youngster sprang to attention. McGirt waived his hand signaling the petty officer to be seated. "How's it going, sailor? Any surprises?"

"No, sir, everything's quiet."

"Any visitors come by during your watch?"

"Yes, sir. Chief Durfee was here about twenty minutes ago. He delivered another food tray. He didn't stay long, just in and out."

"Okay, thanks for the update," McGirt said as he reached for the door handle. He found Lin Yi sprawled out on the top bunk reading a newspaper by the light of a small fluorescent lamp mounted above his bed. A tray of food sat atop one of the desks; it looked barely touched.

"Not hungry?" McGirt asked.

Lin Yi folded the paper on his chest. "No. The meal was not very pleasing."

McGirt studied the tray; dinner was a concoction of chopped beef and egg noodles drenched in brown gravy. There was a helping of rubbery-looking green beans and a half-eaten cookie on the side. He saw that Lin had resumed reading. McGirt recognized the newspaper as the *Navy Times*, the venerable publication of news around the fleet. "Where did you get that paper?" he asked.

"I found it tucked in by the mattress," Lin said. He set down the paper and rolled on his side to face McGirt. "China would never display such details to the public. Do you not worry about security matters, especially concerning your ships, planes and other weapons?"

"Lin Yi, that's a risk in a free society. There is always the chance of sensitive information falling into the hands of bad people."

"My country keeps a tight lid on what data it makes available to the world."

McGirt had some free time before his video conference with the president. He'd wanted to take a short nap before the call but decided to explore things further with Lin. He slid a chair across the room and propped his feet up on the lower bunk. "Let me ask you something, Lin: when you were at Berkeley, did you ever send sensitive information from the school's laboratories back to China?"

Lin Yi laughed. "Are you asking if I am a spy?"

McGirt didn't answer; instead, he raised his eyebrows and extended his arms with open palms gesturing: *Well, are you?*

"We are all spies, in our own right, are we not, Admiral? Whether it is in search of military science information, insider financial data, or for another's personal secrets." He sat up on the edge of his bunk. "There was a girl that I met while studying in the United States. I liked her very much, but she did not seem interested in me, so I decided to watch her from afar to learn more about her. I hoped that after I observed her habits and preferences, I would have a better chance of becoming a good friend. I followed her to her dormitory and watched her converse with other people. Sometimes I would wait in the corner of her dining hall and take notes about what food she liked; I wanted to know what pleased her if she ever decided to acknowledge me."

"We call that stalking," McGirt said. "And it sounds like you were acting like a creep. Do you know the meaning of 'creep'"?

"Yes, I believe that is someone that does strange, distasteful things."

"That's correct. So, tell me, did you ever get to first base with this girl?" A dumbfounded expression draped Lin Yi's face: it was clear that he didn't understand the phrase. "I'm sorry, let me ask the question in a different way: did the girl ever start paying attention to you?"

Lin smiled. "Yes, she did. We became very intimate friends and enjoyed many things together. So, I ask *you* now, Admiral McGirt: Was I a spy when I watched her secretly?"

McGirt was intrigued by Lin's logic. "Well, in the terms you are using, and if nobody was offended, nor damaged, I would not call you a spy." He added, "But I still think you acted like a creep."

"Maybe I was, but I achieved my goal."

McGirt regrouped. "Lin Yi, how does your story apply to espionage? I know for a fact that your country has deployed students at our universities who are seeking privileged information and sending it back to China. Much of that knowledge is being used to modernize the CCP military."

"And we are the only nation doing that?" Lin countered. "The United States does not deploy people to other countries for the same purpose?"

There was an arrogant tone in Lin Yi's voice and it confused McGirt. *Is this guy seeking asylum or is he some sort of decoy?* he wondered. *Could his plane at Subic Bay be a smokescreen to deflect from more critical issues?* He decided to leave those questions unresolved for the moment. "Lin Yi, if you are sincere about living in a free society, you'll have to accept America for its good and bad points. As we like to say, 'Love it, or leave it.'" With that, McGirt stood up and left.

* * *

Dick Moselli rubbed his aching bicep. Doctors had warned that although the bullet wound had healed well, he'd likely experience spasms for the rest of his life. The doctors were right: five years after the incident, he still suffered pain. The Purple Heart and Distinguished Flying Cross he'd been awarded were of little compensation. Moselli had been wounded during the rescue of an American oil heiress held by Muslim terrorists in the Philippines. He and his crew had hoisted the woman and a pair of CIA agents into their H-46 helicopter. In the process, Moselli had been struck by gunfire. One of the agents retired, while the other—a naval officer on temporary duty with the Agency—went on to become a decorated admiral. That officer's name: Johnny Jack McGirt. Moselli had no idea that Admiral McGirt was the same person coordinating his release.

The Americans sprang from their bunks as a gaggle of soldiers, led by their stinking colonel, burst into the trailer. Moselli, Aguilar, and Horton had dozed off after their last meal: a cold lunch of pickled eel served with rice balls wrapped in seaweed. Had the trio not been famished, they would have tossed the slimy blobs into the trash.

Moselli confronted Captain Gao. "What the hell is going on?" he hollered. "The electricity is off again, we have no running water, and our air conditioning is dead...again." He pointed a finger at the colonel. "Damn it, I demand that you connect me with the United States Embassy!" He stood in the doorway and motioned toward the line of house trailers. "Everyone else has power, why not us?"

Gao glanced at the colonel but didn't translate Moselli's words. He bowed his head. "Apologies, please, sir. I will look into that serious matter."

Moselli backed away and watched as the colonel barked instructions to three soldiers that were setting up a video camera. "And what are these men doing? Are you going to film us?"

Gao handed him a sheet of paper. On it were several sentences scrawled in bold, capitalized letters. "You must read this, so we can send a message to your president. Colonel gets emphatic orders from his superiors." Colonel Stink shouted something at Gao. "Oh, yes. These are orders straight from Beijing," Gao added.

Moselli yanked the paper from Gao's hand. "Alright, let me see this." Halfway through reading the message he stopped. "So, who is this freaking person— *Lin Yi*? What does he have to do with us?"

Gao looked perplexed; he turned to his boss. The colonel smiled and approached Moselli; he began speaking in a soft tone. Though Moselli couldn't understand him, the colonel seemed to be almost begging. After over a minute of pleading, he stopped, turned away, and waved a hand at Gao.

"Colonel says he is so sorry, but you have no choice but to obey his superiors. You must read from the paper, or he will keep you here forever." Gao glanced at his boss, who stood firm with arms across his chest. "It would be most helpful for all personnel if you cooperate with the colonel's request."

Moselli considered reading the statement for the camera and then adlibbing to assert he'd only done so under duress; nonetheless, he wanted to know what his crew thought. Horton was the first to offer an opinion. "Hell, Bruiser, what difference does it make? Whatever you say, they'll just edit it so we look like the bad guys."

Aguilar agreed. "I'm with Crazo; just read the damn thing. But commander, you've got nothing to lose by making some demands. Bargain with the bastards: tell them to fix the air and plumbing and give us some clean clothes. I don't know if they've got any decent Western chow on this island, but at least ask for it. Know what I mean?"

Moselli rubbed his stubble. He studied the faces of his copilot and crew chief; the men looked exhausted from lack of sleep, lousy food, and the swelting heat. He realized that he was in the same degraded condition. "Okay, fellas, that's what we'll do."

Captain Gao jabbered a few words to the colonel, who relaxed his pose and allowed a slight grin to slip from the corner of his mouth. Gao gave an order to the filming crew, then addressed the Americans. "Okay, very nice. Stand together close. Senior officer, you forward, please."

Moselli covered the camera's lens with his hand. "Hold it right there! Look, Captain Gao, I will read the statement, but only if your colonel promises to honor our demands: restore our electric power and give us running water so we can shower. And we want clean clothes and better food." Moselli saw that the smug grin on the colonel's sweaty face had spread to a victorious smile. He couldn't resist making one more request. He faced the colonel and said, "And one more thing: I want to inspect my aircraft!"

Gao translated; the colonel's smile evaporated. After Gao had finished, the colonel glared at Moselli then said in crude English, "You winner... that be okay." Gao signaled for the camera to roll.

Moselli gathered his thoughts, then said, "My name is Lieutenant Commander Richard Moselli. My crew and I are being held against our will on an unfamiliar island occupied by the People's Republic of China in the South China Sea. I have been asked to read from this paper, which I will do...verbatim:

"NOTE TO PRESIDENT OF THE UNITED STATES. YOU SHALL RETURN MISTER LIEUTENANT LIN YI IMMEDIATELY. HE IS A MOST VALUABLE AND IMPORTANT PILOT TO PEOPLE'S LIBERATION NAVY. HIS VALUED AND IMPORTANT JET PLANE SHALL BE RETURNED MOST IMMEDIATELY. OR ELSE YOUR AMERICAN HELICOPTER CREW WILL NEVER GO HOME."

Moselli dropped the paper to the floor and faced the colonel. "There, you happy, pal?"

The film crew packed up and left while Gao and the colonel stayed behind. Captain Gao extended his hand. "We thank you very much, Lieutenant Commander. The movie will help you gain your freedom."

The colonel and Gao started to leave but Moselli blocked the doorway. When he saw Gao's hand drift down to his holstered pistol, he backed away. "Is there problems, Lieutenant Commander...sir?" Gao asked.

"No problem here, Captain Gao, but I have one more thing to say: we did our part of the bargain, now you do yours. And tell me: why is this Lin Yi man so important?"

Gao started to speak, but the colonel grabbed his arm and hauled him outside. They got into a vehicle and sped away.

The Americans retreated to the trailer's living area. Moselli sat on the sofa and said, "So, what do you think? Will that video do any good or was it a waste of time?"

Aguilar said, "I can't get a grip on this thing, Bruiser; it feels like we're caught up in a dime store mystery, without enough clues to figure out the ending. But by the way Colonel Stink and Gao bolted, it was obvious you touched a nerve when you asked about their missing pilot."

"Yeah, and from that statement I read, I gather that somebody high on their food chain thinks the guy is 'most valuable and important.'"

The temperature inside the aluminum trailer continued to soar as the men discussed their predicament. Bruiser stood up, unzipped his flight suit to the waist, shrugged his arms and shoulders free, then tied the sleeves in a knot around his waist. He fanned his belly trying to cool off. A half hour later they heard the sound of a vehicle in the distance.

Horton craned his head out the doorway; he saw a pickup truck careening down the dirt road toward them. It stopped in front of the trailer, where a soldier got out and retrieved a cardboard box from the truck bed. He placed it at the foot of the trailer door and then drove away.

"Well, what have we here?" Horton said as he carried the box inside; he opened it and laughed. "Hey, Bruiser, you must have impressed the hell out of Colonel Stink." He held up a tiny battery powered fan, turned it on and waived it back and forth across his face. "Ah...much better!"

"Not a total bust; look what else we got," Aguilar said. He pulled out a plastic jug of lukewarm water, and a single bar of soap. "Guess that's for our shower." He then held up an olive drab tee shirt. "Hell, this would be tight on my eight-year-old nephew." Aguilar dug deeper. "And here's dinner: three cans of Spam and a bag of crackers." He found a note in the bottom of the box; he read it to himself, then handed it to Moselli.

The note read: "APOLOGIES. OTHER BUSINESS MORE IMPORTANT. NOT SO LUCKY TO SEE HELICOPTER TODAY. MAYBE IMPROVEMENTS TOMORROW."

CHAPTER 21

Monday evening
USS Grand Rapids

When he arrived at ICC2 (Integrated Command and Control 2), McGirt saw that the watch section had been cleared out; only Bill Draper and the ship's executive officer—a tall, wiry commander named Comiskey—were present. Both officers rose to attention.

"Carry on, guys. No need for formalities; we're at sea." The XO excused himself and left.

Bill Draper led McGirt to a pair of folding chairs in front of a monitor that had been placed on a rectangular metal table. Unlike the big video screen at the U.S. Embassy in Manila, the monitor was no bigger than that of a household desktop computer. A small camera was secured at its top with a clamp. Two free-standing microphones had been set on the table, together with headphones. Duct tape held the rig's wires together.

McGirt stepped back and evaluated the set up. "Skipper, do you think this Rube Goldberg contraption will work? I mean, cripes sake, we'll be talking with our Commander in Chief."

Draper's face reddened. "Wish we had something more sophisticated, Admiral, but this should do the job. I had our best electronics people hook it up. They weren't very confident with the satellite interface until that tech rep fellow, Dickle, heard them commiserating in the chow line and volunteered to help."

"Dickle? He doesn't have security clearance for something like this, does he?"

"Actually, he does, Admiral. And I've got to tell you, the guy may come across like a nerdy oddball, but he's pretty damn sharp."

"Huh. Did he ask what this was for?"

"Nope, never did. Just showed up with his bottle of Mountain Dew, mumbled a few words and then started plugging things in. Once he'd finished hooking up everything, he channelized the transceiver to the frequency we'd received from the White House communications office. He ran a test with those folks, then placed the unit in standby mode."

"Okay, good," McGirt said.

"After that, I had everyone leave except for XO and me; the MAA posted guards at the entrances, and then we powered the thing back up." Draper shook his head in amazement. "A few seconds later, we were staring at an empty conference table in the White House, with the Presidential Seal in the background." He pushed a button on the side of the monitor to bring it out of standby: the screen flickered, then came into focus; the setting was exactly as Draper had described.

McGirt noted the time. "They should be strolling in soon. By the way, Skipper, that's the White House Situation Room we're looking at."

Draper's eyes widened. "Geez, never imagined I'd ever see that place—and in real time to boot."

"Yes, it can be intimidating when you're inside with all the heavy hitters," McGirt said. "During my first meeting as a rookie on the National Security Council, SECDEF turned to me and asked a question about helicopter aviation. It was something real basic that any pilot could answer, but when I went to speak, my mouth went bone dry. I sort of choke-whispered a reply." McGirt chuckled at the memory. "Secretary Croft smiled, thanked me, and moved on to the next agenda item. A staffer must have sensed my embarrassment; they snuck up from behind and handed me a glass of water."

Draper's expression became dead-serious. "Sir, I'm not planning to speak unless someone asks me to."

McGirt patted him on the shoulder. "Skipper, that's the best strategy." He noticed that a couple bottles of water had been placed on the corner of the table, next to the monitor; he handed one to Draper. "Here—just in case."

The pair put on their headsets and waited. Moments later, a stream of aids swept through the Situation Room, setting folders in front of the empty seats. Then, the dignitaries filed in, led by Secretary of Defense Nathan Croft and Secretary of State Roscoe Depew. President Maxwell Black soon followed. As was his habit, he threw off his suit jacket and loosened his necktie.

"Alright, let's get started," Black growled.

McGirt noticed that the president looked like a different person than the one he'd bantered with the other day. His color was ashen and the dark bags beneath his eyes were swollen. His demeanor reminded McGirt of a man nursing a bad case of indigestion. The president thumbed through a few pages of his folder, then slid the file away. He set both elbows on the conference table, stared into the camera for a moment, then said, "And so, Rear Admiral Johnny Jack McGirt, here we are again." His tone conveyed not a hint of cordiality.

McGirt felt an unanticipated sense of anxiety; he cracked open his water bottle, took a deep swig and cleared his throat. "Good morning, Mr. President," he said with added firmness, hoping that his voice wouldn't crackle. "Sir, please allow me to introduce my host, Commander Bill Draper, commanding officer of USS *Grand Rapids*."

Black raised a hand from the table and said, "Hey, Skipper, nice to meet you."

"My pleasure, Mr. President," Draper replied.

The president leaned back in his chair and turned to Secretary Croft at his side. "Nate, bring these gentlemen up to date with what's going on, will you please?"

McGirt saw Secretary of State Depew sitting on the other side of the president. Depew sat ramrod straight, with hands folded on the table. He appeared bored.

"Admiral," Croft began, "There have been several developments since we last spoke with you. Tensions have increased with Communist China in the Taiwan Straits. We've dispatched two carrier battle groups to the region; the Chinese have two of their older carriers, *Liaoning* and *Shandong*, already on station. Sources tell us that their newest flattop, *Shanghai*, is also steaming to the region. Accordingly, we've upgraded the readiness level of all forces throughout the Pacific theater." Croft paused and turned to the president, who gave an affirmative nod. "That being said, the situation you were thrust into with the Chinese pilot was temporarily placed on the back burner." Croft set down his notes. "Admiral, we're ready to address that issue now."

"Thank you, Mr. Secretary," McGirt said. "I'm standing by for your instructions."

Croft glanced at Secretary Depew. "Roscoe...anything?" Depew shook his head "no" and checked his watch. "Okay, then we'll proceed. Chairman of the Joint Chiefs and CNO are at another meeting, so it will be the three of us here with you and the skipper. First, we want you to know how indebted we are, Admiral McGirt, for stepping up to the plate. Escorting a defecting foreign national would normally be well below your pay grade. We appreciate what you're doing."

The president rolled his hand in a circling motion, signaling Croft to pick up the pace. "Yes, sir, moving on. My staff is considering options about how to garner more information from Lieutenant Lin before turning him over. I'll get to that in a moment, but first, we want to share a video that we've received from our embassy in Beijing. I believe it speaks for itself." Croft pointed to a monitor that had been placed by the conference table. The Situation Room's camera shifted its view and zoomed in on the screen. A grainy, flickering image appeared.

McGirt and Draper recognized the face of Dick Moselli. A background voice said in broken English, "Stand together close..." After Moselli had read the prepared statement, the video faded to another setting. This segment of the presentation was of brilliant, clear quality and featured a slender, middle-aged Chinese gentleman standing at a podium. He wore a well-tailored, dark suit; his hair was styled in a fashion that would make any news anchor jealous. Behind him was a wall-sized world map, flanked by Chinese flags. The man introduced himself as a spokesman for China's president; his English was perfect, prompting Black to quip, "Look at this clown—he should be in Hollywood."

The spokesman reiterated the clumsily worded statement that Moselli had read, but in a smoother, more persuasive manner. He concluded by restating that Lieutenant Lin Yi should be extradited and returned to the custody of the People's Republic, or else the American helicopter crew would be detained indefinitely. The video concluded by fading into a peaceful scene of swaying palm trees and soothing music; the phrase, "Peace through Cooperation" scripted across the screen. The Situation Room's cameraman refocused on President Black.

"Well, there you have it, McGirt: more bullshit from our friends across the Pacific." Black said. He whispered something to Secretary Croft, who nodded and motioned for the president to continue. "We have thoughts about how to proceed, Admiral, but I want to hear what's on your mind after watching the video." Black propped his elbows on the table, rested his chin on his hands and said, "As Ross Perot once said, 'I'm all ears.'"

"Mr. President," McGirt began, "The return of our crew is, of course, paramount. That being said, I'd like to add that I personally know their senior member, Lieutenant Commander Moselli. He's as solid as they come, and by the looks of him and his crew, I don't believe they're in imminent danger."

Black interrupted. "Yes, I agree with you about Moselli." A grin crept from the corner of his mouth. "He reminds me of *another* Navy pilot I know. I think he and his men can sit this out for a few more days if necessary. But what's up with this Lin Yi character you've got onboard? Is it worth going after what he knows?"

McGirt took a moment to absorb what Black had asked. "Sir, if you're referring to the equipment on his jet, I'm not privy to that information."

"Oh, sorry, I jumped the gun," Black said. He turned to Secretary Croft again. "Nate, will you bring McGirt up to speed?"

Defense Secretary Croft summarized the report he'd received from Agent King and her team at Subic Bay; he described how they'd reached an impasse after deciding not to crack open the J-31's laser system. Croft finished by saying, "Admiral, we're faced with a dilemma: if we thought the laser system on Lin's jet was based on technology we already have, an exchange would be made today and Moselli's crew could get back to their ship. And frankly, nobody here would give a hoot if Lin was sent to the gulag, or someplace worse. But after reviewing the report from Subic—and consulting with the Joint Chiefs and their experts—I'm not quite ready to let someone with Lin's knowledge slip through our fingers." Croft turned to the president. "That's all I have to offer, Mr. President."

Croft's words seemed to have buoyed the president: he appeared more energized, and the witty twinkle in his eye that he was known for returned. "Okay, the ball's in your court now, McGirt," he said. "Or should I say, it's fourth and goal with the game on the line. What do you think we should do?"

McGirt had never been faced with such a critical question from anyone above him in the chain of command, let alone the President of the United States. He formulated his thoughts before answering. "Mr. President, if you're in agreement that Moselli's crew can wait it out for a few days, then I recommend that we get Lieutenant Lin back to Subic Bay, pry the information we need from him about his plane, and then go from there."

Secretary Depew rose out of his seat. "Admiral, are you suggesting that we physically threaten the man?" Depew's face reddened and his neck muscles tensed. "Well, answer me, Admiral, is that what you are advocating?"

McGirt found himself speechless. He regrouped and said, "Mr. Secretary, the president has asked for my recommendation, which I've provided...sir. The ultimate decision on Lin Yi's future should come from a higher authority than me."

Depew slunk back into his chair; a defeated scowl covered his face as his eyes shifted down to the table. "Mr. President, I have no further comment on this matter."

Black smiled. "Well done, McGirt. I couldn't have put it more diplomatically. You may have a place in politics someday…although I can't with good conscience encourage a nice fellow like you in that direction." He glanced over at Depew. "This swamp is filled with alligators." The president slapped his hands on the table. "Okay, McGirt, this is what we're going to do: get Lieutenant Lin back to Subic Bay ASAP. Tell him that, depending on how many beans he's willing to spill, he might, and I repeat, *he might,* buy himself a ticket to the U.S.A. I'll leave the details up to Secretary Croft, the Navy brass, and you."

"Mr. President, I'll get right on it," said Croft.

President Black retightened his necktie, stood up and donned his suit coat. Croft and Depew joined him on their feet. "Gentlemen, if you'd excuse me, please. I'm late for an Oval Office meeting with a group of Midwest farmers." He frowned. "Got to keep my supporters happy." An aide appeared to escort the president out, but before exiting, Black stopped in his tracks and leaned back into the camera frame. "And to be clear, Admiral, unless you and Croft can pull a rabbit out of a hat, this Chinese pilot will be exchanged for our guys sweating it out on that sandbar."

CHAPTER 22

It took less than twenty minutes to put the plan into motion. Secretary Croft connected with the Chairman of the Joint Chiefs of Staff and the Chief of Naval Operations. Encrypted movement orders were transmitted to all concerned and *Grand Rapids'* H-60 Seahawk detachment was assigned the mission of flying Admiral McGirt and Lieutenant Lin Yi to the Subic Bay airport. Secretary Croft had suggested that in the interest of time a speedy V-22 Osprey be dispatched, but tensions in the Straits of Taiwan had ramped up, which prompted the CNO to dissent: his two carrier strike group commanders insisted that they preserve all of their assets.

Other than those standing watch, the ship's crew was preparing to hit the rack when the signal for flight quarters was sounded. Sailors that comprised the launch crew hustled into their FRVs and mustered on the flight deck. *Grand Rapids'* air detachment was now led by Lieutenant Bobby Bale in the absence of Dick Moselli.

The same group that McGirt had watched service the H-60's tail section was tasked with moving the helicopter into position on *Grand Rapids'* sprawling flight deck. The aircraft was towed by a battery-powered tug tethered to a hand-held control box; the unit was called "MANTIS." Four safety observers, or "wing walkers," were stationed around the Seahawk: one on each side, one behind, and a fourth by the aircraft's nose. They all carried whistles and had the authority to signal "STOP!" if they believed the evolution had become unsafe. A pair of "brake riders" sat inside the cockpit. The movement was always conducted with great caution, regardless of the environmental conditions: when seas were calm and the flight deck was dry, the procedure could be a snap, however during foul weather or at night, there was a high risk of equipment damage or personal injury.

With the aircraft 'spotted,' sailors secured it to the deck with steel chains attached to each main landing gear. Fuel tanks were then topped off and the aircraft's auxiliary power unit (APU) was started; the Seahawk's four rotor blades were unfolded and its tail section was locked into place. Radios, navigation aids, and flight controls were energized and tested. Inside a compartment adjacent to the hangar, Lieutenant Bale and his co-pilot, a red-haired female named Dorothy Hill, donned their survival gear and briefed the flight plan.

McGirt found Lin Yi asleep and snoring when he returned to their stateroom. He flicked on the compartment's overhead lights and shouted, "Hey, wake up...now! If you want a chance at freedom, get the hell out of bed and get dressed."

Lin covered his eyes with a pillow and mumbled something in Mandarin. He sat up, taking care to not bang his head on the low ceiling. "What do you mean? The ship has entered lights out period." He pulled the pillow clear and glared at McGirt. "Did you not hear, it's our time to sleep!"

McGirt grabbed Lin's blanket and yanked it to the floor. He capped his irritation and said, "I know it's late, but we're flying you back to Subic Bay tonight; I want to see if you really have something to share or if you've been bullshitting all of us. Now get up and get dressed."

Lin Yi offered no further resistance; it was the first time that he'd experienced anything resembling anger from Admiral McGirt. He'd heard the same tone of voice from his flight leader the one time he'd accidentally spent too long eating lunch and was five minutes late for a flight briefing. After an ass-chewing by the squadron's commander, he hadn't been late for anything again—not ever. Lin hopped down and dove into the gear that Chief Durfee had provided: a fresh set of FRVs and spanking new black leather boots. He flashed McGirt a smiling thumbs up and said, "I am ready, Admiral, sir. Shall we depart?"

McGirt struggled not to laugh at Lin's sudden exuberance. "Yes, we shall depart," he said with a grin. He tossed a notebook into his gym bag, which now served as a de facto briefcase. Minutes later, he and Lin Yi met Bale and Hill in the hangar bay.

Bale waved them closer while the H-60's APU whined in the background; he raised his voice to be heard. "Admiral, we're pre-flighted and gassed up. Flight time to Subic Bay airport is about one hour. The ship's weather guesser tells me there's scattered thunderstorms in route, so we'll stay low over the water and use our radar to deviate around them. Any questions, sir?"

"No," said McGirt. He put an arm around Lin's shoulder and said, "Lin Yi, we don't have time to discuss anything beyond this flight. We will talk about your future after your obligations at Subic Bay."

Lin managed a faint smile and nodded that he understood; he followed the group onto the helicopter. A crewman guided McGirt and Lin to their seats and helped them don emergency floatation gear; he then handed each of them a cranial equipped with headset and microphone. Lin followed McGirt's lead and plugged into a nearby jack.

Bale and Hill whizzed through pre-start checks. Minutes later the H-60's powerful turboshaft engines were fired up and the aircraft's rotor blades were engaged. Bale requested takeoff clearance and was given a green deck while a marshaller stood in front of the chopper holding a lighted orange wand in each hand. The marshaller extended his arms to his side, parallel to the deck at shoulder height; he then waved his arms up and down over his head, signaling the pilot to lift into a hover.

Dorothy Hill was the pilot on the controls; she pulled up on the collective lever next to her left knee and made adjustments with the cyclic between her legs. As she did, she applied a smidgeon of pressure on the left rudder pedal to counter the helicopter's tendency to yaw right as the rotor blades' angle of attack increased. Hill established the aircraft in a drift-free hover a dozen feet above *Grand Rapids'* deck. The marshaller signaled a pedal turn to the left, then raised the wands above his head, spun them in a twirling motion and swept them toward the ship's port side. More collective was applied as Hill nudged the cyclic forward. The aircraft crept into the cool night air and climbed. McGirt was relieved when he felt a familiar shudder as the helicopter passed through a phenomenon known as translational lift. Engine and transmission noise subsided when Hill lowered the collective and leveled off. McGirt looked down through a window and guessed they were cruising a few hundred feet above the water.

The pilots completed after takeoff checklists, chatted about keeping a running fuel score, and rechecked the GPS coordinates for the Subic Bay airport. Bale flicked on the autopilot, then pressed his mike switch. "Hello, Admiral McGirt, do you read me?"

McGirt fumbled for his mike switch; he moved the microphone close to his lips and said, "Yes, Bobby, got you five by five."

"Great! Sir, would you like to sit up front for a while?"

McGirt unplugged his headset and sprang forward without answering. Hill climbed out of her seat and helped the admiral secure his safety harness as he settled in. He hollered a "thank you" as she retreated to the cabin.

"Thanks for the invite, Lieutenant," McGirt said on the ICS.

"You're welcome, sir. I figured you'd be more comfortable up here. If you don't mind me asking, are your aircraft quals current?"

McGirt craned his head to peek into the cabin; he saw that Hill and the crew chief were slouched over reading paperbacks under the illumination of their red-lensed flashlights; Lin Yi was staring back at him. McGirt turned around and searched the helicopter's communications panel. "Uh, Bobby...I forgot how to isolate our conversation. Where's the switch?"

Bale reached over and flicked a button. "Just the two of us now, sir. We can hear them, but they can't hear us."

"Okay, that's good," McGirt said. "You wanted to know if my aircraft quals were current? The short answer is 'no'. My last check ride in the Seahawk was two years ago. Since working in Washington, my rear end has been glued to an office chair—unless I'm on some off-the-wall goat rope like this."

"Got it, sir. Thanks for letting me know."

McGirt looked out through the windshield, then pointed at the radar screen. "Looks like the weather guesser was right; I see some action ahead."

Bale fidgeted with a couple dials on the radar unit. "Yes, sir, there's scattered storm activity thirty miles away that we'll have to jink around. I'm not worried about that stuff; more concerned about our approach into Subic." He changed presentations on the screen. "See, there's a strong cell sitting southwest of the field. We'll have to deal with it as we get closer."

"Okay, then you better get Dorothy up here for that." McGirt refocused on the radar. "Say, how'd you get it to display all the way to Subic? We're still far away and at a low altitude. I didn't think your equipment could look beyond the horizon."

"It can't. We're getting a live picture via satellite. This image is likely generated from a ground site near Subic or Manila."

"And in real time?"

"Yup. The airlines have had this capability for years."

McGirt shook his head. "Man, I could have used this back in my day. God only knows how many times I blasted like a dummy through the bottom of a thunderstorm."

"Yeah, these new weather tools are great." Bale added. "They make my job easier."

He saw lightning flashes in the distance and made a course correction to avoid the worst of the convective activity. The helicopter went through a short period of heavy rain and moderate turbulence as it skirted clear of a thunderstorm's core. Bale then made an entry in his fuel log; he confirmed that he had sufficient reserves to shoot two instrument approaches into Subic; if the weather deteriorated below landing minimums, he'd divert to Manila International, where conditions were better.

McGirt peeked back into the cabin again: Hill and the crew chief were still absorbed with their books, while Lin Yi appeared to be napping. He decided that this was the best time to talk business. "Bobby, I'm not permitted to discuss what I'll be doing at Subic other than to say it's very high priority and classified. Our passenger and I will be meeting with a group of officials."

"Copy that, Admiral," Bale said. "May I ask how long you expect we'll be on deck?"

"Not sure, but I hope we won't have to spend the night." McGirt flashed back to all the late-night flights he'd taken as a naval aviator, many times when he was dog-ass tired. He rekeyed his mike and said, "Bobby, this was a short-fused mission on the back side of the clock. How are you doing in the fatigue department?"

"Uh, I'm okay, sir. Dozed off for a while after chow, then had a cup of joe when I found out about this flight. Actually, I feel pretty good."

"How about your crew?"

"I asked if they were ready to fly; got a thumbs up from everyone."

"Okay, that's good to know." McGirt looked at the aircraft's clock. "How soon before we land?"

Bale checked the distance/time readout on the Seahawk's navigation system. "Looks like another twenty or so minutes. We should be in radio range of Subic approach control soon."

"Then that's my cue to give Dorothy back her seat," McGirt said. He undid his shoulder harness but left his headset connected while Bale summoned Hill. "Wish I knew of someplace where you and your crew could zone out while we're on deck. I think you'll have to hunker down in the aircraft."

"No problem, sir. I've logged several hours sleeping on the floor of Hotel Sikorsky. Admiral, one more thing before you leave: I've never flown into this airport. Any tips?" Bale held up a rectangular booklet of instrument flying procedures; it was part of a series of "approach plates" tailored for U.S. military and government aircraft. He turned up an overhead light. "I studied the Subic plates before we left." He found the chart that depicted the airport's layout, complete with runway, taxiways, and buildings; he pointed to the eastern boundary of the field. "Is this the area where you want to go?"

McGirt squinted to see better. "Yes, that's the spot." He pointed to a black rectangle on the chart that represented a hangar. "If you can set down near here, that would be perfect. After your approach, request an air taxi down the runway and make a right at the end; the hangar will be directly in front of you. I'll be on the ICS if you need help."

"Got, it. Thank you, sir."

McGirt swapped places with Hill. He took a seat next to Lin Yi and plugged in his headset; he heard Bale check in with Subic Bay approach control using the call sign of "Merlin Two." The air traffic controller cleared the flight for an instrument approach to runway 07 at Subic Bay International. Bale asked for a ten-degree left deviation from the final approach course to avoid a weather build up. The ride got rough as heavy rain pelted the H-60's aluminum airframe.

McGirt and Guts Gomez had enjoyed a picture-perfect, sunny day on their scenic flight from Manila. This flight could not have been more different: it was pitch black, raining, and windy. McGirt reached for his specs and leaned forward to observe Hill as she hand-flew the approach. He watched the aircraft's altimeter unwind: 400 feet...300...250. Suddenly, blackness gave way to the pulsing glow of the runway's lighting array. Bale reported "runway in sight," as Hill acknowledged, "Got it, I'm visual." She descended to 50 feet and air taxied to the runway's eastern end. Bobby Bale took over for the last segment.

Once he'd sighted the runway from his window, McGirt unstrapped and crouched between the two pilots. Bale had cranked up the aircraft's windshield wipers to their fastest setting for the approach; he left them that way as he taxied through the downpour.

McGirt pointed toward the hangar where Lin Yi's J-31 had been stashed. "Any place close to that hangar will do, Bobby. There won't be a marshaller to guide you, so take it slow and easy."

The three pilots strained to see through the windshield's watery blur. Bale keyed his mike and said, "Admiral, how about I set down next to that civilian chopper in front of the hangar door?"

"That's perfect; just leave those guys enough room to maneuver in case they leave before us."

"Got it, sir." Bale slewed the helicopter's taxi light back and forth to check for obstacles. The area to the east was wide open, so he drifted over to that spot of concrete and set down. Engines were secured, and the Seahawk's four rotor blades came to a stop. Absent the whine of engine and transmission noise, however, the scene was far from quiet: the pounding of thick raindrops made conversation difficult without the intercom.

McGirt took hold of Lin Yi's arm and reached for the cabin door. "Do you need a fuel truck, Lieutenant?" he shouted to Bale.

Bale hollered back. "No, sir, we're good. The OOD told me that the ship will be closing at forty knots; they should be within our range when we depart."

"Okay…just one more thing," McGirt yelled back. "Be ready to get airborne on short notice." He slid the cabin door open, squeezed Lin's arm and jumped to the pavement. He held on to Lin as they sloshed a dozen yards to the hangar. As they got nearer, someone inside pushed open a hatch recessed into the hangar's big steel door. McGirt ducked through it with Lin Yi in tow. The hangar's overhead lights were turned off, but he was able to make out the shadowy image of the disassembled aircraft propped up on jacks; a cadre of men carrying flashlights surrounded it.

McGirt felt someone tap him on the shoulder. He swiped the rain from his face, pivoted, and was greeted by a tall African-American woman wearing coveralls. "Hello, Admiral," she said while extending her hand. "I'm Agent Gwen King. Welcome to our midnight soiree."

* * *

McGirt had spent a good deal of time in the same hangar as a junior officer, and then again as a Detachment Officer-in-Charge. But that was decades ago when Subic Bay International functioned as U.S. Naval Air Station Cubi Point. As his eyes adjusted to the dim lighting, he saw how the building had deteriorated: mold covered its walls, the concrete floor was pitted, and the roof leaked like a sieve. Rain buckets were scattered across the deck; a plastic tarp had been suspended above Lin's J-31. Water cascaded from the tarp's low point into a fifty-five-gallon drum. McGirt realized that he still had hold of Lin Yi's arm. He released it and introduced Lin to King.

"Agent King, thanks for coordinating this evolution," he said. "I'd like you to meet Lieutenant Lin Yi of the People's Liberation Navy."

King extended the same greeting to Lin as she'd done with Admiral McGirt—a firm, no nonsense handshake. "I understand that you speak English," she said. "Is that correct?"

"Yes, it is. I've studied your language since my early age and spent two years at an American university."

"Well, that's a plus." King pointed to the J-31. "Then you should have no problem explaining what the hell kind of death ray is on that airplane." She clapped her hands together and said, "So, let's get to it!"

McGirt blocked her path. "Agent King, my briefing with the White House stated that Ambassador Remington would be on site. I think it's appropriate that he be part of this before we go any further. Where is he?"

"Of course, Admiral. Excuse me for putting the cart before the horse." She motioned to a far corner of the hangar. "Ambassador Remington is over there talking with the Boeing and Raytheon people." McGirt spotted the glow of three cigarettes in the darkness.

He'd crossed paths with Harold Remington twice: at the reception in Manila three days ago, and once at a social event in D.C; he recognized Remington's unmistakable baritone voice and hearty laugh. As he got closer, he noticed that the aviation reps appeared enthralled with the iconic billionaire. He heard Remington say, "Guys, that's my story and I'm sticking to it. Whatever you hear from those dipshits in the press…it's not true." The reps let out a roar. Remington patted them on the back and said, "Now, get back to work!" The men laughed again, then rejoined their coworkers under the tarp.

Remington turned to face McGirt and Lin Yi as they approached. "And here comes the brass; it's damn well about time!" He took a long, final drag from his cigarette, then crushed it on the deck with his shoe. He ignored Lin Yi as he grabbed McGirt's hand. "Admiral, how's your wife? I've heard that she's heading up the orthopedic surgery department at Walter Reed. Please extend my congratulations to her."

McGirt was surprised that Remington remembered him, let alone that his wife was a Navy doctor stationed in Washington. "Thank you, sir. I'll pass that on when I get home." He was about to introduce Lin Yi, when Remington shifted gears from charismatic charmer to sober diplomat: he touched Lin on the shoulder and said, "Lieutenant Lin, on behalf of the President of the United States, I offer my most sincere appreciation for what you are doing. I admire your courage and pledge to do everything possible to ensure your safety going forward."

Lin Yi smiled and started to speak, but Remington turned away and waved a hand toward Agent King; she signaled a thumbs up. "Now if you would, Lieutenant, cooperate and explain the weapons system inside your jet." His tone was cordial yet left no doubt what he expected. King walked across the hangar and escorted Lin to the aircraft.

Remington and McGirt stood together while King introduced Lin to Phil Lombardi of Boeing Aircraft. Remington pulled McGirt aside and said, "Admiral, you need to know something: Ambassador Wu's goon squad is out in town; it goes without saying that they'd love to get their hands on Lin." Remington's tone was all business. "Wu's staff tried to book them rooms at the hotel where King and her guys are staying, up the hill where officers' quarters used to be. Anyway, my people greased the hotel clerk's palm so she'd tell them the place was full and they'd have to go elsewhere."

"Olongapo?" McGirt asked.

Remington grinned. "Yeah, a place called the Marmont. Ever heard of it?"

"Of course. That was a favorite spot for enlisted guys when this was a Navy base. Most officers stayed in the BOQ on the hill, while the youngsters beat feet into town." McGirt's mind wandered back in time. "If I recall, Marmont was about half hotel, half whore house."

Remington laughed. "Yup, still is." He checked his watch. "I'd guess those boys have been well serviced and are sawing logs by now."

McGirt and Remington joined the group where Lombardi was revisiting how he and the other reps had broken down the J-31 but had stopped when they'd reached the core of its laser system. He raised his voice to be heard above the sound of heavy rain. "The readings I took were off the scale on my instruments…and that was from an arm's length away; I was afraid to get any closer." He turned to Lin and pointed to a gaping hole in the jet's fuselage. "Mister, how do you power down this unit so it can be removed?"

Lin Yi bit down on his lower lip; he faced McGirt and then turned to Gwen King. It was his moment of truth, but he appeared unsure of what to do.

After an awkward silence, Remington said, "Lieutenant, I hope you understand how important this is to your future." All friendliness had drained from his voice. "People have traveled great distances expecting you to reveal the secrets of your aircraft. And by the way, some of your countrymen are just a few miles from here; they're ready to take you into custody and put your ass on a plane back to China."

Sweat beads sprung from Lin Yi's brow. He took a deep breath and then moved toward the aircraft. He scaled the step ladder that mechanics had used to reach the cockpit. There was a void where Lin's ejection seat had been. He squatted on the bare cockpit flooring.

Gwen King raced up the ladder and grabbed Lin by the arm. "Hey, don't touch anything until we're able to watch you." She shouted to the men below, "We need a couple more ladders so Lombardi and the admiral can watch this too." Two step ladders were dragged across the floor and set in position. King pulled out her phone and pressed its camera's video record button. "Okay, Lieutenant, go ahead."

Lin unfolded a keyboard from the cockpit's left sidewall; he pressed a button on the top right corner of the device. After a few seconds, the jet's flight instrument display illuminated.

Lombardi threw his hands in the air. "Hell, I never thought of using the keyboard to power up the instruments; I kept poking around 'til I found the battery switch. Jesus!"

Lin stared at the aircraft's digital gauges. He mumbled something to himself, then looked up at McGirt. "Admiral, I will need an exact time signal from Greenwich. My cockpit clock must have stopped after the hard landing. In order to proceed, I will have to match exact Greenwich time to the separate chronometer built inside the jet's weapon system."

"I can handle that," King said. "My phone is synched up with a communication satellite and is accurate to the millisecond with Greenwich."

"Thank you, madam," Lin said. "I will need a time signal for the next rounded minute."

King turned to McGirt. "Huh? What's he saying?"

McGirt thought for a moment. "Lin Yi, do you mean minutes at ten, twenty, and so forth past the hour?"

"Yes, I misspoke my English. The more correct term is a time with a zero."

"Ok, that's easy enough," King said. "Let's see…that will be in about two minutes from now." She extended her phone so that Lin could see the digits as they counted. "What will you do then?" she asked.

"I will type in my military identification code and a password, wait for a prompt, and then enter other numbers and symbols."

McGirt looked down and saw Harold Remington standing nearby with the other reps. Remington had a fresh cigarette dangling from his lips. "You'll have to give us all of those numbers for future use; you understand that don't you, Lieutenant? That's the deal," he said.

Lin nodded. "Yes, I will comply."

"Thirty seconds to go," King said. She counted down the last seconds: "Five, four, three, two, one, mark."

Lin began typing a series of characters and numerals. The screen flashed a rightward arrow symbol, prompting him for more input. He paused for a second, and then entered a lengthy string of numbers and characters. When finished, he leaned back and waited.

"What's it doing now?" Lombardi asked.

"Authenticating. That will take about twenty seconds."

Soon, Mandarin symbols spilled across the screen in rapid succession, then a bold image of China's red and yellow flag appeared. The image blinked three times, then disappeared, leaving the screen blank.

"In one minute, the shroud guarding the laser unit will begin to de-energize," Lin said. He faced McGirt. "Admiral, tell your people to remain clear for another thirty minutes while the de-energizing process takes place. It will then be safe to remove the laser and its capacitor from the airframe."

McGirt and Lombardi climbed down while Agent King leaned into the cockpit and said, "Lieutenant, we'll need to duplicate the authentication codes you typed; I want you to write everything down."

Lin rose from the cockpit and followed her down the ladder. His jaw muscles tensed. "Yes, madam, I will record it for you." A pained expression spread over his face. "But I can assure you that I will never forget what I typed."

"Really? Is there a significance to the code?"

"Yes, it is the names and birthdates of my parents."

As the group dispersed from under the tarp, Remington's phone rang; he answered it and stepped away to talk. He hung up quickly and hollered, "Admiral, you need to hightail it out of here with Lin, and I mean now!"

"Why, what's going on?"

Remington held up his phone. "One of my moles at the Marmont called to tell me Wu's guys just hopped into a taxi and are headed this way. Somebody must have tipped them off."

McGirt grabbed Lin Yi by the arm started for the door. "Let's go, we need to get you back to the ship."

Lin broke free. He reached out to Remington. "Take me to the U.S. Embassy…please. Won't I be safer there?"

McGirt saw hesitation in the ambassador. But after a few seconds, Remington regrouped and said, "Lin Yi, that's impossible. My flight crew has secured for the night and are not available." He took hold of Lin's shoulder. "Your best option is to go back to the ship with the admiral. America cannot grant you asylum while you are on foreign soil."

"Then I will seek protection here in the Philippines," Lin countered.

Remington shook his head. "No, I most strongly advise against that. President Diaz would have already offered you asylum if he had wanted to." Remington turned to McGirt. "Admiral, trust me on this: Diaz is doing a balancing act; he's committed to holding the jet while we analyze it, but that's all. He really doesn't give a rat's ass about the welfare of a defecting Chinese pilot." Remington's phone buzzed again. "Son of a bitch, Wu's people are two minutes away."

McGirt yanked Lin's arm and double timed to the helicopter; he heard rotor blades already spinning. Agent King met them as she came in from outside. "Admiral, I told your crew to fire up and be ready to go," she said.

"Thanks, Gwen. We're out of here."

McGirt and Lin rushed out into the rain and leapt through the chopper's cabin door. Bobby Bale lifted into a hover as they stumbled to their seats. The crew chief helped them strap in as Bale spiraled up to 100 feet, dipped over the nose and pulled full power with the collective. The Sikorsky H-60 rocketed forward and accelerated to its maximum airspeed before it reached the field's western boundary. McGirt put on a headset to check in with the cockpit. "Thanks for being ready, guys."

Dorothy Hill answered. "No worries, Admiral." She pressed some buttons on the navigation gear. "Ship's going balls to the wall toward Subic; estimate overhead in fifteen minutes."

McGirt peeked over her shoulder and located the radar scope. "How's the weather?"

"Looks good, sir. The storm's dissipating; other than a few light showers, we should have clear sailing all the way."

McGirt breathed easier and leaned back in his seat. "Thanks. You guys are great."

Bobby Bale keyed his mike. "Just another day at the office, Admiral."

Bale leveled off at 300 feet and clicked on the autopilot. The ride was smooth; stars poked through the night's scattered clouds.

McGirt looked across the cabin and saw Lin Yi sitting with arms folded over his chest; his eyes were focused on the deck; his face was that of a defeated man.

McGirt motioned for Lin to plug in his headset, then said, "Can you hear me, Lin Yi?"

Lin raised his eyes. "Yes, I hear you...Admiral. I hear you loud and clear, the same way I heard the ambassador."

"I know you're not happy with how this is working," McGirt said. "All I can tell you is to be patient; the game isn't over yet."

The words seemed to buoy Lin's spirits. He keyed his mike again. "If the men examining my jet accomplish procedures as I told them, they will be able to remove the laser generating system without damaging it. What they are capable of doing after that, I cannot guarantee."

McGirt couldn't decipher what Lin was implying. He let the comment slide, then said, "Okay, we'll talk more when we get back aboard ship."

CHAPTER 23

Tuesday
0500 hours
USS Grand Rapids

Grand Rapids raced across the ocean at flank speed. Its two gas turbines and pair of diesel engines pumped water through four jets, propelling the vessel at a speed on par with a nuclear-powered aircraft carrier. Its three aluminum bows sliced through the glassy sea like hot knives through butter. Astern, the phosphorescent glow of a giant rooster tail cast a ghostly haze against the backdrop of the night's moonless sky.

Lieutenant Michelle Perks rose from her Officer-of-the-Deck chair and stepped with caution onto the starboard bridge wing; the blast of cool air felt nice against her face. She took in the heavenly view: a magnificent display of the Milky Way Galaxy unblemished by the light pollution of civilization. Perks glanced back into the bridge where the Junior-Officer-of-the-Deck sat in a high-backed chair studying a computer screen that monitored the ship's intricate systems.

The thrill of a highspeed run prompted Perks to offer a silent thank you to the detailing officer who'd assigned her to the state-of-the-art vessel. Her initial disappointment of not being ordered to a cruiser or frigate soon faded as she became more familiar with *Grand Rapids'* unique capabilities. She loved life at sea and embraced the intimacy of the LCS's small crew. Perks reached behind her head and unfastened the barrette that held her auburn hair in a tight bun. She shook her locks unabashedly in the breeze. She heard a deep male voice from behind her.

"Miss Perks, you're out of uniform!" Michelle turned to see her commanding officer standing in the open hatchway; Bill Draper joined her on the wing. She scrunched her hair into a haphazard knot and shoved the barrette back into place.

"Sorry, Captain. I'm overdue for an appointment with the barber; the regs say 'collar length', and not a centimeter longer."

Draper nudged her on the arm. "Not to worry, Lieutenant, I was busting your chops. With everything going on, I don't have time to be the haircut police. Just wanted to let you know that ICC picked up Bale on radar; he's ten minutes out."

"Thanks, Captain. We set flight quarters about a half hour ago; I'll have my JOOD give an update over the 1MC." Perks leaned back inside and gave the order. Seconds later, the announcement blasted over the ship's master communications system. She then directed the JOOD to slow to a speed compatible with the aircraft's wind limitations for landing.

Perks started for her station on the bridge, until Draper said, "No hurry, Lieutenant: your JOOD is doing a fine job, the tower is manned, and the recovery crew is in place. Everyone is where they should be. Why don't you hang out here for a few minutes and let your people do their jobs?"

Perks moved back to her spot next to Draper on the wing. She realized that the captain was right: she needed to do a better job of trusting her subordinates; it was a leadership trait that Bill Draper had strived to instill with his officers, and a quality that she admired in the man. "Yes, sir. We've got the best view on the ship, standing right here." Soon, the chopper's twinkling beacon and position lights emerged from the inky darkness; the lights grew brighter and brighter as the aircraft sped toward them.

"Wow, he's hauling ass!" Draper said.

Bale's helicopter was bore-sighted straight at them at eye level. At what seemed like the last moment, it broke off to one side and climbed. Perks and Draper felt a rumble beneath their feet as the aircraft thundered out of view.

"Damn hotdogs!" Draper shouted.

Perks followed him back inside the bridge. She grabbed a microphone and said, "Tower, bridge. Do you have the helo in sight?"

A shaky voice replied, "Yes, ma'am. They whizzed past us like a scaled dog; scared me half to death. Looks like they're slowing down and turning back toward the ship now."

"Copy that," Perks said. "Say your winds?"

"Ah…wind is…zero three zero at two-two knots."

Perks glanced over at the captain, who was engaged in conversation with the JOOD. "Okay, give them a green deck."

"Copy, ma'am, green deck." The tower operator pressed a button that changed the deck status lights from 'red' to 'green.'

Perks walked into ICC One, where a monitor displayed the flight deck. A marshaller appeared at the bottom of the screen; their arms signaled Bale's aircraft forward. The H-60 crept into view on the screen, came to hover and set down.

"I'm going down to meet the crew," Draper said. "Officer of the deck, maintain present course and speed."

"Aye, aye, Captain," Perks said, then announced, "Captain's off the bridge!"

* * *

As Draper passed through the hangar bay, he noticed Leonard Dickle seated on a stool, tinkering with a component inside the Fire Scout. Dickle looked up and gave a perfunctory wave. Draper wondered why on earth the fellow was working at this hour, but he wasn't surprised—Dickle seemed to live in his own private world.

The recovery team swarmed around the helicopter in preparation for post flight duties, which included a freshwater wash of engine inlets to remove salt residue, plus the inspection of oil and hydraulic reservoir levels. After that, rotor blades would be folded and the aircraft would be towed into the hangar.

McGirt and the crew chief deplaned through the helicopter's cabin door. Then the two cockpit doors swung open; Bobby Bale emerged from the right side, followed by Dorothy Hill, who hopped out from the left. Draper watched as McGirt turned and went back into the aircraft; he re-emerged with Lin Yi, holding him by the arm. The pair began walking toward the hangar when Lin yanked his arm away, shouted something at McGirt, and continued alone. Draper saw anger on Lin's face as he stomped by.

Draper stood fast as McGirt approached. "Admiral, with all due respect, what the heck is going on?" he asked.

McGirt took off his cranial and swiped a palm over his bristly flattop. "Well, our dear friend was expecting a first-class ticket to the U.S.A. instead of a chopper ride back to the ship." McGirt straightened the collar of his cammies. "Skipper, I'll give you a thorough briefing ASAP, but right now, I have to corral that guy before he jumps overboard." McGirt hustled to catch up with Lin.

Draper walked further onto the flight deck where he found Bobby Bale talking with the air detachment's maintenance chief. He let the pair finish without interrupting. When they were done, he said, "Welcome back, Lieutenant. How was the flight?"

"Sir, everything went as planned. Ran into some rough weather going into Subic where it was raining cats and dogs. Nice ride coming back, though."

Draper slapped Bale on the back and said, "You've had a long day, Lieutenant. Go get some rest."

* * *

The smell of greasy food wafted through the corridor as McGirt trudged to his stateroom. One of the cooks saw him walk by and poked his head out from the galley. "Admiral, we're just starting to prepare morning chow, but I'd be happy to get you something now if you'd like."

"Very kind of you to offer, sailor, but no thanks," McGirt said. He'd been awake for over twenty-four hours and was neither sleepy nor hungry, so he ducked into the wardroom and poured himself a cup of black coffee. As he stood at the counter, he debated whether or not to track down Lin Yi. Common sense prevailed as he reasoned: *Where the hell can Lin go, anyway? And if the guy decides to jump overboard, he's not my problem anymore.* McGirt finished his coffee, then sprawled out on the wardroom's sofa. He relished the solitude until Leonard Dickle burst through the door.

"Howdy, Admiral, sir. Say, I passed the Chinaman in the hallway, and boy, did he look pissed. Guess things didn't go so well in Subic, huh?"

McGirt recoiled at Dickle's insolence. Flat out of patience, he snapped, "And what the sweet Jesus does it matter to you?"

Dickle stepped back. "Ah...no disrespect intended, Admiral. I was just commenting that—"

"Mister, you'd be best served to mind your own business."

A pall fell over the room until one of the ship's junior officers came in carrying a tray stacked with food; his face was flushed with cheeriness. "Good morning, Admiral." He held up his meal as if it were gold. "The cooks whipped up some fine-looking waffles. Sure beats the usual slop. Sir, can I get you a plate?"

McGirt couldn't help but smile at the youngster's joyfulness. "No thanks, son. I'm good."

"Hmm...waffles?" Dickle said as he slinked toward the door.

But before Dickle left, McGirt felt the need to reach out after their dustup. "Hey, Leonard, when we landed, I saw you working on some black boxes inside the Fire Scout. What's going on?"

Dickle leapt at the opportunity to talk about himself. "Matter of fact, sir, I think I'm on to something big, and I mean *mega big*. I've been toying with a new encrypted satellite link that will be a breakthrough for controlling UAVs."

"Oh?"

"Yes, sir. Not bragging, but I think it will surpass anything our military has."

"Really? Better than the Chinese? Sources tell me that they're a generation ahead of us in that department."

Dickle smiled ear to ear. "What I've devised will leave the Chi-Coms spinning in circles. I'd be happy to give you a rundown after chow."

"Yeah, I'd like to hear about that." McGirt checked his wristwatch. "I've got some calls to make. How about we meet in the hangar at 0900?"

"You got it, Admiral. See you then."

CHAPTER 24

Tuesday
Aircraft carrier Shanghai

The topic of Lin Yi's defection had slipped from its number "1" position to "2" on Commissar Han's hand-written list of priorities. With China's potential invasion of Taiwan taking center spot on the world stage, he cursed the traitorous pilot for what he'd done—not only for defecting, but for taking his top secret jet with him. *As if I don't have enough to worry about,* Han lamented.

The commissar hadn't left his stateroom for two days: he had the luxury of his own private head, and when he got hungry, he picked up a phone and ordered food from the ship's galley. He'd spent most of the night studying teletyped messages from Beijing and updated readiness reports from *Shanghai*'s air boss. When reveille sounded, Han was drinking the morning's third cup of strong tea; the ashtray on the corner of his desk overflowed with cigarette butts.

Han heard two soft knocks followed by the creaking of his stateroom door as it opened. He didn't bother looking up from his work; he knew it was Captain Song. Not another soul on the ship would have had the balls to enter his space without an invitation. "Bulldog, I was hoping you'd stop by. How goes our cherished *Shanghai*?" Han said.

Captain Song held out a pack of cigarettes and shook it until a couple filter tips popped out. Han had thrown in the towel with trying to quit; he nodded a "thank you" and lit up. Song joined him.

"You look like dog crap," said Song. "When was the last time you got a full night's sleep?"

Han sucked in a deep drag, held the smoke in his lungs, then exhaled to one side. "Probably the night before Lin flew the coop. We had not yet received orders to the Straits; flight ops had secured, and we shared a good meal in your stateroom."

"Ah, yes. We toasted the Party Chairman with a shot of that good Scotch you'd bought in Singapore."

Han smiled at the memory. "Something tells me that we won't be toasting anything for some time." The happiness left his face. "Bulldog, we may be on the brink of war."

"That's why I came to see you, Commissar," said Song. "If you have a moment, may we discuss the situation?"

"By all means. I've been reading dispatches from Beijing but have not received any updates in the last hour. What's on your mind?"

Captain Song pulled a small notebook from his pants pocket. "First things first: as you know, we've been placed on an elevated state of readiness. The morning launch got off without a hitch. Additional flight crews have assembled in their ready rooms and are awaiting instructions."

"Very well, Captain. I trust that the pilots have put Lin's defection behind them?"

Song grimaced. "Not entirely. Air Officer Lu has put out word that Lin was lost at sea, but I don't think our flyboys are buying that explanation."

"What about Yang Chen?"

"Yang has been confined to quarters and will be flown off the ship. If he knows what's good for him, he'll keep his mouth shut."

Han took another long draw from his cigarette, butted it out, then emptied the ashtray into a trash can. "Okay, then. It sounds like you've got your vessel prepared for the worst case, Captain. Let's get our ducks in a row concerning other issues."

Han motioned for Song to move closer to better see his priority list. "With the Lin situation on the back burner for the time being, we are free from that mess and can concentrate on more critical matters. That brings me to the current situation. Our two other aircraft carriers have arrived on station." He unfolded a map of Taiwan which encompassed the Straits and extended to the east coast of the Chinese mainland. "*Liaoning* and *Shandong* have taken positions on the island's eastern coast, while we're here on the west side." He slid an index finger down an imaginary line that bisected the body of water that separated Taiwan from mainland China. "*Shanghai* and the rest of our surface forces have been ordered to remain clear of this accepted buffer line in the Straits."

Song was already aware of what Han was covering, yet out of respect for his commissar, he allowed him to continue without interrupting. After a pause, he asked, "What about our landing force?"

"Ah, yes." Han pointed to the Chinese port city of Fuzhou, located across the Straits, 250 kilometers from Taiwan's capital, Taipei. "Our amphibious forces are standing by and ready to deploy on a moment's notice."

The men studied the map in silence. They knew it would not be a cake walk if Beijing gave the order for an assault of the "rebel island." Intelligence reports had confirmed that the Taiwanese military was on high alert and bolstered by U.S. forces and other allies.

Han read Captain Song's mind. "And of course, we are not alone in these waters. Two U.S. carrier strike groups—one off the shores of Taipei, the other guarding the island's western flank—are prepared to render a counter assault on our naval forces."

"And the Japanese?" Song asked.

Han shuffled through documents on his desk and held up a stack of photographs taken by Chinese surveillance satellites. "Our Asian brothers have dispatched two carriers, *Izumo* and *Kaga*, that are rendezvousing with the American ships." He handed one of the photos to Song.

Captain Song donned his glasses and held the picture closer. "I knew they had contracted with the Americans to purchase F-35s." He counted the jets staged on *Izumo*'s flight deck. "But, damn, I didn't realize they had so many." He set down the picture and turned to Han. "Considering what the Japs have, combined with the Americans' F-18s and F-35s..." His face blanched as he said, "If we go to battle, our pilots will be tested."

"They certainly will," Han added. "Our best defense against that type of air power would be the laser system that Lin Yi has developed. But if the Americans seize that technology..." Han's gaze drifted to the deck; the fact that Lin's jet was in foreign hands drove home the stark reality that the J-31's weapons system had been compromised.

Captain Song stood up to leave. He gave Han a caring squeeze on the shoulder. "We've got a couple of hours before the next update from Beijing, Comrade; allow yourself to rest."

Han rose to shake his friend's hand. He eyed his bed and said, "Thank you, Captain. I know that *Shanghai* is in good hands."

* * *

Dick Moselli woke from another fitful night of sleep; his body was drenched in sweat. As he emerged from slumber, he realized that the clanking and pounding that he thought had been part of a dream was in fact real. "You guys hear that?" he hollered above the commotion.

Aguilar shouted from the far end of the trailer, "I don't want to get too excited, but I see a couple soldiers unloading an A.C. compressor. Miracle of miracles, it looks like Colonel Stink came through."

Horton joined Aguilar at the window. "Yup, our prayers have been answered, Bruiser. Now if we could get some running water and decent chow."

Moselli got up from his soggy bunk, wrapped a towel around his naked body and met Aguilar and Horton in the living room; there was a knock on the door. "Well, the surprises just keep coming, don't they?" he said with a snide laugh. He opened the door and was greeted by Captain Gao.

Gao stood at the base of the steps, smiling. "Good morning, Lieutenant Commander. Colonel wants to thank you for the cooperation."

"Cooperation for what?" Moselli said.

"The movie that we made of you and the others. The colonel is most appreciating." Gao's smile grew wider as he held up a paper bag. "I bring you more American food, like you have requested. May I please come inside?"

Moselli waved Gao in. "Sure, mi casa es su casa."

Gao returned the greeting with a dazed expression. "Yes, of course, as you say."

Horton grabbed the bag and shook it upside down; three hockey puck sized items wrapped in aluminum foil fell onto the kitchen table. Horton tore into one. "Looks sort of like a breakfast sandwich." He separated the two doughy pieces that held it together and sniffed. "Smells a little funky, but I'll give it a try." He took a tiny bite and chewed. "Uh... spam and eggs maybe?"

Gao nodded enthusiastically. "That is most correct. The cook found a box of eggs, added water and cooked in a pan. Do you like?"

Horton hesitated before rendering a verdict. He looked at Moselli. "McDonalds got nothing to worry about, but it ain't half bad." He tossed sandwiches to Aguilar and Moselli.

Aguilar started eating while Moselli set his aside. "So, that's our reward... breakfast?"

"Oh, no, there is more news to tell you," Gao said. "Colonel has received order for...how do you say...a swap."

Aguilar dropped his food. "Are you telling us that we're going to be released?"

Gao's smile widened further. "Yes, that is most correct. I have come to drive Lieutenant Commander to the helicopter."

Horton stood up and pointed to Aguilar. "What about us?"

Gao's smile faded. "So sorry, but that is not possible. Colonel says that just your leader for now. Other two later."

Moselli saw the dejected look of the men's faces. His crew hadn't been separated since they'd lifted off *Grand Rapids'* flight deck. He felt like a dad abandoning his kids. "You sure they can't come with me?" he asked.

Gao shook his head. "Colonel says only you."

"For how long?"

"Colonel did not tell me." Gao lowered his voice as if sharing a secret. "I think to prepare helicopter to fly."

Horton shot up from his seat. "Damn straight! Time to get the fuck out of here!"

Moselli headed for his bedroom to get dressed. He'd rinsed out his underwear and white athletic socks with the bottled water they'd been given, then set them on a chair to dry. The items felt clammy as he slipped them on. He'd neglected to wash his flight suit; its green fabric was stiff and crusty with dried sweat. With flight boots on and laced, he walked back out into the living area. He caught the eyes of Aguilar and Horton. "Guys, I'll see you when I see you. Enjoy your breakfast."

The drive in Gao's open-air jeep took longer than Moselli had expected; he'd forgotten that the trailer complex was on the opposite end of the island from where he'd landed his aircraft. He took the opportunity to survey the sights: the building projects that the Americans had observed during their walk appeared to have expanded; the cargo ship they'd spotted at the pier had been replaced by another vessel—this one looked double the size. Ten minutes into the drive, they slowed down to allow a backhoe to cross in front of them; a three-person working party lugging shovels followed close behind. One of the men stopped in his tracks when he spotted Moselli.

"Hey, Gao, isn't that the man that flew in with us?" Moselli said.

Gao slowed the jeep. "Yes, that may be him. There are many people from other countries that work on our island."

Moselli spun around in his seat and yelled, "Salid...Salid, is that you?"

Salid Alonto burst into happiness at the sound of Moselli calling his name. He dropped his shovel and started running toward the jeep until another man caught up and held him back. Captain Gao shouted something at them, then gunned the motor.

"Gao, why the hell did you do that?" Moselli said.

"Workers cannot speak up without permission," Gao said. He kept the gas pedal floored as they bounced over the gravel road. "You do not understand, sir. That man who you recognized...he is lucky." Gao's tone lost all friendliness. "He is lucky that Colonel did not dispose him."

Dick Moselli realized that Gao was dead serious. He asked, "Does that man have something to do with why we are being held prisoners?"

Gao ignored the question. After a long pause, he said, "Lieutenant Commander Moselli, if you and your people wish to leave, do not ask me that again."

"Okay, I get it. I won't ask." Moselli decided to change the topic. "How much further until we reach my helicopter?"

"Your helicopter is around the next corner," Gao said as they took a wide swing to the right. The pitted dirt road transformed to a smooth asphalt surface.

Moselli spotted his aircraft a few hundred yards ahead. A flatbed truck was parked alongside the chopper, together with a forklift, which was unloading steel drums. He saw Colonel Stink standing next to the aircraft; Stink's arms were folded across his chest as he watched the drums being lifted off the truck and set on the concrete landing pad. A platoon of soldiers was gathered nearby.

Gao parked the jeep clear of the pad. As Moselli got out, he saw the colonel jogging toward him. Stink had already worked up an early morning sweat.

"Ask him what's going on here," Moselli said to Gao. But before Gao could speak, the colonel launched into an animated rant; he waived his arms toward the sky, then pointed to the helicopter.

Dick Moselli stood by, clueless as to what was happening. The colonel finally stopped talking. He got closer, flashed a mouthful of bad teeth, and extended his hand. Dumbfounded, Moselli shook it.

"He said that negotiations have concluded, and you are released," Gao announced. "Also, Colonel says the People's Republic wishes you good luck and charm."

Moselli chuckled at Gao's odd phrasing then said, "Uh...Captain Gao, what are those men doing to my aircraft?"

"They are delivering petroleum to you. We do not yet have a fuel station constructed to refill airplanes."

Moselli counted a string of ten fuel drums along the aircraft's left side. A pair of soldiers were inserting a hand-cranked pumping device into one drum; at the soldiers' feet were a long hose and nozzle. They attached the hose to the pump, then searched for a place on the helicopter to plug in.

Moselli hustled toward the fuelers. He yelled over his shoulder, "Gao, tell those men to stop what they're doing; I will help." Gao cupped his hands around his mouth and shouted; the men set down the hose.

Moselli had never refueled an aircraft by himself, but he'd watched it done hundreds of times. He took a long shot when he said to Gao, "Tell the colonel that I need my crew chief and copilot here to assist me."

Gao translated; the colonel shook his head. "Only you now. Others can come when we do swap."

Curiosity about "the swap" almost got the best of Moselli, but he'd resolved not to ask questions and delay things further: the task at hand was to get fuel into his aircraft's depleted tanks. The job would have to be accomplished by the gravity method instead of the much faster pressurized procedure used aboard ship. But Moselli had two issues to contend with: first, he wanted to verify that the fuel was compatible with his helicopter, otherwise there was a risk of fouling the aircraft's engines; and second, he needed to check the fuel for contamination. He scanned the drum's labeling for the fuel's specifications, but the words were written in Chinese characters. "Will you ask the colonel, what type of fuel this is?" he said to Gao.

Upon hearing Captain Gao's translation, the colonel snarled and started hollering at Moselli. "It is the same petroleum used by our airplanes and helicopters," Gao said. The colonel grunted a couple more sentences. "Colonel said to tell you that he is not a stupid person; it is JP...jet propulsion."

Moselli acknowledged the colonel with a polite smile. "Thank you; that's good. And please tell the colonel that I do not think he is stupid. He has my respect."

Gao translated; the colonel mumbled something and gave a curt nod. "Colonel says he accepts your apology," Gao relayed.

The soldiers had confused looks on their faces as they gripped the hose. Moselli showed them where the gravity fueling port was on the aircraft's left side, just aft of the cabin door. One fellow started to insert the nozzle, until Moselli stopped him.

"There is no disrespect, Gao, but it is customary to always check the fuel for contaminants before filling the tanks." As soon as the words left his mouth, Moselli thought, *Now, how the hell am I going to do that?*

Gao conferred with his boss, then shook his head. "Colonel tells me he does not understand."

Moselli got an idea. He took hold of the cabin door and said, "I would like to get something from inside if that is okay." The Colonel nodded his approval.

Once inside the aircraft, Moselli poked around his seat until he found what he wanted: an empty, clear plastic water bottle. He turned it upside down and shook; it was bone-dry. He jumped down from the helicopter and held up the bottle. "We will use this to do the test. Gao, ask the men to turn the crank slowly so I can fill the bottle this far." He pointed a finger two-thirds up the bottle.

After more interpreting, Colonel Stink consented. One of the soldiers turned the pump's handle while the other held the hose nozzle over the bottle. The nozzle was wider than the bottle's opening, so a few ounces of JP splashed over Moselli's hand.

"Okay, okay, that's great!" Moselli shouted. He held a thumb over the top and shook the bottle before emptying it on the pavement. He motioned for the soldiers to repeat the process. When the level reached a couple inches from the bottle's top, he signaled the pump man to stop. The event went smoother this time, just a few drops were spilled. Moselli then swirled the sample until a vortex appeared inside the bottle. He held it at eye level and examined the fuel for evidence of contamination. It looked perfect: no dirt or water droplets spinning on the bottom. He helped insert the nozzle into the fueling port, gave a thumbs up to the colonel and said, "Let's do it!" No translation was necessary; the colonel waived his hand and the fueling began.

Moselli made an educated guess of how much remained in the tanks when they'd landed; the system's "low fuel" warning had come on during the approach, so he knew the rough quantity. Rather than do the math for a specific amount, he told Gao to have the men keep pumping until the tanks were full.

Gao's men shared the work of cranking the hand pump. The left tank required almost three drums; the forklift driver repositioned another three drums to the right side. After a half hour of manual pumping, both tanks were topped off.

"Okay, what's next?" Moselli asked. A satisfied expression filled the colonel's face as he strolled over and opened one of the cockpit doors. He gestured for Moselli to get in.

Moselli looked at Gao for guidance. "What does he want me to do?"

"Colonel says he wants you to start the engines and spin blades," Gao said. "Make confident everything works."

Moselli saw that the soldiers that had been standing off to the side had put on their helmets and cinched up their gear. They spaced themselves evenly around the landing pad's perimeter, assumed the prone firing position, and aimed their rifles at the helicopter.

Moselli climbed aboard and strapped in. The colonel continued holding open the cockpit door while directing an animated harangue at Gao. When he'd finished, Gao took a breath, then spoke. "Colonel says take your time to do your job; run the helicopter for five minutes and then stop the motors." The colonel said something in a low voice to Gao, then turned away. "And one more thing from Colonel: do not try funny business or you will be shot from the sky." Moselli rolled his eyes. Before he could reply, Stink slammed the door closed and walked clear of the pad.

It became obvious to Moselli why Aguilar and Horton hadn't been allowed to come with him to the chopper: the colonel knew that he wouldn't fly away without them. He guessed that the rifle squad had been assembled as an added layer of intimidation.

Dick Moselli hadn't performed a startup procedure without another pilot sitting next to him since his solo flights in a prop trainer as a student in Pensacola. He pulled out a checklist and began reading through a list marked "Prestart Checks." He read the challenges and responses out loud. Hearing a voice, albeit his own, seemed to evoke a sense of calmness and routine. When he'd reached the step to start the helicopter's auxiliary power unit, he donned his helmet and plugged in its mike and headset chords. Instinctively, he turned on the aircraft's radio and dialed up the frequency for *Grand Rapids*.

Captain Gao bolted toward the aircraft and pounded on the cockpit door window. "Colonel wants to know what you are doing with helmet on." He swept his arm in a wide arc. "Men will shoot you down if you try to depart. Colonel must give permission before flight."

Moselli took off his helmet; he saw nervousness in the officer's eyes. "Captain Gao, there is nothing to worry about," he said. "When I start the auxiliary power unit and engines, there will be a lot of noise. I must wear my helmet so that I can listen to the aircraft systems and confirm they are functioning." He tried to speak in basic terms that the soldier could understand. Gao stared at him for a moment, then pivoted to his boss and yelled a few words. The colonel threw up his hands, then pointed to his wristwatch.

"Go ahead and wear the helmet. Colonel says spin the blades for five minutes, then stop them." Gao waved a finger: "And no funny business!"

Moselli gave an exaggerated thumbs up. "Right! No funny business. I got it!" He shut the door and put his helmet back on while Gao trotted clear and stood next to the colonel. He then worked his way down the lengthy checklist. The APU was started, followed by the H-60's two turboshaft engines. All that remained was to release the rotor brake and advance the engine power control levers. "Here goes," he said to himself. Once hydraulic pressure was removed from the brake pucks, the aircraft's four rotor blades began spinning; Moselli glanced up and watched the tips of the blades swirl from right to left. He moved his left hand to the pair of power levers and slid them forward slowly. A few seconds later, the helicopter's rotor system was fully engaged.

Moselli guarded the collective with his left knee, then turned up the radio volume and keyed the mike switch on his cyclic stick. "Bronco, Bronco, this is Merlin One, do you read?" He heard nothing but static; he tried again. "Anyone on this frequency, do you read Merlin One?"

A faint, static-laced, reply came through his headset: "Merlin...Bronco tower..." followed by more garbled static.

Moselli persisted. "Bronco, Bronco, say your position?"

This transmission came through better, but choppy: "Merlin, Bronco, nine five miles ...playmate Merlin Two ETA...Zulu..." But then *Grand Rapids'* radio cut out. Moselli tried to reestablish communications but failed; he realized that the range of his aircraft's radio was limited while sitting on the ground. Regardless, he'd heard enough to buoy his spirits: the ship couldn't be that far away. What he didn't understand, though, was the fragmented second phrase about the detachment's other helicopter, Merlin Two. He'd heard "ETA," but couldn't make out the time.

Moselli scanned the aircraft's engine instruments; everything looked normal. Likewise for the helicopter's flight instruments; the bird was ready to fly. He stared at the blur of rotor blades spinning above him. The blades' rhythmic pulsing coupled with the familiar whine of the helicopter's engines and transmission induced a sense of control that he hadn't felt since being forced down by the Chinese jets.

A pounding thud on his right side jolted Moselli from the euphoria. He turned to see the colonel's angry, dripping face. Stink waived an open hand under his chin, signaling him to shut down. Moselli went through the procedures: fuel was secured to the engines and the rotor brake was applied. After the blades had come to a stop, he shut down the APU.

The colonel yanked open the cockpit door, backed away, then shouted an order to the soldiers surrounding the aircraft. The men gathered their gear and filed away.

Captain Gao met Moselli as he stepped off the aircraft. "Colonel is very happy that helicopter runs. Does everything look satisfactory to fly?"

Moselli leaned back into the cockpit and set his helmet atop the cyclic. "Yes, it will fly very nicely. When can we leave?"

Gao lowered his eyes and said with a furrowed brow, "Not so sure. That would be up to the colonel, and when other persons arrive. In meantime, I will take you back to the trailer so you can prepare for departure."

Moselli wanted to ask more questions but decided against it. All signs were that he and his crew would soon leave the island. He hopped into the passenger seat of Gao's jeep. Their path was blocked as a parade of heavy equipment lumbered by. The vehicles parked a short distance away from the landing pad. Moselli pointed to the activity. "What are they doing?"

"No time to install pavement, so machines will press down dirt hard and smooth so other helicopter can land on that location."

"Oh…okay." Moselli smiled and tapped Gao on the leg. "That's a good thing."

Gao returned the smile. "Yes, and you will go home very soon. Good thing for everybody."

The return drive to the trailer was pleasant. The road's potholes felt less jarring as Gao sped along. Moselli tilted back his head and let the warm breeze brush across his face. The thought of eating a cold Spam McMuffin almost seemed appealing.

* * *

Dick Moselli was overwhelmed when he opened the trailer's door; the place was meat-locker cold and filled with mist. He heard Ed Horton singing a Beatles tune from inside the shower.

A towel clad Don Juan Aguilar emerged from the fog. "Yeah, while you were hanging out with Colonel Stink and Gao, some guys showed up and fixed everything: air conditioning is set to max, and the water is hooked up." Aguilar reached for another towel to dry his hair. "So, what gives on the other side of fantasy island? We going back to the ship or what?"

Moselli sat down on the sofa. "It's starting to look that way. The colonel had barrels of JP lined up and a crew standing by to refuel us. I convinced him that we needed to fill both tanks, but it took forever doing it with a hand pump."

Aguilar palmed his hair into place, and then sat down at the kitchen table, "Okay, boss, so what can we expect?"

"I'm not sure, Don Juan. Stink had me start engines and spin the rotors for a few minutes. Said he wanted to make sure everything works."

Aguilar laughed then said, "Well, did it?"

"Yes, the spirit of Igor Sikorsky was with me; everything spooled up as advertised. I even managed to raise the ship on the radio."

"Great! What'd they tell you?"

"The transmission was garbled, but I think they said they were nine-five miles away and Merlin Two is flying to meet us this afternoon. That makes sense because after I did the runup, a crew started preparing a dirt pad next to the paved one we landed on."

"Any word about the swap that Gao was talking about?"

"No, not a thing. Whoever it is, though, must be mighty damn important to the Chi-Coms, considering all the fuss they're making."

Horton had stopped singing and emerged from the mist. As he went to sit down, his towel fell to the floor. He picked it up, covered his private parts, then sat next to Moselli. "I heard most of that from the head. So, we're standing by to stand by?"

"Yup, it looks that way, at least for the moment," Moselli said as he stood up. "Now unless you two bozos drained all the hot water, I'd like to take my turn in the shower."

CHAPTER 25

Tuesday afternoon
USS Grand Rapids

Commanding Officer Bill Draper settled into his bridge chair and delegated ship handling duties to Michelle Perks. Earlier that morning he and Admiral McGirt had participated in another video conference with the White House; a final determination had been made regarding the exchange of Lin Yi for the release of Dick Moselli and his crew.

Perks got up from her station and stood next to Draper. "Captain, with your concurrence, I'd like to decrease our speed to provide a better launch envelope for the chopper crew." She read the latest weather report. "Skies are forecast to stay clear, but the high surface winds we're experiencing should continue for several hours."

Draper looked up from the small green notebook that he always carried. "Sure, whatever you think is necessary, Lieutenant. Go ahead and do it." The morning's glassy waters had roiled into a white capped, gusty sea state. But after twenty years of serving aboard Navy ships, it took more than today's swells to cause him concern. Draper went back to reading while keeping his ears open to the OOD's commands. Perks ordered a minor course change, which together with slowing down the ship, resulted in ideal wind conditions for the rotary winged aircraft.

Draper tucked away his notes, then leaned over to switch on the monitor next to his chair. He called up a live video of the flightdeck where he saw a flurry of activity: a mechanic was securing an access panel on the helicopter's tail rotor while one of the crew chiefs finished his preflight inspection. At the base of the monitor, Draper noted the crash and rescue detail donning their silver aluminized fire suits. He turned to Perks and said,

"What's the latest from our pilots?"

"Wait one, sir." Perks grabbed a microphone: "Merlin Two, Bronco, say time for engine start. Over."

Bobby Bale's voice filled the bridge's overhead speakers. "Bronco, Merlin; crew is ready to go. Just waiting for our two VIPs; once they're strapped in, I'll call you back."

Moments later, Dorothy Hill transmitted, "Bronco Tower, Merlin Two, request permission for engine start."

The ship's tower operator—a crusty chief petty officer named Blanchard—replied, "Merlin Two, cleared for engine start." After both engines were started, Hill requested permission for rotor engagement. Blanchard answered, "Merlin Two, wind zero three zero at two zero knots, cleared to engage rotors."

The cockpit crew completed after-start checklists, received takeoff clearance, and departed. Perks announced over the 1MC, "All hands secure from flight quarters. Standby for short notice recall."

Captain Draper watched as the crash and fire detail stripped off their bulky gear while the rest of the launch crew stood down. Some retreated into the hangar, others sprawled out on the safety nets that encompassed the flight deck. Lieutenant Perks gave the order to set course for their designated rendezvous point.

* * *

The Americans were bored stiff as they awaited word from Colonel Stink. Moselli broke the monotony by conducting a preflight briefing, but there wasn't much to discuss: other than the gusty winds, the weather was fine; the helicopter had performed as expected during the short runup, and it had enough fuel to fly over three hundred miles if necessary.

The men picked through another box of snacks that Gao had delivered when he'd dropped off Moselli. They'd polished off all the goodies except for the dried eel. Horton had thought it was beef jerky, but after taking a big bite, he'd gagged, ran to the door, and spit it outside. But as time passed, one by one, they'd drifted back to their bunks and fell asleep to the drone of the trailer's new air conditioning unit. It took a half dozen poundings on the door by Captain Gao to wake them.

Gao was ecstatic when Moselli met him in the doorway. "All conditions are satisfactory, and it is time for your departure," he said while motioning to the string of vehicles parked on the gravel road: three open-air jeeps, plus a large, canvas-covered troop truck. "Colonel says, you each get your own transport. He wants you to be most comfortable."

Moselli heard commotion on the other side of the trailer as Aguilar and Horton bounced out of bed. "Let's go guys," was all he needed to say; they ran past him and jumped into their vehicles. Gao escorted Moselli to the lead jeep. As he climbed in the passenger seat, he noticed a flap of the truck's canvas cover creep open. Through the gap, he saw the faces of soldiers. One of the men plied the flap further open with his rifle. "Gao, why are there armed soldiers in that truck?" he said.

Gao answered, "Ah, yes, the soldiers. Colonel does not want to take chances of your escape. That is why."

Moselli laughed. "Oh, I see. Let me ask you, Gao, do you really think we are foolish enough to take off without the colonel's permission?"

Gao reacted with a deadpan reply. "Lieutenant Commander, I would hope that you are not that foolish. That would be a very grave mistake." He started the motor and assumed the convoy's lead.

Moselli stayed quiet during the ride. Along the way he saw that the new runway appeared several hundred feet longer, and the airport's control tower had grown in height. The Americans had been held captive for just three days, but within that short period, the island complex had expanded by leaps and bounds.

When Gao navigated the final stretch of road, the first thing Moselli noticed was the colonel standing alongside the helicopter. A horde of military vehicles were parked outside the pad's perimeter, together with a big yellow firetruck and a pair of vehicles that looked like ambulances. An orange windsock had been erected between the paved pad and the new dirt one. The dirt landing zone had been graded, compacted smooth, and painted with white markings.

Gao steered the convoy to a spot behind the firetruck. "We go to the colonel now," he said to Moselli as they climbed out of the jeep. Aguilar and Horton joined their boss and marched shoulder-to-shoulder to the aircraft, until Horton broke from the group and sprinted ahead. He slapped a hand against the H-60's fuselage and said, "You're one beautiful looking machine, honey!" He then smacked a kiss on the aircraft's nose section.

Aguilar opened the left cockpit door and hoisted himself into his seat. He turned to Moselli. "Looks like everything's the way we left it, Bruiser. Want me to do the preflight items?"

"Sure, go ahead. You and Crazo work the checklist down to starting the APU. Let's hold off on that for now."

Moselli approached Gao who was standing beside the colonel. "Okay, so what's the plan, gentlemen? When is the other helicopter scheduled to arrive?"

Gao did the translation. The colonel pointed to his wristwatch, then launched into a lengthy spiel. When he stopped talking, Gao asked him a couple questions, then turned to Moselli. "Colonel says that our radar equipment is not installed; you can power your radio to listen for other helicopter as it approaches." The colonel interrupted and mumbled a few sentences to Gao, who nodded and continued the instructions. "Colonel wants you to know that your transmission to the ship this morning was under recorded monitor. So be most careful what you say." He pointed to a truck with a tall antenna protruding from the roof of its cabin. "Our personnel are listening."

Moselli glanced at the truck's antenna, then looked over at the colonel, who had a smirking grin on his face. "Okay, I get that, Captain Gao," he said. "Just tell me *when the fuck* the other helicopter is going to land so we can be ready."

The vulgarity seemed to confuse Gao, but he regrouped and said with a smile, "Yes, I understand what you are asking. Land time about thirty minutes."

Moselli responded with an emphatic thumbs up. "Thank you, Gao. Now with all due respect, may I join my crew?"

Gao relayed the question to the colonel, who grunted his answer, then waved a hand toward the helicopter. "Of course," said Gao. "But do not start auxiliary power plant until given permission. It is too noisy to hear discussion on the radio."

"Okay, fine," Moselli said. He joined Aguilar in the cockpit and donned his flight helmet. "Test one, two," he said over the ICS. "You guys hear me?"

"Got you loud and clear, Bruiser," Aguilar answered. "Same here, boss," Horton piped in.

Aguilar flopped his pocket checklist onto his knee. "Crazo and I completed exterior and interior pre-flights down to APU start. Tuned up the radios on battery power; nothing from the ship or our playmate yet."

Moselli settled into his seat and flicked the communications panel switches where he wanted them. "Okay, then we'll standby until we hear from somebody."

"Where'd Colonel Stink run off to?" Aguilar said.

Moselli pointed to the truck with the antenna. "He headed over there. Gao told me they are monitoring our radio."

Horton poked his head into the cockpit. "Yeah, well, that's not all they're monitoring. I see a couple of goons with binoculars next to Stink's truck. Looks like they're scanning the skies."

"Not surprised," Moselli said. "I'll bet dollars to donuts they know exactly where the ship is; they're just not telling us." Moselli checked his watch. "Alright, let's see if our guys are in range." He keyed the radio and said, "Merlin Two, Merlin Two, this is Merlin One, do you read?" No reply. He waited a moment, then called again.

Copilot Dorothy Hill answered, "Merlin One, this is Two; we got you five-by-five. Great to hear your voice, Commander! We've departed Bronco and are headed your way. ETA one nine minutes."

"Damn straight!" Horton shouted. "Start this freaking whirlybird and get us the hell out of here!"

"Patience, Crazo, patience," Moselli said. "Take a look at that rifle team surrounding us. We're not doing a damn thing until we get approval from the colonel."

"Yeah, I got that, boss. Sure would like to know who this guy is that they're trading us for. Must be a pretty important dude."

"I think that's way above our paygrade," Aguilar added as he strained his eyes hoping to spot Merlin Two. He then turned his sights to the colonel's truck where he saw one of the lookouts pointing to the northeast. Captain Gao and the colonel jumped down from inside the truck; they raised their binoculars in that direction.

Moselli keyed his mike. "Merlin Two, say again your ETA." There was no reply. He followed up with another transmission. Again, no answer.

Finally, Dorothy Hill's trembling voice came over the airwaves. "Mayday, mayday, mayday! Merlin Two declaring an emergency."

Moselli and Aguilar stared at each other. "Holy shit," was all Moselli could muster in response.

A garbled sentence followed, then Bobby Bale spoke in a shaky tone, "Tail rotor drive is failing; we've lost all tail rotor authority! I can't control it!" Hill's voice could be heard shouting in the background, "Get us down, Bobby, get us down!"

Horton forced his way between the two pilots. "Jesus Christ, look there… twelve o'clock, high above the horizon." The trio spotted a dot in the sky with a line of smoke trailing behind it. The image began corkscrewing down, gaining speed as it plummeted toward the water. Seconds later, it disappeared from view.

Moselli squeezed the mike trigger on his stick. "Merlin, Merlin, say your status…say your status!" There was no reply. He tried another avenue. "Bronco,

Bronco, this is Merlin One on the ground, do you read me or Merlin Two?" Again, the airwaves were silent.

"Bruiser, did you switch to the upper antenna?" asked Aguilar. Moselli nodded that he had. Aguilar hung his head. "Son of a bitch, there's nothing we can do."

The pilots heard a cabin door fly open, followed by a cursing Ed Horton slamming his helmet to the floor. Horton ran in front of the aircraft; he turned toward Moselli and Aguilar and extended his hands in a pleading gesture; his face was contorted with grief. Dick Moselli had never witnessed such a sorrowful expression on the hard-nosed sailor. He and Aguilar removed their helmets and unstrapped; they joined Horton on the tarmac.

Tears welled in Horton's eyes as he spoke. "Ah, fuck, we gotta get out there!"

The crew heard shouting in the distance. They turned toward the commotion and saw the colonel, who'd hoisted himself atop the truck's cabin roof. His free arm waved wildly as he talked on a mobile phone.

"Christ's sake, Stink is giving a blow-by-blow of what happened," Moselli said. After a couple of minutes, the colonel hopped down and beelined toward the Americans, with Gao close at his side. The colonel started hollering at the flight crew.

Gao ran ahead and addressed Moselli. "Colonel has received orders for him to investigate and rescue our man." Gao then faced his boss and said something. The colonel stood resolute with arms folded across his chest. He spewed a few words at Gao, then got nose-to-nose with Moselli. Moselli wanted to back away from the man's foul odor—but he held his ground. After a brief standoff, the colonel stepped back and motioned for Gao to translate.

Gao said, "You will fly Colonel and me to the spot where other chopper went down."

The sight of the aircraft spiraling into the sea was etched in Moselli's brain. Deep in his heart he knew that the odds were slim that Bale's crew had survived the water impact. But there was always a chance. Moselli turned to his men and said, "Let's go guys, saddle up."

He started to lead his men back to the helicopter when Captain Gao jumped in front of them and blocked the way. "Just you, Lieutenant Commander, and the man in back to operate rescue. Other pilot stays here."

Aguilar forced a snide laugh. "Oh, I get it, lucky me. I get to stay behind as the ransom. They're afraid we'll toss their sorry asses into the drink and then fly to the ship." Aguilar grabbed Moselli by the shoulder. "You got no choice, Bruiser. You and Crazo have to take them to the crash site…that is, if you can even find it."

"You're right, Don Juan." Moselli said.

Horton added, "Boss, we don't have any other options."

The colonel hopped into Aguilar's seat while Horton explained to Gao how to put on a headset and plug into the interphone. The colonel toyed with Aguilar's helmet but decided not to put it on. Instead, he accepted a headset from Horton. Moselli breezed through the rest of the checklists, started the APU, and then lit the bird's engines. The rotor brake was released and Merlin One was ready for takeoff.

Moselli saw that rifle team had cleared the area. Likewise—except for the firetruck and ambulances—the remainder of vehicles had backed away. Aguilar stood at the edge of the pad, bracing himself against the rotor wash; he signaled Moselli a thumbs up, then rendered a salute. Moselli returned the salute, then pulled the aircraft in a hover. He made a pedal turn in the direction of where they'd seen Merlin Two go down, then yanked an armful of collective and dipped the nose; the aircraft pitched and yawed through the gusty winds as it accelerated. Moselli glanced to his left and saw that the colonel had a death grip on the glare shield; his face had turned white.

"Gao, you better say something to calm down the colonel," Moselli said on the ICS. "Tell him that it should get smoother as we climb, and the temperature will cool down." Moselli thought to himself, *I don't want the son-of-a bitch to puke or crap his pants; he smells bad enough as it is.*

Gao repeated what Moselli had said. The colonel slid open his side window and focused on the horizon. The fresh air seemed to help settle him. He fumbled with the cyclic, searching for the ICS transmit button. Moselli leaned over and pointed it out. The colonel keyed it and shouted into his microphone.

Gao leaned into the cockpit. "Colonel said, 'thank you', and wants to know how long before we reach the helicopter crash."

"I don't know for sure but tell him about ten or fifteen minutes. Then we will begin a search pattern and look for survivors." Moselli waited for a response after Gao had translated. The colonel nodded that he understood, then swept a palm over his dripping face; his complexion had changed from pale to a greenish-gray shade; he appeared on the verge of vomiting. For a brief moment, Dick Moselli felt sorry for the guy; the thuggish army officer was completely out of his element. Moselli guessed that the flight had not been Stink's idea, but rather the result of a direct order from his superiors.

They continued on a northeasterly track. Whether it was Moselli's innate sense of direction or sheer luck, Ed Horton spotted something in the water. He tapped Moselli's shoulder and pointed to the right. "Bruiser, my eyes may be playing a trick, but I think I see some debris over there."

Moselli banked the aircraft then rolled wings level. "How's that heading look?"

"A tad more right...there, that's good."

Moselli followed Horton's directions; he slowed to 50 knots and descended, leveling off at an even 100 feet on his radar altimeter. "Yes, I see it too."

Gao had relayed the conversation to the colonel, who appeared to have recovered from motion sickness; his complexion had returned to normal and he'd stopped sweating.

Gao wedged himself next to Horton. "Colonel asks you to go low and slow to get pictures." As Gao spoke, the colonel pulled out his smart phone and began thumbing through applications; he aimed the phone's camera lens straight ahead.

The debris was less than a hundred yards away as Moselli slowed to a crawl. He glanced down through his side window and saw the shimmering image of a fuel slick; there was no doubt that they'd found the wreckage. He put the aircraft into a shallow bank to trace a wide arc around the site.

"Aw, hell, boss, there's nothing left," Horton said. He'd slid open the helicopter's right side cabin door and was leaning into the airstream while tethered by a strap. "Those poor bastards must have really hammered in. All I see is a bunch of junk floating on the surface."

Moselli crept closer to the wreckage; he descended to 50 feet and switched on the Seahawk's automatic hover system. The aircraft stayed rock-solid motionless above the wave tops. Now relieved from manipulating the controls, he was free to search the area with his own eyes. What he saw made him nauseas: fragments of charts and maps bobbing with the swells, plus some wire bundles and scattered airframe parts that hadn't sunk. He steeled himself and asked Horton, "Do you see any bodies?" The words caused a bitter taste in his mouth as soon as he said them.

"No. I do not. Just a whole lot of...." Horton's voice began to crack; he couldn't finish the sentence. After a long pause, he said, "I do see a chunk of the airframe that's still on the surface. Yeah, looks like a side panel; I recognize our squadron logo on it."

Moselli had started a peddle turn to get a better look, when he felt the colonel slap him hard on the shoulder. Gao said on the ICS, "Colonel sees something off to that way." Gao nudged himself into the cockpit and pointed to the left. The colonel began snapping photos in rapid succession as Moselli changed directions and inched closer to a green colored blob on the surface. The colonel started hollering as he took more photos. When finished, he handed the phone to Gao.

Moselli placed the helicopter over what had captured the colonel's attention. He saw an object with bright red and yellow symbols contrasted against olive-green material. "Gao, what do those symbols mean?" he asked.

Gao held the phone for Moselli to see; he zoomed in on the screen's image with his thumb and index finger. "Mandarin characters say it is property of Navy pilot Lin Yi…the man we wanted to make swap for."

Moselli grabbed the phone. The characters meant nothing to him, but he recognized the olive-green item on which the symbols were written: it was a pilot's helmet bag, similar to the one he'd lugged with him his entire career. He reached down and held up his own bag, then turned to the colonel. "I think this is what you see." No translation was necessary. The colonel bit down on his lower lip. His eyes conveyed a hint of sadness.

Horton closed the cabin door and came forward. "Hey, Bruiser, we've been down in the salt spray for a long time. You might want to get us higher before we foul an engine."

Moselli handed the phone back to Gao. "Yeah, you're right." He clicked off the auto hover, accelerated and climbed to 200 feet. He took some deep breaths in hopes of clearing his mind before speaking. "Captain Gao, we can't stay out here all day; what does the colonel want to do?"

Gao and the colonel exchanged words, then Gao replied, "Business is done here. Colonel says fly back to the island. He must await further instructions."

Moselli wrapped the helicopter into a tight bank and accelerated to its maximum airspeed. He said a silent prayer for his lost shipmates.

CHAPTER 26

There was no conversation as they flew back to the Scarborough facility. Moselli made a pass over the landing pad to check the winds; the fresh-out-of-the-box windsock was hanging limp and wavering from side to side, signifying that the gusty breezes had tapered off to just a few knots. As he lined up on final approach, he noticed that nothing had changed: the rescue equipment was still in place and the soldiers lay prone on the deck with their rifles ready. The colonel bolted from the aircraft once the engines and rotor blades were shut down. Gao followed close behind.

Moselli worked his way through the checklist, though considering his two thousand hours in the H-60, he could have performed it from memory. Nonetheless, he stuck with habit and read each item aloud as his index finger slid down the page. He stopped short of the item that read "Blade fold." He was startled when Aguilar yanked open the cockpit's left door. Aguilar had the anxious look of someone hoping to receive good news but knew in their gut that the opposite was about to be delivered. He hoisted himself into the copilot's seat.

"Nobody made it, Don Juan," Moselli said. "We searched the whole area; nothing recognizable but a few parts and some papers on the surface. We did spot the Chinese pilot's helmet bag, though. Stink took a bunch of pictures of it with his phone."

Ed Horton leaned in from the cabin; his eyes were bloodshot and moist. "I hope they hit the water so fucking hard it knocked them unconscious." He choked backed tears. "And they didn't have to go through the agony of drowning."

The crew sat in silence, remembering their shipmates that had perished. Horton was the first to notice Gao as he jogged toward them. "Great, now what the hell does he want," Horton said.

Moselli held open his door. "What?"

Gao's usual smile was absent. "Colonel says it is time to redo the plan. I will take you back to trailer."

Horton flung his flight gear against the cabin's aft bulkhead. "Jesus Christ, here we go again!"

"But there may be good news in the future. Colonel is talking with his superiors now." Gao started to smile but erased it from his face. "I know this is a sad time for all personnel." Moselli simply nodded his head.

Gao led the Americans to his vehicle. The day's scorching heat had lowered a few degrees, and the construction crews had secured. When he dropped them off at the trailer, Gao's parting words were, "Be well. I will return when news from the colonel."

* * *

Commissar Han couldn't remember the last time he'd gotten a full night's sleep. Captain Song had made it a point to look in on his old friend as much as possible; however, the tempo of operations in the Straits had occupied most of his time on the ship's bridge. *Shanghai*—together with the CCP's two other aircraft carriers—had been conducting an aggressive display of flight operations off Taiwan's coast. In response, two U.S. flattops, *Reagan* and *Lincoln*, had matched China by doing the same. The Japanese carriers—a pair of helicopter ships converted for fixed-wing operations—were coordinating their efforts with the American strike groups. On the Chinese mainland, a massive amphibious landing force was awaiting orders to deploy.

Han heard Captain Song's distinctive footsteps in the passageway; he got up from his desk and opened the stateroom door before the skipper knocked.

Song fanned the stale, smokey air as he entered. "This place is disgusting! You need fresh air in here, Snake!" Song reached up to the overhead air vents to ensure they were open.

Han slouched in his chair. "I can't pull myself away from this work, Bulldog. The Party is burying me with information."

Captain Song placed a hand on Han's shoulder. "I thought you'd want to know that we've temporarily secured flight operations for the rest of the afternoon."

"Really?"

"Yes. Air Officer Lu has informed me that the tempo of operations is taking a toll on our pilots and flightdeck personnel. He fears that if we don't give them a break, somebody will get hurt."

Han gave a weary smile and said, "Lu Zhong is a good man. You were wise to take his recommendation."

Captain Song couldn't take his eyes off the commissar; Han appeared to have aged ten years over the last week. Chain smoking and poor eating habits were ravaging the man's rail-thin body. "Well, in case you were wondering, it's a beautiful day outside," said Song. "When's the last time you took a stroll on the flight deck?"

Han shrugged his shoulders. Song chuckled. "That's what I thought; come on." He took a gentle hold of Han's arm and helped him to his feet.

The pair navigated a myriad of passageways and ladders enroute to *Shanghai*'s flight deck. Sailors pressed their backs against the bulkhead to make way for the ship's two most senior officers. Many had stunned looks on their faces: they'd never actually seen the reclusive Party Commissar.

Han shielded his eyes from the afternoon sun when Song opened the hatch that led outside. The flight deck was still: dozens of jets and helicopters sat idle as *Shanghai* glided over smooth, following seas; there was barely a wisp of wind noise.

Captain Song motioned toward the ship's bow. "Let's go this way. I always enjoy peering over the deck edge as this big monster plows through the water. Much nicer view than with that ugly ski jump ramp on our old flattops." They walked in silence. When they'd reached the bow, there wasn't a soul nearby.

Song reached into a pants pocket and retrieved his phone. "The Lin Yi problem may have taken care of itself," he said. He thumbed through photos until he'd found what he wanted, then offered the phone to Han. "These just came in from Beijing: images of what's left of the American chopper that was flying Lin Yi to Scarborough."

Han took the phone and paged through the pictures; he then viewed a video where he could hear the colonel's voice hollering above the aircraft's noise. "Who took these?" he asked.

"Colonel Fu Quancheng, our Army construction officer heading the Scarborough build out."

Han scanned the photos a second time. "These images are very convincing." He then gave Song a suspicious look. "Tell me what you know about Fu."

"From what I've gathered, he's a very senior colonel in the People's Army. He's had some tough breaks and was passed over for promotion. I think this billet overseeing the Scarborough project may be his last chance to redeem himself."

"What kind of tough breaks?"

"Apparently, when he was the officer in charge of another project, three of his men were killed by a crane boom that collapsed at the work site. The investigation found that one of Fu's subordinates had forged the equipment's maintenance records: periodic safety inspections had been logged as completed, but they'd never been performed."

"And those inspections fell under Fu's responsibility?"

"Yes. The only thing that saved him from prosecution was the fact that his wife's father held a high position in the Party. Fu got off the hook by claiming he was an alcoholic and wasn't in full grasp of his faculties at the time. His father-in-law greased the skids for him to go through dry out treatment. He bounced back as lead engineer at Scarborough."

Han shook his head. "Lucky bastard. Anyone else would have gone to prison. Their family's social scores would have tanked, and they'd be destined to live in shame."

"Not in this case. It appears that Colonel Fu turned the corner and has been towing the line...at least as far as we know."

Commissar Han stared off toward the cloudless horizon; a cool, late afternoon breeze helped clear his mind. He took a deep breath of the clean, ocean air. "Bulldog, give me your gut feeling about these pictures; can we trust what we are seeing?" He handed back the phone.

Captain Song pursed his lips while thinking. "In my professional opinion, the odds strongly favor that Lin has been lost at sea. Did you notice the shot of his personal gear?"

"Yes, the helmet bag. I zoomed in on that."

"The colonel said that he heard the crew's distress call over the radio and witnessed the chopper spiraling into the water. The crash occurred several kilometers away from Scarborough; however, based on the photos that Fu took and what he stated in his report, the helicopter impacted with such force that he doesn't believe anyone could have survived."

Han took another deep draw of salt-laced air. At moments like this he longed for his old job as commanding officer of a warship, when he could mingle freely with his crew and was immune from Communist Party obligations. The words *That was then, and this is now,* passed through his mind; the adage brought him back to reality. "Skipper, the way I see it, even if Lin somehow survived that awful crash, his knowledge is of little value. We suspect that the Americans have already broken down the laser weapon and analyzed it. That being said, our experts are confident that the blueprint for the metal alloys used in the device's core, the capacitor, is nearly impossible to duplicate. And now that our nation controls the rare earth mines in Africa, it could take years for our adversaries to harness the processing formula and materials. In the meantime, we will outfit our fighters with the laser weapon and achieve global air superiority."

Captain Song laughed. "You've said a mouthful, comrade. I think the fresh air has done you good. Getting to another issue, what about the Americans at Scarborough?"

Han stood erect with his trademark perfect posture. He thought for almost a minute before saying, "I anticipate that Beijing will want my input on that matter." He paused again then said, "Based on what we now know, I will recommend that Colonel Fu release the Americans. They are of no further use to us."

* * *

Moselli's crew spent the next two hours wasting time and gnawing on another batch of snacks Gao had provided. Horton woke up from a nap and walked to the window. "Well, looks like it's fixing to be another romantic sunset." He turned to the pilots. "You ladies care to join me by the seawall?"

Aguilar stood up from the kitchen table. "Why the hell not? Nothing better to do." Moselli followed them outside. Before reaching the shoreline, they spotted a billowing cloud moving along the dirt road; Captain Gao's jeep emerged from the dust. Gao brought the jeep to a jerky stop and jumped out; he ran toward them waving his phone in the air.

"Hey, guys, I think something's about to go down," Moselli said.

Gao struggled to catch his breath as he said. "My gentlemen...I believe...the colonel will call...very soon." On cue, Gao's phone rang a few seconds later. He held it away from his ear as the colonel spoke.

"Wow, I can hear Stink hollering from here," Aguilar said. "Man, he sounds hot!"

After a series of head nods, Gao hung up. He couldn't hide his happiness. "Colonel says you may go now. I take you back to the helicopter."

No explanation was needed; the men ran inside to get their gear, then piled into Gao's jeep. Aguilar shouted from the rear seat. "Bruiser, do we have any idea where the ship is now?"

"Not a clue. You know anything, Gao?"

Gao held both hands on the wheel as he swerved to avoid a pothole. "I am not so positive. Colonel was speaking very loudly. I think he said one fifty kilometers away."

"How far is that, Bruiser?" Horton yelled from the back.

"That would be…about a hundred miles."

"We got enough gas?" Aguilar asked. "Do you remember how much you burned?"

Gao interrupted. "Forgot to mention, Colonel said, if you need more petroleum, he will give it." A broad smile spread across his round face. "Colonel said, 'no charge.'"

Moselli chuckled at Gao's attempted humor. His own happiness about leaving the island had temporarily replaced the sadness of losing his shipmates. "I don't want to take any chances," he said. "Yes, Gao, tell the colonel to fill the tanks again."

Captain Gao dialed the colonel to relay Moselli's request. When they'd rounded the final bend in the road, they saw that a pair of refueling crews had already hooked up; two JP drums had been positioned on each side of the aircraft.

"Yahoo!" Horton shouted. "Looks like somebody found another pump."

It took just a handful of minutes for the Americans to strap in. "No need to read the whole checklist, Don Juan: she flew in, she'll fly out." He turned to Horton. "Crazo, do a quick check of the rotor head. We need to get the hell out of here ASAP." He turned on the aircraft's battery and noted the fuel quantities. "We didn't burn that much gas; it shouldn't take Stink's guys long to top us off."

As Horton scaled the aircraft, Moselli noticed another jeep approaching. The colonel got out and sauntered onto the landing pad; he carried a sheet of paper. Gao met him in front of the helicopter, where they had a short discussion. When they'd finished, the colonel made eye contact with Moselli. His head dipped ever so slightly as he raised his right hand. He held it there until Moselli returned the gesture, then pivoted and walked away. "Huh…I think that was some sort of farewell sign," said Moselli.

"Yeah, I think you're right, Bruiser," Aguilar said. "And I'll bet he can't get rid of us fast enough." Aguilar laughed. "Look…he beat feet to his jeep and tore outta here."

Horton hopped down from inspecting the rotor head and rejoined the pilots inside. He was surprised when Gao jumped aboard behind him. "So, what gives,

Gao? Do you want to go with us?" he said. Captain Gao leaned into the cockpit and handed Moselli the sheet of paper that the colonel had carried.

Moselli studied the paper; he turned it left, then right and upside down. "Geez, Gao, I can't read this, it's in Mandarin."

Gao took it from Moselli's hands. "I will interpret. It says that your ship was at this location at this time." He pointed to a string of geographic coordinates and a date time group buried in the middle of the message.

"We can work with that," Aguilar said as he took the paper from Gao. He punched in the GPS coordinates. "Yep, according to this, they're about a hundred miles to the north." He scribbled on his knee board, then checked the aircraft's clock. "And...the message's time stamp was over an hour ago." He turned to Moselli. "Bruiser, if the ship is steaming in our direction, they shouldn't be very far away."

Moselli gave a thumbs up and said, "Let's get the hell out of here."

Gao jumped out and stood by the firetruck. The crew whizzed through the abbreviated checklist, lit the engines and engaged rotors. A minute later, Moselli lifted the aircraft into a hover, peddle-turned to the north and whirled away.

Horton came forward during climb out. "You guys might not have noticed, but as we departed, Gao stood at attention and saluted. I think he's going to miss us."

Aguilar pressed his ICS switch. "Well, I'm sure as heck not going to miss him. He seemed like a decent fellow, but I don't care to ever see him or Stink again." Moselli and Horton clicked their mike switches in agreement.

* * *

Salid dropped his shovel to the ground and stared at the helicopter as it flew past; he wished that he were on it. Earlier in the day his new friend Hashim had shared a rumor that foreign workers would be allowed to leave the miserable island hellhole once construction was completed. Salid held tight to what Hashim had told him. He closed his eyes and remembered the phrase his mother had told him as a child: "My fate is in the hands of Allah Almighty."

* * *

As they leveled off at 3000 feet, Aguilar re-tuned the ship's radio frequency. "Well, here goes...Bronco, Bronco, Merlin One checking in. Do you read?" Nothing but hissing static, so he tried again. This time Chief Blanchard's voice boomed back, "Merlin, Merlin, we got you loud and clear!"

Before Aguilar could respond, another voice came up on the net; he recognized it as Michelle Perks. "Merlin, Bronco here, radar is painting you at four-five miles. Captain has us rooster tailing to close the gap. Come right ten degrees and prepare to enter starboard delta. Red deck while we recover an Osprey."

Aguilar acknowledged with, "Roger, wilco." He then said over the intercom, "Osprey? Is she kidding?"

"Last time I checked, the ship was still 'Emergency Only' for those guys," Moselli said. "Too heavy and its exhaust heat can damage the flight deck. But I remember reading that modifications were in the works to fix that."

Horton threw up his hands. "Well that's just great! Watch them melt a big hole in the deck and then we have to fly back to fantasy island."

"Keep the faith, Ed," Moselli said. "Draper and his people are better than that."

Soon, the ship's profile came into view as the sun edged below the horizon. Merlin One entered a holding pattern on *Grand Rapids'* right side. Moselli leveled off at 200 feet and switched on the autopilot. There wasn't anything else to do other than fly a lazy circuit until the flight deck was clear.

"There they are...nine o'clock high, a couple miles out," Horton said while pointing toward the Osprey. The cockpit was silent as the helicopter continued to orbit. The flight crew caught a glimpse of the big tiltrotor as it set down. "I don't think they're refueling," Horton added. "Wait a minute, they just lowered the boarding ramp. Yes... I see three people running out from the hangar; they just got aboard." The crew lost sight of the ship as they flew upwind of the bow and the autopilot commanded a right turn. They heard the Osprey's pilot request takeoff clearance. By the time Moselli's aircraft rolled out of its turn, the V-22 had lifted off and sped away to the east.

"That didn't take long." Aguilar said.

Before Moselli or Horton could comment, the tower chief said, "Okay, Merlin One, cleared to land. Wind zero three zero at one five."

Moselli switched off the autopilot and called for the landing checklist. Half a minute later, the H-60 Seahawk was on final approach. Aguilar called out altitudes as the flight deck loomed closer: "One fifty, one hundred, green deck, cleared to land." He read off the final numbers from the aircraft's radar altimeter gauge. The ship started rolling a bit, so Moselli held a ten-foot hover until the deck stabilized. He lowered the collective, nudged the stick forward and touched down with a controlled, yet definitive 'thump.'

The chock and chain gang ran out to secure the aircraft. Aguilar read the checklist as fuel was cut off to the engines and the rotor brake was applied. He and Moselli completed post shutdown items over the ICS, then removed their helmets.

"Say, what's going on?" Horton called out. He and the two pilots watched as one of the hangar doors was raised; a crowd led by Captain Draper burst out and ran toward the aircraft.

Aguilar had a dumbfounded expression. "Jesus, there's another Seahawk in our hangar. I can't believe it...looks like they've already replaced Bobby and his crew."

Horton flung open a cabin door and jumped out. He shouted back to the cockpit, "Well, if they did, they found Bobby and Dorothy look-a-likes!"

Aguilar craned his neck and saw that Bobby Bale and Dorothy Hill were hugging Horton as if he were a long lost relative. Seconds later, the cabin was crammed with sailors, all laughing and high fiving each other.

Captain Draper pushed his way forward and grabbed Moselli's hand. "You made it Bruiser, you made it!"

Moselli took in the commotion. He attempted to acknowledge Draper, but the only words he could muster were, "They're alive. Thank God my guys are alive." He felt people pounding on his shoulder, but their congratulatory words became undistinguishable chatter in his ears.

Lieutenant Commander Dick "Bruiser" Moselli was a tough, hard-nosed officer, who seemed immune from the stresses of naval aviation. But after realizing that his people had survived, he bowed his head, covered his eyes and wept.

CHAPTER 27

Hours earlier...

By 9 p.m. local time, most Washington politicians and government bureaucrats had made their way home, had a cocktail or two, eaten dinner, and kicked back for a few hours of relaxation with their families. President Maxwell Black and the National Security Council were not part of that fortunate group. Black and his team had been working around the clock strategizing their moves as the situation grew more intense around the island nation of Taiwan. When McGirt saw the look on Black's face after the president took his seat in front of the video camera, he had a hunch that this meeting would be a short one. The dark rings under Black's eyes seemed to have grown larger and puffier since their last conference. As Black began to speak, it was clear to McGirt and Bill Draper that the man's energetic fighting spirit had been depleted. McGirt recalled one of the fiery Midwesterner's campaign slogans that, "It's time to put hay in the barn." Sadly, Black's hayloft looked empty.

"Hello, McGirt, Skipper," Black began. He nodded toward the two men seated at his sides. "No introductions needed, you know Nate and Chuck," he said, referring to Secretary of Defense Secretary Nathan Croft, and Chief of Naval Operations Admiral Charles Timmons. "Gentlemen, we don't have a lot of time. My staff has arranged a teleconference with the Japanese and Australian prime ministers in fifteen minutes, so let's get right to it." Black pointed a finger at the camera. "Last chance, McGirt: give me a good reason why we shouldn't swap this Chinese pilot for our guys today."

McGirt stayed quiet until he was sure that Black had finished, and the satellite link's delay had passed. "Mr. President, I understand your concerns. This situation has gone on long enough; it's time to take action."

"So, you agree that we should give up Lieutenant Lin now?" Black said.

"Well, sir, not until after I present some information that you and your staff may not be aware of."

Black frowned. "Like what? Does Lin have a magic cure for cancer... or maybe he can guess the winning numbers for the next Powerball lottery?"

McGirt noticed that Croft and Admiral Timmons had turned away from the camera to shield their grins. He was happy to see that the president still had a shred of humor in him.

"I know your time is precious, Mr. President, so I won't beat around the bush. Lieutenant Lin has told me that even though our people at Subic have analyzed the laser weapon, they'll encounter a multitude of obstacles when they try to duplicate the composition of the unit's capacitor, which is the guts of the system. Lin claims that only he and a handful of Chi-Com scientists know the formula for the metal alloys used in the capacitor, and—"

Black interrupted. "And he won't reveal the details until he's a free man on U.S. soil, right?" The president shook his head. "McGirt, you've got to do better than that." He looked over at Secretary Croft. "Nate, are you buying any of this?"

Secretary Croft leaned forward and said, "Admiral, it's true that our engineers in the Philippines are stumped by the composition of the capacitor. But that doesn't mean that over time they can't replicate it."

"No doubt, Mr. Secretary," McGirt replied. "I have great confidence in American ingenuity. That being said, it should be recognized that until we can duplicate the lethality of Lin's weapon, we risk losing air superiority over China."

McGirt saw that President Black appeared even more irritated than when the meeting had begun; He leaned back in his chair with a bored expression. "Anything else that you can provide...Admiral?"

Johnny Jack McGirt realized that his entire career might rest on his next words. He stared into the eyes of the two men seated alongside the president; they were both battle-tested professionals with little tolerance for mistakes. "Mr. President, I would like your permission to employ a plan that I believe has a better than average chance of gaining release of our men while at the same time retaining Lin Yi. It will cost us some assets in terms of dollars; however, in the larger scheme, those assets will be trivial."

After an uncomfortable period of dead time, McGirt felt an elbow jab his side. Bill Draper whispered, "With all due respect, sir, I believe they're waiting for you to finish."

McGirt was about to continue when an aide appeared on the corner of the video screen. She approached from behind the president, said something to him, and then left. President Black rose from his seat and cinched up his tie. "Gentlemen, I have to attend another meeting." Black placed his hands on the conference table; he leaned forward and focused straight into the camera. "Admiral McGirt, I'm delegating this to Secretary Croft and the CNO. They have my approval to do whatever they think is appropriate." He started to leave but stopped and faced the camera again. "I hope your plan works, McGirt, but if it blows up, I'll take responsibility; that perk comes with this job."

After Black had left the room, Nathan Croft said, "Okay, Admiral, tell us what you've got."

* * *

Leonard Dickle dropped a socket wrench to the floor. "You want me to do *what?*" His buggy eyes glared at McGirt.

McGirt pointed to Dickle's pride and joy: the MQ-8 Fire Scout parked in the ship's hangar alongside the air detachment's H-60 Seahawk. "Like I said, Leonard, I have complete authority to do whatever I see fit to secure the release of our crew held by the Chi-Coms."

"Is this for real, Captain?" Dickle asked.

"Yes, it is," Bill Draper said. "The admiral and I have devised a plan to gain their release without swapping the Chinese pilot. As Admiral McGirt just explained, we will stage a fake crash of our helicopter by using the Fire Scout."

Dickle moved next to the MQ-8; he rubbed a hand across its nose as if he were stroking a pet. "This aircraft is worth several million dollars. And you want to trash it...like an old toy?"

"Leonard, we don't think of it that way," McGirt said. "It's being sacrificed for a higher cause." He saw that Dickle was still in a state of disbelief. "I'm aware that you hold a top secret clearance in order to do your job, but this operation goes way beyond testing satellite communication relays and sonobuoy signals. And if it's any consolation, the Fire Scout Bravo models will all be replaced by the Charlie version over the next year. You yourself have complained about how outdated the Bravo models are."

Dickle slid his hand off the aircraft's nose panel. "Yeah, I guess you're right on that one. The Charlie will fly rings around this guy. So what do you want me to do?"

"We have about six hours to get this thing ready," McGirt said. "Lieutenant Bale and the maintenance chief will give you the details, and our mechs will help with the airframe modifications. I need to know if you can command the UAV to do what we want it to do."

"Which is what?"

McGirt held out a sketch that he and Bobby Bale had drawn. "We will launch the Fire Scout first and then the Seahawk. The ship will be out of visual range of the island so the Chi-Coms shouldn't be able to observe the operation."

"What about their radar?" Dickle asked. "Won't they be able to figure something's up when they paint two aircraft?"

Captain Draper said, "Our intelligence satellites have done several flyovers of the island. To date, no radar configurations have been detected. The facility is still in its early stages of construction."

"But there is a risk that they won't buy the ruse," McGirt added. "In which case, we will be required to fly Lieutenant Lin to the island and make the swap." He set the sketch on Dickle's workbench. "Both aircraft will climb to five thousand feet: the Seahawk will orbit over the ship, while you steer the Fire Scout to within visual range of the island, say ten to fifteen miles. At the coordinated time, Bale will simulate a tail rotor gear box failure and follow emergency procedures by initiating an autorotation; you will program the Fire Scout to begin a rapid, spiraling descent."

"Okay, I can do that," Dickle said. "Then what?"

McGirt glanced at Draper before answering. "That's when the tricky part begins. We're confident that the Chi-Coms will be monitoring radio transmissions while awaiting Lin's arrival. Bale and his crew will make a distress call over the frequency to give the scene authenticity. But we will need visual displays to make the operation believable." McGirt placed a hand on Dickle's shoulder. "Leonard, you've been touting a new satellite link that you've developed; do you think you can provide a remote signal that could detonate a smoke canister attached to the tail boom?"

Dickle rubbed his chin. "I…can't guarantee it, but I'll sure give it a try. What else do you need?"

"That's it in a nutshell," said McGirt. "We don't have a heck of a lot of time; the swap is scheduled for sixteen hundred hours this afternoon. I've instructed the maintenance chief to work with you and attach some gear to the Fire Scout that will remain on the surface after impact."

"So, if I understand, you want it to hit the surface hard enough that everything sinks except for a few items?" Dickle asked.

McGirt smiled. "Yes, exactly. Can you program a free fall from a couple thousand feet?"

"Why, of course, if that's what you want." Dickle chuckled. "A free fall from two grand? Yeah, that should pretty much smash her to smithereens."

The men turned in unison and faced the Fire Scout; there was an extended quiet period as they absorbed the plan. McGirt broke the silence. "Skipper, let's not dilly dally. Time to get Lieutenant Bale and his folks down here."

* * *

As acting officer in charge, Bobby Bale huddled his people next to the Fire Scout for a briefing. He gave them a concise explanation of the operation, stressed the importance that all hands work expeditiously, then delegated the plan's implementation to his maintenance chief petty officer. Leonard Dickle wired a radio activated initiator to a smoke charge, which the detachment's airframe specialists mounted to the aircraft's tail rotor section. Another group painted the unit's logo on both sides of a three-foot by two-foot section of the drone's aluminum airframe; strips of Styrofoam were bonded to the panel's edges. Dickle and the maintenance chief devised a method to secure the panel well enough so it would stay attached during flight but could break free when the Fire Scout struck the water. The same method was used to attach a bundle of navigation charts and aircraft manual pages to the inside of a loosely hinged access door; the door would spring open on impact, allowing the material to scatter on the surface.

With an hour to go before launch, Admiral McGirt hung up his phone call with Secretary Croft and returned to the hangar bay. Bale's working party snapped to attention. "Carry on, ladies and gentlemen," McGirt said. He then called Dickle and the maintenance chief aside; he held out Lieutenant Lin Yi's empty helmet bag. "Sorry that I didn't remember this earlier. Do you think you can rig this on the aircraft so that it will float along with the other items?"

The chief inspected the green vinyl bag stenciled in Mandarin with Lin's name. "Sir, we'll give it our best shot." He took the bag and laid it out on a worktable. After the chief and Dickle had a disagreement on what to do, they compromised on a solution: thin strips of foam were stitched to the interior, then the bag was turned right side out, pressed flat and mounted to an inspection panel, that like the others, was rigged to break away from the airframe before it sank.

McGirt ran a palm over the flattened helmet bag; it protruded a fraction of an inch from the Fire Scout's skin. He turned to the chief and nodded his approval.

Flight quarters were set. The Fire Scout was spotted on deck and readied for launch while Bobby Bale and his crew pre-flighted their helicopter inside the hangar. McGirt joined Leonard Dickle at the Fire Scout's control station in ICC2 below the flight deck. He watched as the tech rep typed a string of commands on the station's keyboard. Dickle powered up the aircraft's BRITE Star camera and swiveled it through its range of motion with a joystick.

Leonard sat back in his chair. "I never imagined that my time at sea would end like this, Admiral." His face had a sad expression as he said, "You and I will witness the MQ-8's suicide in living color."

"Yeah, this wasn't listed on my agenda when I left D.C. last week," said McGirt. "Leonard, would you mind talking me through the steps as you go?"

"Sure, no problem, sir." Dickle confirmed that the flight deck was clear. Once given permission from the tower, he fired up the Fire Scout's engine and rotor system. His fingers raced across the keyboard. "I'm initiating the takeoff sequence now." Both men watched the flight deck monitor as the aircraft lifted off.

"How high are you hovering?" McGirt asked.

"I've programmed fifteen feet. The tower chief has given us permission to depart to port, so now I am typing in the next command, 'perch proceed.'"

The UAV pitched over a few degrees and began to climb; it exited the scope of the tower's camera. McGirt saw that Bale's launch crew wasted no time; the image of his H-60 inched onto the screen as it was towed from the hangar.

"Not much we can do until they get airborne," McGirt said. He reviewed the script that he, Bale and Dickle had pieced together. Dickle programmed the Fire Scout into a holding pattern at 1000 feet overhead the ship.

A few minutes later, the H-60's rotor blades were spinning, checklists were completed, and Dorothy Hill called for takeoff clearance; Bobby Bale was at the controls. He lifted off and departed. Dickle programmed the Fire Scout to climb to 5000 feet and then entered the coordinates for the Scarborough Shoals facility into the aircraft's nav system. "Well, here we go," he said.

"How soon before we can see Scarborough on the monitor?" McGirt said.

Dickle made some adjustments to the Fire Scout's nose-mounted camera. "It should come into view in about twenty minutes, sir. The BRITE Star has excellent resolution." The pair sat in silence as time passed. Dickle squinted as he watched the BRITE Star's screen. "There...the shoreline is coming into view now."

McGirt adjusted his eyeglasses and stood up to get a closer look at the monitor. "How far away are we?"

Dickle checked the aircraft's navigation readout. "Says we're eighteen miles out."

McGirt and Bale had agreed to communicate on a discrete frequency, while simultaneously monitoring the ship's channel. "Okay, Bobby stand by for my call," McGirt transmitted. "About three minutes to go."

Leonard typed in a descent command to zero altitude but did not activate it. When the Fire Scout was at fifteen miles, McGirt keyed his mike. "Bobby, execute now!" He tapped Dickle on the shoulder and said, "Start the descent, and begin the rotation like we briefed."

Dickle executed the command to descend to sea level, then typed "lateral command" and entered a new compass heading to simulate the loss of tail rotor authority. On the ship's frequency, he and McGirt listened as Hill and Bale read aloud the procedures for a tail transmission oil overheat. They followed up by carrying out the steps to perform an autorotation and emergency landing.

"Trigger the smoke, now!" McGirt shouted.

Dickle's fingers danced over the keyboard as he ignited the smoke charge and said, "Good God, I hope this works." He then began typing repeated heading commands to maintain the MQ-8 in a descending spiral.

McGirt focused on the Fire Scout's camera display which showed the UAV in a constant turn. The image of Scarborough came in and out of view as the aircraft rotated.

"Can you spin it any faster?" McGirt asked.

Dickle wiped the sweat from his brow. "No, sir, that's as fast as the software can process my commands."

"Okay, what's our altitude?"

"Passing through thirty-three hundred at a descent rate of fifteen hundred feet per minute."

"Thanks. At two thousand, I want you to kill it."

Dickle looked up at McGirt; his face had a pained expression. "Yes, sir. I understand." He loaded the command, "Flight Terminate," but held it in abeyance. He continued reading out altitudes: "Twenty-three hundred, twenty-two...two thousand. Executing flight terminate!"

Dickle joined McGirt on his feet as they stared at the image projected from the Fire Scout's camera. The "flight terminate" command shut down fuel supply to the aircraft's turboshaft engine. Absent energy to its rotor system the Fire Scout transitioned from a flying machine to a free-falling object. Its nose fell below the horizon and drifted further down until the airframe was in a twisting, vertical dive. The BRITE Star camera relayed the event with crystal clear accuracy.

McGirt felt the urge to turn away—it was an image that a pilot never wanted to see: the nightmarish sight of plummeting face first into the ocean. But he forced himself to watch as the wavetops zoomed toward him. Foamy bubbles filled the BRITE Star's lens as the Fire Scout impacted the water. The camera's monitor blinked a couple times, then went blank.

CHAPTER 28

McGirt caught a glimpse of Moselli's helicopter through one of the cabin windows. He lost sight of it as the Osprey made a sharp turn to the east and transitioned to airplane mode. The V-22 seemed to labor as it accelerated and climbed; McGirt guessed that its fuel tanks had been filled to the max for the long flight.

The decision to relocate Admiral McGirt, Lin Yi, and Leonard Dickle had come directly from Secretary of Defense Nathan Croft. With the crisis in the Taiwan Straits at an impasse, Croft had convinced CNO Timmons to once again free up *Reagan*'s Osprey to fly the group to Andersen Air Force Base on the U.S. territory of Guam—a distance of sixteen hundred miles from *Grand Rapids'* position in the South China Sea. Captain Draper had delivered the news to McGirt. He'd entered the admiral's stateroom while waving a classified movement order. "With all due respect, Admiral, it's time for you and your roomie to get the heck off of my ship!" Draper had said with a laugh. Lin Yi had slid down from his upper bunk, said something in Mandarin that sounded joyful, and started to dress. He had nothing to pack: the Navy FRVs and steel-toed work boots were his only possessions.

McGirt stuffed the set of khakis that he'd worn from Manila into his gym bag along with his toiletry items; he wondered if the big suitcase he'd left at the Rizal Park Hotel would ever find its way back to his home in Washington.

Leonard Dickle's name appeared at the bottom of the teletyped message that Draper had delivered. It read: "Tech Rep Dickle to detach with Admiral McGirt. Depart with personal items only; Fire Scout tools and support equipment to remain onboard *Grand Rapids*." The message failed to mention Lieutenant Lin Yi by name, instead referring to him as "Admiral McGirt's associate."

The Osprey was manned by a pair of enlisted crewmen and its two pilots. A few minutes after departing *Grand Rapids*, McGirt motioned to one of the crewmen that he wanted to enter the cockpit. The sailor nodded and helped him strap into the aircraft's snug jump seat. As the admiral had gotten up from the cabin, he saw that Lin appeared to be sleeping, while Dickle was busy tearing into the box lunch that *Reagan*'s cooks had provided for the flight.

McGirt plugged into the interphone system and extended his hand to the aircraft's mission commander; it was Stretch, the same pilot who'd flown McGirt from Subic to *Grand Rapids*.

"And so we meet again!" McGirt said. "How'd you draw the lucky number for this flight, Stretch?"

"Our ops officer asked if I wanted the flight since I'd already flown you once. I said 'of course.'" Stretch motioned to the pilot next to him. "Got another copilot this time; Admiral, meet 'Gomer.'"

McGirt shook the lieutenant's hand. "Great to meet you, Gomer."

"Pleasure's all mine, Admiral."

McGirt located the directional compass on the aircraft's instrument panel and saw they were flying due east. "I know that we're going to Guam, but I didn't know the Osprey had the legs to fly that far."

Stretch said, "No, sir, it doesn't. Sixteen hundred miles is about double our normal range. We'll need to refuel inflight at least once, maybe twice."

"Oh…that wasn't mentioned on our movement order." McGirt glanced ahead at the darkening nightfall. "Is that something you do on a routine basis?"

Stretch leveled off at cruise altitude and switched on the autopilot. "Sir, my quals are up to date. I've done two daytime hookups and one at night in the last month."

McGirt patted Stretch on the shoulder. "That's reassuring to know," he said with a laugh. "So, tell me, what's our enroute time?"

Gomer unfurled a lengthy computer printout; he reached up to focus a map light on the papers. "At this speed and altitude, roughly seven hours of flight time, plus another twenty or so minutes for the refueling."

"That's a long time to be strapped in," said McGirt.

Gomer nodded. "Yes, sir, it is, but Stretch and I will likely meander back to the cabin a couple times to keep the ol' blood flowing."

McGirt wondered how the crew would handle personal comfort issues on such a lengthy mission; he hadn't noticed a toilet in the cabin. "Pardon me for asking, but how do you deal with…you know…biological issues on a long flight like this?" Both pilots roared.

Gomer reached down and pulled out a plastic sack from his helmet bag. "This here is what we call a piddle pack, Admiral. Pretty basic: you do your business, and this here powder in the bottom sops it up; turns the liquid into something like mushy jello."

"Well, that's one way to handle the issue," McGirt said. "In my day, most aircraft had what we called a relief tube under each cockpit seat and one in back for the crew." He checked his watch. "How soon before we rendezvous with the tanker?"

Stretch punched some buttons on the Osprey's GPS unit. "Um…we'll hook up with a Marine KC-130 in about two hours. Admiral, you're welcome to stay up here for as long as you wish."

"Thanks, Stretch. I'd like to check on my folks in back and then return for the refueling, if that's alright with you."

"Great, see you then," Stretch said.

McGirt unplugged his headset while Gomer helped him unstrap; he returned to the dim cabin. Lin Yi appeared as if he hadn't moved since takeoff; he sat ramrod straight with his shoulder harness cinched up tight. His eyes were closed. Dickle had sprawled out on the floor with a jacket propped under his head for a pillow. The two aircrewmen were playing cards under the illumination of a flashlight.

McGirt sat across from Lin and reached for the box lunch that a crewman had handed him when they'd boarded. Inside the box he found a sandwich wrapped in cellophane; he took a cautious bite. The sandwich consisted of a thick slab of ham between two slices of buttered white bread. He washed it down with a tiny can of warm grapefruit juice while wondering why Navy box lunches hadn't improved since he was an ensign. He took a few more bites, then tilted back his head. The pulsing drone of the Osprey's massive proprotors soon lulled him into a deep slumber.

* * *

This strange assignment wasn't what officers of McGirt's high rank would have expected in the normal course of duty. A cordial meeting between dignitaries in the cozy confines of the Manila's U.S. Embassy had morphed into bizarre trial of aircraft rides, time at sea, and the handholding of a Chinese pilot seeking political asylum. Had the Commander-in-Chief not personally requested his services, McGirt would have fought tooth and nail to turn down the job. After over a week on the other side of the globe, he was exhausted and wanted to go home.

When Stretch nudged his shoulder, he awoke feeling cold and disoriented. Stretch gave him the hand signal for refueling: the fingers of one hand pressed against the open palm of the other, forming a sideways "T." McGirt unstrapped and followed him back into the cockpit.

"Ten miles out, Admiral," Gomer said while pointing into the moonless night sky. "That's our guy."

McGirt strained to see the tanker. "Heck, I can't see anything. Do they have their position lights on?" He glanced at both pilots and realized they'd already donned night vision goggles (NVG).

"No, sir, they don't," Stretch said. "We were ordered to treat this as a covert mission with exterior lights off." He reached into his flight bag, pulled out a black case and handed it to McGirt. "Here's my backup pair of NVGs."

Gomer showed McGirt how to turn them on, then said, "Admiral, I don't think we can mount them securely to your cranial; you'll have to hold them like a pair of binoculars." McGirt had played with a set of night vision goggles when a group of Army pilots had made a presentation to his old CH-46 squadron in the early 1980s. The officers were part of a development team advocating the use of NVGs during low level night flights. He remembered how cumbersome and heavy the goggles were; these were feather-light by comparison.

"Wow, what an improvement!" he said. "We used these a little bit when I was a junior officer, but if you wore them on your helmet for more than a few minutes, the extra weight gave you a bad neck ache." He looked ahead and spotted the KC-130: except for the colorless, white-grey tint, the image was clear as a bell. He grinned like a kid who'd been given a new toy. "We sure could have used these back in my day."

Stretch laughed. "Yeah, that's what all the old guys say when they first put them on." Stretch realized what he'd said. "Uh, sir, I apologize for that comment. I didn't mean to imply that—"

McGirt laughed. "Hey, don't sweat it. But remember the adage: 'you have to live a long time to get old.' So, what's the next step? Talk me through it if you would."

"Sure," Gomer said. "Stretch will be doing the flying. I've connected with the -130 crew: it's just a matter of getting into position and plugging in."

McGirt gave a thumbs up. "Can't wait to see this." He watched as Gomer extended a long refueling probe that reached several feet out from the right side of the Osprey's nose. The probe had a small light at its tip.

"Okay, let's do it," Stretch said. He turned off the auto pilot and increased airspeed to close in on the tanker, ultimately positioning the Osprey in loose formation about fifty feet behind the KC-130, and below its left wing. The tanker crew unspooled the refueling hose from an elliptical-shaped pod mounted to the underside of the wing, and to the left of the outboard engine. Attached to the end of the hose was a funnel-shaped basket, called a 'drogue.'

"Admiral, do you see the illuminated symbol on the back of the refueling pod?" Gomer said. "It looks sorta like a Y."

"Yup, got it."

"That's the signal telling us the tanker is ready. After Stretch plugs in, that Y will change to a circle, confirming that there's fuel flow."

Stretch keyed his mike. "We're lucky tonight, sir. The air is smooth; turbulence can make this a challenge." He closed the gap until the Osprey's probe was just a few feet from the drogue; he sped up a tad more and aimed for the center of the basket. Closer, closer, until the probe hit the edge of the drogue and bounced away.

Stretch clenched his jaw. "Darn it! Thought I had that one." He backed away and said, "Gomer, take the controls for a second, will you?"

Gomer took over while Stretch shook out the tension from his hands and arms. He regripped the controls. "Okay, I have it back."

Gomer held his up hands, signifying that Stretch had the aircraft. His silky drawl whispered over the intercom, "Nice and easy, bubba…you got this one." Stretch inched the probe closer. He gauged the drogue's motion, then at the seat-of-the-pants moment he felt best, added power; the probe slipped straight into the drogue's center.

McGirt spotted a satisfied grin on the pilot's face as the pod's lighting array changed just as Gomer had predicted. Stretch flew the aircraft in formation with the drogue as the transfer began. Minutes later, the process was complete and the Osprey was topped off. The tanker crew retracted the hose back into the pod.

"There they go," Gomer said as the trio watched the tanker accelerate ahead of them; it banked to the northwest and flew out of sight.

"Where do you think they're headed now?" McGirt asked.

"Not sure, sir, but I think they're based in Japan," said Gomer.

Stretch switched on the autopilot and removed his NVGs. "Geez, glad we got that one under our belt." He reached to his side and retrieved a large chrome plated thermos bottle. "Coffee anyone?"

Gomer fished out three paper cups from a cubby hole behind his seat. "Dang, the galley didn't give us any cream or sugar." He turned to the admiral. "Sorry about that, sir."

"No worries, I've been drinking the stuff black since when I was in flight school."

Stretch poured while Gomer held the cups. McGirt had considered going back to the cabin and trying to get more shuteye, but he nixed that idea; the excitement of observing the inflight refueling had energized him. He decided to stay on the jump seat and chat up the pilots, yet he felt obligated to see how Dickle and Lin Yi were doing. He buzzed one of the crew chiefs and asked them to check on the pair. The sailor reported that Dickle had woken up and was reading a magazine; Lin Yi looked like he was still sleeping. McGirt asked the crewman to give Lin a nudge to make sure he was alright.

The crewman called back on the ICS. "Admiral, I kicked him in the foot and he opened his eyes, so I guess he's okay. He retightened his harness and then went back to sleep."

McGirt, Stretch, and Gomer spent time swapping stories about flying, their favorite sports teams, and the places where they'd grown up. The pilots were enthralled when McGirt shared that he was a member of the President's National Security Council. He told them a few humorous tales about life on Capitol Hill; they were especially interested in how McGirt dealt with the assortment of political characters in Washington. He praised President Black, the CNO, and Defense Secretary Croft, but when asked his opinion of Secretary of State Roscoe Depew, he smiled and said, "I'll just say that he's not on my Christmas card list."

Whether it was the familiarity of being with fellow naval aviators, or the effects of the caffeine, the time passed quickly. When McGirt looked down at the GPS's "distance to go" readout he saw they were three hundred miles from Guam. He asked, "How we doing on fuel, Gomer?"

Gomer had been working with a handheld calculator and scribbling notes on his kneeboard. "Admiral, it's Stretch's call, but I think we're in good shape and won't need to plug in to the tanker a second time. We've had a nice tailwind and made up twenty minutes; plus the weather is still good at Andersen. We should touch down with a solid hour of reserve fuel."

Stretch said, "Then let's send a message to waive off the Air Force tanker and press on."

An hour later, Guam's twinkling lights came into view; the local time was 0400 hours. Stretch started a descent and then passed the controls to Gomer, who landed on one of the airfield's long runways. Andersen's ground controller instructed them to taxi to a remote location on the far side of the airport.

Stretch took over and followed the marshaller's signals to a parking spot next to a twin-engine Gulfstream Five passenger jet. The shutdown checklist was completed and the aircraft's proprotors coasted to a stop. Two MPs and an Air Force major arrived and stood on the tarmac next to the Osprey's boarding ramp. McGirt unstrapped and met them.

"Good morning, Admiral McGirt," the major said while saluting. The man introduced himself as the base duty officer. "We're at your service, Admiral, what do you need?"

"Well, Major, the flight crew needs transportation to billeting. Myself and the two gentlemen traveling with me are connecting to the States." He motioned to the G-5. "Is that our ride?"

"Yes, sir, it is," the major said as he reached for his phone. "Excuse me while I make a call." Minutes later a van arrived to take Stretch and his crew to their quarters. A fuel truck lumbered behind the van and parked next to the Osprey.

"Admiral, your flight isn't scheduled to depart for another hour and a half," the major said. "And I believe your pilots are still in operations doing their flight plan. Would you like to wait in our VIP lounge?"

McGirt looked across the tarmac and saw that the Gulfstream's boarding stairs were lowered and its interior lights were on. "Thanks, Major. I think we're in good shape. We'll stay here until the pilots arrive."

The major saluted and started for his sedan, but halfway there, he turned around and hustled back. "Sorry, Admiral, I almost forgot to give you this." He pulled an envelope from his pocket. "It's for a...Leonard Dickle of Northrup Grumman. Is he onboard?"

"That would be me," a voice hollered from inside the Osprey. Dickle emerged carrying a tattered suitcase. He dropped the bag, grabbed the envelope, tore it open and unfolded the message inside. "Well, what do you know...my boss says he doesn't want to see me for another week, and to proceed home at my convenience." He waved the note in the air. "I'm on full per diem and there's a prepaid ticket for me at the airport. Yee-hah!" Dickle picked up his suitcase and turned to the major. "Hey, sir, can you give me a lift to a beach hotel where the pretty girls hang out?"

The major laughed. "Son, I'll drive you to the passenger terminal where you can call a cab. You're on your own from there."

Dickle said a hurried goodbye to McGirt and then sped away with the major while Gomer and the Osprey's two crewmen piled into the van. Stretch approached with Lin Yi at his side. "Admiral, he seems confused; I want to make sure you have him before we leave."

"Thanks, I've got it from here. Stretch, how long is your layover?"

Stretch unrolled a strip of paper fresh off the aircraft's printer. "They only gave us twelve hours on deck. Then we do the whole thing in reverse and fly back to *Reagan*."

McGirt grabbed the pilot's hand; "I can't thank you enough for getting us here. Good luck to you and your crew. Fly safe!" Stretch rendered a salute, pivoted, and double-timed to the van.

Lin Yi and McGirt stood alone as dawn's blazing sun cracked the horizon. Other than the muted sound of traffic arriving on base, the setting was still. Lin Yi pointed to the G-5. "Admiral, is that how we will fly to America?"

"Yes, it is. We'll be landing in San Francisco."

Lin's face lit up. "My old home. I will be happy to reside there."

McGirt led Lin toward the jet. "Lieutenant, there are some issues we have to address before takeoff. Follow me."

As they stepped onto the aircraft, a stocky, caramel-skinned man greeted them. He wore a starched, short sleeved white shirt, dark trousers, and a black tie. An identification badge hung from a lanyard around his neck. He introduced himself as Mr. Ozawa.

"Ah, the notorious Mister O. So we finally meet!" McGirt said while shaking the fellow's hand. "You guys had to hustle to get here after my conference call with Secretary Croft."

Ozawa chuckled. "All part of the gig, Admiral. You've been in this game long enough to know that the only thing for certain, is the uncertainty." Ozawa held a black binder in one hand. He motioned with it toward two sets of opposite facing leather seats separated by a small coffee table. "Admiral, if you are agreeable, may we begin?"

The three men sat down: Ozawa on one side, McGirt and Lin on the other. Mr. O set the binder on the table. His pleasant mood disappeared faster than a drop of water on a desert highway in summer. He stared at Lin Yi for several awkward seconds before speaking. "Good morning, Lieutenant Lin, my name is

Edward Ozawa. I represent the Central Intelligence Agency of the United States of America. I've been told that you are fluent in English. Is that correct?"

Lin sat motionless. A tiny smirk crept from the corner of his mouth. He matched Ozawa's stare and held it.

Ozawa leaned forward and said in a louder voice, "Do you understand me?"

Lin muffled a laugh. "Of course I understand you, and I know what you are about to ask: It is the details of my plane's laser weapon and the metallic formula that comprises its capacitor. Do you understand *me*...Mister O?"

Ozawa stiffened. He turned to McGirt and opened the binder. "Well, then, we can skip the preliminaries and get right to the point: Do you have the weapon's specifications on your person?"

"No, I do not."

"Okay, then to be blunt, if you can't produce details and schematics, you will be turned over to the Chinese embassy in Manila." Ozawa closed the binder. "This jet can fly in that direction just as well as it can to San Francisco."

Lin's face went blank, like that of a high stakes poker player. "But my country thinks I am dead."

"So what?" Ozawa snapped. "The crash that was staged can be explained as a misdirected error. Trust me, it will be ironed out by representatives of our nations over a bottle of Scotch, and you will be subject to the consequences."

Lin glanced at McGirt, then turned to Ozawa. "I can produce the information. It is being held in the United States."

"Where? Where is it located?" Ozawa pressed.

Lin smiled. "Why would I tell you now? I thought the deal hinged on me gaining asylum in America."

McGirt interrupted. "Lin Yi, you *are* in the United States.; Guam is a U.S. territory and has been for over one hundred years."

Lin shook his head. "I am sorry, Admiral, but this is not the United States that I want to see."

The group heard the squeal of brake pads as a military sedan stopped next to the Gulfstream. The aircraft's two pilots got out and began their preflight duties; they avoided eye contact with anyone in the cabin.

Mr. Ozawa reopened the binder, then took out a pen and laid it on the first page. "I'm going to cut to the chase, Lin. I assume that you know the meaning of that idiom?" Lin nodded. "This document is a promise to grant political asylum. If you sign it, you will be given a new identity and recognized as a naturalized American citizen. You will be employed by the United States as an independent research consultant." Ozawa leaned back with arms folded across his chest. "But, as stated in the agreement, if you cannot produce the information my organization wants, then this document is null and void; there will be no deal…nothing, and I mean *not a thing.*"

Lin stared at the papers in front of him. Images of his parents and brother flashed through his brain. He pictured the face of the young women he'd met while studying in the U.S. "Gentlemen," he began, "You must trust that I know where the information is being held, but I will not give you directions."

"Okay, Lieutenant, can you tell me how you got the data into the United States?" Ozawa's tone carried a shred of warmth.

"Yes, I can do that; it was quite simple. I was detached from my aviation squadron to attend administrative training in Beijing. While I was there, I befriended an American cargo pilot who was staying in the same hotel as me."

"So, does this person have the information?" said Ozawa.

"No, if he was honest, he does not. He was flying trips between the U.S. and China that month; we saw each other in the hotel gymnasium numerous evenings. I asked if he would mail a letter to my friend in the north section of California."

Ozawa's jaw dropped. "You told him to put the information in the *U.S. mail?*" He turned to McGirt with a dumbfounded expression. "Are you buying this, Admiral?"

McGirt avoided answering Ozawa's question. "Tell us, Lin Yi, does that letter contain the laser information?"

"No, but the thumb drive I included with the letter does: blueprints, specifications, and formulas; everything needed to reproduce the weapon."

Again, Ozawa was flabbergasted. "You asked someone to put a thumb drive…with top secret information…in the U.S. Mail?" It was more of an acknowledgement than a question. "Lin Yi, how can we be assured that the letter and thumb drive were mailed to your friend?"

"When I saw the pilot the following week at the gymnasium, he handed me a receipt from the Los Angeles postal office. I did not want to keep the receipt in my possession, so I destroyed it."

Ozawa looked Lin straight in the eye. "But you are confident that it was mailed?"

"Yes."

"What is the name of the person you mailed it to?"

Lin hesitated; his eyes shifted between Ozawa and McGirt. "I know her name and I know where she lives."

"Okay, then tell us," said Ozawa.

"No, not until I am in California. But I will tell you this, Leanna and I met when I was a student at Berkeley. When we communicated last year, she told me that she had moved to her family's vacation home after finishing her graduate studies. She wanted to take some time off and has always wanted to write a book of fiction, a novel."

McGirt sensed that he might be anticipating Ozawa's next question when he said, "What would have prevented this woman from opening the thumb drive and reading the information?"

Lin shrugged his shoulders. "Nothing would have prevented that, but I asked her not to in the letter. I wrapped the drive inside plastic and sealed it with glue. I told her it contained very personal information."

One of the Gulfstream's pilots leaned out from the cockpit. "How we doing, Eddie? We still going to the West Coast?"

Ozawa sighed; he paused for a moment before saying, "Admiral, what do you think?"

McGirt noticed that one of Lin's hands had begun to twitch. But the young pilot's resolve appeared undeniable: there was not a hint of fear or panic in his demeanor.

"Agent Ozawa, the decision rests with you, but I can say this: I've spent the last several days at close quarters with Lin Yi; I find him to be an honorable man. I believe he is telling the truth."

Ozawa stared down Lin Yi the same way he'd done when they'd first met. He held the gaze even longer this time; again, Lin matched his stare. A thin smile emerged from the agent as he said, "Lieutenant, a high-ranking officer of the United States Navy has given you his endorsement. If your story is good enough for him, then it's good enough for me."

Agent Eddie Ozawa called out to the cockpit, "San Francisco it is, boys. Fire 'em up!"

* * *

McGirt fell asleep before the Gulfstream had gotten off the ground. He awoke two hours later to the smell of coffee brewing and to the soft hum of the G-5's twin turbofan engines. He raised his seat from its inclined position and glanced around: Lin Yi had moved across the aisle and was tucked underneath a blanket; Agent Ozawa was seated in the rear of the aircraft reading a newspaper. Ozawa made eye contact with him, smiled, and then returned to reading.

The coffee's enticing aroma helped bring McGirt back to consciousness. He gazed down at the Pacific's blue waters and reflected on how the last week had unfolded. What had begun as a cursory diplomatic meeting in Manila had evolved into the adventure of a lifetime. A grin spread across his face as he recalled his flat-hatting Cobra ride with Guts Gomez along the Luzon coast. Likewise, he savored the two Osprey flights, especially the one with Stretch and Gomer where he'd had a front row seat to a nighttime aerial refueling. The unexpected reunions with Kathleen Torres and Jimmie Posadas, plus his dealings with Captain Bill Draper, Bobby Bale, and Leonard Dickle would be added to the long list of fond memories he'd compiled during his career.

McGirt's orders to the President's National Security Council were due to expire the following year. He was hopeful that his performance in that highly visible job would open doors for other prestigious assignments and a possible promotion. Yet, despite the thrills he'd experienced over the past several days, he felt the longing for a more peaceful life. An old salt had once told him that military service was "a young man's game." Now in his fifties, those poignant words rang truer than ever in McGirt's mind.

As a newly selected flag officer in the Navy's Medical Corps, McGirt's wife, Gina, was anticipating orders to another duty station. The couple had always dreamed of retiring to their cozy, Spanish-style home in Coronado. He pondered, *if Gina can swing orders back to San Diego, maybe it's time for me to call it quits.*

McGirt carried that thought as he followed his nose to the plane's galley. He poured himself a cup of black coffee, faced Ozawa with a tired smile and said, "I'm getting too old for this, Eddie. I want to go home."

EPILOGUE

The bucolic northbound drive on California Highway 101 passed quickly for Lin Yi and the two FBI agents that had assumed control of him on the tarmac at San Francisco International Airport the previous evening. With the aid of a strong tailwind, the G-5 had flown the 5800-mile distance in just over nine hours. All hands had checked into an airport hotel for the night. McGirt and Ozawa caught commercial flights to the East Coast in the morning, while Lin Yi remained in the custody of the federal agents.

"Sir, you need to take the next off ramp and then turn left," Lin said from the front passenger seat of a black SUV. A couple of miles further, he instructed the agent to turn off of the paved highway and to follow a narrow dirt road that ascended into a wooded area.

"You sure about this, fella?" the agent seated in back asked.

"Yes," Lin said without hesitation. "This is the way."

Minutes later, the dense woods thinned out and a log home shrouded by tall evergreens and ornamental bushes came into view. Slivers of the Pacific Ocean shimmered between the trees.

"This is very beautiful, Mister Lin, but are you sure that somebody is living here?" the driver said.

Lin motioned to continue forward. "Her car should be parked on the other side if she's home."

"I'm not comfortable with this," the agent in back said.

Lin Yi turned around and saw that the agent had drawn his handgun. "Sir, you will not need that. I can assure you." As they drove to the other side of the home, Lin spotted a faded green compact car. "That is her vehicle."

The driver inched closer and read the car's bumper stickers: "'Give Peace a Chance,' and...'Save the Planet.'" He parked alongside the car, and said, "Oh, great...another hippie from the Bay. Why am I not surprised?"

Lin Yi reached for the door handle. "May I get out?"

The agent in the rear seat leaned forward and said, "Well, we didn't come all this fucking way to gather pinecones. Mister Lin, you have exactly ten minutes to do your business, then we're getting you out of here."

As Lin stepped onto the home's porch, he saw Leanna's startled face as she peeked from behind a curtain; when she recognized him, she burst into elation. The door flung open before he could knock.

"You're back, you're back!" Leanna said while hugging him. The young Asian-American woman matched Lin Yi's short height. Her raven hair was done up in a haphazard bun atop her head. A well-used cooking apron covered her tee shirt and blue jeans.

Lin Yi kissed her on the cheek, and then nudged her away gently. "But only for a brief time." He motioned to the SUV. "My friends offered to drive me here so I could retrieve what I mailed to you. Did my letter arrive?"

Leanna wiped her tears with a corner of the apron. "Yes, it did. But when I picked it up at the post office, I didn't recognize the handwriting on the envelope. I was afraid to open it until I read the words, 'Sent from Lin Yi' on the back.' The post mark said 'Los Angeles.' Is that where you live now?"

"No. I do not live in L.A. I asked someone I met in China to mail it when he returned to California."

"Oh, I see. Well, I have it tucked inside a dresser drawer. I read your sweet letter but didn't open the item you'd wrapped in plastic." She looked over Lin's shoulder. "Would you and your friends like to stay for dinner? I'm baking lasagna."

Lin smiled; lasagna was his favorite meal that he'd discovered while attending Berkeley. "No, we really do not have time for that. In fact, we are on a rather tight schedule and must return to San Francisco today. May I have the item I sent, please?"

Leanna couldn't hide her disappointment. The happiness drained from her face as she said, "Of course. I'll get it for you."

Lin Yi stood alone on the porch while she went inside. He turned to face the SUV and saw the agent in the rear seat stick out his left arm and tap his watch. Lin nodded that he understood. A couple of moments later, Leanna returned with the flash drive, still sealed in plastic wrap.

"Until I read the part in your letter asking me not to unwrap this, I thought you had sent me a gift." She shrugged and handed it over. "I suppose that I got my hopes up prematurely."

Lin shoved the flash drive into a pants pocket. He asked, "How is your writing going?"

Leanna perked up at the question. "Oh, it's coming along. Not as easy of a project as I had thought." She giggled then said, "It's just a drippy romance. Probably nothing that you'd ever want to read."

Lin held her shoulders affectionately. "I'm sure it will be a wonderful story. I look forward to the day when I read it." The SUV's motor started up. Lin turned and waved a finger signaling that he was almost ready.

"I wrote down my new phone number," Leanna said as she dug a piece of paper from an apron pocket. "Believe it or not, I get good cell coverage out here in the wilderness."

Lin accepted the paper, then held her hand. "I wish that I could spend more time with you, Leanna, but that is not allowed on this day. I must go." He pulled her close and kissed her again, this time on the forehead. "I am so, so, sorry," he whispered. Their dark eyes met for a second, then he turned, stepped off the porch and jogged to the SUV. The driver did a quick turnaround, then started down the hill.

"I'll take what she gave you, Mister Lin, including the note," said the agent in back. Lin Yi handed him the flash drive and Leanna's phone number.

As they drove away, Lin Yi looked into the side mirror. He saw Leanna still standing on the porch; she was waving goodbye. He held back his emotions and focused on the dirt road ahead. "You must take two right hand turns, then one left to reach the paved road," he instructed the driver. After they'd merged onto the southbound 101, Lin Yi looked toward the tree covered hill where Leanna lived. He wondered if he'd ever see her again.

The agent in back said, "Off the record, Mister Lin, was she the reason why you defected?"

Lin Yi kept his eyes focused on the road as he said, "There were many reasons."

* * *

The punishing effect of jet lag was the final nail in the coffin that trashed McGirt. Between double digit time zone changes and the lack of sleep he'd endured during the stressful mission, his fifty-five-year-old body finally threw in the towel. He'd taken a taxi from Dulles Airport and was met by his wife in the doorway of their Georgetown Brownstone apartment. Gina presented him with a handwritten note from the White House Chief of Staff that read: "Take as much time as you need to recover. Welcome home." Gina had encouraged him to play hooky for a solid week, but she knew she was wasting her time: Johnny Jack McGirt got antsy after two days of sitting in his easy chair watching TV. He called his secretary and informed her that he'd report for work the next morning.

He sensed an unexpected lighthearted mood as he cleared security at the White House. Staff members seemed cheerier as they greeted him in the passageway: one elderly female tugged on his elbow and whispered, "Good on you, Admiral!" McGirt felt confident that he'd completed his assignment satisfactorily; however, he wasn't prepared for the hero's-like reception he was getting. When a Secret Service agent spotted him, the man knocked on the Oval Office's door, gave a thumbs up signal to the president, and ushered McGirt inside.

President Maxwell "Mad Max" Black sprang from his seat behind the Resolute Desk and gave McGirt a bearhug. "Welcome home, sailor! If you hadn't already earned forgiveness for trouncing my Badgers on the gridiron, you've most certainly earned it now." The president shook McGirt's hand and then motioned for him to take a seat in the chair closest to his desk. Defense Secretary Nathan Croft and CNO Charles Timmons shared a nearby sofa along the wall. Black returned to his desk, yanked off his suitcoat and loosened his necktie before sitting down.

McGirt saw a buoyant energy in the president's disposition that he'd found absent during their video conferences while aboard *Grand Rapids*. The dark circles beneath the man's eyes appeared less severe and Black's complexion looked rosier. "Great to be back, Mister President," he said. McGirt gave a nod to Croft and Timmons. "Gentlemen, nice to see you as well."

President Black placed his hands atop his head and leaned back. "Nate, Chuck, I'd probably screw up the details so why don't you two tell the admiral what we learned late last night?"

CNO deferred to Secretary Croft. "Will do, Mister President," Croft began. "Admiral, yesterday afternoon, we received a report from our West Coast Boeing and Raytheon reps that they've completed their preliminary analysis of the flash drive that Lieutenant Lin handed over." Croft made brief eye contact with the president, then continued, "I've searched for the most accurate, single word to describe the contents of that information; the best that I can come up with is *exquisite.* It's as if Lin had a telepathic understanding of our engineers' questions. He presented such a detailed description of the laser weapon—most notably the layout of its energy storage and the composition of the unit's capacitor. If you recall, Mister President, those are the two items that have baffled our folks for years. It now appears that we will be able to duplicate the entire system, with notable improvements, within months."

"And if I might add," Timmons said, "With the capability to utilize laser energy in place of convectional missiles, bombs and bullets, this will neutralize China's air superiority."

Black pounded a fist on his desk. "Damn right! Once good old American ingenuity kicks in, we'll bring those commies to their knees for good!" Croft, Timmons, and McGirt muffled their laughs at the president's exuberance. The man had the look of a youngster about to hop on a rollercoaster at the state fair. "But that's not the best of it, McGirt, wait until you hear this." There was an awkward pause until Black said, "Go ahead, Nate, tell him about the Chinese planes."

Croft leaned forward. "Of course, Mister President. In addition to the laser weapon schematics that Lin gave us, he also provided the names of other potential defectors. Apparently, there's been a covert plan to defect by several Chinese pilots. Like Lin, many of them had lost loved ones as a result of China's brutal treatment of its citizens during the pandemic." Croft turned to Admiral Timmons, "Chuck, what's the latest tally?"

Timmons read from his notebook. "As of 0700 this morning, another seven pilots have made a run for asylum in Taiwan. The first two were shot down by Taiwanese fighters: one pilot perished at sea, while the other ejected and was rescued by one of our destroyers in the Straits. However, after Taiwanese air defenses received the names that Lin provided, when those pilots identified themselves on the radio, they were escorted to Taiwanese military bases. So far, Taiwan has recovered three J-15s fighters and two J-31s."

Secretary Croft took over. "That information will be released to the news media later this morning. Our surveillance satellites have confirmed that after the defections, China's air operation have stood down, and their surface ships have retreated from Taiwan's coast. Also, our intelligence agents on the ground report that Chinese forces that had mustered for an amphibious assault have been put on hold."

"And you were instrumental in bringing all that to fruition, McGirt," Black said. An elated air filled the room as the president stood up and extended his hand. McGirt rose to meet him. "Admiral McGirt, I thank you, and a grateful nation thanks you. Well done, sir."

McGirt had walked into the office with the notion of tendering his resignation as a member of the President's National Security Council, but he realized that this was neither the time nor the place to take that action. "Just doing my job, Mister President," he said. "It's an honor and privilege to serve you."

Croft and Timmons offered their personal thanks. As the pair headed for the door, McGirt said, "Gentlemen, I know it's water over the dam, but whatever happened to Lieutenant Lin's jet?"

CNO Timmons began to speak but checked himself as President Black sauntered toward McGirt; he had an impish grin on his face. "Well, I can tell you this: I received a phone call from Ambassador Remington with the answer to that very question. Harold told me that every nut and bolt on Lin's jet, absent the laser, has been put back in place. With that done, Ambassador Wu demanded immediate diplomatic clearance for a Chinese pilot to fly it home. But President Diaz refused and had the jet craned onto a China-bound freighter tied up at Subic Bay."

"Perfect," McGirt said with a grin.

An aide carrying an armful of folders poked his head into the Oval Office. "Whenever you are ready, Mister President," the man said.

Black returned to his desk. "McGirt, I think our little meeting will prove to be the highlight of my day." He put on his eyeglasses, then said, "Send that guy in as you leave, will you please?"

On his way to the West Wing, McGirt experienced an epiphany: the conviction that he'd felt about retiring had faded. He still had another year left on his tour at the White House, plus his wife held a primo position at Walter Reed Hospital. They both longed for the day when they could return to the snug comforts of Coronado, but that would have to wait. He knew they'd eventually get there.

A perky intern was waiting as he stepped into his office. She held a large, sealed envelope stenciled in bold red letters with the word "CLASSIFIED." "Welcome back, Admiral," she said. "I've been instructed to hand carry this to you."

McGirt signed for the document, thanked the girl, and sat down. He opened the envelope and wondered where his next adventure might take him.

Meanwhile...

A Type 096 nuclear submarine departs China's Yulin Naval Base and slips deep beneath the surface of the South China Sea. It carries a dozen JL-3 long range missiles that are capable of reaching the continental United States.

THE END

I hope you enjoyed reading **Acts of Deception**. If so, I'd appreciated your feedback on Amazon.com and I invite you to visit my website at www.LarryCarello.com.

Larry Carello
Jacksonville, Florida

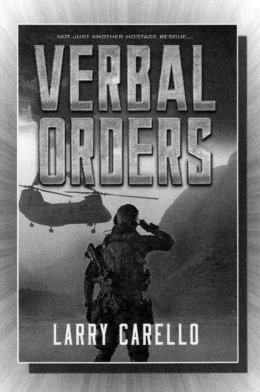

FROM TODAY'S MASTER
OF CARRIER AVIATION FICTION

KEVIN MILLER

Midway as never told before!

www.braveshipbooks.com

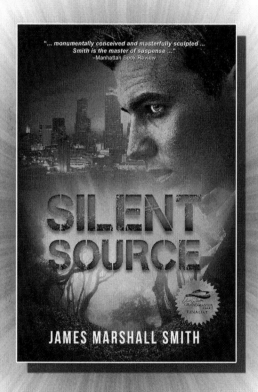

THE WAR AMERICA CAN'T AFFORD TO LOSE

GEORGE GALDORISI

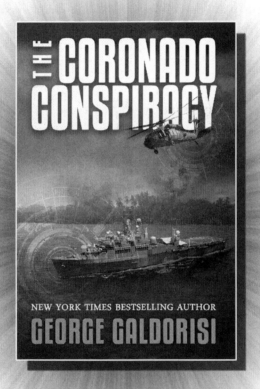

Everything was going according to plan...

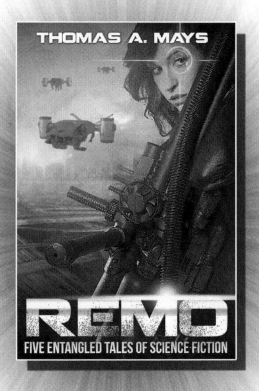

**THE THOUSAND YEAR REICH MAY BE
ONLY BEGINNING...**

ALLAN LEVERONE

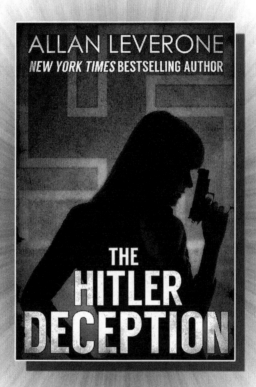

A Tracie Tanner Thriller

www.braveshipbooks.com

Made in the USA
Columbia, SC
12 January 2025

51636124R00159